W9-DBL-529

For Max and the Guerrero Street Gang

Books by Barney Rostaing

Phantom of the Paradise, Bantam Books
Bill Walton's Total Book of Bicycling, Dell books

With unlimited thanks to Paul Bresnick, Peter Walker, and Dr. Mehmet Oz, without whom this book would not exist.

*A high degree of spirituality goes
hand in hand with the stud farm.*
— Henry Miller

I am he as you are he as you are me and we are all together
— Lennon-McCartney

I

1

Mcgoohey Construction, Inc. occupied a one-story building that sat like a fort in the center of a big unkempt lot in a bad LA neighborhood. The offices were hewn in the man's own image, rough and rowdy: cheap wood paneling over concrete blocks, big loud AC, and no suggestion that a major business enterprise operated there. Papers were stacked in loose piles on his big metal desk. On the desk were three big heavy old cord phones, red, green and yellow, one for each construction site. The man sat squarely at his desk, large and tough, not yet fifty, with thick iron gray hair.

In the adjacent office, smaller and completely organized, sat Alice Smith, surrounded by towering beige file cabinets. Alice was the glue that held McGoohey's dreams together, a tall, blonde, quietly attractive and dignified widow in her late forties, liked by all, whose perpetual fiancé did something dark for the military. Alice took all land-line calls, evaluating them and prepping McGoohey. Where he was forgetful, her mind was a clean machine, long adapted to his impulsive and shifty methods. She was also one of only three people with the number of his second cell phone, a tiny one that did not ring but vibrated in the breast pocket of whatever he was wearing. His business cell phone played Danny Boy loud enough to be heard on a construction site operating full-bore. McGoohey gave Alice little thought, blaming her when things went wrong, and he had no idea that she was critical to his success. Alice stayed with McGoohey because it was convenient, she was unaffected by his moods, and because he was the toughest, sneakiest, most resourceful sonofabitch she'd ever met, including her straight-arrow fiancé. He was also a laugh a minute, which her betrothed was not.

The third party to McGoohey's private cell phone was Len Thomas, who trained his string of thoroughbreds, the only black trainer anyone had ever heard of. The owner had no use for racing protocol, and Len Thomas was the only trainer he could get along with.

Responsible for many overpasses, cloverleafs, sections of freeway and similar projects, McGoohey took simple, primal satisfaction in creating these things. He freely enjoyed the money that went with it, though it had complicated his life by leading to his marriage with a beautiful and socially adept young woman half his age. The former Jasmine Felter took pleasure in being the prime trophy of this earthy and easily manipulated goy, and also had darker feelings about her husband, as did his trainer. But she enjoyed being rich, driving around in her Porsche and shopping on Rodeo Drive. They had no children because Jasmine liked her body the way it was and took something prescribed by her physician, a relative by marriage who specialized in cosmetic surgery. The couple's only real issues were McGoohey's mid-life obsession with begetting an heir and their lack of social standing.

Through the glass that separated their offices Alice saw that this would be a bad Monday. Sharing wasn't his way, but McGoohey's old-school tough-it-out style didn't fool her. He was a man waiting for bad news, and with a great deal at stake. McGoohey was an ambitious man, a player to the bone, and his vision of social mobility began with his undistinguished string of thoroughbreds. The day before at Santa Anita that dream had been blown away as the jockey on his demented gelding Popsicle had a near-death experience when the horse tried to force his way into a non-existent gap between the rail and the horse in front. The jockey had kept him from flipping over the rail, but it had been close. In the heat of the moment, McGoohey had bellowed an obscene oath in his penetrating blue-collar voice, a brutal, industrial-grade voice developed to cut through the roar of pneumatic drills, cement mixers, pile-drivers, truck rumblings and so forth. No one within fifty feet missed a word and there was shocked silence in his box. His box full of people he needed to impress. He cut off this memory with an effort of will that left him rigid.

Okay, he'd lost it, and he'd pay for that because the commissioner who doled out contracts had been in his box. But McGoohey was a self-made man, aggressively optimistic, and his success was not built by dwelling on disasters. Soon he was thinking ahead. He had the dream, and a general plan, and whatever people thought of him today, he was sure that one break could change everything. Like that first municipal contract seven years ago. A Derby-quality foal, its career noted in the media, would gratify all parties, especially Jasmine, who longed to move in Eastern circles and summer in the Hamptons. The foal's ascent to stardom would be their own. His business success had been a kind of miracle, and now he wanted another one. Full of ideas that felt new and fresh, he was thinking Saratoga. Taking his mare Arabiche up there and hooking her up with a top-end stud. Everyone would be there, and the big allowance race would have all the top mares, including Black Ice. A third place would be significant and offset her uneven record... pull a third in that one, mosey over the clubhouse and meet some people without lookin' too bad. I may be the son of an illiterate hod-carrier, but now I learned it ain't all about money, which I got. It's bein' at the top, and I'm getting' there by fuckin' horse . . .

The flashing light on the green phone caught his eye as Alice prepared to let a call through. Looking up to the window between offices he saw her holding up an oversized file card on which was printed: COMMISSIONER BULLITT.

Big Jim Bullitt, who'd been in his box yesterday when he'd lost it. He'd forgotten to tell told Alice to hold his calls, so he had to take it.

"I've got bad news about those storage facilities, Pat," said Bullitt without preamble.

"Yeah. Well, that's life, right? I've got some other things I can turn to. Who finally got it?"

"Looks like Jed Kline. The State got involved because of the funding."

A brief, dry chuckle came out of McGoohey's tight throat like a death rattle. Jed Kline. Jed Kline, whose cell phone played a choral arrangement of Hava Nagila. Jed Kline, who'd brought his cousin Jasmine to an convention cocktail hour, setting in motion a chain of events that seemed to have no end, including the McGoohey-Felter nuptials and Jed's addition to a dinner with the Commissioner. Losing a job to Kline unnerved McGoohey. The bastard was just too smooth. Like Jasmine, he had great wavy black hair that always looked right, but unlike her, he was always smiling. No heavy lifting for Jed Kline. No enemies either, and the bastard had access to dozens of friendly young women who professed to admire big strong clumsy captains of industry with big strong clumsy wives.

It hit him then that he might have to lay off the third crew, a blow that would reduce him as a man. Bullitt talked on, McGoohey drifted. Him and the boys shooting up to Saratoga to pull off something that would make this old fart remember who really deserved those friggin' contracts.

"You there, Pat?"

"Yeah, got a call on my cell I've gotta take. No hard feelings, Jim," replied McGoohey in a fairly solid voice. "I wasn't counting on it, truth be told. Sorry if I embarrassed you yesterday with my language. Damn horses, they really get to me."

"Not at all, Pat. It's your passion."

Meaning you are dead until further notice, you dumb Mick.

"See you in Church, Jim. I'm goin' East for a while. Saratoga."

Hanging up the phone he was furious. His passion? What the hell was that? If he had a passion it was Latin pussy. What the hell was wrong with Jim Bullitt, using an artsy-fartsy word like that? Bad enough killing the deal, he didn't have to come on like Father Flynn talking about The Christ.

It passed. Fuck Jim Bullitt. Len Thomas was right there with him, cool-headed, smart and solid. Warned him off Popsicle, shoulda listened. You couldn't think of him as an inferior, even if he was one – call a spade a spade and you could end up in court. Didn't steal, and a damn sight more fun than Big Jim and that wife. And with this fine negro's help, he, Pat McGoohey, was on his way to Saratoga with his favorite horse and a sure-fire plan. In her office, Alice skewered another note on an old fashioned spike.

The Dead Heat was a dark old Pasadena bar with a good selection of hard liquors and beers, though thin on wines. It also provided chili and burgers, and served as a mail drop for patrons in good standing. The Heat catered to hard-core racing professionals, and its dark wood smoke-mellowed walls were covered with framed photographs of the greats, going back to Man o' War. The women were few, hot, and available, sharing a taste for small, intense men high in testosterone, and they deployed in a pattern that allowed convenient approach.

McGoohey and his trainer arrived together and took a booth. They were an odd pair, a hulking, freckled white man and a soft-spoken, composed African-American, lean but not large, with a distinguished beak and an intelligent bearing. It was early evening, and the room was half filled with owners, trainers and jockeys, all of them familiar with this pair, all of them on good terms with the trainer and wary of the owner. A waitress showed up immediately with a bottle of single-malt Bushmills from which she poured the owner a double, leaving the bottle on the table. Len Thomas took a bottle of mineral water.

"Gonna send Arabiche to Saratoga," said McGoohey, as if he'd thought it through and decided it was a good plan.

Arabiche, 'Biche to her friends, was a good-looking lazy little mare with a record that did not suggest an expensive Saratoga trip. Caught off guard, Len nodded slowly, as if this was an interesting idea with real possibilities. McGoohey opened a big old satchel and produced *The Saratoga Conditions Book*. Both men were uncomfortable with technology, and Len worked with a small notebook in which he made sparse notes that would make no sense to anyone else. It was an object of fascination for McGoohey, whose few notes were jotted illegibly on scraps of paper that only Alice Smith could decipher. Len's notebook was fine-grained black leather, of a size to fit a back pocket of the chinos and jeans he normally wore, and it was refillable, with gilt-edged pages and a slim black mechanical pencil in the spine. In McGoohey's eyes it outclassed any electronic device hands-down. As he sipped Bushmills, his trainer drank mineral water and took some notes. Watching him write, the owner again saw that negro wasn't the right word and nigger was all wrong, his long-dead father to the contrary. Len might sound like a soft-spoken street black minus the profanity, but the owner knew he was a genuine top of the line African-American, and totally reliable.

"Gettin' rid of Popsicle, got a couple bids," said McGoohey. "I'm goin' with the best offer by Friday. Friggin' disgraced me. Until Tamari heals up, Arabiche is what we got, basically, gonna concentrate on her. Get some results up in Saratoga and get her covered by a top stud."

Len nodded his apparent-agreement nod, concerned first of all about his job. Arabiche in Saratoga was a strange notion and Len knew that when McGoohey talked wild and leaned forward with that spark in his eye, life was going high-risk. Saratoga was Mission Impossible territory because 'Biche didn't qualify for a top stud, nor would Saratoga change that, barring a miracle. Caution wrapped itself around him like an invisible shield.

"Maybe oughta look at some numbers first an' talk in the morning," he said.

McGoohey rolled over this exit strategy like a toy and went on about Bold Ruler, in his grave these many years, and his son, Seattle Slew, also become history. Danzig as well, more recently. Arabiche had these and other fine bloods on both sides, as did many mediocre horses. Distracted and disturbed by the new plan, Len recalled simpler, happier times. Roll a bone and smoke it without a care.

McGoohey was pointing at the open *Conditions Book*. Len knew what was there for them – two races, one plausible, the other a very big stretch.

"Whaddaya think?"

"On her record she belong in the fifth Saturday, prob'ly do okay. Sunday the big one. Black Ice and Margiedaw tunin' up for Breeders Cup. Eclipse candidates."

This dry, minimalist, generic-black way of speaking was a kind of scrim that Len had developed, behind which he concealed the thoughtful, well-read Llewellyn Thomas. It was reliable, easy to work behind, and felt like his real self when that was the appropriate way to feel.

"So what you're sayin' is, there's no point in the first and she's outclassed in the second. That's some fuckin' choice, *Llewellyn*."

"Dunno," said Len, ignoring the provocation. "She always inna top half, might as well be top half a good race. Real speed horse in there, field split early, an' she ain't gonna make that up. Bad for her state of mind, get whipped real bad. Maybe talk to Paco "

"That's a chance we're gonna haveta take, 'cause I ain't

6

flyin' her out to run third to a bunch of pigs. What're ya doin' t'morrow night?"

McGoo didn't normally cut into his evenings. Time for a low blow.

"Finishin' a book – *Seven Pillars of Wisdom*. T.E. Lawrence. Then I got a date." After a silence he added, "a.k.a. Lawrence of Arabia. He wrote it."

"Oh yeah, Peter O'Toole. Good movie, we seen it on cable last year. He was a fruit. Lawrence, I mean, not O'Toole."

Len saw an irrational wave sweeping his boss to the high ground of this doomed Saratoga soufflé. Other owners were just as likely to take the challenge as an opportunity, but no point bringing it up. McGoo finished his drink and poured another while Len considered the personal benefits of a trip East. Meeting friends he rarely saw, avoiding the attentions of a woman who was all over him lately. Possibility of a job offer that would release him from indentured servitude to this redneck across the table. Not too damn likely. He felt his stomach tightening up.

"We can change her training around, get her so she breaks faster and don't get lost in the starta that Sunday race," said McGoohey hopefully.

"Worked for Seabiscuit," said Len said seriously, as if it was a new idea.

"That was a good book," he added. "Woman who wrote it, invalid all the while she was writin' and searchin' out people t'talk to. I mean serious sickly. God wanted that woman to write that book same way He wanted Seabiscuit to win that match race."

This was all perfectly understood by McGoohey, including the implication that he never got through a book, but he felt good. God wanted a book written and it got done against the odds by a sick lady. Plus a great movie. If God was in the mood, 'Biche could foal a champion. Would, with any luck.

"Sunday race longer," noted Len, searching for positives, wondering how he'd get through this without losing his job, which was a miracle that would not happen twice.

"Mile and a quarter, her distance," he added thoughtfully.

McGoohey was smiling his full and frightening gap-toothed smile, up a gear now with God on their side, which was about the edge his trainer figured they'd be needing.

"Change of venue might light her up. Yeah, we enter both," said Len. "I ask around, prob'ly pull out the Saturday race when I find out who runnin' Sunday."

McGoohey smiled. He enjoyed driving Len up the wall. It was relaxing fun at the end of the day, and he'd let him in on the rest of the plan later. No question, this trip was the right thing to do. Change of scene, different faces, fresh country air, rub elbows with the big boys. Then he caught himself for a moment. What about Jasmine? His lovely wife knew how to travel, find good places, always knew just what to bring. Smart. That *yiddisher kopf* – get it on your side and you really had a weapon. Too late. The mission was locked in his mind as an all-male venture. First the mission, then maybe a little party if it all worked out, and *then* maybe an infidelity, but not with Jasmine on the same coast.

Another idea struck him.

"You think she'd wake up and run if Jimmy had, you know – a machine?" he said quietly. By this he meant a device that delivered an electrical jolt that could sometimes improve performance dramatically. For this reason, machines were illegal and would lose a jockey his license. Tossed ones were often found on the infield. Len heard the hesitation in McGoohey's voice and looked his boss firmly in the eye.

"License all Jimmy got. Lose his license, that's the end, no tomorrow."

He kept his eyes firm but not challenging, and McGoohey switched tack.

"Try someone else?"

"I dunno. Lotta jocks hangin' round Saratoga lookin' for a ride, sell you out in a minute. Plus Jimmy get along real good with other jocks," he added, meaning that he was a devoted conniver who could keep his mouth shut. Both men knew that buying third place was the only way, but the owner wanted it to be Len's idea and didn't want to know anything about it, and he knew Len would never say a word. It would be simple and smart, a handshake cash loan initiated by Len, which would inoculate the owner to a polygraph if things went wrong.

Both men were good at silence. Len allowed this one to

extend until he saw uneasiness on the other side of the table. It wasn't often he could play McGoo, and it made his stomach feel better immediately. So far their dealings had been legal. This was not, and he didn't like it. And the owner was helpless without him, simple as that. He had a sip of mineral water and was silent, as if in serious dialog with himself. At length he squared up to the table and spoke.

"Somethin' on mah mind, Pat. Feel embarrassed askin', but Ah'm in kind of a jam," he said, in a warm, friendly, embarrassed tone, as if for a microphone.

"Financial problems?"

Len nodded.

"Got a number?"

"Middle five figures, not sure yet."

"No problem. Just give me a call."

McGoohey's smile was genuine and confident. If there was a third place to be had with that sweet little horse, Len Thomas would get it done. Then it would be up to him, the owner, to seize the day. Get her covered by a champion. He had one in mind.

Len had already guessed his shoot-the-moon plan and knew it wouldn't work. He was flipping through his notebook, relieved that his end of this game came down to buying some jockeys. Crooked but fairly routine, and not dangerous. No getting out of it.

"Change of venue," intoned the owner with mellow satisfaction, tasting the new word. "Think that might be a positive thing? Mentally, I mean."

"Could be. She too level-headed – maybe all that strangeness get her wired up. Ain't no guarantees this business, but we ain't yet seen her full flat-out. Maybe she give it up this time."

McGoohey nodded, in a rare good mood. He liked *venue* and would add it to his vocabulary. He put a short fat index finger against the side of his meaty, up-tilted pixie nose, regarding Len across the table with a hard mission-twinkle in his squinty green eyes. They were both on the same page, and the risk was where he wanted it.

Sitting in his old Impala afterward, Len reviewed the situation. The man was going to do it his way, like buying Popsicle against all advice. But no matter what the owner came up with, he had to keep a firm grip on this relationship, because there was no replacing Pat McGoohey. No one else would hire a black trainer. Give him credit for that, he mused soberly. Man loves his horses and he trusts me with them, knows I can do the job. Gotta keep that in mind all times.

What would Wink do? He leveled himself off by reflecting on the totemic Jimmy Winkfield, a.k.a. The Black Maestro. Wink was the last great black figure in the sport, and Len Thomas's model. A hundred years ago when Southern aristocrats controlled racing, Winkfield had won everything, including back-to-back Kentucky Derbies. Then a Jim Crow cabal had squeezed blacks out. Stable hand, hot walker, groom, exercise boy – that was it for blacks now.

Stay cool and you can beat it, that was Wink's lesson. But you might have to be a little creative. Winkfield had beat it by going to Russia, winning as usual, and marrying an aristocrat. Caught in the Revolution, he'd moved south to further victories in Poland and France. His picture hung on the living-room wall, a smooth, calm face with large thoughtful eyes.

2

It was a little past ten of a fine Kentucky morning, and Annabelle Lee "Dixie" Dixon, queen of Lee Farms, was looking forward to her first of the day. It would be blended into an exquisite compote of fruits from orchards around the world, available through a catalog she and her friends had discovered some years back and all took up together. The chime of a little bell broke the sunny silence of the room, and when she decided to open her eyes, the compote was by her bedside. At fifty, Mrs. Dixon was a beautiful, buxom, vigorous honey-blonde, as well preserved as money could achieve through medical, dietetic, and all other available means, including massage, exercise, sleep therapy (Switzerland), and cosmetic surgery (LA). The cornerstone of her programme was bourbon whisky from a small distillery in which her father had a silent controlling interest. Like all Lee activities, the distillery had a dual agenda – excellence and a strong liberal bent, manifested in this case by early retirement for several notorious bigots who had long reigned like petty slaveholders. The only exceptions were a pair reckoned to have irreplaceable palates.

Blending smoothly with the juices of the compote were two ounces of whisky from this distillery that had been aging about half as long as Mrs. Dixon, and a pinch of brown powder. She sat up in bed among her multi-colored pillows, made herself comfortable, and very gradually the hair of a great dog slipped down her smooth throat, along with the fruits and their juices. The tall, spacious room was very bright, its subtle pastel mango-and-blue faux-impressionist walls warmed by the mid-morning sun. She took a minute to appreciate what she and her invaluable assistant had achieved here, resumed the compote with relish, and then slipped off until the bell chimed again. She pressed a button, and soon a slim, pale-cinnamon-colored young woman entered bearing a tray surrounded by a halo of coffee vapors. Next to the Spode cups was an oval dish with two thin slices of dry, toasted, home-made, multi-grain bread, rich in vitamins, minerals, enzymes and natural fiber, each with a small dab of home-made grapefruit marmalade.

"Good Morning, Dixie."

"Good Morning, Holly dear. Isn't it just a lovely morning?"

"It surely is," said Holly St. Cyr, going on thirty, honors in art history, in charge of creating new environments, handling correspondence, and anything involving numbers. Dixie's ex-husband, an investment advisor, had pocketed several million that went unnoticed until one day he disappeared on a newly acquired and seaworthy boat, on which he was assumed to be drinking himself to death with his presumably gay skipper and manservant. Dixon had put up with his spirited wife until it was let be known rather widely that his sperm were not motile. This was not a true fact, but Dixie's tactful doctors were not about to tell her that untreated teenage gonorrhea had fried some essential reproductive components.

"I always enjoy morning coffee so much with you, Holly," said Dixie with a smile. This was fact, and behind it another fact. When Holly brought the compote to her mistress, which was almost every morning, it included a small addition of brown powder from the heart-shaped gold locket that nestled between her discreet but nicely formed breasts. New Orleans born and bred, the intelligent and artistic Holly was heir to a Creole tradition of spells and potions, and she didn't sell it short. Her large, round, innocent eyes made such thoughts unthinkable. Dixie's feelings toward Holly were very real, and she was delighted that Holly remained single, encouraging this with bonuses, little favors, and good yearly raises. The last thing she wanted was to lose her marvelous executive assistant.

"Do I look well this morning, Holly? I don't feel quite myself."

"You know you do, Dixie. In this wonderful light you are absolutely radiant."

"I hope to be in a couple of hours. I'm going down to the stables with Daddy, and I do so want to make him feel proud. And for God's sake, sit down and have some coffee with me!"

Her assistant smiled, poured herself a cup, and sat down in

a wicker chair next to the bed. Making Daddy Tom feel proud was a general obligation at Lee Farms, and Dixie was Lee to the bone, regardless of the married name she stuck with. Holly accepted it all. She had a job to die for, and the price was right. If she didn't quite have it all, she had as much as an intelligent, good-looking, not-yet-thirty black woman could sanely expect. Her family, to whom she sent a check each month, thought her wildly successful. In her spare time she painted in a neo-impressionist manner, and she kept up her French by reading magazines and books. But she did wonder lately how it was she didn't want to change the world, go into finance, have a baby, or even just leave the South. Instead, she squirreled away her money, played currencies, and made herself indispensable.

Holly had a head for numbers, and she'd picked up a business minor which turned out to be useful. Over time, with Dixie's approval, she had gained access to the details of family finances, which she explained to her employer in terms she could understand. She also had access to insider tips that came their way, which were frequent and reliable, and which she often tailgated. Ronnie Pitt, the family-friend financial manager, was qualified mainly by social proximity, and his management of the family money was rudimentary by 21st-century standards. He didn't seem able to grasp that the nineties were over, and that technology, energy, and third-world slave labor were driving everything. His security was rudimentary, and trust moneys could easily be diverted by a knowledgeable person with the code words for specific trusts, but Holly saw no reason to point out this embarrassing fact. Fair, fat and forty, Pitt had fallen into this lucrative relationship when Mr. Dixon left. He knew his limitations and was under Holly's spell, meeting with her frequently, often following her suggestions. Socially astute, he understood the benefits of standing in well with Holly. It was all part of the easy, unbusinesslike family feeling old Tom Lee encouraged.

3

Len was relaxing on his front porch enjoying the mid-day sun, which he loved, equating it with sex, cognac and winning long shots. His warm mahogany skin seemed to require sun for genetic reasons that seemed obvious to him. Laid back for his afternoon break, he let his mind drift to the old, pre-9/11 world, before routine paranoia and terrorists. Fat years, gone forever, fool in the White House talking war.

At forty-one, Len Thomas looked younger, a slim, fit, short-haired, clean-shaven man with an oval face, and a prominent aquiline nose that he would have liked to understand better, everything else about him being typically African-American. Arab, he guessed, encouraged by his mother. He lived in Arcadia, a multiracial enclave where he was known and respected, first of all, for having ascended to the very white turf of thoroughbred training. To supplement his income, Len played poker and craps semi-professionally and put his money in the bank. His neat three-room apartment with its floor-to-ceiling wall of books was testimony to his mother's influence, and that of an unusual high school teacher. It was she who had christened him Llewellyn, to balance the brief last name. The name brought him grief as a boy, but the nose had stood him in good stead with women.

Len's need for sun and an ongoing problem with the many Irish of his native Boston had eventually taken him to southern California, where he'd prospered. He loved reading, horses, pretty women, and select herb ingested with care and caution, having in his late, wild teens, developed an opiate dependency, or "Jones," as it was called at the time. He was determined never to be arrested again, but if he was, the charge would probably be murder, and the victim Padraic McGoohey III, self-made multimillionaire. McGoohey had no idea of Len's ambivalent feelings and regarded his trainer as an exceptional member of his maladroit ethnic group, experienced in horse matters and much easier to get along with than his wife.

He dressed in trainer mode for the afternoon's business: lightweight navy blazer, yellow turtleneck, gray slacks. Looking in the mirror he saw a cool, smooth, man, a little under five-ten, with a distinctive nose and a straight back. Nobody's fool. As he was about to leave, his home-phone rang; it lacked Caller ID, so he let it take a breathy message from Charlotte. Lily-white Charlotte, breaching decorum by calling so soon after their lengthy afternoon. He listened to her rich, demanding voice telling him how nice he was. Rich, white Charlotte. Liked black men and had settled on him. Used to getting her way, woman past thirty, mammal with need to breed and no idea what that involved in this case. Also wanting to be married, with absolutely no idea what interracial marriage really meant, either. The stress. The goddamn *stress*, like it was a criminal enterprise.

Saratoga beckoned, a fine town in late summer, perfect place for a time out. He was damned if he'd be Charlotte's fool. It wasn't love, and she had to know that.

Jimmy Broughton was a bigot without borders, for whom the n-word was not only acceptable but integral to his thinking. He drank too much instead of eating, and fought to hold his weight, his moods evaporating as Pluto Salts and lesser laxatives stripped his guts to keep him at 112 pounds. He'd taken some getting used to, but Len had come to books late enough in life that it didn't interfere with his reading of people. Himself a bit of a miser, Len saw that Jimmy's words meant nothing, his generosity everything. The jockey loved mankind with a simple innocence, but felt obliged to conceal this abnormality.

Walking from his old brown Impala to the Patch barn, Len moved slowly, homing in on the jockey's peculiar wavelength. He was an ageless little man of fixed habits, a miniature farm-boy, tough as nails. His life centered around the track, where he often slept, waking up to breeze horses at dawn. He did not maintain a cell phone, and his rooming house was mainly a place to park his gear and dry out. To reach Jimmy, you left word at the Heat or his rooming house, or looked for him at the barns as Len was doing. Suspicious of outsiders, he fit perfectly into the racing world. His

15

alliance with Len was long-standing, and they would do each other a favor without expecting anything in return. What mattered for Len was Jimmy Broughton's essential character – his generosity to people in need, and his basic humanity.

He found him standing alone in the warm late afternoon looking into a stall at the far end of a long line. It was dark in the middle of the shedrow, and the still air was spiced with hay, feeds and horse manure. Grooms moved patiently around the barn trundling bales of hay, replacing water buckets, and mucking out stalls. The jockey was having a look at the horse that nearly killed him. Popsicle's eyes were perfectly calm as he gazed at Jimmy without recognition. They were looking at each other when Len walked up, approaching this private dialog with respect.

"Got a minute, Jimmy?" he asked after a while.

It was natural for them to meet, but Jimmy responded with cautious hesitation, as he did to any unprepared encounter. Off a horse, he was a slow processor, as if new to the language. He wore new, too-big jeans that clashed cheerfully with a green K-mart T-shirt; he owned several of each, purchased on sale, enabling him to appear in fresh, identical attire each day. His feet looked huge in a pair of heavy work-style cowboy boots bought for durability. In a profession noted for a certain style, Jimmy Broughton was a hay-seed, oblivious to appearances. It was generally assumed that head injuries were involved, which was not the case. Len slowly nodded, a vague wordless gesture of agreement.

"Yeh," said Len, as if continuing a conversation. "Look like we goin' Saratoga this weekend."

Jimmy smiled. Though he disbarred many ethnic groups from full humanity, along with several family members, people from certain states, extra-large people and rich ones, he had a special category of good guys in which a man's gene pool was irrelevant, and Len Thomas was prominent in this group.

"Saratoga. Hey, that's great, very cool. McGoo idea, huh?"

"Yeh, he gonna run 'Biche."

"Claimer?"

"Allowance."

"What's he thinking about? She don't belong up there." After a long pause he added sharply. "Hey, not the one with Black

16

Ice and all them!? He'll break her heart. I don't wanna do it, man. That ain't fair."

"I know what you thinkin' but the man gonna do it. I got a plan."

"C'mon Len, you don't need a plan, you need a   miracle."

"Start out, need some cooperation."

A wave of disbelief roiled Jimmy's pale eyes.

"No *way*! Black Ice an' Margiedaw people ain't gonna talk to us, fer Chrissake."

"'Course not, just wanna get in the money. McGoo want a third is all. Set her up for a high-class stud."

Jimmy got it and nodded. His eccentricities did not affect his standing with his fellow jockeys, and he was a well-liked insider.

"They're all gonna be class horses, Len, know what I'm sayin'? 'Biche – I mean, who's kiddin' who here?"

"Yeh, well, you get with your buds up there and see what you can do, right?"

"Okay. No harm tryin'. Y'ain't got yer pipe somewheres? I wanna drink bad, but I can't, I'm up near two   pounds. I 'bout shit my pants Sunday, started shakin' on   the way home, and got blitzed at the Heat. Think I ate some, too."

"Meet me out back in five, Jimmy. Out by where they load, right?"

"Way cool! I dunno what you got in that thing, but it sure works."

"Varies," said Len, who understood mankind's yearning for mystery and magic and his obligation to help with this. Waiting in the old mud-colored Impala, he considered what Jimmy Broughton had to surmount to accept his authority as a black trainer, and he fully understood what it said about their relationship that Jimmy had admitted his fear with such candor.

It was breaking dawn as Paco Gonzalez, groom and horse-whisperer, led Arabiche to the track, his gut resting comfortably on a wide belt. He handed the reins to his teenage cousin Carlos and tightened the saddle girths. Curious about what they could hope for, Len decided to work her himself. He mounted, entered the track, and slow-cantered, waiting for the owner, who showed up a minute later and gave him a nod. Len made a little *chirrup* and Arabiche took off. 'Biche moved smoothly at any speed and had no bad habits. She had no acceleration, either, picking up speed with ladylike decorum. If she got to the front in a race, she was passed in the stretch, usually by two or three horses. Of her two wins, the first was ancient history, the second a fluke in which she ran around three entangled competitors to win. She never 'exploded', as McGoohey put it, never gave that beautiful, terribly exciting burst that everyone understood, including other horses. She could run forever, but she lacked the sacred madness. 'Biche didn't care; she had too much horse sense, a quality not prized in thorough-breds.

Sitting on the rail watching his horse work, McGoohey was expressionless, as if sprayed into place like the thick, wavy, iron-gray hair that topped his blunt powerful frame, but he radiated rude energy and determination. Len and Paco had long agreed that 'Biche was a natural breeder, and with his assent, they were all on the same page. She might not have the class, which was essential-ly a matter of spirit and will, but she was exceptionally sound and did have fine blood. Not especially knowledgeable in horse mat-ters, the owner was increasingly convinced his Saratoga plan would work, and she would bear a great foal by a celebrated sire, transporting him, Padraic McGoohey III, to that heady world of highfalutin' LA celebrities he secretly wished to join, a desire implanted by his wife with effects he didn't fully grasp and wasn't inclined to think about.

His horse galloped by more or less full-bore, then Len pulled her up to be hot-walked by Carlos. As usual, her fractions were no more than decent. McGoohey ignored her, his silent obses-sive stare loaded with demand. Len wanted success as badly as anyone, but as Paco had observed, this particular horse would have to be doped to the gills to give everything. No one wished to abuse the lady and get them all thrown out of racing for life, so she went on as the stable favorite, getting endless carrots, apples, and sugar cubes.

After a small eye-opener from his flask chased with the bottled water his wife left for him each morning, McGoohey broke his silence with care.

"Best blood in the string," he observed in a reasonable but transparent tone. "Only one that looks right. Breeder. Popsicle wasn't cut, might have used him."

"Yeh, she got that blood," agreed Len tactfully, thinking that all of McGoohey's horses lacked something essential, in this case testicles.

Paco, standing slightly behind the two at the rail, nodded to himself. Overweight and underpaid, Paco was not a talker around the owner. He was a dreamer, subject to visions, fearless, moving at his own speed. He smoked weed excessively but he always knew what to do, and he had the best hand with horses of anyone in the barns. Everything had slipped into place when Len hired him. At times it was almost magical, which McGoohey would never see. But the job beat hell out of construction, he could smoke discreetly, and he had his horses to talk to. McGoohey thought they were his horses, but Paco, Len and the horses knew better.

An unmistakable screaming whinny ripped through the soft morning. Fifty feet away was the useless Popsicle, cautiously surrounded by new owner, trainer, grooms, and a doubtful exercise boy. Unhappy with his new support group, his eyes rolled madly, jaws wide, haunches swinging as he tried to line up for a kick or bite, his crazed whinnies cutting through everything. Then he went silent, hooves planted in an unnatural, wide-splayed stance, vibrating with rage as one groom held the bridle while another tightened the girths. Then he locked his hands for the exercise boy's left foot so he could throw the other leg over, and everyone stepped quickly away as the horse went into a raging fandango, half bucking, half rearing, then prancing sideways onto the track.

Misses Paco, thought Len, and shifted his attention to Carlos, hot-walking 'Biche, who hardly needed it. As usual she had plenty of gas left in the tank. Her lack of desire was one problem, and the solution was breeding her. But Len knew McGoohey was the real problem, cantankerous and raw, standing squarely in his own way. The custodians of that classy nut-case blood instinctively closed ranks against him. As Len settled himself at the rail to observe the fragile Tokyo Tamari breeze, the owner passed him a two-day-old Racing Form.

"Missile Man. Record syndication," said McGoohey with devout respect. "Gotta be the most expensive jism on the market."

"Yeh, he the one. Line form to the right. Lee Farms horse. Lee Farms up there with Winstar and Claiborne. Gonna be next Calumet with Double-M. Already got his daddy, the Commander. Hot blood."

"Perfect for 'Biche," said McGoohey passionate and transparent, revealing the Saratoga secret agenda, which Len had already figured out. His part was to open the door by having 'Biche run well against Missile Man's stablemate, Black Ice, a big favorite. Then the owner would talk to the Lees. Like most of his schemes it was simple, tainted with fantasy, and relied on his relentless drive to carry the day. Lee Farms was one outfit McGoohey hadn't alienated, and the pairing made sense. 'Biche had the soundness that was always in doubt for Missile Man, a sickly two-year-old that had come around dramatically to run away with the Derby, tying Secretariat's record. The legend began that day, and both men knew it by heart. But Double-M was the Prince, and 'Biche was just another pretty girl, which her owner didn't get. The Emperor McGoohey was a powerful dreamer, and it had helped him bully his way up through the construction business. In the world he dreamed of entering he was a boring lout.

Len sat motionless, projecting sanity and calm. *Chill, Pat, get a grip. This barely minor league ball we got here.* But telling the emperor that he was missing his clothes when his emerald eyes were radiating this heady dream… that was not an option.

He excused himself to confer with Paco about Tokyo Tamari, and visit him in his stall. He was a friendly beast, swift and flawed, and he allowed both men to examine his delicate ankles. "Swelling's been gone two days," he observed. "Real workout tomorrow?"

"Still don't feel right. Like you sprain your wrist, swelling is down but wrist don't feel right. He too willing, hurt himself again 'cause he like to run. Lotta heart. We jus' breeze him, get blood moving "

"McGoo gettin' impatient."

"Nothing new, right? I tell him, he find fault. You trainer, plus he like you. Never talk to me, like I am peon."

Len nodded. "So I tell him, no problem. Like to put Toky's head on 'Biche."

"McGoo always buy horse with problem, save money. Popsicle was stud, be perfect for 'Biche. How come he got this attitude on me, Len? I no fuck up."

"How he is, man. You ain't alone. Any dreams about Saratoga?"

"Just now hear about it, sound crazy to me. He need Step program."

Len sidestepped a Step lecture and drove home to shower.

Had it been better working construction? The mood was still with Paco when Len and McGoohey left in mid-morning. He set Carlos at his tasks and left to kill some time with his old friend Juan, also known as Don Juan or DJ, because of his endless success with women. He had the top floor of a small house in a safe neighborhood, and an easy cheerful mood prevailed. Tall, and thin, Juan's true calling was women, which had extended his active life into his sixties. He lived alone, a friendly *soltero*, and there was often a group hanging out in his front room, some between jobs, some to be away from their families for a while. Paco jogged up the two flights of stairs to see how he'd feel, and saw that he wasn't really ready for construction work after all. He caught his breath, then knocked.

"Door is open."

Inside was the lanky DJ, his green recliner at half mast, smiling as usual. On a long brown corduroy couch were two young Mexican-Americans he'd met before, junior guys, both in construction, looking to learn. Everything was old and comfortable, the room spacious and neat. Mellow in here, thought Paco. *La Raza*. Home. He said hello to everyone.

"How you doing, Paco?" asked DJ.

Paco shrugged and smiled as well as he could, and went into the bathroom to relieve himself and slow down. Still unsettled, he re-entered the front room as one of the guys on the couch was lighting up and sat down to join the circle. Like himself, DJ had a special kind of knowledge, and not just about women. He always knew what Paco meant to say, no matter how the words came out, and he knew about his daytime dreams, which struck him as a further gift.

"Tough morning, huh?" observed DJ. Paco nodded and accepted the bone for a refresher hit. His expression quieted the others.

"*Coño!* Fucking ethnic shit getting me down. Boss too much. Man ignore me, every day find some new way to insult, like hobby. Old days, someone keep up this shit with me, I just stick him."

The dark energy in his voice was deadly calm. They all knew about it and except for DJ, they lived with it. The two on the couch, murmured agreement, Paco's status was understood. Everyone knew he had a big gift for horses, and his knuckle-dot tattoos said that he'd been in a gang. Their respect was evident, and Paco felt better.

"This boss," remarked DJ, "he probably got no idea what he's doing to people. Just bein' himself. Maybe not ethnic at all, just bad person."

"Know what he's doing every second. Man is fool about horses, no love. This thing I got, he needs it, and he blind to it. Now has this crazy idea, go to super-big east coast race with mare she don' win at home. Good blood, jus' won't run. We talk about it, she know I am unhappy but she is born breeder, drop first class foal. Owner finally gets it, then act like his idea. But black guy trainer, we talk, he listen, no problem. One smart thing boss does, hire this guy. But me, no respect."

"Yeah, I see," said DJ in his peaceful voice: "But you got to use your gift. Obligation to use it."

"Your thing man, nice obligation to have, women all over you since forever. Where you get this from?"

"Who knows? God give everyone something, horses for you, women for me, magic hands for my brother the thief. Don't use it, goes away like muscle. You born with it."

Paco spoke for the young guys, who expected it.

"Yeah. Just always like animals, not afraid of animals, make friends easy, but mostly I learn it from stepfather. Mother meets Miguel, passing through from Jalapa, horse country. *Vaquero*, always with horses. He going north, so we all go together. Good guy. What I got, I learn from Miguel. He just tell me, you and horse basically the same, minor difference, can communicate. Special language – body and voice, eyes. Also teach that horse can get scared, confused, misunderstand, an' maybe you get hurt. One day show me how to take horse off his feet, put on ground, make him see how it is. I skip school, follow him around, learn from him."

"Like you learning a job?" said one of the young laborers.

"Like learning everything need to know," said Paco. The temperature of the room was perfect, the weed delicious, and Boss Pat forgotten. DJ smiled and spoke.

"Someone coming over, guys," he added. "Have to clean up a little."

The evil mood was gone and Paco wanted to be with his family for a while. Then wash his Camaro, eat dinner, find a Meeting, go out and talk about the Steps.

4

One section of blazing airport tarmac far from the terminal had been set aside for deplaning horses and a pair of long horse vans. It was high noon, fiercely bright, a day to Len Thomas's liking. In a strip of shade provided by one wing of an antique prop-jet stood a handful of grooms, trainers and assistants. Under the other was a group of reporters and photographers exchanging disinformation, all with dark glasses to fend off the relentless glare. The media men wore mostly khakis, loafers, and dress shirts without ties, and had jackets slung over their shoulders. Several jacketless New Yorkers wore designer jeans and expensive sneakers, and made more frequent trips to the beer cooler. DeQuincy, internationally acclaimed winner of three straight classics on the continent, was just arriving via specially adapted Boeing 737, in a large, heavily padded, gyro-stabilized stall that rode free within the fuselage, reducing sharp motion. Simulated daylight and dark came and went at appropriate computerized times. DeQuincy's pony-friend was in similar accommodations, and they could get a head and neck into each others' stalls for friendly dialog.

The plane was unmistakable, a suave pale silver with bold scarlet Arabic markings. It rolled gently to a stop and the press strolled out of the shade with notepads, Nikons and video cameras, hoping for some Muslim arrogance that might jump their work to the front page. DEFIANT SHEIKH LAKHAM WILL NOT CONDEMN TERRORISTS, SHRUGS OFF INQUIRIES ABOUT COUSIN. With the anniversary of 9/11 approaching, that would be perfect. Two of the New Yorkers, both skilled Fox employees, had prepared a number of gambits for baiting the Sheikh (who was also a Prince). Research had confirmed him to be a distant cousin by marriage of a talented and newsworthy terrorist. It also confirmed that the two had not spoken for many years, but this fact had no journalistic value.

Lakham was always a story, starting with the handsome

young Sheikh and his blondes. Within Arab racing circles, their centuries old and very respected operation was a great thorn in the side of Makhtoum's tricontinental Godolphin Racing empire, the largest thoroughbred operation in the world. The Lakhams regarded them as *arrivistes*, without style or wisdom, a family of no consequence until an oil company arrived to provide revenues in the vicinity of ten million dollars per day. If Makhtoum showed up and could be induced to chat about that terrorist Lakham cousin, Team Fox was ready. A tiny video cam developed for spies peeked through a hole in the photographer's many-pocketed vest as the media strolled over. Within minutes an elaborate ramp with padded side-rails was set up by a silent three-man Arab crew. Several silent armed guards descended to create a perimeter, followed by DeQuincy, a sleek black stallion well aware of his celebrity. He was led by his portly British trainer, trailed by his pony and two assistants.

An airport veteran, DeQuincy proceeded to shake his head, look around, and then walk about with a light, easy step, loosening up at the end of a shank held by the trainer. He was in fine fettle, unaffected by his flight, presently trotting smoothly in a big circle on padded rubber shoes, a well-schooled and self-possessed horse with fine, lustrous eyes. The press got their pictures and rearranged in a loose semi-circle in front of the passenger exit, waiting for his owner. The Sheikh-Prince watched from behind one-way glass with a blonde and waited for them to leave. He had never liked that cousin-by-marriage who went bad, and would have said as much, but he knew that it would be wiser to let his horse speak for him.

While the media waited him out, eleven California horses were stepping into the heavy mid-day sun from a McClintock plane several hundred yards away. By ones and twos the press gave up on the Sheikh and went over to watch. Arabiche was third out, graceful, head high, in her usual good mood. Several reporters wondered if this was a dark horse being smuggled in, but only briefly. Len could pass as a serious character in his tailored khakis and Italian silk-and-wool jacket, but he was the wrong color. Paco they saw as Sancho Panza on holiday in super-baggy ghetto jeans and vintage Cheech-and-Chong T-shirt. McGoohey was absent, closing down a site, getting leased machinery returned and paying off the men, and had yet to service his wife in hopes that this would *keep her on the reservation*, in his words.

Soon the area around the McClintock plane was full of horses, several urinating, one evacuating its bowels. Then they began loading into battered six-horse trailers as DeQuincy followed his pony into his personal trailer. The California loading took a long time, with two bad actors full of testosterone dancing around as if they'd never seen a trailer before.

Stupid horses, reflected Len irritably, watching this show with Paco and waiting for 'Biche to be loaded. His careful observation of DeQuincy had stuck in his mind, and these animals reminded him of kids hanging around the street corners of his adolescence. He turned to Paco, who had found an old stingy-brim straw hat to replace his Dodgers cap. Its sweat ring irritated Len, who had much on his mind.

"Okay, you know where she goin', right?"

"Same as others, main barn, number forty-seven," replied Paco. "Hey man, you not coming? What if is problem?"

"Like what? We all confirmed, faxes in the envelope."

Paco shrugged, a unique shrug that required no physical movement, and Len decided to skip the beer at Madam Jumel's, which would have been ideal in this weather. Just one beer, real German beer, and not too damn cold. But Paco was right, he owed it to horse and owner not leave her with a gifted but disoriented groom who spent all his money on weed and automobile-enhancement while his family subsisted on the largesse of the state. Paco alone had the power to make Len Thomas into a Republican. How had illiterate Paco qualified to become a citizen, and what did that say? Tax money from hard-earned wages, his wages, was stripped monthly by the state to be distributed to Paco-people. In this mood, Darwin became prominent in Len's thinking, along with Spengler's *Decline of the West*. Two years he'd kept at that pair of tomes, understanding bits and pieces, rereading and thinking, developing his inner Nazi, unable to finish them but never returning them to the library. A skilled swimmer in life's waters, Len was unbothered by Spengler's grim Teutonic vision, but now his stomach was tightening up. Paco's seed ought not be cast so widely, much less subsidized by the state.

"You wanna smoke?"

"No, I do not wanna smoke, and I don't wanna car fulla smoke, either. I wanna see 'Biche feelin' okay about things, get inspected, and then get in her stall."

"Man, I only *ask*."

"You got your answer, right?"

Paco knew how to needle Len, and enjoyed turning him into this weird black gringo bastard. Not many years ago, when he was a gang member and out of his mind on cocaine, it would have been dangerous to address Paco this way, but life had taught him flexibility. A wetback at five from tiny Tica de Gualpa, little Paquito had found himself in a strange land full of miracles where people spoke a new language taught by cold, towering foreign women. When Miguel died, his adroit mother struck up a relationship with a good-natured well-connected older man who became his second stepfather and got him legalized. Paco attended school for a while and learned enough English to get by, but his soul lived a stateless, under-the-radar existence, still Indian. Flunking out in ninth grade, he had fallen in with the Cabs, short for Caballeros, a junior branch of the Clantons. Graduated to full colors and certified gang-tough after a knife fight, the teen-age Paco was doing a brisk business in weed and hosting fine parties until he attended a wedding where he met Conchi, fresh from Mexico. Pretty and cooperative, she joined him in a sexual tornado followed by a shotgun wedding, kids, construction work, and finally a Step program to wean him from cocaine. His fatalism became mystical, laced with Step mottos.

With marriage, debts and eleven-hour workdays had come the first dreams.. Vivid, beautiful daytime dreams that came unexpectedly, sudden visions of things to come, often accurate. His present job had followed such a dream, a dream full of happiness and horses. One morning a foreman sent him to deliver an envelope personally to McGoohey, who had not arrived. As Paco wandered the shedrow, Len looked on and named him: Paco Gonzalez, Horse-Whisperer, and Equine Rights Advocate. He loved horses, it was reciprocal, and he was fearless, even with the savage Popsicle, who greeted him with friendly snorts. By the time McGoohey arrived, Paco had made friends with them all, and Len had hired him to replace a worthless groom, his first major initiative. He was off the wheelbarrows, effective immediately. A dream had brought him his horses and a great new job, erasing all doubt about their miraculous power. Right now the job was chafing, though.

"Okay-okay," said the horse-whisperer. "I jus' need something for my nerves, everything so different here man, never come here before."

"Right. So you gotta be alert. Mister McGoohey ain't spendin' all this money for you to smoke weed in Saratoga, *chaparrito*. Bright eye, bushy tail, that's what he wanna see."

And now *chaparrito*. Okay, his legs were short, so naturally he was short, but Len usually spared him this kind of shit. No sleep, no smoke, and now these jabs. Okay, play with him.

"Yeah, right, Len. How come we here, anyhow? She never win up here. This worse than Santa Anita, man."

"Better, Paco, not worse," said Len slipping into the chilly, educated voice he saved for dealing with certain situations. "Saratoga is a top venue, one of a kind. Saratoga is the Tiffany's of horse racing, located in a beautiful town near a seat of higher learning."

"Who this Teefany?"

"Top jewelry store in US. Like Winston diamonds, bluegrass horses."

"Si," murmured Paco, impressed with Len's knowledge and perspective, putting aside his grievance, relieved to have avoided this responsibility.

"You got a woman up here?" he asked when they were on the highway.

"No. No woman up here. We here to take care of business. 'Biche get third in her race is all that matters."

"How she get third in Teefany if she fourth in Wal-Mart?"

"Arabiche no Wal-Mart horse, Paco. McGoo break you in half, he hear you say that."

"Lotta fourth place though."

Len said nothing, putting on a wise face and extricating himself from the smoky and seditious world of Paco Gonzalez, horse-hypnotist. Having allowed McGoohey to believe that third place in a serious race was possible for 'Biche, he had a serious problem, especially since the owner believed this would create an opening to Lee Farms and Missile Man's services. Heads could roll if third place didn't happen, and the plan was doomed even if it did. McGoo would approach Missile Man's owner and embarrass himself again. Len couldn't wait for Jimmy to show up.

Dixie had an aversion to any house that did not feel both fresh and lived in, so she'd sent Holly ahead to open the Saratoga house. But two long days of phone calls, Saratoga rumors and difficult decisions without Holly reminded her how much she depended on her quick wits and little jokes. And no one else could get the compote right, and she couldn't sleep worth a damn.

And the Eclipse Award. Theirs to loose barring bad luck or a big ugly Texas mare named Margiedaw. Dixie couldn't relax, and by the third morning she really missed Holly's morning chat and the pleasant stimulus of her quick, ever so compatible mind. Edgy didn't begin to describe her condition. The morning before they left she came awake from a steamy dream about Holly. It was right up there with Katie Spencer at boarding school, going out for field hockey and breaking a tooth to be with her. She just didn't feel right when she was away from Holly, so why should she be? And it had to be mutual – she just knew it, and she so loved that delicious slim little cinnamon girl. Loved her half to death. Outrageous, but what the hell, she'd always been that. And she still got off with men sometimes, it wasn't as if she was some hard-core dyke. Just somebody who needed love. Holly's.

With coffee she became her normal, focused self, dealing with whatever came up, wanting to be up there already, with Black Ice whipping Margiedaw and those pretenders down the stretch. The Travers all over. God, let there be a speed horse to wear down Margiedaw, dumb Texas animal that just had to have the lead.

Studying her husband across the table, Jasmine McGoohey didn't really know what was on her husband's mind, but since the Popsicle nightmare she was noticing that these horses, so exciting and prestigious during their whirlwind courtship, were a financial drain and an ongoing disturbance. She sensed that her husband would be *doing a geographic*, as the Step people said. Getting away and making Popsicle history. Fine, but that episode stayed fresh for her, because she had a soft spot for innocent Jimmy, and she'd seen him close to death. Seconds later she'd damn near puked on the Commissioner.

"Gotta go East couple days, talk to a few owners," said McGoohey, as if it was barely worth discussing. They were having one of her vegetarian dinners, and he was politely munching on a simulated hamburger with simulated satisfaction. "Need some new clothes, too. Somethin' appropriate for a classy Eastern club-house, y'know."

At that point his wife sensed an agenda beyond simple escape. He didn't want to say exactly where he was going, but that was just him, and it didn't bother her. Clothes were not a problem – she knew just how to clothe his burly aggression in a way that gave him a citizenly gravitas. Once she'd caught him at the hall mirror looking pleased with the effect.

"I'll be glad to pick some things up, Pat. I made a *dobsche torte* for dessert (his eyes lit), but remind me to check your measurements. I want my honey looking good for those New Yorkers."

"I ain't gained a pound, word of honor, but who said anything about New York?"

"I just assumed. If you're going out to Long Island this time of year, that's a different sartorial story, Patty-poo."

His face darkened with exasperation at the last.

"Don't go ballistic, Padraic, you know I'm just teasing."

"Anyhow, neither one. I'm goin' t'Saratoga, gonna give 'Biche a chance to see how the other half lives."

Left out! Instantly she was so angry, jealous, insulted and hurt that she could only lie about it, which she did perfectly, as if she'd never heard of Saratoga.

"I'll get on the computer and check it out. I should be able to get shots from last year if I look around. I'll dress you so you fit right in."

Being left out was just fine, she decided. She could be as self-amusing as the next narcissist. She extended her research past the time when McGoohey began to feel sleepy in an unhappy way, Thursdays being informally understood to be lucky sex days.

Falling asleep exhausted over his coffee, aware that he'd blown it again, he remarked on the extent of her research.

You can wait for it, big guy, was her unspoken reply. Aloud she said, "It isn't as if they have pages and pages on what to wear in this ditzy little town that happens to have a race track."

"Yeah, I should've planned this better. I'm gonna go in and lie down, watch the news."

This was exactly what Jasmine had in mind. She knew perfectly well what Saratoga was, and that she could be useful there while enjoying herself, letting rich men from ripe old Eastern families glimpse delicious bits of her lovely body, getting them invited to the right places and generally facilitating her husband's awkward ascent, the selfish bastard. As she operated her smooth silver laptop, she reviewed her relationship with the feral but inspired capitalist she'd married. Well educated, Jasmine kept it to herself, relying on looks and charm, bypassing her education to make swift decisions on an instinctive childlike basis.

She'd married McGoohey because she'd never seen anything like him before and had outgrown her respectable middle-class family, which, while it had its lawyers and doctors, was founded on accountancy and was pretty damn dull. Jasmine was a gifted consumer who could use a McGoohey to full advantage, but she still recoiled from her husband's remarkable mental and physical coarseness. His skin fascinated her with its freckles, red spots, and variations in texture. But she'd seen him for a winner, a winner on a scale none of her family could match, respecting his manic creativity and gift for gain. The Felters came from a diffused but proud Sephardic tradition of decorous flirtation and affairs conducted with Proustian finesse, and her mind was active in all aspects of a relationship. She reflected that of the McGoohey operation, its leader was actually the least attractive in sensual terms. But of course subordinates were off limits. Brooding on Sunday's catastrophe, cause of this Saratoga excursion, she remembered her terrible fear for little Jimmy – the smell of death when that crazy fucking horse nearly took him down. Jimmy, with his strange tunnel-vision reality and inability to conceal his attraction, was her favorite. Jasmine thought him cute, in his homely way, and romantically courageous, right out of a movie. As she saw it, Pat had endangered Jimmy's life with that crazy horse just to show off for the Commissioner.

On the plus side, it made her feel good that her husband worshipped her even as he lied to her and did stupid things like excluding her from this trip. As her mind roamed, another self was planning phone call follow-ups to the orders she was placing, setting up morning fitting appointments. The right people at Saratoga would be dressed like star-spangled lollipops, which worked better with slender men, but her Pat would look the part.

5

Call it a mansion, that's what it's about, thought Holly, infatuated with the Saratoga house. She loved wooden houses, and this one was a classic, a white Victorian three-decker that Dixie's grandfather had picked up for a song after the Crash of '29. It sat back from the road at a perfect distance, with green shutters and fine flowerbeds to set it off. But it was high-maintenance, and the new caretaker couple had done nothing. Mr. and Mrs. Salmon were living like moles in the servant's quarters and hadn't even thought to air the house. Inspecting it room by room, Holly's pleasant mood was replaced by a hard, cold anger as she saw the job ahead. In the kitchen afterward she stood looking over this dull blobby pair with her cool gaze, started a list on a legal pad, then drove them without mercy. Two days of bossing white folks around; what a smile, even if they were only a pair of townie chuckleheads. But Dixie had come up a winner with this idea, no doubt about it. A little project all her own, and two days without horse talk and pre-race jitters. Holly addressed her victims with civil contempt and cool composure, all three standing.

"This kitchen is not clean. Mrs. Dixon would notice that immediately and hold me responsible. Everything will have to come out of the cupboards, they'll be washed, and new shelf paper laid in. Then we'll see what can be saved."

Not very much, because Holly skimmed a fifteen percent commission in the process of replacing anything, money destined for her well placed investments. The recession had barely touched her, and she'd seen those Enron crackers headed off a cliff the minute the California governor talked about sueing. But later, standing in a big shop full of beautiful colors and cutting a deal for daily flower replacement with a screaming-gay florist who compared her to the young Diana Ross, she was aware of discontent. She missed her little group of friends at the Blue Lantern, and she missed *flirting*. Out there somewhere was a man or woman she could stand waking up to, and she didn't care which it was. And a job where kissing ass was not included, although, dammit, she missed Dixie.

She's my significant other for now. I can live with it, but I didn't get my fancy degree to sell my ass, and it's over six years now.

These were troubling thoughts that sent her to a zone rarely visited. The Lees appreciated Holly's unusual detachment and sophistication, but took it for granted as part of her intelligence. That was one element, but behind that detachment was experience, a high school experience she would never forget. At seventeen, Holly had been *broken in*, as the man put it, to *the life*, as it was called. Ageless Little Isaac had picked up pretty, bookish Holly after school in his pale blue convertible, seduced her, then kidnapped her and installed her in his fine Atlanta apartment. After that he had beaten her for some imaginary insult and put her on the street for nine days that shattered the precocious and inexperienced high school girl, introducing her to normal-appearing Caucasian clients with needs she could never have imagined. When she ran off to the bus terminal with five hundred dollars the fifth day, Little Isaac was waiting, and beat her again, skillfully avoiding bruises. Several days later he was found dead in his hotel apartment by an associate who was expediently charged with the crime.

Afraid to go home, she had showed up dazed on the doorstep of Cousin Gentian, the strangest, strongest, and least righteous of her relatives, a believer in magic. She spent several days calming her niece, and then somehow quieted her mother. When Holly returned home to rejoin her class and catch up in her schoolwork (it was assumed she'd been pregnant), she was much the same, except that the expression in her eyes was calm and level beyond her years and she didn't date any more. Several months later she graduated Salutatorian, won a scholarship, and sailed through a good Northern school with honors, learning quickly in and out of classes, having an affair with a faculty member, and developing a cool aplomb that stood up in all weathers. Offered an astounding yearly wage by Annabelle Dixon, a graduate and patron of the college, she went for it.

Who would I have been without that? she wondered, driving

from shop to shop in the rented blue BMW convertible. She returned refreshed and resumed the pleasures of sadistic but civil bitchery. After rattling off a new task list, she left again, saying she could be reached on her mobile phone.

Mrs. Salmon, shapeless and huge in a gray work outfit, stared at her in the doorway. She'd heard tell of cell phones, but *mobile* – what was that? Holly held up the phone, wrote down the number, and left to check out a place called The Rafters, her cinnamon shoulders succulent under a fuchsia hat. The place turned out to be a big disco room jammed with skinny, raucous near-midgets. Then Sperry's, offering a selection of gaudy, gawky, rich white people with Madras jackets and Lily Pulitzer dresses and not a Brother to be found except in some menial uniform. *Shit!* The restless boredom started up again, but when she returned it was very satisfying to see Mr. and Mrs. Salmon in their matching gray outfits hauling a filthy old rug through the door like field hands. Upstairs, she looked through every closet and bureau with sharp eyes and a sensitive nose. If she kept driving them, the place would be perfect, and after a few days without her special compote, Dixie would deeply appreciate her accommodations, a drink complete with magical ingredient, and herself, the perfect companion.

So why don't you just give me this nifty house, cause then I can live my own life and maybe really love you, bitch! One more degree and I could talk myself into a job at Skidmore and seduce myself a cute little Waspy professor complete with pedigree and trust fund, and show him a few things he wouldn't want to do without. Or rent rooms to select students and have my own little world.

Which could never happen, because Dixie was a demented, jealous, rageaholic who liked her company too much to give it up. In this mood Holly's mind gravitated to the wild and crazy possibility of diverting some of those trust moneys into an offshore account. It was something she periodically fantasized about when irritated with her employer. Holly was strongly risk-averse though, so this remained a fantasy, but it continued to amaze her that all that money was protected only by a toothless guard-dog family friend who probably had the code-words scribbled on the wall. In a meritocracy, Ronnie Pitt would be a smiling doorman or clerk; in his present role he was a temptation to white collar crime.

Her business courses and a steady diet of *The Wall Street Journal* and *The Economist* told her she could do his job much better.

The mood passed, and she went back to harassing the Salmons, but after assigning their new tasks she felt ashamed of herself and came to an unexpected dead stop in the large, old-fashioned third-floor bath. Here she fell abruptly into despair, then tears, then black rage. As she looked at herself in the mirror considering cosmetic repair, the rage simmered. Closing her eyes she wondered: would she ever in this life, for one whole minute, feel truly free? What did it feel like to own your own life? Did Dixie herself actually feel free, or just powerful? Opening her eyes, Holly perceived a dangerous lack of clarity in them and realized she was exhausted and vulnerable. The rage fell away, and she went to her room to collect herself and write up a final list of chores and errands. Then she found the Salmons, whom she couldn't stand to look at any more, and told them they were free until eight the next morning.

Out of the blue it struck Len that it wasn't just McGoohey and his frecklebrained antics and insults and hard stare. After eighteen years, he'd had enough of the horse game. Outgrown it. As he watched the old vet checking slobbery horse mouths for the numbers tattooed on their lips, he was offended by the rich, rude backstretch aroma hanging in the steamy air and the presence of too many horse-people. It was taking forever, and he'd wasted another afternoon. He wanted a shower. No, a *bath*. In a big sunken tub with water jets. Another horse's mouth opened, lip bared, and the animal was checked off. *Boring!* Boring and dangerous. Before he hit fifty, Len wanted to be doing something else in a different world. Once he'd been a halfway decent piano player, good enough to play high-school gigs. Got himself busted, avoided jail by going into the Army. Sayonara keyboard dreams.

What else would he need for this new life? Maybe he wanted a house. Brand new idea. Another horse stepped up and he speculated that he could probably make it as a jewel thief to the rich and famous. He'd tended bar and waited tables, and when required he could speak good American English. Boston had been a hundred and ten percent nasty, but his widowed mother had taught him to read, and the notorious school-busing program had projected him into a mysterious world of well-to-do whites, where he'd studied hard and made the most of it. His ear picked up language and accents, making top-end Step'n Fetchit easy. High school had been high stress, but he'd learned a lot. His gay English teacher had never made a pass, but got his full attention with a single comment on his term paper, "Black Writers of the Americas."

I cannot give an honors grade to a paper with this title that omits the self-educated Machado de Assis, equal or superior to any writer you have named. Try Epitaph for a Small Winner.

Self-educated. No wasted words, little sting to it – it had tightened his belly. That shrewd Mr. Johnston had also given him a copy of his personal reading list through grad school, complete with his ratings and comments, which Len still had.

Step, fetch, filch. Then back to Europe, where he should have stayed after his discharge. He'd find himself a bohemian-type woman with a taste for black men. Charlotte with a little *je ne sais quoi*. That was still a popular model, went way back, and he had naturally good manners, which worked over there. It wasn't too late for a move. Take a chance and be that guy.

He liked it. Out of the horse game, out of this fat ignorant country that twisted black people out of shape from birth. And who knew what he'd find inside himself? Step one, get out from under all this damn *crap*. Infinitely rich males in some of the loudest, silliest threads he'd ever seen. Carefully tailored off-the-wall oranges; bellowing reds, glaring limes, and bizarre plaids; plump bellies and thighs ready for basting and roasting. The women looked better in their flowered dresses and the large statement hats that protected them from the sun that was battering the mostly balding middle-aged skulls with rays they couldn't handle. Len was, by Saratoga standards, under-dressed. Featherweight summer tweed jacket, tan button-down shirt, medium-bright paisley tie and his Italian loafers, which were suffering in the damp soil. Classic, but no edge. Many other trainers had a similar look, as if afraid to outshine the exuberant owners. He was the only black trainer, ignored as usual. Fine. He wished he had a horse that would blow their heads off instead of a cute lazy little mare that lacked class.

And here was Margiedaw. The notorious Margiedaw, known for constant, grinding acceleration throughout a race, right to the finish. Rarely beaten, never cracked. Only Black Ice could get by her in those stretch duels. A great beast of a horse, sound and solid. *Big.* Suddenly he hadn't had enough of the horse game after all. This ugly, mottled-buckskin gray excited him. Bred to the teeth for power, front-running, and attrition. Proud animal, suspicious of the old vet, who'd easily calmed the other horses. He made some friendly sounds and patted her on the neck, and eventually she allowed access to her unlovely lips. Then she danced back on the shank and left with her groom, both stepping high.

A horse like that, thought Len. Make you forget everything else, give you something to think about every morning, keep the ladies in perspective. Or that DeQuincy, horse of a lifetime, win from in front, come from behind. Missile Man's natural rival if they hadn't retired him to stud. Arabs losing their ass everywhere, but they sure got some horses. And he had important work to do with Jimmy. Tricky unaccustomed work in a foreign environment, with McGoo due soon. Stress.

Finally Arabiche appeared with Paco, a pretty horse with enough distinction to merit a second look, and Paco looking right for once. He'd changed into khakis and a passable open-necked navy sport shirt. As he led 'Biche to the vet, she as much as smiled at the man. Perfect manners, make some rich girl a great hack, thought Len. Learns fast, probably jump too. He joined Paco as they went to her stall.

"Lookin' good there, my man."

"Yeah, well – Saratoga, right? Teefany time. You me an' 'Biche lookin' good, McGoo we see about."

Len was surprised at the edge Paco could come up with if you got him off his round-the-clock herb. All business this afternoon. Then an inquiring look.

"Yeah, okay, private stock, you earned it," Len responded.

In the car on the way to their rooming house Len lit the pipe with his gold Zippo and inhaled lightly. Paco ended his fast with a pair of humongous tokes, each one held for the absolute limit, and was his usual smiling foggy self when they checked in.

"5:30, backstretch, right?"

"*Si.* Blue-jean an' sneakers okay?"

"Long as we clean. Oklahoma trainin' track, just a breeze. Thinkin' we trick her a little, don't ask her to run hard, maybe she do it on race day just to be cute."

"Good as anything. She like a little game, this lady, all mental. Like pretty girl want to get married before she give it up. Drive you crazy."

6

Holly woke from her nap fuzzy-brained and mean, relieved to be alone. After two cups of strong coffee she was skimming the local paper and feeling frisky. Marcus Wheatley was playing a room called the G-Spot, and she knew for a fact that any reasonably hip African-American would want to escape the prevailing local paleness in Wheatley's company. He was so fine a player on his juiced Hammond that she and her mother could actually agree on it. And the G-Spot claimed to be New York State's soul-food center north of Harlem. Trusting to that, she ate half a tiny peanut-butter sandwich, took a leisurely bath in a vast old tub, dabbed herself delicately with a Parisian scent from her employer. Then she was out on the town, still ravenous, her short, lustrous hair sprayed into place. She drove off into the warm evening with the top down in hopes that some educated attractive person would notice her and maybe just vault gracefully into the car with a smile at a stop sign. None did, but the G-Spot turned out to be a classy black club sprinkled with white patrons. At the still half-empty bar, she ordered a red wine and some ribs with a side of greens. Halfway through this genuine treat came the first miracle: a strong, confident black male voice speaking her name in this town full of strangers.

"Holly St. Cyr?"

She dabbed at her mouth and turned deliberately to see a face that sent her back half a lifetime. Howard Budney, a tall shy boy she'd dated before Little Isaac knocked her out of alignment. She'd helped the handsome athletic Howard with his homework and been envied in her little clique. She seemed to recall that he'd gone to college on a football scholarship, leaving early to turn professional. One of those tall, quick ones that harassed other tall quick guys trying to catch the ball for the other side. Known as Flash to his many fans.

"How's the prettiest girl ever come out of Medgar Evers High School?"

"If that's me, she's doing fine, Howard. How about Flash Budney?"

"Me too, babe."

He plonked his large self into the next seat without waiting politely for an invitation in case she just might be waiting for someone. He'd been a star at each level in the football world and lost his manners, but he was a damn good-looking man now, and he still had that nice smile. It just wasn't shy any more. When his long fingers reached for a rib, she looked at him with a kind of schoolmarm expression that stopped him, made him smile and willed him to ask if he might. When he did, she laughed and cut a section for him.

"That's *much* better, Howard." Then she handed him a napkin.

His story was well-practiced: good contract just as he was flunking out, then doing great, putting money away. Bought a house for his mom, then banged up his knee in the middle of his fifth and best year. Came back next year, team made the playoffs on a Budney interception. League Championship, final playoff for the S-Bowl, and sho nuff, got the *other* knee. Doctor shot it up but it wasn't right, and his backup was worse, so no Bowl that year. And that knee never quite made it back, so there he was at a little college a hundred miles away, finishing his degree with education courses that would let him teach and coach.

A lengthy narrative with a downward tilt at the end, but his permanent smile still slipped into that disarming kid-grin from time to time. Holly kept eating and listening. Football had done more or less the same thing with Howard as Little Isaac had with her, though making him rich in the process. A Biker For Jesus now, he had given up his wild ways and held on to his money, of which he was proud, and referred to with pride, smug caution and subliminal fear.

"I come down with friends, if y'like to join us," he said politely, then asked about her doings, which she cut to an ultra-modest paragraph that left him guessing.

"You sure lookin' good for someone got her a nothin' job

with some rich old white folks," he said as they crossed the room. He walked without a limp, Holly noted, on guard now, thrown off by his size, vitality and animal intent. His casual confidence and energy seemed to obliterate people in his vicinity.

Further down the bar Len watched them leave with regret. He'd spotted her on entering, appreciating her poise and flawless cinnamon skin, noting the fearless application of hot sauce and the neat carnivorous way she did in those ribs. But there was something beyond all that, something about her that slipped his defenses. He wanted to understand what that thing was before making a move, and he'd outsmarted himself. He sipped his brandy, knowing that his interest wasn't going away. East Coast, that was part of it. College town, might be faculty. And so *fine*. So extremely fine. And now with brash big-butt Flash Budney, said to be out of the game with those bad knees, but still with that youthful magnetism. And money, of course. Bad luck. *Terrible* luck.

Len had chosen a stool with a good view of the big room, including the bandstand, where the group was setting up. The view included Budney's table. His friends were young salt and pepper followers. Quiet and thoughtful, Len looked away from the happy table and searched his face in the bar mirror. Dissatisfaction. With his love life, his employer, and those flawed horses the man gave him to work with. Dissatisfaction with his limited, mediocre existence. Flash Budney had not been mediocre, he'd been a rising star, stopped only by bad luck. True fact, move on.

Something French about this woman, he decided. Civilized and proud.

With this much clear, knowing where he stood, he felt free to make his move. *Obliged* to. But he also knew at a glance what Flashy Howard was all about. Dumb, dangerous, and sniffing hard. It puzzled him that they seemed to know each other; that didn't compute. Then a deep throaty blast from that hot-rod Hammond lifted the small hairs on his neck. Wheatley's theme, *Wheatstraws*, a tight little blues in disguise. Larry Young school, thinking man's organ. Fresh air swept through Llewellyn Thomas's synapses, restoring his perspective. *Came here to play tonight, not fall in love.* Just one last thing. He caught the bartender's eye and put down a twenty.

"Gotta go outside a few minutes, like to hold my seat."

"Got your name on it, man," smiled the baby-faced white boy. Sounded silly, but the kid meant to be friendly.

Outside was a light evening breeze, a pleasant reminder that his work was done for the day. He slipped his daily Marlboro Lite behind an ear and strolled the empty sidewalk, swivel-lid pipe in one hand, gold Zippo in the other. At the corner he glanced around, kept walking, and lit up without stopping. One enormous toke, Humboldt County earth-grown. He held in the smoke Paco-style while pocketing the pipe and meditating on his vice. He didn't like juiced Amsterdam weed, and wished he could experience the legendary varietals old-timers spoke of like fine wines. Acapulco Gold, Panama Red, Purple Pango, Punto Roja. The Mouton-Rothschilds of herb, replaced by unnatural designer herb developed by fish-belly-white Caucasians who should never have been let in on the secret in the first place. Skunk, Hydro, Canadian Sticky, whatever. He just didn't care to have his head knocked off.

After the long-delayed exhale he lit his daily cigarette and circled the large, pleasant, safe, small-town block, making it back to his seat just as Wheatley was going into a Larry Young classic, playing it so close Len found himself waiting for the Sam Rivers tenor solo. Barely into the first set and the room was pulsating. Again his eyes fell on Holly St. Cyr, most of her obscured by Budney, who was into a dead-serious pitch to get his ashes hauled.

On account of she'd been the one girl always understood him. Len could just about hear him. Well, she wouldn't be the first beautiful woman to succumb to a tall, rich, handsome semi-celebrity looking to settle into a classier lifestyle.

Thank God for Marcus Wheatley. The organist executed a remarkable two-handed criss-cross run to open his next chorus, lifting Len from this world long enough to obscure everything unattractive. His drummer was cooking up a solid meal with the local guitar player, who'd obviously memorized all the Master's works, most of them blues and standards, like an uptown New York group of twenty years back. It was Len's preferred taste – rock solid, but with an edge. Music you could dance to, too, some of it.

He ordered another brandy. A pretty girl down the bar smiled at him. Buy her a drink? No, he was targeted. The bartender

43

brought him a nice big Remy Martin and Len half closed his eyes, resting his soul in the G-Spot's throbbing musical cocoon. The next tune was a slow-dance number, seized upon by Budney as an opportunity to get his gnarly paws on Cinnamon Girl. Len stayed put, calming his devil and closing his eyes again, the better to enjoy the music and avoid watching her deal with Bigfoot. He was aware that between this woman, his pipe, and the hard liquor, he was in a pleasantly dangerous twilight zone, a nice private place except for this moronic steroid football nigger wrapped around the lady in question. He opened his eyes after the tune ended and saw that his rival was gone. Cinnamon girl was sitting toward the edge of the banquette a little apart from the others. The band went into one of Wheatley's big hits, a medium shuffle.

Mood I'm in, might do any kind of foolish thing, thought Len. Before cowardly thoughts could intervene, he walked straight to the mysterious stranger, smiled gently, and asked her for a dance. She returned a ladylike smile, taking his hand as she rose to her feet, the picture of grace. From the frightened silent faces of those in the booth, Len knew he was in very deep water, but the lovely round eyes said that she was bored with Bubba Howard, which was all they had to say.

And prim slim Cinnamon could get *down*. Smooth and cool, not a whole lot of motion, but in the zone, eyelids lowered. Words would just be superfluous, and Len Thomas had initiated many seductions on dance floors. He had no problem reading her classy little East Coast style, and shortly, with no change in expression, she began to open it up a little. No problem, no words. Hippest couple on the floor, Budney's friends aghast. He picked up on her and moved back just a little so she could see what he was doing, then threw in some things the younger set was doing in LA., which she picked up quickly, then getting a little more intricate with her foot thing, which he observed with respect. Little *test*. He hooked up with it, making the shift as the band started a fresh chorus.

Hot, thought Len Thomas. Man, this woman is hot.

Cool, thought Holly St. Cyr. This guy is fun.

Then the flicker of a glance, and the slightest change in her expression, and then another change of expression that made no sense at all until he felt a heavy hand resting on his shoulder. A

44

deep, unnaturally controlled voice spoke quietly:

"Cuttin' in."

Along with words, he'd forgotten all about Bad Knees Budney. Two hundred and thirty pounds of jealous Rottweiler. Len danced around the intrusion, gaining seconds, nodding a gracious *okay* at Howard Budney, having one last look at those lovely eyes telling him he'd better leave. She was concerned for him, worried about him, it was obvious and touching. He smiled and thanked her, and then she was gone, blocked off by Budney, a master of direct body language.

So busy dancing I forgot to get her number! Holly. Holly Sincere, something like that.

As he was leaving the pair turned, and he smiled at The Flash as if they were all members of a jolly little group with lots in common. Then he retreated to the bar to see him trying to keep up with the only woman to throw Len Thomas off the rails in more years than he wanted to think about. And he didn't even have her name, only knew she could dance her little feet off, and didn't care a bit for Handsome Howard.

I really need to get to know that woman, he decided, seated at the bar, avoiding eye contact as the tune ended and the dance floor cleared. He noticed that the club was filling up with people he didn't feel like looking at. Something told him to go, and he did, leaving enough money to cover his drinks and a big tip for the college boy. Then he walked around the parking lot half-buzzed and tried to guess what car she'd come in. The HBUD plates on a big BMW spoke for themselves, but that was as far as he got. Then a strange wave of relaxation engulfed him. He was going to see that woman again, he was sure of it.

Trudging through Albany International Airport in late afternoon with his carry-on bag, McGoohey was hung over, sour and surly, with a drink-sweated look, dressed even worse than usual. The energy drained out of Len as he looked him over. The immaculately tailored racing crowd were dressed like peacocks on angel-dust, and this owner was not. He looked shoe-horned into the suit, and no tailor could ever adjust for the chip on that sloping, meaty shoulder. The polyester was okay this year, but the tired maroon was completely out. He wasn't headed to the baggage claim, and the carry-on bag could not contain an alternate wardrobe. Obviously the plan for Jasmine to dress him hadn't happened. A wave of fatigue settled over the trainer. Moving closer through the sparse crowd, Len spotted white, tasseled, patent-leather loafers. Above these was the first pair of black dress socks he'd ever seen on McGoohey, and too-short uncuffed pants.

Hasn't worn this outfit for years, thought Len. Hid it away from Jasmine at the office. Put on weight and it shrank when he had it cleaned. And he's wearing the belt above his gut, which pulls the pants up level with the tops of those short little socks. New haircut, too, thatch roof look. 'Biche could win the damn race, and no one would want to talk to him.

McGoohey sensed his presence and looked around.

"Where the hell you been, Len?"

Tired little green eyes starting to harden.

"Lookin' for you, Chief. Gettin' afraid you missed your flight. Gimme that bag, Pat."

The valet act comfortably hypnotized McGoohey, who began to relax after handing over the bag, feeling more like an employer again. No longer disoriented and irritable, he aimed himself at the bar. Half a step behind, Len saw him coming together in a reasonable condition. As they entered the bar, a dull-looking local woman with a flat, bored face was smiling emptily into the dimmed room from behind the nearly empty bar. McGoohey took a seat toward the end and glanced inquiringly at his trainer as she came over.

"Answer is Yes," said Len.

Against his will, McGoohey had to smile.

"What was the question?"

"Yes, I want a drink. Bushmills neat, water back."

"Me too," said McGoohey, and the woman left.

"Also, Yes, you were right. She traveled fine, lookin' good. Plus Yes, Jasmine got you a good room, checked it out, best place in town. And Yes, entries in the box for both races. Only thing, we got to wait and see about which one."

"How about 'Yes, one fuckin' dull airport bar,'" said McGoohey, but in a mellow tone. "I hate the East Coast. Just something about it."

"Yeh," agreed Len. "How come Ah left Boston."

"Better out by the track," he added, satisfied with McGoohey's mood. The drinks arrived quickly and were small. Len looked down at his briefly, shook his head, and downed it in a single swallow. It was an unprecedented act, catching McGoohey by surprise and making him smile broadly. It was all turning into exactly that change of scene he'd been needing. Presently Len was half smiling, lightened by the alcohol on a near-empty stomach. His employer saw that he had it all under control as usual, and after a second drink allowed himself to be taken to the Gideon Putnam, a fine establishment where he lay down for a pre-dinner nap that became a long-delayed full night's sleep in his suit.

The Lees were settled in, Dixie and Holly in second-floor bedrooms, old Daddy Tom and Frank, a tall, thin, black, aged man, in the ground floor suite.

"You've done some things here, I see, Holly, and about time," said Daddy Tom, standing at one end of the long, perfectly proportioned main room. "Whenever I'd look at that old brown rug I was embarrassed to invite anyone over. Looked like something left over from the Truman administration. This new one has some life in it. Nice rich colors."

Then he steered himself to the big old chair near the fireplace as Frank brought in their bags. Dixie, relaxing quietly, observed other small improvements.

"Glad you saved this chair," said Tom Lee. "Fits like an old shoe."

Dixie smiled and Frank went to mix drinks. Holly expected horse talk, but Dixie sat silent until the vodka tonics, with an unreadable expression.

"First time I've relaxed in a week," she said then, with quiet intensity. "I don't know what it is, Holly, every room you touch feels better afterward. That Sheikh was just *raving* about you last fall."

"Talk about someone making a person nervous," said Holly. "My mother's not sure I'm a good enough Christian, but that little harem of his made me born-again on the spot."

Even the seriously religious Frank laughed, and Holly spoke again.

"Let's forget restaurants if it's all right with everyone. I've got a surprise we can enjoy right here without running around and dodging drunks."

This would be an omelet she'd been planning since fighting off Howard Hot Pants the previous night after concluding he was just another over-the-top black jackass, dumb as ever.

"Perfect," said Tom Lee with his FDR smile. "Music to my ears."

The St. Cyr women could all cook, and the Lees ate ravenously. Afterward the old man relaxed with the local paper, a smile lingering. He spoke again in a warm, heartfelt baritone.

"That was *marvelous*, Holly. Better than I've had in any number of so-called top restaurants. I know you're an educated woman, but I'm going to do the unspeakable and turn on the TV. It's news time, and I love to hear what people are talking about up here."

Frank brought the remote control and the old man found a local politico in a toupee going on about Homeland Security.

"*Germany*," said the old man in mock-rumination. "Now *that* place was *secure*. I think these new Texas fellows learned a lot from that gang."

Then came DeQuincy.

"Just *look* at him!" said Tom Lee quietly. "Dixie, don't you wish we'd let Double-M run one more year?"

"I do now, Daddy, looking at that DeQuincy horse. Can't look away from him. These damn business decisions. Harry and I were going over times and fractions, and there's no question, Missile Man and DeQuincy would've been the race of the year, World Championship. If both horses were sound. But that fetlock. Daddy, I don't care what the vets said, Double-M was always a little fragile, and that would have been a cruel chance to take. Worst case, could have been the end of the Commander line. The best of it, anyway."

"Just look at him!" said her father, still looking at the screen. "Knows exactly who he is, that fellow! I don't see our Sheikh anywhere, just his trainer."

"Well, you know who his cousin is, Daddy. Those reporters are loaded for bear."

"Better headline than another fake jewel robbery," agreed Lee. "Get those every week."

Then came the President, and off went the TV without a word. For a moment the room was silent, as if someone had passed wind. Then Dixie giggled and everything was fine.

Dixie's wine at dinner contained a pinch of the substance in her executive assistant's locket, and she was feeling herself for the first time in days. As the men headed out into the warm dusk for a short walk, she leaned forward in her chair and whispered to Holly.

"If you had any idea how much I missed you – I mean, you are the *fun* in my life, Holly, it's as simple as that. These sweet little things you think of, like that omelet for Daddy. It just settles us down, honey."

An obscene picture flashed before Holly as she smiled. Chubby rarely came right out with anything unless she was ticked off. Another glass of wine and Holly broke out her best pussy-cat smile, adapted from an old Eartha Kitt movie. *I'm sparking on my own tonight*, she thought. And we'd better keep it quiet, because Frank's got to be a light sleeper.

"I missed you, too," she said quietly, not completely lying. "Bored to death. I drove those poor Salmons *way* upstream. I wonder if they went off to spawn."

"Looked too tired to me," Dixie giggled, leaning toward Holly, exhilarated and boozy.

"Frank doesn't say much but he can mix a drink. Sometimes I'd swear he knows everything that goes on at Lee Farms."

Knows exactly what I'm thinking, thought Holly before replying.

"Frank's got that special gift of not knowing what you're not supposed to know. Anything that can't be said in church never quite reaches consciousness."

"I love education. The sound of it. Holly, I could jump on you right this minute, in case you haven't noticed."

"That's two of us, but we've got to tuck in Daddy Tom and kill some time."

"Honey, you take charge of all that." Dixie's eyes were glittering with lust as she whispered. "Best I can possibly do is be patient and smile, and try not to start squirming. I am so *hot!*"

7

Stepping out of the sun into the cool dark world of Madame Jumel's lifted Len's spirits. The big faux-saloon featured a long bar and lots of tables packed with jockeys and exercise boys, himself among the tallest at under five-ten. It was a sea of little men: Americans, Hispanics from everywhere, proletarian WASPs, the usual Brits and Irish, and a few Continentals. Bonded by chronic near-starvation, athletic talent, courage and a taste for risk, they were different from other men and well aware of it. But not here at Madame Jumel's, the air charged with hot Latin music, their voices loud and free. Happily at home in this rough, wild scene, Len was completely comfortable for the first time since arriving, mellow and sharp. These were men who could understand and sympathize with his mission. Eyes roving, he worked his way through crowded tables, all with drinks on them, a caloric disaster to be sweated out in steam room and sauna, along with purgatives if anyone got drunk enough to eat. But right now everyone was having a good time, Saratoga being a very cool stop on the circuit.

Len slipped through anonymously, searching for Jimmy Broughton. He didn't want to set anything in motion without Jimmy, who was a very good mixer, and key to the negotiations. Jimmy was always welcome, and his trusting, slow-minded smile had a mesmeric warming effect on horse people. Len was relying on him, which in his foggy way, Jimmy would assume, knowing Len did little by chance. Long before getting on the plane he'd known he'd have to do something, and that he'd do it. Long as it wasn't one of those damn *machines*, because *that* could lose him his *license*.

Still without his beer, Len spotted Sam Gwynn, an exercise boy and former protégé he'd been tight with years ago, parting on very bad terms. Sam had had the size, guts, and natural gift to be a great jockey, and would have been but for his honey-gold skin. He also had a low flash-point and very quick hands, and being denied his true calling had begun to sour him by the time he picked a fight with Len that changed their lives. Spotting Len now, he leaped to his feet and wheeled to face him. Len braced himself, but Sam smiled and threw his arms around him.

"Len Thomas! Man, I thought I never *see* you again! I bet you think I forgot about that fifty I owe you! I ain't forgot, man."

Len experienced a strange sensation, the presence of someone who knew him from hand-to-mouth days. Sam introduced him, ordered a round, and announced to the table: "Len Thomas – owed this man fifty dollars since back in the eighties, an' he finally shows up!

Over that fifty dollars they had fought toe-to-toe for six or seven minutes nonstop before the other grooms broke it up, and both had been fired from good, steady jobs at Aqueduct. Sam had been drunk to the point of forgetting the debt, and Len had been amazed that a man so drunk could fight so well.

"Here y'go man," said Sam, pulling a fifty out of a well-packed wallet on his hip. Then he pulled out another, and stuffed it into Len's handkerchief pocket, calling it interest. Len waved it at a waitress and bought a round for the table.

"Man fought like a *bear!*" cried Gwynn from his chair. "Three days before I was right again, and I was a kid, never felt nuthin'."

"You still a kid in you mind," said a fearless Hispanic jockey on the other side of the table.

Sam smiled. "You wasn't so valuable I break you in half, Ramon, but then some Whitney or Vannerbilt have me put away or somethin'. Hey, you still on Novetta? She been flyin'. I was thinkin' I put somethin' on her. How she goin'?"

"Si, Novetta. Works good last week, owner tells me stay with the Ice till she run down Margiedaw. She don't catch them two unless they fall down. Got to go from the gate, an' she ain't no mile-an'-a-quarter horse."

"Maybe save my money," said Gwynn, and turned to Len. "This man here – I was a kid, he took an' taught me everything I know."

"Everything 'cept the left hook," said Len. "Born with that hook, gave me a two day headache. How come you didn't go in the

52

ring, make some money, Sam?"

"Yeah?" replied Gwynn. "You ever see my uncle, you see why. Retina come loose. 22-0, right. Then the doctors picked up on it. First one eye then the other, got one eye now."

Len nodded, aware of someone at his shoulder. Looking up he saw Jimmy Broughton, a mild, unsure smile on his homely face.

"Jimmy! Hey, these are some people I met. Ramon here is on Novetta Sunday. Ramon Ortiz, second richest man in Mexico. Sam here is my old Boston brother, beat the crap out of me at Aqueduct fifteen years ago over nuthin' at all."

Having got everyone's attention and bought a round, he cut to the pitch. "Jimmy and me both workin' for McGoohey Farms in LA, brought a horse out," he said, nodding. "Little mare, Arabiche, Sunday allowance race," he added.

Next to him Jimmy Broughton settled down and began to smile more fully.

"Novetta, huh? Won a few weeks ago in Florida, real fast time?"

He had memorized all the information collated by Len, and knew Novetta was a prime target, a speed horse that could break a race open.

Ramon shrugged slightly. "Arabiche is what? I never hear this Arabiche."

"Yeh, good little horse, jes' coming on lately," said Len vaguely.

Then Jimmy did something that Len had seen him do before, always unexpected and incomprehensible. Jimmy looked at Ramon with an empty expression, like the dumbest shitkicker north of Texas, his eyes wide, round, artless and magnetic, showing precisely the correct amount and quality of respect, plus a wild fun quality prized by men who risked their lives on a daily basis.

"I guess that's what Mr. McGoohey brought her here to find out," drawled Jimmy in his perfectly square voice. "'Biche-girl, we got her under cover, see, she ain't done nothing big yet, and he wants t'see how she goes up here with some real horses, I guess."

And Ramon Ortiz, who rarely smiled, nodded. Barrio-bred in Mexico City, unscrupulous, funky, frequent object of suspicion, distrusted by all but his true peers, Ramon was a man at the top of his game and could pick his mounts. Jimmy smiled again for no particular reason, and Ramon smiled back, a kind of slanted grimace of acknowledgment. Journeyman Jimmy Broughton was okay with him, a standup guy with cool friends, crazy eyes, *un hombre simpatico y peligroso.*

One down, thought Len, but as he listened the glow faded. Other mares with fine résumés and designs of their own on the Breeders Cup would be showing up, because a good third in the sixth on Sunday would be an invitation to the big dance.

Outside Madame Jumel's under the pure, clear sky of a northeast summer twilight, Jimmy spoke his piece.

"Ramon, ten thousand and he hold Novetta fourth, he don't care, don't like the owner."

"Few others we gotta talk to. Think Ramon gonna help us more?"

"Maybe. Prob'ly. Gonna cost, man, he'll want a percentage. Big race."

With fifty thousand of McGoohey's money pinned into his pocket and ten more on his hip, Len knew he should have asked for more.

"You and Ramon jes' keep talkin', man. I come up with the bread. Don't gotta be all of 'em."

"May-bee," drawled Jimmy Broughton, knowing that each of those other horses had won or placed well in fast company. His expression was transparently doubtful. After a glance around, Len opened his hands, pipe in one, gold Zippo in the other. Jimmy couldn't figure out how they'd got there.

"Yeah," he said, pleased by this surprise. "I ain't had a drink this week, or hardly et anythin' either. Like to make one-eleven."

"Still gotta eat, just a little. Oatmeal without stuff in it line your stomach, little piece fish an' some greens, no salt, no oil. You do that, you be okay, Jimmy."

He looked at the jockey until he nodded, then lit the pipe and sipped at it, passing it to Jimmy, who inhaled gratefully. After a long pause he exhaled.

"Nice idea, comin' out here. Never been before. What you think this is gonna cost him?"

"Top Mercedes, all options. We gotta get the man his third place."

"Yeah. Gonna be tough, even with Ramon on our side."

"It ain't the World Series, Jimmy."

"Yeah, everybody wanna be on Ramon's good side, that don't hurt."

Len nodded his little genuine-agreement nod. Everything was in place, and no more could be done until tomorrow. At best they could buy four or five horses out of ten or eleven, and they needed six or seven.

Sonnet, Fatalistica and Gracie Too were holding Len's attention in the foggy dawn at the training track, but he lost focus as two remarkable women appeared from nowhere. Blonde, luxurious Annabelle Dixon and a subtle, slender, delicately tinted attendant. Last night's unforgettable mystery woman! Each had a nice spring in her step, having enjoyed the reunion and begun the day with plenty of strong coffee and compote. It was Len Thomas's second look at Holly St. Cyr, and he was never quite the same man again. Everything he'd felt and guessed in the dark of the G-Spot was confirmed and enhanced in the soft morning light.

He looked away to conceal his reaction as the pair proceeded toward Harry Armstrong, the Lee trainer, a heavy, quiet southerner. The women drew all eyes, giving Len a moment of privacy, during which he stood completely still, mind and heart racing. McGoohey saw only the powerful Annabelle Lee Dixon, empress-to-be of the racing world, whose family's horses had won all the triple crown events, plus Travers, Wood, Breeders and other classics. The Commander had made Lee Farms a dynasty of priceless seed, and his son would add to that. To McGoohey's provincial eye, his owner was a queen who owned the ground she walked on. Unable to look away, he completely missed his trainer's strangely vacant expression.

Waiting to go was the queen's favorite, Black Ice, a tall, elegant bay so dark that an inspired sports writer had dubbed her the Dark Lady, a name that stuck. Aristocratic in every way, she was the obvious star of this workout, timed to avoid contact with Margiedaw. Owner spoke to trainer, who nodded and gestured to the exercise boy, who maneuvered her out onto the track.

"*Annabelle Dixon*," murmured McGoohey in reverent envy.

"Yeh, that her," agreed Len from very far away. "Missile Jism, Inc." He was on auto-pilot, under the spell of her companion who was as cool now as she'd been hot the night before. Recovered from his first reaction, he felt young, motivated, full of energy. He stole another glance. Better yet. The club lighting had masked the glow of her complexion. He saw her mouth as if for the first time. Perfect. Small, full, refined and sensual. Round relaxed eyes full of intelligence. He forced himself to look away as she started to turn toward him. How to play this? Not at all, for now. They were the only two blacks, a tricky situation without protocol.

"I'm gonna talk to Dixie if Arabiche shows," announced McGoohey quietly.

"About Missile Man," he added, as if his trainer might not understand.

Len nodded. *Good luck, Pat*, he thought, trying to look impressed while following Holly St. Cyr as she passed. And there it was. Contact. Just a brief, cool crossing of glances, the moment of acknowledgment. Almost a little smile. As McGoohey muttered on, Len turned to show his profile. *Nose, do your thing.* Then he looked squarely at the owner and delivered a second nod of thoughtful appreciation, as if bowled over by his remarkable plan.

In the Dixon group there was an agreement of glances, a nod at the jockey, and Black Ice took off, tall and graceful, quickly on the rail, eating up track with her long legs, passing other horses smoothly. Len focused on her and the coming race. The Lees would want a speed horse in there to set up her stretch run at a tiring Margiedaw. It had worked twice in their three confrontations. That would be Novetta, already bought and paid for, but it didn't seem to matter. Who *was* this mystery woman? Nothing ordinary about her. Personal secretary? Assistant? More than that. *Confidante.* That was the word. Picked it up in a book. In the nature of things, the queen needed someone like that, smart and trustworthy, and in the South, he knew, the races sometimes reached a special rapprochement when a powerful white person wanted it. Thomas Jefferson, for example. These two were a team, and if he was going to make a real impression on this cool *confidante*, McGoo would need that pretext to approach Ms. Dixon. Be rejected probably, but the situation would open a door for his brilliant trainer.

As he stood there, a new and very different Saratoga game plan came into being. Third place went from urgent priority to absolute necessity. Arabiche was just a damn *horse*, a lazy one that for once was going to do what she was born to do, run like hell. Holly St. Cyr was releasing energies in him that he didn't know were still there. Arabiche was going to get crazy for once, change his world. Open the door to Miss Cinnamon. The new Len was decisive and a little grim. He smiled though: *New Plan* was a favorite McGoo line.

Len knew how it was done, any trainer did, but he had never injected a stimulant into a horse or even thought about doing it. Now he did, in detail. As trainer, he could guarantee total privacy while Paco did the deed, having had hands-on experience in Mexico. ("*All the time at Mexican track, horses are high, ees normal. Bes' place under here, good spot, not near heart, goes in system smooth, like – you know, slow and easy...* ")

His face a mask, Len caught himself, rocked by his thoughts. Was she worth it, this woman? Risk his job? His barely begun career? He knew in his guts that she was, and it wasn't just physical; several friendly women already had that covered. It was her unique effect, the decisive boldness she released in him.

Dixie paid no attention to either man, but Holly was considering the well-dressed Llewellyn Thomas, stopwatch in hand. Great dancers were one thing, but a black trainer? Who could dance like Satan? That was strange. As he turned, she noticed the nose, that distinctive aristocratic beak. How had she missed that? An Arab nose, and a damn good-looking man. Darkish but classy. And really smart. Had to be. And energy coming off him in deep quiet waves.

As they watched the workout, Len spoke quietly to McGoohey.

"Gotta pass some water, Pat. Back in time for 'Biche."

Then he started for her stall, destabilized and revitalized by the shocking plan this woman had triggered. One big roll of the dice. And one last review, after which the good Len was replaced by his evil twin, and he knew it.

Waiting there all along, he thought.

In the still half-dark barn Paco was sitting alone on a wooden box with a friendly but abstracted look on his face.

"You be smokin' off premises Ah hope," Len began.

"Oh, yeah. Saratoga, right?"

"Wanna talk serious with you alone. Where's Carlos?"

Paco whipped out his new company cell phone and dialed.

"Time to baby-sit," he said. "*Si,* now. *Andale!*"

"Be waitin' on you out back where people go t'smoke," said Len in his coldest business voice. "Be quick, hear."

A life full of risk had taught Len Thomas to think carefully. He could create a scenario, detail it, rehearse it in his mind, see where it might go wrong, and work out contingencies. In this case there were none; he'd get away with it or he wouldn't. Calm again, he considered his horse first. His understanding with Arabiche was deep, and he knew she was deceptively strong, with deep reserves. Could she handle it? Paco had said so more than once. Step one, McGoo would have to be prepared. He couldn't be totally surprised and start running his mouth. He needed to hear how Saratoga was having a wonderful unforeseen effect, that the workout times were deceptive, that 'Biche really wanted to run for a change. Jimmy would hear nothing, because he'd refuse the ride. He'd find out when it was too late to do anything about it, and he'd be as crazy as the horse when the cork was pulled and he felt that big *zing*. He'd be ready to pull off the miracle, which Len calculated would definitely happen, with Novetta and four others in his pocket. All the money being on the two stars and the rest around 10-1 or worse, Arabiche in third wouldn't stink up the place and cause an inquiry. It would pay, too. Big time. Ten thousand times five or ten.

Stretching out his daily cigarette in the smokers patch, slightly away from the half-dozen exercise boys and grooms, Len was just about fully irritated when Paco finally showed up. He put a Marlboro Lite package in his hand, jarring him.

"I stop, you know – is *hard*, tobacco. Hard to stop, easy to start again. They got Step Program for all problem. First thing is accept Higher Power."

Paco crossed himself, and Len nodded once, his danger nod. Paco continued, oblivious. Len didn't pretend to knowledge of the Higher Power and this was a bad time for such thoughts, but he allowed Paco to relieve himself by reviewing the Steps once again, stressing the fourth one.

Why was he going ahead with this? Because he couldn't stop himself. Because he'd glimpsed a path out of what now felt like a crappy, pointless existence. To rescue his one and only life. To escape McGoo-world, from which he'd probably be fired if third place didn't happen. Because he'd been fully alive for ninety seconds dancing with that woman, smiling quietly into those calmly interested eyes, and it had happened again this morning.

"Is like Confession, fourth step," continued Paco with feeling. "Exact same thing, make you feel clean inside with good intention."

Len reminded him to light up, since no one came here except nicotine addicts. "Do like a President, don't inhale."

"Also no relation with young girl, eh?" Paco was extremely happy at having such a full hearing on the fourth step. Then he was suddenly cautious. Len never listened to Step talk. He noticed that they'd drawn away from the others.

"Is problem, Len? Horse is good. We talk already, she like special Saratoga feeling, nice air. Feet dancing when she move around."

"She gonna be *real* special tomorrow, Paco. You gonna find us some juice."

There was a long silence.

"Here? Saratoga? Venue of Teefany!"

"Yeh."

"Man, she not win a race all *year*, they gonna *know*."

"Keep your voice down. Ain't gonna win, Paco. Ain't gonna place. We gonna *show*. Otherwise we all lookin' for new jobs. Now without lookin' surprised or confused or runnin' your mouth, keep my smokes, put 'em in your pocket. Ten fifties inside. What I hear, Stenamina ain't on the list. Old bike-racing drug."

"*Si.* I heard sometimes test shows in blood, but not saliva and urine. Only European test. Got masking agent, too."

Paco nodded as he spoke, placing the cigarettes in the bottom of a side pocket, deeply pleased. Len was heeding him, giving him proper respect, taking his advice. The drugs wouldn't cost more than a couple of hundred, so he'd have even more to bet, and 'Biche, was good for third, easy. Very easy with five horses bought off.

"Next thing. Don't bet at a window," said Len. "*Private bet.* You got it?"

"Right, quiet. LA people place bets for me."

"Okay. What I just say?"

"We gotta show – place third or we outa work. Don' bet at window. Hey, Len, don' worry, I understan'. I spread money around. Phone call home, my friend Pete handles it. Family, married to cousin."

"Right. And stop lookin' so *happy*, man."

"Right. You wan' me to do it? I am experience'."

"Yeah, I do. Now get it and chill. Only two people know about this, an' if you ever talk we all be off the track for life and you still got me to deal with. No braggin' rights on this. *Nobody* – 'specially Pete Suarez. He still a gangbanger, an' you got a career to protect."

He dropped his cigarette and ground it out in the packed earth, then hardened his eyes. Paco intimidated was Paco at his best. That was what life had done to Paco, Len reflected. Except when gripped by a vision. Then all bets were off, these being messages from Above.

"Jes' remember, Paco, anything go wrong we ain't alone."

"Unnerstan', serious business, but is okay, Len. She got very strong insides, that lady."

"Okay, an' you better be right, Paco. About what she can do."

"She do it man, just need to shut brain off."

Alone a minute later, he thought it through again.

I need that woman to help me change my life. We clicked last night, and now she knows I broke the color line as a trainer. Trainer with no big results, but she took a second look at me and let me see her doing it. This is our *minds* touching, too, and I need that feeling bad. That *lift*. Not just my joint liftin'. Everything, head to toe, which I ain't felt in years. This is a jail-break. Inside, the sky is a little square in the wall – outside it's everywhere, all yours. In between's that great big risk. Unavoidable, because if third place doesn't happen, Pat will need someone to blame, and there's no way this crazy new Len Thomas will hold still for that shit any more.

But it was beautiful, this moment. Special rare. What was that song?

Somewhere. Old Archie Shepp-Bill Dixon recording, beautiful, full of hope. Leonard Bernstein tune.

8

Rain!

Powerful sheets of driving rain were drumming on Pat McGoohey's windows, waking him with a joyous heart. One thing they all understood about 'Biche was the strength and stamina packed into her, that she could lift her legs and maintain stride forever against the suck of a muddy track when quicker animals flagged. Paco always prayed for rain before her races, and her best ones came on soggy tracks. And this rain wasn't stopping, it was hammering. Beautiful! Lying on his back, McGoohey looked around the room Jasmine had found for him. It felt good to his relaxed eyes. Spacious and tall. And nice *appointments,* as she would say. Rarely alone, he was having an unusual experience, a moment of calm in the eye of his personal hurricane. A nice mood, justifying the whole trip. A different – whatever. A real pleasure. Lying there listening to the rain, he finally looked at his watch. Six on the dot. He went to the window and saw a sodden gray landscape, trees bending in the wind. The rain could stop right now and the track would stay soggy, and it wasn't stopping. He called valet service to have his suit pressed, then showered, dressed in jeans and tee shirt, and ordered a big breakfast to see him through the day. Then he picked up the phone.

In his modest room down the street, Len was already showered and dressed, in an equally good mood, sipping black coffee.

"*Dreadful* weathah," he answered, in a good mock-English voice.

"Heh-heh. For some people, huh?"

"Last thing Paco said, he was looking for a church so he could pray better for this rain. It was supposed to be light, y'know; I wasn't hopin' for this."

"Power of prayer. Come on over and eat a real breakfast for a change, bro," said McGoohey with real warmth.

Bro? This was a very loose McGoohey. For now, anway.

"Yer gonna get wet but come on over. Think Paco's

awake?"

"No workout today, gonna let the boys sleep. Be there less than half hour."

At the desk of the Gideon Putnam, dapper and unsmiling with his folding umbrella, waterproof, khakis and commanding nose, he impressed the clerk.

McGoohey greeted him with a manic, energy-draining smile, and gestured at a morning feast on covered silver platters. There was no avoiding the eye-opener.

"To the little lady," he said. "Mudder today, mother-to-be pretty soon."

"Fairest of them all," said Len, surprised at McGoohey's wit. He glanced at the window, through which wind-driven rain could still be heard. The boss was in a rare mood.

"Ain't no guarantee," the trainer noted. "Don't hurt, though. Not one bit."

McGoohey nodded, looking out the window, thinking that it was amazingly easy to talk to Len Thomas compared to most people. Jasmine at this hour – Jesus H. Christ. The mood was mutual, and Len was finding his employer pleasant company. He decanted most of his eye-opener unnoticed into the dark rug behind his chair after the first sip.

"What I heard, at least three of these other horses don't like it wet," said McGoohey, standing at the window to view the saturated wetness of the land.

"Correct," said Len, naming them. "But those other two, they don't mind."

"Well, they ain't part of our calculations. But wouldn't *that* be somethin' – come in between them two?"

"That case, I be agitatin' for a raise," replied Len in a light tone. *Or getting investigated and ending my career.* The owner had another small nip, and they began eating a meal that would have fed four. Len stayed with the fruit and toast, but in the spirit of the moment he also got down some scrambled eggs and sausage. It occurred to him that while this room was commensurate with the standards of Mrs. Dixon's lovely *confidante*, his own resembled an upgrade on what touring black bands often experienced in the South.

"What's the serious look?"

"You eat this way every morning?"

"Christ no, Jasmine would kill me."

Len nodded and walked to the window, thinking it would be nice to have the lady present to calm her husband. "Rain end pretty soon," he said. "Startin' to clear to the south. Prob'ly sun before noon, but that track's gonna be jes' right for our girl." He paused and added, "all day."

"One eleven even," remarked Jimmy with satisfaction, still pink from the steam. It was mid-morning, with a still-overcast sky that gave a greenish gray cast to his pale face.

"Long time since you hit one eleven. Strength okay?" asked Len gently.

"Yeah, I done the fish and salad last night and a little plain oatmeal this morning. It's the thirst. Boy, am I thirsty."

"For a beer," said Len maliciously.

Jimmy emitted something between a chuckle and a giggle.

"One glass of water, my man. One glass, and you sip at it like a beer."

Jimmy sadly waggled a tiny bottle of Saratoga Springs water at him.

"You and me goin' for a drive."

In the rented blue Malibu, Jimmy announced that Ramon had bought four other jockeys, getting 10 percent on people he delivered.

"You got him that low?"

"Ramon's cool, man. All gravy for him. Twelve thousand, ten, ten, ten and eight. That's fifty, right? Ten percent is five more, for Ramon, right?"

"*Si,*" said Len, "but now we over feefty – what McGoo say now?" His Paco imitation was close to perfect, and the jockey broke into a whinnying laugh. Then he abruptly stopped.

"You ain't just bein' funny t'day," he said. "This thing ain't locked up by a long shot, and we both know it. Eleven-horse field so far, all of 'em pretty damn good. Ramon says two of them are there for exercise, plus he's holding his horse, but that's still seven. Minus the two is five."

"Maybe not minus the two."

The car rolled down a country road in silence for several moments.

"I don't get it," said Jimmy. "Whaddaya mean, Len?"

"Horse you on today ain't gonna be like any Arabiche you ever seen before."

There was another silence as Len let the cat find its way out of the bag.

"What I'm thinking is real strange, Len," said Jimmy in a hard, quiet, very disturbed voice. "You sayin' it's another horse I'm gonna be on, or yer gonna make her into another horse?"

"The latter," said Len in his educated middle-class voice, freezing the jockey and creating another silence that he deliberately waited out.

"Lose everything," said Jimmy in a beaten voice. "Everyone knows they do a lot of checking up here. Saliva, urine, sometimes blood. We'd be gone, Len, out of racing for life, all of us."

"I said not minus the two, right?" continued Len in the educated voice. What I'm saying is that you will be okay if you *hold* that horse, because we've never once seen what she's really got. *Third place.* No better and no worse, that's the arrangement. *Third place* – that's where we have no risk."

"No such animal, 'no risk'. I ain't doin' this, Len. I ain't *got* nothin' but my license, man."

"Got your *friends*," replied Len with easy weight, setting up the big lie in his usual voice.

"I sure don't like this too much. This ain't *like* you, Len."

"McGoo get outta racin', I'm out the bes' job Ah'm gonna get my time of life, an' you out half your rides. Paco's okay. Mexico, anyone can talk to horses and shovel shit got a job."

Jimmy could not help snickering at that.

"That's what we'll all be doin', Len, except they won't let us even do *that*."

"That's why she gotta come *third*, Jimmy. Anything less, McGoo out the horse game. Wife's on his ass. He ain't gonna say that, but that's it. Popsicle gone, we down to 'Biche, Tamari an' the three little pigs. Gettin' close to no more McGoohey Farms. Turn this ride down, one thing for sure – you never ride for McGoo again, my man."

"This's *dirty*, Len, this ain't like you."

"You think *I* come up with this shit? Black trainer?"

"That fuckin' Mick!"

"You ain't s'posed t'know, an' I sure wouldn't bring it up if I was you. She gotta show her potential, set her up for a class stud. Only way – he right about that."

While the jockey struggled with it, Len saw just what he was doing to his friend to re-start his own life. His job was at stake, but it was just as much to with Cinnamon Lady. Enhancing the respect he'd seen in those lovely eyes this morning. Or was that just the natural look of a beautiful woman who knew how to play any situation? He put that aside.

"Sorry, Jimmy. Life get pretty dirty sometimes."

Then his tone changed..

"But Paco says this gonna work, an' we sure ain't never doin' it again. That was my conditions."

Good solid lies to a gullible and trusting friend. Len regretted it deep in his guts, with an unaccustomed self-loathing. But his words were so clearly accepted that the regret simply went away, and he felt only relief. *Another problem solved.* A big one, because Jimmy had to be in control. Most thoroughbreds were genetic freaks, bred to run themselves half to death with much encouragement. 'Biche didn't care, and even Paco didn't know what she could do if she ever got crazy.

"Paco says she got more than anyone ever guess, and this is her kind of track. Read my lips, Jimmy. If he's right, which he always is, she gotta be under *control*. Third place – no better, no worse."

"I guess this is one time she don't finish with gas in the tank," observed Jimmy. "Just hope she don't do a Ruffian."

It froze Len. Ruffian, a legendary and undefeated filly, had run herself to death in Florida some years ago. But Jimmy was already accepting the situation and considering how this ride had to go. Tuck in behind the front-running Margiedaw, and hang on. Sure, perfect, except everyone else would be trying to do the same. But still and all, God might like little 'Biche like everyone did, 'cause she was a sweetie. It could be like the nice parochial-school girl who decides to take a drink and runs wild for the weekend. Or she just might not change a whole lot. He'd heard of that happening. He took a measured sip of bottled water and decided to place his bets through a buddy at the Dead Heat.

Len was silent, thinking about Ruffian. He'd seen it on tape and felt sick to his bones. No dope involved, just too much heart, ran herself to death. *Happens,* he thought. *But if Paco's wrong and 'Biche goes down, I'll never forgive myself.*

The bright white Saratoga grandstand harks back long gone to an America when robber barons were still new and interesting. Set against high sun, blue sky, and the deep greens of full summer, the classic wood structure has a gracious elegance from back beyond Teddy Roosevelt, Edith Wharton, and the Spanish American war. The setting suggests a very long tradition of refined civility. A world in which the young Scott Fitzgerald would be just another bright young Ivy League upstart, and Hemingway another talented fast-track bully. But a fine gravitas enables Saratoga to absorb all sorts, down to the lowest. It comes of money so mature, respectable and secure that there is no need to proclaim itself. The ease of the place exposes Churchill Downs' twin minarets and merciless media hype as clearly over the top. And it seems that no matter how many are present Saratoga never feels crowded.

Classy. Very classy, as Dutch Schultz observed.

Taking in this fine world, Len Thomas waited to see where his life was headed. *Big stage*, he thought. Big and funky. The smell of gambling drew a crowd of track-trash drifting and clustering everywhere – pickpockets, touts, pimps, gigolos, disbarred members of the racing world, car thieves, jewel thieves, townies who cashed tickets for taxpayers, whores of all sexes, and Schultz's successors in black sedans and limos from Detroit.

The Lee box was on the finish line, near that of the Sheikh, who had been smuggled in past the paparazzi. He smiled and waved a little European wave, and the Lees waved back. Close by was a box full of St. Jameses, to whom he also waved. Eleanor St. James's mismanaged operation had been on its last legs until big Margiedaw beat Black Ice to challenge for the Eclipse Award.

Under perfect rides by Tom McGovern, Black Ice had won their first two meetings, each time by a neck, but Margiedaw's win on the big Belmont track had been impressive. Given a small field, wide turns and room to run, she had taken control early, unleashing a gradual but endless acceleration until there was no getting past.

Following a furious ugly-drunk tongue lashing by Dixie, McGovern was about to suggest a new venue for stabling her horse, but had held off as Tom Lee led his daughter from the room. McGovern's agent had doubled his rate, and the jockey said no more than *morning* or *afternoon* to Dixie. But he stayed on the horse because she was a winner and he loved the old man. The Belmont race had been Margiedaw's all the way, but Black Ice still had the top team in Armstrong and McGovern, while St. James decisions were strongly affected by Eleanor's sleek blond alcoholic son. They were a throwback to an earlier day, a warm, gun-loving, spend-thrift crowd that gave classic, unbelievable Texas parties featuring famous politicians falling drunk into the pool, *flagrante delictos* out in the tumbleweed, a billionaire pushed into the barbecue pit by his wife and requiring plastic surgery, and similar incidents.

The two ladies smiled brightly at each other when their glances crossed, then looked away. It drove Dixie half mad that Eleanor was able to *enjoy* herself, that she wasn't truly *serious* about this holiest of quests. She wanted to say that to someone who would understand, and that would be Holly St. Cyr, all in white, seated with a double pepper Stoli at a table on the clubhouse patio.

This was fine with Holly, but not satisfactory to the Lees. Missing someone so close and special in the box had become a delicate issue, temporarily solved by packing the box with people who arguably could not be excluded, owing to the Missile Man syndication. Handsome Bill Pater, the clean-cut, well spoken young attorney, chief expediter of that process, was socially impeccable, a highly functional adornment, and of course Adolph Pufmann spoke for the syndicate. Mrs. Pufmann was there to take up space, and of course Armstrong.

That was a boxful, and Dixie had made a point of conferring with Holly about the seating. Holly understood perfectly and had no desire to be in the box, because there was no point advertising the special relationship. Her idea of seating the dull Armstrong between the duller Pufmanns had brought a smile to Dixie's face. Republicans right, Dems left, lawyer in the middle. What a subtle mind lurked under those curly black waves! And one day soon, by God, she'd *be* in the damn box. Next year, and not just at some juvenile tryout. The hell with what people said.

Dressing, weighing and saddling up, Jimmy Broughton knew this race would be with him 'til the day he died. The rain had felt like an omen. Anyone who knew him well would have noticed how quiet he was in the changing room. He felt strange to himself, going through the familiar motions, but the second his leg swung over his mount and settled himself, he felt 'Biche's skittery edge, and she was unhappy with the lead horse on the way to the gate. He was indeed on a very different horse, sweating and switching her rump impatiently, as if she wanted to dance or kick someone. The sun had been out several hours, but when he'd checked the track it was still well-soaked, perfect for 'Biche. She had an outside slot, which was fine, because the field would stay together – No Lie was a no-show, and Novetta was bought and paid for. She entered the gate smoothly as usual, and broke with her usual clean move, but hard and sharp, and a rough wild sound rose up from Jimmy's chest.

The early pace was cautious, and he had her sixth within a hundred yards. They were all waiting out the rival queens, and an unknown in sixth was no threat. Ahead of him was Fatalistica, a medium-serious contender, and as they rounded the first turn he glimpsed Big Ugly in the lead, grinding away at Gracie Too, followed by Sonnet, who hadn't been bought, and maybe the horse he had to beat. Then came Black Ice, perfectly placed and running smoothly, all these leaders more or less single file, all eating mud except Margiedaw.

He couldn't believe it when 'Biche announced her disdain for Fatalistica completely on her own, fighting her way up outside until they were running together. It was turning into a hard little duel until the other jockey made a quick calculation that 'Biche would burn out by the last turn and let her go. Ahead, Black Ice was starting to move up on Gracie, but under Jimmy was a fine fresh animal that had been saving it forever and was finally ready to splurge.

Damn! By now his green and purple silks, face, and goggles were heavily mud-splattered, and he flipped the goggles down for a fresh pair Bonded tightly to the horse, he was in perfect balance. Their positions held until Black Ice entered the final turn and let Gracie know she was going to have to prove it. Amazingly, 'Biche felt this and responded, driving harder, Jimmy still letting her run her race. Black Ice was good on turns and Gracie wasn't, running wide and sliding back, giving Jimmy wild ideas, but coming out of the turn Gracie rallied and still had a long neck up on 'Biche. Gracie didn't mind the mud, and it was looking tough for McGoohey Farms, because Gracie was always up there in the money. Jimmy remembered young Wally Jenks, too young to shave, damn bug-boy, didn't weigh anything. Classy kid, refused Ramon, polite but firm. A quiet parking lot conversation in which Jenks repeatedly shook his teen-age head. Gracie was a horse with a future, and the kid was under identical third-or-bust orders. Jimmy remembered Jenks shrugging his skinny shoulders, a frail, talented kid with a big novice weight advantage, a real good horse, and a future of his own.

Motherfucker! muttered Jimmy, and for the first time called on his baby to come again. Instead of reluctance he got instant response. Gracie kept on at the same speed, which was not slow, and Jimmy went to the crop. Arabiche was beyond horse sense, digging deep. Seeing the dark little animal coming up on the rail, Gracie fought back. 'Biche fought harder, gaining by inches. Unbelievably, Gracie faltered, and Jimmy felt a wild surge, drunk with power, taking aim on the favorites, his mind empty of everything but the magnificent possibilities of this best-ever lifetime ride. Sure as hell never had this much horse under him before.

And now Sonnet, third favorite after the rival queens. Was she sliding back? Yeah, a little, thought Jimmy. Good finisher but she's tired from the mud. There was a long way to go, and he felt the lightly-raced 'Biche digging into untouched resources, actually *gaining*. Awesome! Then Sonnet picked up on her and rallied.

"*Yaaaah!*" screamed Jimmy, giving his horse a single perfect whack.

You're dead, bitch, he muttered as he sensed Sonnet's perfect stride starting to break up. But not quitting – all these class horses had heart. Then he saw the air going out of her balloon – too far to go in the mud. Seconds later, side by side, Sonnet seemed to implode. As he passed her into third place, Jimmy saw that he was actually gaining on those two great ladies just ahead, and something popped in his addled brain. His long arm brought the crop down again, and 'Biche responded, continued gaining. And there was Margiedaw's wide gray butt, Black Ice's sleek dark one inside, almost even. Everything was gone for Jimmy except those two horses in front of him and all that track ahead. Just a pair of bitches in his way. His face twisted into a primal snarl as he went to the crop again, and 'Biche was still responding.

Fucking flying! he thought. Through the mud he saw, amazingly, that he was overlapping Black Ice's left flank, and there was room on the rail as Black Ice, unaware, moved out to crowd Margiedaw just a little and rattle her.

Shitagawdamn! sang Jimmy's soul.

9

"Jesus Christ!" The words sprang from Holly St. Cyr in furious prayer as she saw it happening on the huge screen. Off the turn Black Ice was perfect, challenging on the inside, big Margiedaw having swung wide as always. McGovern had Black Ice right next to her, at the edge of fouling, knowing the big gray liked space. But Margie wasn't yielding. Even when her nemesis got to her shoulder, she kept driving in undisturbed rhythm as if the Lee horse were not right there crowding her. As this duel moved away from the rail, there was just room for the dark little unknown, still moving up, perfectly placed, still fresh. And that little horse was actually *challenging* Black Ice, who was still drawing up on the ugly buckskin-gray as planned.

Then it was falling apart. Black Ice had her head at Margiedaw's withers, gaining slowly, and then more slowly for a dozen strides, then head-to-head. But very slowly the St. James horse was fighting her off. A nose, a head, half a neck, grinding it out. Black Ice didn't crack, but humiliation loomed. The little no-name horse running down low glued to the rail was going stride for stride with the tall Dark Lady, *pushing* her, an unfamiliar distraction. Maybe gaining a little. Full of heart, the Lee horse had no quit in her, losing ground by inches as Margiedaw won strong. It was a photo for second.

Holly was frantic, eyes no longer round and calm, but twisted tight by stress and fear. Dixie had been on a dangerous edge since arriving, super-horny and crazy, ready to tip any which way. Now she, Holly, and McGovern had to deal with it. But the jockey didn't live under same roof, and he did business through an agent, wasn't a damned *slave*. A bottle of whiskey would be down before dinner with no apparent effect. Then the thunderbolt could strike anywhere, anything, anyone, herself included. Losing was bad enough. It could be the end of a second Lee Farms Eclipse Award in the new century. Black Ice had been dominated for the first time head-to-head, and she'd been ready, training well. McGovern's flawless ride had set her up, and Big Ugly had whipped her anyway. Whipped her going away, leaving her challenged by a complete unknown at 40-1. Taken to a photo, *maybe beaten for second!* It had looked to Holly as if the little bay horse was winning that battle. At worst she'd made the Queen look like a pretender, emphasizing Margiedaw's raw Texas dominance.

Old Tom could be sporting about a setback, even one like this, but not his hellion daughter. Daddy's girl was vengeful. There would be one godawful howling-screaming scene, because that was how Dixie got rid of things. Holly didn't scare easily, but she knew she couldn't handle Dixie right now, no matter which way that photo went. Her world was up for grabs and she couldn't think straight. Blind and vicious, Dixie could be so foul, nasty, and insulting that Holly thought she might have to resign, and without references. Minutes ticked by, no word on the outcome. The computer part of Holly's mind began toting up her investments on its own. Barely into six figures. Then it was apples (suck it up and get into those trusts) versus oranges (defining herself as just another thieving black bitch who used her education the wrong way). *And where was the goddamn call on that photo?*

OK. She could Tom her way through. Or she could raise the stakes if attacked, resigning with dignity before the Big Bang. Being near-indispensable in so many ways, she'd probably be rehired on the spot if Daddy Tom was in earshot. Guess wrong, and she'd be on her own, cut off from her roots after the seven fat years. And those had become real roots, she could feel them, she was family. No real career option, either. Out of school to become a house servant? Peculiar. All wrong, that's how it would look. Something lacking, weak, defective. Earlier, she'd have lived on grits and got the MFA. Should have, but she'd gone for the money and the glamour.

And why not admit it bitch – the challenge. The fun and frolic of a no-bullshit madwoman as sharp as herself who went ballistic from time to time, leaving bodies behind. And now owned her ass. Unmoving in her seat as the patio crowd swirled and jabbered, Holly saw her life from afar. That good little college where she'd done so well, been so pleased with herself, courted by young and old, both sexes, in that innocent, clumsy-crude academic way. Couldn't face the damn thesis. Afraid of the thesis. Couldn't write, no flair. Not *creative*, dammit! Quick, smart, demon researcher, good-looking, a winner. But not a true alpha. A goddamn interior decorator.

Even as he stood to be ruined, Len Thomas had been stealing glances at Annabelle Dixon's young confidante, recalling the magic of that dance and the size of his balls that night. Flash Budney could put you in a wheelchair for life and get lawyered into community service. And the way she'd tripped his switch again at the Oklahoma track. The insane chance he'd taken to command her attention in a more serious way and get her for himself. Now the wild, heady satisfaction of this gorgeous moment, Sonnet dying in the mud, third place clinched.

Time for Jimmy to hold her. But no. Time was suspended in an eerie slow-motion nightmare. Then slow-motion shock and a sharp vision: No jailbreak, no big sky freedom. Busted. No job, career over.

Still waiting for the photo call, he came out of it, calmly recalling the previous afternoon. Those thoughts about changing his life before it was too late. He'd had enough of Pat McGoohey to take this chance. No regrets, even now, except for Jimmy, who'd lost his mind when he should have been holding that horse. Crazy damn cracker. Had he tried? Len couldn't be sure what he'd seen, but he half-remembered something his mother had once said about his father, one of her indirect "signifying remarks" indicating some dark element, some dangerous thing that had been survived, bonding them for life. Something out-of-control, not discussable and maybe illegal. Whatever it was, Len knew what she'd been getting at now. He'd never suspected he could risk everything on a hope at this point in his life, and he knew it wasn't something he'd ever do again.

Then it was all howling sirens again, train wreck full of bloody screams as he was suddenly convinced that 'Biche had indeed passed Black Ice. It had been evident down the stretch that she could. *Crazy Jimmy!* In the tide of uncontrolled fear rolling through him, Len finally forgot the woman who'd tipped him into this mad zone. Dazed, he heard a fat, smug, East Coast lackey voice leading up to the result with endless empty words. He was limp when the prissy voice finally announced Black Ice's second place. *Saved!*

He dipped his head, remembering his mother again as the wave of fear passed. What she'd say about this deed, how her face would look. When he noticed Holly St. Cyr's absence, he never wanted to see her again. He felt like a man coming out of transplant surgery with somebody else's heart, shaky and disoriented.

And he still hadn't had a look at his splendid little horse.

Stands and clubhouse buzzing, slender stylish Eleanor St. James and her handsome son left their box trailing media like a bridal train. She was slim, modern, and dark-haired, a good-looking widow in her mid-forties, dressed to the nines in elegant chartreuse, her son a handsome Ivy League Wall Street failure, both of them attractively dissipated. They made their glamorous happy-tipsy Dom Perignon descent through the stands to cheers, clapping, and genteel euphoric tumult, followed by their greatly relieved trainer. It was a classic Saratoga moment, which Dixie sat through with a proud fixed smile.

As they made their way, Margiedaw was being led into the winner's circle, larger than life now with pride of victory, all cameras firing, everyone smiling. The horse dominated by sheer forceful size and calm. As the owners joined the scene, the horse celebrated with a resonant fart, loud enough to be heard through the hubbub. *Forget style*, it said: *Big Ugly's here.*

Happy-happy-happy! None of these happy alcoholics had to deal with the dangerous-when-drunk Annabelle Lee Dixon, who had in earlier life fired a pistol with intent twice in a public bar and run a man down with her car for sleeping with a special friend. Holly's bitterness and fear flowed unchecked as she found a spot in the stands where she could watch the winner's circle assemble. How to dance these next rounds with the eight-hundred-pound gorilla? Love it to death, play within herself, absolutely no blinking. It was Atlanta again, under the will of Little Isaac. She walked away from the crowd until she was alone, lit a cigarette, and saw that this luxury – this *necessity* – of some privacy, was not allow-able. She had to be there for that flower of Southern Womanhood right now. Slip up alongside and unobtrusively squeeze her hand with all the sympathetic sensitivity of a top-end whore. If at all pos-sible, she had to *cry* at some appropriate point. Cry on behalf of this horse that lived better than any field hand ever had and this mad-woman. Crying was not do-able, she knew. Before Little Isaac she'd cried easily enough, but never since, not even at her father's funer-al. She stepped forward and began working her way through the crowd, so cold and focused that people got out of her way.

Len felt hollowed out, Godless and weightless, innards turned to Styrofoam, unable to steel himself for the drug-test delay. He knew how the testing should go if the rules hadn't been changed or Saratoga didn't have some of its own. Which could be; he'd been in his California cocoon for a long time. Stenamina was-n't on any list he'd seen; it was European, and almost unknown, a bike racer's drug years ago. But this particular third place was very unlikely, and 'Biche's dramatic challenge definitely qualified as suspicious. McGoohey Farms was a joke, so there just might be an investigation, and maybe additional testing if some well-connected party made a stink. The purchased jockeys would tell appropriate stories, no problems there, but he was dazed, walking on eggshells. *Just barely a nose! Had Jimmy lost his damn mind?* In the minutes between finish and photo results, Len had seen his carefully con-structed life explode in full detail. Career gone, professional exile, end of a legally clean quarter century, and worst of all, dragging Jimmy with him. Beautiful, trusting Jimmy, whom he'd used with-out mercy. Paco could go straight to Mexico and be welcomed for this *coup*. McGoo – fuck McGoo. The Commish would cuff Pat around a little, blame the ethnics, and it would ease itself into his-tory. Nothing like rotten concrete or a collapsed overpass.

And 'Biche. He walked over and watched her hot-walking from a distance. To his eye, she looked like a horse was supposed to look after giving everything, which meant that she wasn't quite herself, because she never did that. Not exactly shaky, but her head was drooping. *Horses look like that all the time after a hard race,* thought trainer Len, but alter-ego Llewellyn lodged a protest.

Paco observed 'Biche from closer, eyes shuttered as Carlos led her along. Behind the shutters was a calm glow that told Len she was okay. Still totally conflicted, Len quietly walked away, not ready to deal. Where was Pat? Not that he really cared. McGoo would be bursting with booze, triumph, and dreams of glory. Len went to the smoking area for his daily cigarette, not wanting to be around the owner now that he knew his horse was all right. He knew this mood would be sitting over him like the low-pressure area preceding a tornado until the test results were in. He ground out the half-smoked cigarette like a robot, walked to the car, and lay down in the back seat, as exhausted and unfocused as some street hustler with no place to crash. After twenty minutes or so he pulled himself together and walked back for another look at 'Biche.

About to enter the hazy light of the shedrow, he saw three figures entering from the other end, the sun behind them, not recognizable but with an air of authority. He passed the entrance without breaking stride and continued around the barn. Their backs were toward him when he got to the other side, and one of them was talking with Paco. Purtees, DeQuincy's trainer. The tall slender man was Sheikh Lakham, Prince of the Blood. One of dozens, but still a Royal. And the big man standing back to view both entrances would be his security. Paco was looking just right, though. Happy smile, confident bearing. More so than his own, Len knew. He also knew exactly what Paco would be saying, because he'd written the script: Arabiche had been recovering from a sickness, hard to say exactly what, but then rapidly achieved the great form that comes of a sound, healthy animal with excellent blood on both sides. And if she had only moved earlier, she might even have won, his little baby 'Biche, because of the excellent and patient training strategy of Mr. Thomas, who had had this very race in mind for months.

The visitors listened politely, looking into her stall, feeding her treats that Paco supplied, the Sheikh actually *chatting* with Paco now, taking his time, a man on a relaxing and enjoyable mission. Or he might always look that way. Len thanked God, his lucky stars, and Kismet that the Sheikh hadn't had a horse in *that* race. As he came up to them he heard his name, his full name this time, correctly pronounced by Paco. He introduced himself, thinking that Paco had set it up perfectly. Lakham made a playful joke about cameras.

"It was probably better without them," he said. "A horse-man has the wisdom to see which horse is winning."

"We should have gone earlier, but I'm not unhappy," said Len. "It was a great field. What we want to do is breed her, though."

Then the security man reminded the Sheikh of an appointment, and they were gone after a friendly smile from the Sheikh. Then a pool of quiet.

"Going to be okay," said Paco quietly. "Sheikh don't visit suspicious horse. He like her, how she take mud and don't give up. He see she is special."

Len said nothing, and was about to return to the car when McGoohey appeared, living his dream. Paco handled this, too, taking the pressure off Len.

"The Sheikh was here to look at her," he said.

"The Sheikh?" said McGoohey in a hushed voice as if referring to a Papal audience. "Sheikh Lakham?"

Len found his voice. "With his trainer; told Paco she was a fine little horse."

"Him – not the trainer? The *Sheikh* said it?"

"As I was walking in. Well, she run good, Pat."

"Good? She was *great*! She done it all, she was so close, I swear, if Jimmy had gone earlier she'd have been – she'd've been *past* the Ice, and the way she was goin' – am I crazy?"

Dope tests looming, Len could not bring himself to provide flunky homage. As usual, he got no congratulations for this event on which he'd staked his career. His reply was measured, in his usual track voice, but a little slower, with just the suggestion of an edge.

"He give her the right ride, Pat. Perfect ride. Look at her. Didn't leave no gas in the tank this time. Took the two best in the country to beat her and she took Black Ice to a photo."

McGoohey nodded, liking the sound of that, then moved on abruptly.

"Okay, gotta find the Lees now," he said in his executive voice: "See ya at the yearling sales, Len."

As he walked off, Len went into the stall thoughtfully,

breath taken away by the arrogance. It hadn't even *occurred* to the man that he might want his brilliant trainer along to facilitate the miracle he was hoping to arrange. Brilliant trainer wouldn't get to shine for Cinnamon Girl today, which he'd really been counting on.

He stored it away, and looked at his horse carefully, an arm around her appreciative neck, then feeling her legs carefully, down to the hooves and listening to her breathe. Paco was right, she was fine, and looking pleased with herself the way people did after good sex or some fun three-on-three hoops on a schoolyard court. It gave him something to feel good about. Pulling a pair of sugar cubes from his pocket, he felt relieved and ashamed when she nuzzled him, thinking about the line between illegal and evil. Evil striking an innocent creature, especially. He'd been spared that, at least, but that was luck, too. Little heart valve problem, little slip in the mud on that magnificent final turn. Any little thing could have done it, totally stretched out as she was.

"Gotta go, Paco. You did great. You and Jimmy."

"You think some day McGoo say something   good to me?"

"Same day he say somethin' to me I like to hear. Same day he have good word for Jimmy. Jus' don' hold y'breath, right?"

Both men smiled dry, angry smiles, and Len left for his room. Still absorbing McGoo's abrupt departure, he lay down to reassemble himself. Ambivalence about what he'd done was grinding against his frustration at being left out of that meeting. Armstrong, the Lee trainer, would damn sure be there. He started to doze before it occurred to him that the money he'd put on this race had become a vast sum, his biggest single score ever by far. Either he'd be trading the old Chevy and buying some nice things to wear or he'd be a ruined man. As a gambler, he understood his situation perfectly. What he didn't understand was how he had come to *do* such a thing. Crime of passion? Temporary insanity? Just went ahead and did it. And then locked out of the big meeting.

If you black, get back, he thought, tasting it to the full. But unless she failed the tests, he still had his job, and probably a little raise.

And anything not nailed down, he decided. Spoils of the

race war. McGoo was asking for it; leaving him there with Paco had made it personal. His stomach was a raging knot full of acid.

McGoohey started his search in the vast clubhouse, standing a moment in the doorway, suit freshly pressed, smiling genially and beaming optimism as he scanned the tables. It was a room full of bold dressers, dapper Manhattan-based operators elbow to elbow with blazered bankers in Bermudas, unfettered males everywhere chatting up the choicest of imported working girls. McGoohey went unnoticed, except for the white patent-leather loafers. Jasmine had been trying to get rid of them since the marriage, but they were his special lucky shoes, party to his first blockbuster deal, of impeccable Italian lineage, perfect for a Napoli Don. His well-rehearsed game plan, absolutely secret and discussed with no one, was modesty personified, a carefully worked out line incorporating a respect bordering on servility. *Frankly, I never thought my little horse would come side by side with Black Ice – that was a big moment for me, Miz Dixon. It won't happen again, though; I think she's really for breeding, with all that Bold Ruler blood...*
There was a lot more of it, but no Annabelle Dixon to say it to. He also had an eye out for Armstrong, but he wasn't there either. McGoohey smiled. Armstrong must be suffering after seeing his horse get stuffed like that and just barely holding second. McGoohey knew *that* feeling, and he was sure this Dixie woman had a mouth on her. He strolled through several seating areas, checking everywhere with the quick eye of an outdoor man as everyone stared at the huge video terminals. Passing through, he said hello to a couple of people he recognized, but to his keen disappointment, not one remarked on Arabiche's sensational closing charge in the best race of the day. DeQuincy was getting all the play for his runaway victory in the feature, and there were comments about Missile Man's early retirement for no obvious reason, implying that Lee Farms had dodged DeQuincy.

No matter, Lee Farms couldn't ignore Arabiche. They'd seen her go the distance, blow away contenders and challenge really hard. But as McGoohey toured the clubhouse it struck him that the high-end owners would have their own gathering place. There was a Lee colt running the next day, though, and at worst he'd find her then. He let himself drift for a moment, feeling every inch a winner. The ride of Jimmy's life, slick as John Velasquez. Should have taken second, but great as that would feel, it would have been a bad mistake. Or would it? Knock off the Dark Lady and they'd fuckin' *have* to respect him. What the hell – it was a great day, his team had come through, another crazy Pat McGoohey plan was working out just fine, thanks to his excellent judgment of men. Len Thomas might slur and mumble to the point where sometimes it was almost like he was putting it on, but he ran a good crew, and today was the proof. Now it was up to him, and sooner or later he'd find the lady and work it out.

Passing the bar on the way out he spotted Barry Carney, with whom he'd always have a drink. A good trainer, close to McGoohey's own age, Carney was still waiting for the horse that would make his career, and he'd obviously seen 'Biche flying past all those name-brand contenders. McGoohey clapped him on the back; Carney was big and solid enough to take it. Then he stood him a drink of the special Bushmills, which they naturally had here. Harry was pleased to accept a double. McGoohey might look a little out of place, to put it mildly, but was definitely to be court-ed now that his little mare had taken the Dark Lady to a photo.

"Damn nice run your horse had in the sixth, Pat. Went earlier, might've taken the whole thing. Icy-hot was lucky. You've got to breed that little lady."

McGoohey nodded. "I'm here t'do just that. I'm thinkin' Missile Man, for the closing speed."

"You'll have to get in line there, y'know," said Carney diplomatically.

"I can wait," replied McGoohey without thinking.

"Do you really want to? There's Tory Commodore, kind of similar, Commander blood."

"Yeah, but all that Alydar and Slew in there, Double M's just right for her."

Carney nodded, wondering. Did this unconnected con-struction bully really think he could pull this off on the basis of one good race? Already a great champion, Missile Man would be a great sire. The Commander line was famous for it. But the man did have a way of getting things done, little as he knew about horses, and he might be wanting a more experienced trainer of a different color if things went a certain way. Time to divulge a bit of information that was no secret.

"You'll probably find the lady at Spuyten Duyvil. Dollars to bagels she'll be at the yearling sales. She's knowledgeable, Dixie is. Great lady, too. Chrome steel magnolia. Might be kind of irritable today though. Tomorrow might be better."

McGoohey struck a thoughtful pose and paused.

"Hell, worst she can do is say no, or put me off for a while. That Sheikh, the DeQuincy Sheikh, he was over lookin' at my little girl, took time to talk. He's got studs, big operation, but this case I wanna buy American."

"Still and all, that's what I call a hell of a fallback, Pat."

Len waited patiently for his employer at the grassy site of the yearling sales, staying busy, conscience and resentment at bay as he strolled through the fine northeast late afternoon, the heat of the day finally breaking to a tasty twilight. He looked over the horses carefully and systematically, making cryptic notes in his little black book as he went, happily free of McGoohey's strong views. You couldn't tell a great deal about a horse in a stall other than from the eyes, but you could find out where it came from and go from there. Len priced horses in his mind, knowing McGoohey would never come up with the kind of money to play in this league but letting his fancy roam, committing about two million to an imaginary Len Thomas string, contingent on bidding of course. Moving from horse to horse, he listened to voices carefully, style being especially critical if you were black. You had to have that down, and it had to be second nature. He'd have to do a high-end trainer the same measured way Colin Powell did Eisenhower, for example, before they cleaned his clock, or Tiger Woods as a rising young Republican bank executive. And *threads*. There had to be a Len Thomas style, within bounds but *cool*. Like his mother's description of Duke Ellington, say, or Quincy Jones. Bespoke Brit blazers, Italian leather for the feet.

He stopped to look at a roan Commander colt being led on a shank. The speed was in his eyes, the wild hot blood that ran in Missile Man. He absolutely needed this one too, which put him well over two million. And face it; though he was a qualified train-er whose horse had been the surprise of the day, he could not even speak with the people around the colt. That was a fact. Black and unknown, he held just one card, dealt from the bottom of the deck. For which he might be eighty-sixed for life tomorrow, tarred and feathered on the evening news, out of town on a rail. If it came to that, he'd just take the rap and swear no one else had any idea. *Did it to save my job.* Say it often enough, hang his head, roll his eyes sadly, and it could stick. Maybe get Jimmy off, who didn't look smart enough to be trusted with serious information.

And just maybe let on that McGoo knew. Not exactly say so, but let it slip out between the lines. Len smiled. In a calm way, he was about as seriously angry as he ever let himself become. He could have swung a length of two-by-four against that thick skull with pleasure. Not to kill him, just get his attention.

10

Spuyten Duyvil was not intimidating. Not super-big or fancy, not Spago or the Four Seasons, just a good classy restaurant, and a full one at cocktail time. Many tables, many faces, mostly a bit flushed. McGoohey entered confidently, surveying the room, thinking now that it might have been handy to have Len there, the Lees being notorious liberals. The maitre d' approached.

"Looking for the Lee Farms group," said McGoohey, rich of voice, unctuous, transparent, primal, and powerful, nailing the man ever so briefly with his business stare.

"The Lee party is at the rear table nearest the window," said the maitre d', and instantly regretted it. McGoohey didn't belong. Not now, not at that table. The shoes alone disqualified him. The Lee party, drunk as they might be, completely belonged. He glanced back. It was quiet drinking at that table, and everyone knew why. It hadn't just been Margiedaw doubling down her Belmont win, but their Eclipse candidate just barely salvaging second. He was about to step in front of this customer, but without any appearance of haste, McGoohey was gone. As he watched the tail of the too-short jacket bobbing over McGoohey's substantial rump, the maitre d' regretted his hesitation. Avoiding awkwardness was his job, and he'd been bluffed. Another group entered to claim his attention and he let it go.

By deduction and telepathy, Annabelle Lee Dixon knew who the churl in the tight suit had to be. His horse had been working at the Oklahoma track the morning Black Ice had, and she never forgot a horse or anyone who dressed so badly. Without breaking off her discussion of Missile Man's matings, each one evaluated as seriously as a Royal coupling, she observed McGoohey's long, graceless progress, shoulders squared, tassels flapping. She hated him in a special, creative, southern-woman way, with razor-edged aristocratic intensity. The first mood change since that God-damned humiliation at the track froze her solid. The bourbon finally kicked in as she followed his progress in her peripheral vision.

Two tables away was the Sheikh and his group, tall and slim, not unlike his terrorist brother-in-law. On his left was his big silent security chief, Alberto. The chat continued as McGoohey came closer, but all of this group were following closely. His progress was impossible to ignore for several reasons, starting with his brash style, bad suit, and rude confidence. They weren't eating yet, because an Alberto assistant was also the taster, and they were still in the waiting period. Since 9/11, there was always that possibility for a Muslim in the U.S.

And this crude man was the owner of that very nice little mare, thought the Sheikh. Inappropriate, but he could see the man's strength as well. America was truly astounding to him, utterly out of control, but always an interesting challenge, and he had decided that Lakham's focus for the new century would be here, asserting Arab strength on his own terms. It might last the rest of his life, given U.S. determination to control mid-east oil while undermining his religion and culture. His interest in the McGoohey–Lee meeting quieted conversation at his table.

"Mrs. Lee, I'd like to introduce myself," McGoohey began.

Even had her name wrong, Dixie thought, looking up as if noticing him for the first time. As if he were of acceptable appearance and demeanor.

"Well, who are you, then?" Just the faintest edge, but not unfriendly, almost jovial, democratic in spirit.

"Pat McGoohey. I'm a fellow owner."

"Nice to have met you, Mr. McGowan," she replied with a rich smile on her flushed round face, flashing some perfect teeth and turning immediately back to counselor Pater. Pater was out of Princeton, in his late thirties, married to a lesser Whitney, cute as hell, and a shrewd advisor on the syndication.

"We can talk about the details later," she said to him. "I don't see any reason we couldn't do business with the Ettings soon. Give them a little priority, and if the horses take care of *their* business, we could all be proud parents. We've seen Josetta twice, Daddy and I, and we both noticed how she's awkward out of the gate but strong enough to catch up and run with the leaders.

Results on the board aren't everything, we know that. What matters is the right combination. Ah b'lieve in that 'zmuch as Ah do anything on this earth, Missah Pader."

With the slurred last line, McGoohey grasped that she was drunk. When she left him standing there, he decided she'd simply forgotten he was there. If she had designs on fancy pants in the Madras jacket, that was fine, they could talk later.

"If this is a bad time, we could arrange to meet later sometime to talk some business while I'm in town," he said with warm formality. She turned to face him.

"Ah don't recall that we *have* any business Mister McCoy," she said, and turned back.

"We should," said McGoohey, drawing deep on his patience and self control. "I'm interested in Missile Man myself."

This got a thin, dangerous smile and another look.

"So are lots of people. You weren't thinking of that little mare that fouled my horse this afternoon, I hope."

McGoohey felt a sudden awesome fury deep in his soul but he didn't crack.

"She didn't come *close* to fouling. Do you think a California owner would get a fair shake from stewards in your backyard if there was anything on the tapes?"

She hitched her chair slightly to face him and struck, her voice charged and clear, no sign at all now of having drunk the larger part of a quart of whiskey.

"There's just something not quite right about your little horse, Mister McGarry."

"McGoohey, and what do you mean by – "

"I don't give a damn what you call yourself. Missile Man – well, your little horse just isn't in that *world*, Mister McCooley."

McGoohey feared that he might kill or maim. Not her, but some fool who got in the middle. His rage was blinding, but still controlled. What the *hell* did she mean by something "not quite right" about 'Biche? He regrouped again.

"I want to breed my horse, and I don't care about the price or conditions. I know that Missile Man is the right sire, and it's the horses that matter, whatever you think about me."

Saying that in a civil tone took a lot out of him, but instead of bringing about a more businesslike dialog, he heard a laugh welling up, amused and dismissive, rippling her handsome chest. McGoohey knew that one glance toward the maitre d' was all it would take. He mastered himself.

"My money is as good as anyone's," he said with quiet politeness. "We both know my mare had yours in her sights and if my jockey wasn't a fool she had her beat."

"Ah think y'all know where you can put your money, my California friend. You don't just come around the owner of a horse that *your* horse fouled as if nothing happened. Next time try ordering a round from the bar, and if the party happens to invite you over, the only words from your mouth should be gentlemanly acknowledgment that your little spoiler – "

"SHE DIDN'T FOUL YOUR FUCKIN' HORSE! BLACK BEAUTY RAN OUTTA GAS!"

They were on him all at once, the maitre d' directing, with two college boys from the kitchen advancing on the flanks, one white, one black, both on football scholarships. At the Sheikh's table, Alberto and his assistant invisibly removed pistols from belly holsters, holding the weapons below table level.

"Is this man causing inconvenience Mrs. Dixon?" purred the maitre d'.

"What do you *think*, Gesualdo? You let me sit here waving at you like a fool and just took *forever*!"

The shadow of a smile crossed McGoohey's silent face. She'd done no such thing. But he enjoyed confrontation, and these three did not impress him. Not many years ago he'd been working side by side with his single crew, men who knew how to fight no holds barred. Without turning, he jammed an elbow into the neck of the white boy, taking him out of the equation. His gagging sounds and blind backward staggering alerted everyone to the escalation. It was a sporting crowd and they knew right away that even as the hot-tempered fireplug suckered the white boy, the black one had seen it coming, and almost simultaneously slammed a big fist into McGoohey's lower ribcage, which was braced for the blow, protected by a tightened belt of muscle and fat. The angle was bad, and a shock ran up through the boy's wrist, numbing the arm. He stood for a moment, confused by the useless arm, but

McGoohey, while upright, was unable to breathe, and could not gather himself for the lunge that would get things down on the floor, where he was at his best. In that moment the black man struck with his good arm knocking the off-balance McGoohey to his knees with a fine hook to the temple. No referee being present, the maitre d' produced a short thick black stick, actually a slim leather truncheon filled with lead shot. As McGoohey was about to throw himself into his opponent's knees, a measured tap to the skull sent him the rest of the way to the hardwood floor, face down, dazed but coherent, knowing it was over. The Sheikh's men holstered their weapons at a small gesture from Alberto. Christians battling Christians. They found it encouraging, and the taster, still alive and healthy, began to eat as Lakham nodded, lifting knife and fork.

"Okay," grunted McGoohey.

Standing up slowly, a man on each elbow, he got in a last word: "I'll get you for this, lady."

Clear and malevolent, delivered in his hard, heavy voice, but ignored by Dixie, who was already back with the young attorney, inviting him to a party in case they lost contact at the yearling sales. Dixie realized that she'd probably reached her limit, fine as another drink would taste at this moment. She slid a little further into her chair, exhausted by her difficult day. Her breeding served her well, and her appearance changed only slightly as she slipped into a nap. The trainer shifted his chair, allowing him to support his employer enough that she wouldn't slide to the floor. He glanced at Holly, who nodded in a way that said she'd help out as soon as possible. The thunderbolt had missed her and she was content. Padraic McGoohey III was long gone, spirited out a side door as if he'd never existed.

Len was starting across the grass to the little amphitheatre where people were gathering when Gala's Boy caught his attention. Then he saw McGoohey beyond the horse, carrying himself strangely, with an expression Len had never seen before. Shaken, with pain control written into his face. He had a roughed-up look, sprayed hair askew, and he wasn't walking quite right. Not drunk, but not himself. Len looked down at his black book to look busy, pretending to write. In half a minute, McGoohey appeared at his elbow, pretending everything was fine.

"How much ya spent for me here so far?"

"Two mil, maybe lil' more."

"Gonna have t'wait a year or so."

Without looking directly at him, Len was sure that McGoohey had been manhandled, an event that would take some doing. But how? Why? It could happen to anyone, but no mugger would take on Pat McGoohey, and this was Saratoga, not LA.

"Yeah, we're not gonna get any of that Missile jism. I talked it over with Mrs. Lee, they call her Dixie. She was nice about it, but his foals, well, they got a line of mares from here to Pasadena waitin' on him, and they gotta keep him at a certain limit of course."

The lie rolled on, totally transparent, Len far ahead of it, seeing that he had risked everything, only to have this fool drop the ball again. He nodded briefly and followed with a small shrug.

Did it his way, came up empty, and I never got near that beautiful woman, he thought, looking back at Gala's Boy. But I will. The horse stopped moving for a moment to look at him. Len made a faint chirruping sound, and the horse pricked his ears. Not the next Missile Man. The Lee Farms people were approaching, and the owner's silence was getting awkward. Then he heard Dixie's voice, saying good-bye to Pater, who came into view with the bewitching Holly St. Cyr, and Len temporarily lost his mind again. He turned slightly, and when her glance caught his, there was no question in his mind that her eyes held contact longer than necessary, and that she damn well knew who he was now. Ghost of a smile, right under her boss's nose. He turned and got hold of himself. McGoohey was talking some nonsense that he barely heard. He could not resist this woman, and it was dangerous. Crazy. But fuck it, that quiet little half-smile had fully recognized his coup. To achieve that, he'd risked everything, including good friends. Now she was walking off with a tall handsome rowing-type white man. But not before that smile.

Then he saw something hard as steel pass swiftly over Dixie's face, after which she rather abruptly led her group into the amphitheatre. Slim, stylish Eleanor St. James was approaching with *her* group, a larger one, mainly exuberant Texans. They seized center stage, radiating inebriated triumph. Len felt McGoohey tensing up, still wordless, and felt sorry for him in the newly acquired misery of his meaningless millions.

"All set with 'Biche?"

It was a shaky voice full of self-doubt, totally wrong for an owner whose troops had just provided the best day of his sporting life.

"On the way to the airport. Meet Jimmy two hours."

"Okay then. I need a shower. We didn't do too bad here, did we? Good job, Len. I was right about the little girl, wasn't I? She showed 'em. See ya back home."

And he abandoned the field, unable to carry on in the presence of such concentrated wealth and power.

Strolling over with his group, the Sheikh observed the exchange, and the trainer's tact. Len turned and the nose caught the Sheikh's eye, but Len didn't notice, preoccupied with McGoohey. Pat was not himself. Whatever had happened, it was big, and Len knew depression when he saw it. He didn't suffer from it, but he knew what it was in a general way, and that it was a kind of epidemic, providing a huge bonanza in pharmaceuticals. McGoohey's solution would be old-school, snarling his way out of it in a manly manner, passing the load onto people around him. You could take that to the bank. He allowed himself a final look at Holly St. Cyr walking slowly away, talking with the rich guy in the Madras jacket as if she completely belonged. She had a step on him, no question. *Time in grade* they used to call it. Experience, knowing how things were done. But the door was open and he knew what it would take. He'd have to become the Llewellyn Thomas she imagined on the basis of what she'd seen. Calm and thoughtful, he walked to the car and drove to Madam Jumel's to pick up Jimmy, roaring drunk but allowing himself to be carried off to the plane by Paco and Carlos, laughing, giggling, waving, and shouting friendly obscenities.

11

Alice Smith sat in her office looking well, half-listening to a McGoohey phone call while working. She was wearing a medium-blue business suit with a bit of floral material at the neck that revealed her natural flair while concealing a slight looseness. Jasmine's good friend Dr. Ron would restore that at virtually no cost, and she was considering this as she listened to McGoohey while impaling notes on different spikes. Refined and reserved, she liked straightforward men of action. An awkward, direct manner was no issue, and she liked to see men happy, which McGoohey was definitely not. She was puzzled by her boss's unaccountable mood following that remarkably successful Eastern trip. His voice lacked resonance, and Alice paused to listen more carefully. It was a voice he used when cutting corners and taking chances.

"The little girl proved it at Saratoga," said McGoohey in an aggressive but subdued tone, cradling the phone away from the door between their offices and sounding dishonest. "She's gotta drop a foal and it's gotta be the right stuff; that decision is made."

Never gets tired of saying it, she thought.

"No. I think I mentioned that Missile Man is not available to us at stud presently," he said after a pause. "I didn't get a chance to tell you the full story before my flight, but we had a conversation, me and Dixie, and her position is that a horse whose best recent result was coming third, even in that class of race, didn't qualify, owing to the widespread demand for her horse's services. I pointed out that she ran with Black Ice and Margiedaw all the way, but – "

The false tone triggered Alice's further enhanced her curiosity. What had actually happened on that trip? And who was her boss talking to in this peculiar way?

McGoohey was silent, half listening, recalling that great finish, his little 'Biche whipping Fatalistica, Sonnet, Bobo's Girl, and

Maidenform. About to whip Black Ice, too. Did he imagine that little hesitation at the end? Was that Jimmy? After that perfect ride?

Then the awful scene at Spuyten Duyvil came to him in perfect replay. It came back every time he felt the rib the black kid had cracked, and whenever he dreamed. *Clothes make the man*, he was thinking. Somebody smart said that. Why hadn't he picked up the clothes Jasmine bought? Because he was just another grunt in a Mercedes. Why hadn't he brought Jasmine, who had a sixth sense about these things? Same fuckin' answer.

"Yeah, hang on a second."

He spun his chair and pushed the door to Alice's office closed with his foot a little harder than necessary. Alice pressed a secret button that allowed her to hear McGoohey's voice in the room. Her fiancée had rigged it at her request to help her keep current with McGoohey's often forgotten commitments, and this felt like trouble. With the door closed he was more direct.

"She put me down because I'd had a couple and I was a little, y'know, *motivated*. Hungry. These people, they're never motivated, not really, they don't have t'be, never been hungry in their lives. I wanna motivate her ass in a few years, whip it with her own Double-M blood."

Another call came in, and Alice had to give up her eavesdropping to explain a bill, missing part of the call.

"I *know* there's other class studs out there, we already had that conversation I don't need a fuckin' list."

"Yeah, steal it if necessary."

Steal what? wondered Alice.

"Yeah, I know you said it as a joke, but it's a damn good idea."

"Of *course* I mean you! You think I'm gonna go outside the family for something like this? You're the man. I know it can be done, maybe just a fat bribe, it happens, no one gets hurt."

Another call came in, diverting Alice.

"Yeah, okay, maybe not that easy, but I know you can do it. You're prob'ly the only person I know *could* do it, and it's ten large plus a percenta what comes out of it. Ten percent ownership of the foal and all earnings.

"Direct and indirect, yeah, okay."

A long pause, during which Alice returned.

"Whaddaya mean? said McGoohey. "You look like getting caught, you got a pint of Jack and you pour it down your throat. Smell drunk, act drunk, they throw you in the slam overnight. Anything real bad, I spring bail and hook up an attorney knows what he's doin'. Those hicks'd never figure out what was really going on."

"Okay then, twenty."

"Yeah, okay, ten up front. Now here's the thing: If they connect *you* to *me* in case of a problem, then they can hang both of us. You gotta get some kind of trail from your relatives back East, like you been there on a some kinda regular basis, y'know what I mean? You bein' black, they're not gonna expect a lot of proof, just like you got drunk and went off the reservation. No insult, Len, just bein' realistic."

"Of *course* you're not fired if you don't pull it off. Just give it a good shot. You're the man, ain't I seen that just a couple days ago?

"Just think about it, okay? The *potential*. 'Biche can run forever, she's got the juice, just like Paco said, and she just proved it, right? Problem's all *mental.* And she's so *sound*, never gets sick or has all those fucking knee and hock and all those problems, the shin thing, the lungs, the viruses. That's fuckin' hard to find, a sound thoroughbred. Perfect breeder."

Alice decided it would have to be Len on the line, but what exactly was he agreeing to? Pull off *what*?

"Well just think about it, okay?" said McGoohey. "You got time. The idea's a winner though, right? How hard can it be? You're smart enough to get it done. And a ten percent ride, baby, off the top, no expenses. This ain't really about money for me."

"Forget fifteen, I'll go twelve percent. Of a friggin' gold mine."

McGoohey's green phone rang. Alice tapped on the window between the offices. Half a minute later she stood at the glass door holding up a sheet of paper, willing McGoohey to focus in much the same way that Len might in dealing with a difficult horse.

"Gotta go, Alice is wavin' a Commissioner Bullitt sign if ya can believe it. Maybe I got that Santa Barbara deal. See ya in the morning."

Len sat for several minutes by his phone hating his employer. Then he dressed casually, drove to the quiet of the library and learned of the artificial vagina, stroking of the ampullae, digital manipulation, seminal vesicles, and the all-important prostate. After that he visited several bookies, each of whom he bought as many drinks as they were in the mood for after paying off his Saratoga winnings. Crime paid, all right, at all levels of society. He just didn't like it for some reason. More so since Saratoga.

The main Lee barn was a subtle, weightless, tan-gray, quietly stating the civil and restrained dominion of properly aged Kentucky blue-grass money. The peaked slate roof was like nothing you'd ever see in LA. Maybe up in the wine country, Len thought. Vast flowerbeds and endless lawns that would require a master gardener with assistants. Perched in his tree, Len took photos with a tiny camera and imagined working in this world, living under one of its solid roofs, secure as few employees could ever be in this century. That was the secret of the fine, confident finish on what God had given that Holly woman to start with. Through his father's old Zeiss binoculars he saw a white boy in his teens leading a big, serious-looking stud horse out the wide main entrance. Space Commander, Missile Man's sire. Matured late but ran for many years, improving with age, winning many big races. Good jism, *fine* jism, but coals to Newcastle, because 'Biche was solid anthracite. To bear a super-foal she needed a fiery stud.

He put down the binoculars and swiveled around to survey the orchard behind him again, left and right. No one. From his carefully chosen pear-tree he had seen seven men and a young girl, all horse-people, all of them around the barns, sheds and workout track. Bales of hay, loads of manure, and sacks of grain moved around at a nice pace while gravel was raked. The layout was simple – one big barn, one small, the track beyond them. Couple of small storage buildings, no security types. They'd be obvious to his Army-trained eye, sharpened by his year as an MP. He knew the style – vigilant, if not too observant, always a little tight. So far he'd seen only electric fence. No problem, but these days there were all kinds of little cameras and black boxes. Probably a computer room in there somewhere. This spread, was, when you thought about it, up with today's best. In breeding terms, second only to legendary Calumet Farms, and Calumet was of the last century.

Looking at history up here in this tree, he thought. They didn't have their Citation or Secretariat, but they had the reigning sperm-king and his heir apparent. Lee Farms was the real deal, and so was Dixie Dixon. Whatever that plump-titty blonde did to Boss Pat, she did it good. Put Len Thomas up in a damn tree.

Uneasy thought, then a good, practical one. There were Lee Farms tours, and he guessed that these tours would include showing off that security room, where some whitebread whiz kid would be sitting at a computer sipping Red Bull. Paco's cousin Miguel, known as Mike, was studying computers and good at it. It was hard to believe they shared any genes, but Mike's unacknowledged father was a French gentleman-jockey, now deceased. *That Crazy Frog,* to Jimmy. Young Mike was smooth, smart, cool, and well-spoken, with no accent. On scholarship and always broke. Mike could do that visitor's tour and have a look at that security room if there was one. A plane trip and a long weekend plus some spending money would sound terrific to Mike.

Having these thoughts while trespassing and planning the crime was making Len fidgety. The big old Zeiss binoculars were a dead giveaway, beside which he'd been there a while and his bladder was filling up. But before descending he tucked the binoculars under his shirt, hunkered down into the tree, and uncapped a small flat pipe containing a blend of Humboldt and kif. About to light up, he thought the better of it, climbed down, and made his way back through the trees to the electric fence. Why didn't they keep it armed in daylight? Mindless confidence?

Mission-think receded as he strolled back to the car, and his thoughts went to Dixie's beautiful cinnamon confidante. Smart, he imagined. No, he knew that. Real problem finding a beautiful woman that was smart and not bitchy. He told himself she was too smart to be really bitchy unless you brought it on by acting like a fool. And calling her now would be crazy even if he had her number.

God, those smiling glances! Just a dream for now. The reality was near future high risk crime, even with the alarms out courtesy Cousin Mike. Group McGoohey collecting the goo on their own, because approaching an employee would be stupid; they'd looked too happy. High risk because Paco's experience as a gangbanger didn't include anything like this, and Carlos was just a kid. They wouldn't draw attention like black guys, but had no sense of what this gig would demand. Amateurs, no discipline, sign of the times. No military experience, that was part of it. Paco belonged to the Cheech and Chong tradition.

The car was just as he'd left it, half a mile away, in a section where the shoulder extended well off the road, shaded by tall pines from the afternoon sun, the windows down an inch to reduce heat build-up. Still hot as hell. He started the motor with a feeling of relief strong enough that he forgot about his bladder and just sat there for half a minute coming down. As he was about to step out and relieve himself, he felt a car pulling up behind. In the mirror was a local cop. The binoculars went under the seat and he stepped out of the car wearing an earnest, businesslike expression, thinking about his presentation: loafers, khakis, quiet blue sport shirt. Middle-class without being ridiculous. The cop climbed out and walked over and Len evaluated him: big, clean, young, blond, dumb, born asshole.

"License and registration, please."

This is that profiling thing, and this is the South.

He removed them from his wallet, all in order, all false and of good quality. The cop examined them briefly.

"Like to ask what you doing here, sir."

The trained-in politeness was more threatening that bubba-bluff.

If you knew you'd shit those khaki pants and bust me for a promotion. Pipe right here in my pocket. Camera, too.

"I used to live in Louisville as a boy and come out here to work summers before the family moved. I just wanted to look around, see how it changed over the years. I'm on vacation, officer."

This was the rarely heard Llewellyn Thomas, civil, genteel and respectable. Hearing this voice, the cop saw before him a Good

Negro, apparently with some education. Respectful, no tattoos, face-hair, Afro or corn-rows, and speaking darned good English. Obviously employed, at ease with the Law. Felt like an accountant, something legitimate like that. Probably had some college, a lot of them did, probably knew a good attorney or was capable of finding one. His story was reasonable, and he didn't have any attitude at all. No need or excuse for a search. The man obviously did not fit a criminal profile.

"Routine," he said, in his careful young law enforcement voice. "Had a little trouble out here recently, we're stopping people we don't recognize as local."

But do recognize as cullud. No probable cause though. Sorry, Off'sa Whitebread. Not your day.

The cop was nodding, as if agreeing with himself about something.

"Not going to write this up, but this is a highly well-policed area because the property and livestock are highly valuable to the owners."

The highly well-placed owners. Everybody seems to be high out here, officer. Not you, of course.

"I understand."

A subliminal nod acknowledging the problems of law enforcement.

"This is not racial profiling, Mr. Johnson, I am simply informing you of a situation we're concerned with."

"Understood."

The cop turned on his heel and walked back, shoulders squared. Len climbed into the rented car, stomach knotted, glad it had not been rented in his name. He'd played everything right, but now he was becoming angry. He detested being forced to act like a white man, preferring to keep at a distance. Having lost control of how he would speak, he was beginning to lose control of critical back-brain processes, and rage was blazing up out of control. Rage and fear going back to his Boston childhood balling-up in his stomach, along with an uncontrollable hatred at being violated, at having this role forced on him. Beyond reason, he completely forgot that he was doing reccon for a major crime.

Whitebread motherfucker bitch! You and your goddamn gun

piss me off!

It came up from deep inside in a muttered, raging fury as he watched the cop drive off. He didn't want to speak *that* way, either, dammit, but he was even angrier than he'd been with McGoohey for leaving him out of that Saratoga meeting and his mouth felt wrong from all that false talk. It needed to be rinsed with alcohol, which would then need to be swallowed. Almost any alcohol would do in this state of mind. His reaction was reverberating uncontrollably and he drove off with shaking hands locked on the wheel. After a couple of minutes he wiped down the pipe, a nice little pipe he had carved for himself, and tossed it out the window with a quick flip that shot it deep into high grass, well away from the road. Evidence gone, but he felt the tension building in his stomach, cutting into his confidence and sense of himself. He hated feeling vulnerable, and feared what it released in him: the knowledge that he could, in the right circumstances, kill someone who brought it on.

Seen by a fucking cop right where the crime gonna go down! And with that different-looking nose that people remembered. Goddamn McGoo and his crazy schemes! But even now he had to respect McGoohey's raw, bold intelligence. And the cleverness of putting *his* black ass on the line whenever convenient, thank you very much. Bastard would be having dinner at Spago while he, Len, was risking his intelligent, well-read personal self with a couple of very unqualified guys. For twenty large and twelve percent. McGoo had known his price, the sonofabitch.

And all his own idea! A little joke that McGoo had snagged and become attached to, until there was no avoiding it, just getting what he could out of it.

Hoist on my own petard! he declaimed, wondering again what a petard might be. Anyway it was Shakespeare, studliest of them all. Len was a great admirer of the Bard, who could always change his mood. Stupid kid-cop had really got to him, though. He wondered how long it would take to fully wear off.

Not really a criminal and don't want to be, he mused. Making it up as I go along. Amateur mistakes. Damn car parked too close, crazy to bring the pipe and those big old binoculars. Unprofessional. Lucky it wasn't some for-real cop.

Coming home had been hell for McGoohey, and it wasn't getting better. The photo-finish shot had made the LA Times and everyone was complimenting him, and it tasted like dirt. His crew came through and he failed. He played the video several times daily and carried a copy with him in the glove box of the Mercedes. Each time he watched the last furlong, he felt the same raw sorrowful pain. A perfect ride, and he knew it by heart. And if Jimmy had just really whacked her a couple of good ones right at the end there! But he'd followed orders – his own stupid god-damned orders. Of course they wanted to beat Black Ice! He'd been out of his mind not to see it. That Dixie bitch would've had to respect that, and they'd've had a whole different conversation. And if only he'd been wearing the clothes Jasmine picked out for him! And he'd brought her along! Instead, total humiliation and everyone telling him how great it was. He had looked into another world, and everything in his own now seemed like a bad joke.

And he couldn't talk to Len! Len had laid down strict rules, including telephone silence. No trail. No evidence that he or anyone else connected with this caper had ever been in touch with LA. Phone records were so dangerous that Len had left his cell phone at home.

It had started to sprinkle by the time the exercise boy was ready with Tamari. An odd development – he couldn't remember the last rain. He got up on the rail, hatless in the spiffy jacket and slacks Jasmine had bought for Saratoga, letting the occasional tepid drop fall on his head. As he took out his stop-watch, he had a strong impulse to smash it. Omitting his eye-opener, he had a swallow of bottled water. Paco watched and wondered from a safe distance. The McGoohey he knew would always drink from his silver flask before the water, exult in a good workout, and sometimes temporarily change personality for the better. This man had been wearing the same stare since Saratoga. Even Tamari's healed feet and solid workout didn't change it.

The owner's expression hadn't changed even when the Commissioner gave him a job that would keep his third crew together. The new Padraic McGoohey saw only that he owned a great little mare destined to dam a champion and change their lives. That was his new world, and job one was getting her the right juice. It required total focus and allowed no daytime drinking. The previous evening it had again forbade him to exercise his husbandly privileges with the beautiful young woman he had married. His focus was total, his heart was pure, and he felt very strong. He thought he might go to church for the first time in years and do a reasonably honest confession. Somewhere out of town, because God's servants were known to have a drink and a chat, along with the choirboys.

As he watched Tamari being hot-walked, his number two cell phone played his favorite Irish air.

Let it be Len. That was his first thought when any of his phones rang. But the caller ID had a local number, one he didn't recognize.

"Pat McGoohey speaking."

"It's just me, Paddykins. I'm on my new phone that takes pictures. If you had one I could send you a picture! I just feel so alone since you came back, and I just now saw you took out the clothes I bought for your trip, and I felt so *sad.*"

"Don't feel bad little Jazz. I'm wearing them, and they look great. I really shoulda remembered them, and I paid for that. Them clothes, they were what I was missing. And y'know what else? Throw out those friggin' white loafers, I felt like a jerk in 'em."

There was a pause while Jasmine, sitting in bed with her second cup of coffee, tried to process these unnerving remarks. It was as if she'd been at the wheel of a great big red vintage V-8 El Dorado ragtop and it had turned into a black Bentley saloon, quiet, unfamiliar and inhibiting. She didn't know this suddenly considerate impersonal husband, or what to do with him.

"How about we go out tonight, Jasmine? Someplace nice."

How about you go back to the way you used to be? she wanted to say, having spurned the attentions of Dr. Ron for days on end only to be ignored by her husband.

"That'd be so cool," she said obediently. "You want me to make reservations?"

"If you don't mind. Not too early, maybe eight-thirty or nine?"

If you don't mind?
"Sure, hon. Are you okay?"

"Never better. Any calls for me?"

"No, baby."

"I'll be home around seven. Wanna bring anyone with us?"

With her husband's query about bringing others to dinner, Jasmine was positive her marriage was in trouble. He was a hardass, a suspicious man full of secrets, not sociable by nature, and had nothing you could call a circle of friends to invite from. This was about shirking his husbandly obligations, which had to be about Another Woman. She was going to have to have a damn baby after all. Get Big Red's libido up and running again and let it happen. She went to the medicine cabinet and took a tranquillizer. Walking away, she decided that was wrong, what she really needed was something to break this mood weighing her down. She added one of Doctor Ron's anti-depressants and washed it down with grapefruit juice and a touch of vodka. After her marmalade toast she was back on the phone.

"Mom, I've got a problem."

"What else is new?"

"Seriously. I don't know what to do about Pat, he's like, *different*. Like friendly but distant?"

"So he met someone in Saratoga, some shiksa?"

"Maybe – he's like, I don't know, got religion I guess."

"So religion means you can't have sex?"

"Mom, he's Catholic, what do we know about that?"

"I'm not the one that turned down some very nice Jewish boys, little girl. Queers running everything? Maybe not the Pope, but all those priests and bishops, and they get to be cardinals. Give me a rabbi with a normal weakness any day. And they helped ruin a good president, for what? A little petting she asked for?"

"That was some other Christians, and we're getting off the subject. Should I have a baby?"

"You bet, bubby; he's always talking about it, according to you. And if you think I don't know about Ron, you're wrong, his cousin is very close to Rachel, and she saw you together. I'm not criticizing, I'm just saying. He's sandy-haired too, a little red in it."

"*Mom!*"

"It's so awful? He's a nice Jewish boy, very nice, and *smart*, a doctor."

"If you think Pat's dumb, you're *way* wrong. Totally! Put them both on a desert island and you'd see, he'd get the natives off their butts and have a beach-front development going by the time they were found. Ron, they'd eat. Besides which, there's the little issue of genetic identity. All he needs is a little suspicion."

"Okay, but why suspicion?"

"What do you think?"

"Oh. *Him?* Really?"

"Did this ever happen with Daddy?"

"Are you kidding? Tax time every year, or if he lost a client, or I missed a period."

"He's taking me to Spago tonight. I'm *afraid*, Mom. He's not himself. We never go to Spago anymore. I don't want a divorce, I can't go through all that, I'm too old."

"What do you know from old? You come from good stock, Jasmine. Just remember that your grandmother in the Russian winter walked hundreds of miles across ice and snow to get out of that Revolution. You think about that, Miss Sensitive. She was skinny, too, you take after her."

It reminded Jasmine of one of her father-in-law's potato-famine stories. *Nothing but immigrants, all of us,* she thought sadly. As various chemicals worked their way through her system, she found herself crying.

"Oh, I did it again," said her mother. "I keep forgetting about the artistic side, which you also take after one hundred per-cent. Just sit there, I'm coming over. Don't move. My little girl is going to come out just fine. Just sit. We'll have that man prancing around like a bitch in heat. That's backward, but you know what I mean. He's a man, he just needs reminding."

12

Coming down from the cop Len still felt like the doomed space shuttle, glue melting, tiles flying loose as it passed into the troposphere and immolation. He rarely experienced fear, and his disarray now was as bad as he could remember since he'd moved West. Very aware that he was irrational, driving carefully at the legal limit and trying hard to think clearly, he spotted a nice restaurant set back from the road. A drink. Right. Hadn't had one in a week. He needed that one drink, and this looked like it might be the right place, decent-looking, not too fancy, might be color-blind for a well-dressed middle-class person of color like himself. Just a few cars outside, clean-looking but nothing special. He guessed this was where you went after work if you didn't drive a German car. Look in the door, check the vibes, split if they felt wrong. He parked behind the building where the cop wouldn't see the car if he drove past.

Stepping into the big, dark bar a minute later, he heard an old Miles Davis side playing. The super-smooth group with Wayne Shorter and Tony Williams. Taking in the subdued atmosphere, he felt he could finally breathe freely. Long classy wooden bar, spacious room, eight or nine black and white people interspersed and getting along. *Hallelujah!* A few more sat together at a banquette looking relaxed. The place was perfect. Seated alone at the short end-section of the old bar, Len ordered a Remy Martin from a quiet young white boy with short hair and a neutral manner. It arrived promptly in a very nice snifter, and by its luxurious aroma he recognized the real thing.

Down the bar were two attractive women sitting together, one white, one mocha, speaking frankly about life, lovers, employers, and the mischief various people had been up to lately. After listening a while, he thought about making some kind of approach. The women were in their early thirties, right where he liked them, old enough to be realistic, definitely not on the slide. But of course he shouldn't even *be* in the damn bar, it was just more people to recognize him. The thought physically chilled him. The cop could be driving around the building, spotting the rented Chevy and waiting for him to leave with probable cause on his breath. A single cognac, sipped slowly. After the first sip his bladder went mad.

He stood a long time relieving himself, approving the bathroom and its mild medicinal aroma and pulling himself together. Quick shake before washing hands. Okay, the cop had a plate number, and good luck with that, because it wasn't rented in any traceable way and his name wasn't Johnson. He went to the mirror and inspected himself. His usual face, maybe just a little remote. Stomach still in a knot. The cop had depleted him, leaving him with a strong urge for human contact. Returning to the bar, he saw that the two women had been joined by a third. He couldn't see her face, but he liked what he saw of her dress. Almost an evening dress, medium-dark blue, perfect for the cocktail hour in a refined little town full of money. Mocha lady, white lady, new lady, all in a row, the new one furthest away. Pick of the litter, he guessed, but he couldn't get a look. His right foot was strongly inclined to walk over and sit next to her, but the left one reminded him where his drink was. And flirting was guaranteed to set him in memory. Sipping his cognac, he decided on a modest goal: satisfy his curiosity about the girl in the blue dress. Then he analyzed his situation. Simple, really. He was destabilized and craved human warmth after that roadside cop scene. The relief of touching and being touched, laughing together at something on the tube. Friendly sex, humanity in a favorite and reassuring form.

And really dangerous. After delicious inhalation and another taste, Len consulted his facsimile Rolex and glanced at the trio. The two nearest women were leaning back, laughing at something the third had said. And that third female was none other than Mrs. Dixon's bewitching cinnamon confidante, Holly. Holly Sincere? Something close to that. He was shocked at the perfectness of it, and lifted his drink to cover his expression. On full autopilot, he stood, walked down the bar, sat next to the beautiful Holly, and addressed her in the quiet, respectable tone he'd employed with the cop, this time voluntarily.

"I think I recognize you from Saratoga – with Mrs. Dixon?

I'm Llewellyn Thomas, trainer with McGoohey Farms in California."

Holly turned at the sound of his voice, nodded, and smiled just enough. Not chilly, just waiting, obviously remembering. College all the way and not very interested in horses, he guessed.

"I never did get your name before your friend cut in that night," said Len

"Holly St. Cyr," she replied in a cultivated and not unfriendly voice, and he could feel Bad Knees Budney disappearing, consigned to the bottomless chasm of big crude men who talked too much. "How did you do up there?"

Perfect again, deadpan cute, and really dangerous. She knew damn well what 'Biche had done to Black Ice, her last smile had said so. That coolness, he was thinking. That coolness that heats you up and leads you by your desperate member like a dowsing rod near an underground flood.

"Came third in the sixth on Sunday – almost second, but ran out of track."

"Oh, yes. The bay. Pretty horse. We had two seconds, really disappointing."

As if she cared. New subject, right now, before she turns back to her friends.

"I'm on vacation visiting friends in Louisville and had an idea to drive through the area. Black Ice is a Lee horse, I believe."

"You *know* that." She paused, almost smiling. "Yeah, our gang were pretty upset. If your little horse had beat Icy there'd have been hell to pay."

Our Gang. Funny. The informal *Yeah* was promising, too, and when she almost laughed, it was perfect. Everything since the cop was perfect. She could call Arabiche his little horse, he decided. She could do anything she damn pleased and knew it.

"Any live music around?" he asked. "Seems like all the good music comes from out East."

"Nothing like Marcus Wheatley."

Understated *intime* smile. She turned to her friends.

"Emmy, Trish, this is Llewellyn Thomas, who trained that bad little California horse that nearly embarrassed us at Saratoga."

Then she turned back to him in a very positive way just as

the bartender was asking if he'd like another, and Len was permitted to buy a round. All the women were drinking vodka tonics made with a vodka he'd never heard of. They all chatted, and he was as charming as he knew how to be, talking about scouting horses for his employer, who hadn't found exactly what he wanted at Saratoga. With that, Holly barely managed to fight off a laugh. Whatever happened to McGoo that day, Holly St. Cyr knew all about it. Did she know what happened to Len Thomas every time he was around her?

The women briefly debated local music, then the craziness of the Sport of Kings, all parties enjoying the   happy hour.

High water mark right here, announced an inner voice Len had come to trust over the years. He got out his black book, nailed those wide eyes with a solid look, then went into the little pocket for his personal card, which had only his name and the number of his cell phone.

This is my time, he thought unexpectedly, mind very clear. As he handed her the card, he leaned slightly forward to be heard through the music.

"I'd like to see you when I'm back East again."

"Certainly, Llewellyn."

Formal but flirtatious. *Get a grip,* man, said that inner voice. He lifted his snifter in a tiny toast, then began orchestrating his departure. This involved a brief, fanciful tale of his East Coast trip, which involved a meeting he could easily be late for. Holly listened, said nothing, and produced a tiny black beaded bag, into which was worked a golden horse in a wonderful airborne full-stretch gallop. Lee Farms logo, had to be a gift from Mrs. Dixon. Bells rang on pure intuition. With a smile balanced perfectly between personal and professional, she extracted a card and placed it gently but firmly in his palm. Might as well be palpating my damn soul, thought Len Thomas as he put it in his wallet.

Done and done, said that voice. *Get out while you ahead, baby.*

Outside in the heavy afternoon sun he was extremely pleased to have made his escape without some miscalculation, blunder, or confession of undying love. Just that risky chat. Holly would never bring him up with the Lees, but while his stomach was finally relaxed now, the safe feeling was gone. He'd had two drinks, was badly in need of food, and it was time to find a motel. On the road, he reset the rear view mirror to get the glare out of his eyes and kept driving until he was in the next county, where he stopped at the first available food, a Taco Bell, where he stood quietly salivating before buying a pair of miniature burritos. Before starting the car he bolted one.

As he drove, the food leveled him off, leaving him in a kind of robotic daze. But just as the sun was getting low he spotted the perfect Motel Six, half a state away from Lee Farms. His front lasted until he checked in, after which he collapsed on the big bed and found himself re-living his near arrest. In the silence he could feel a powerful echo of his fear and rage, and it wasn't going away. Locked in that zone, he heard his mother's firm voice:

Pray about one thing at a time Llewellyn, and don't be praying all the time over nothing.

He wished he could remember how. Still lying on the bed face down, he worked it out. At least two prayers were in order: one for his deliverance from Officer Kid-cop, which was a miracle, what with the evidence right there in his pocket and his father's binoculars under the seat. Then a thank-you prayer for that perfect twelve minutes with Holly St. Cyr, which had settled him down and set him up when he really needed it. He'd been *unstrung*, as his old teacher Mr. Johnston would call his post-cop condition. Walked in unstrung, left in perfect tune. Not a chance meeting at all, but another miracle, a reminder that the books were still open on Llewellyn Thomas.

Still got game, baby. Conscious and deliberate, he ate the rest of the burrito, stood, rinsed his face at the sink, looked at himself calmly, then filled the tub with steaming water. Very strange day. Really tested him, but luck had gone his way. Nothing holding him up but a tightrope of smooth talk.

You acting, motherfucker, admit it. Good liar, nice smile. Lot of that smiling lately.

In the tub with only his sweat-beaded head out of the fiercely hot water, he wondered what his mother would think about prayer in his current circumstances. In the background he wondered about all this *acting*, which came easy, and which he'd never really thought about much. Mr. Johnston had never bothered acting, but he was white upper crust, didn't have to.

Shut up and do it, man.

Right. Sweat poured down his face. His mother was always right when it really mattered. Like when she got him into that excellent hell-on-earth high school where he'd finally learned about real racism, and how to think and speak. Now she wanted him to pray. In a short while, dry but still naked, he was down on his knees in an un-Christian posture, head touching the floor, eye-sockets resting on his knees, hands knitted, with a sensation as strange as the day itself, but glad he could still do this. After formally thanking God for these remarkable events, he asked to be freed of the ugly thoughts the cop had released. After that he apologized in advance for things he was planning to do, in which only money and horses would be involved, no violence or doping. Nothing like that ever again.

Into his blue-checked pajamas, he then sat at the little desk and tried to plan the sperm-jacking, using the easily-removed middle sheet of his little black book. Sketching out the barns, track, and orchard, he found himself appreciating the wisdom in McGoohey's suggestion about hooking up with his East Coast roots. Still more luck – some of these were in the Louisville area. With modest financing he could work up a decent alibi, and it would be family. Another plus.

Finally he turned on the tube and found a *Law and Order* rerun he'd missed. Then he was off to dreamland – a Marx Brothers comedy, with Carlos masturbating Missile Man into an enormous thermos jug to preserve the priceless semen while Paco whispered incantations and he sat waiting for them at the wheel of another rented car.

13

Waking up at noon in the Dead Heat with an extreme hangover, Jimmy Broughton quietly sipped Diet Coke, alone in the dark of the bar re-living the finish again, along with that same feeling of being crazy-happy and sad at the same time. Things rarely went as planned in his life, but 'Biche had done herself proud, his bets had paid off, and on returning he'd bought and paid for the best pussy, booze, and blow that money could buy in Tijuana, along with many drinks for friendly people. He'd returned to awesome respect and offers of very good rides, but first had come that heroic, international movable feast exploding piñatamof a party and this mighty hangover with blown-out nasal passages. Apparently he had eaten real meals during those fifty-odd hours, ballooning him to one-sixteen and losing him a number of lucrative rides. All okay, fine, except for this *dream*, which kept coming around, different each time, always leaving a sad sense of failure. The first time it had been the last furlong in slow motion, that wild wonderful feeling that everything was working out as planned. 'Biche giving everything she had, Ice and Margiedaw ahead going stride for stride. Ice fading! Fighting but fading, and 'Biche creeping up. Moving along that sweet section of track just out from the rail, but with Len's will resting like a heavy hand on his shoulder. *Third place, no better and no worse...* and him like some bug-boy apprentice, doing what he was told. That was one version.

Another began at the start of the last turn. 'Biche ready and willing, three horses in front of her, letting the race come to him, knowing third was sewed up. In this version he went to the whip early, committing before the turn, because that little lady loved the turns and never *ever* had the wheels come off late in a race, just lost interest. Catching the Dark Lady earlier, and getting that big gray locomotive dead in his sights with a long ways to go. She didn't have the big finish, Margiedaw, just ground you down, and 'Biche wasn't grinding down that day, dammitall she was *flying*, doing whatever he asked! *Could-of, should-of, would-of won that race!*

Okay, maybe not win, he thought, seeing his homely face in the bar mirror. But *challenge*. Get that photo with Big Margie for first, because Ice was finished. No way you could be sure of it that early, but if he'd gone with his guts…

"What's your weight now, Jimmy?"

He nearly lurched off his barstool but with an athlete's quickness let it appear like a pleasant surprise. McGoohey, the big bastard! The last company he wanted, with that big red face and hard little money-color eyes.

"Ready tomorrow," he lied automatically.

"Yer gettin' too valuable, Jimmy. Everybody seen your ride at Saratoga, I gotta raise your rate. What I was thinkin' was, could you allow yourself a short one from the private stock?"

On the stool alongside like a smiling bear, smelling of mouthwash, cutting him off from anyone he might *want* to talk to. He would not breathe freely until the owner left or he started drinking again, after which dangerous things might be said.

"Betcha got a real hangover, huh?"

Jimmy nodded, hangover-weak, feeling his mind being read, dominated by the broad face and big smile, because he knew McGoohey. More than twice his size, probably had a three inch dick and never forgot it. There was no protection with a bastard like that staring into you.

"Thought I'd take a minute t'say you earned your fun, Jimmy. Len told me how you helped out, and I seen how you rode."

Back on his game, Jimmy waited. McGoo liked to cat-and-mouse a guy. What the hell did he really want? Their deal was done.

"Yeah, I hope you had a good piece of change down on it."

Which he knew. Jimmy nodded. Maybe there was nothing behind this. But he didn't let his guard down. Owners were never easy except after a win, but this one telegraphed his shots.

"Yeah, I looked at those tapes, and next thing I thought was, if you'd've went earlier she'd'a been past the Ice and goin' up to that big gray. I musta watched it a dozen times."

Cheap, thought Jimmy, but I seen it coming.

"We'll never know, will we?" he replied, in the subtly taunting voice of a professional. McGoohey backed off and Jimmy wished he felt free to smile.

"Done the ride I was told t'do," he said quietly. "Maybe she coulda had second, but that – doin' that'd put us right under the microscope. You, me, Len."

And Paco, who had appeared on McGoohey's free side. A more confident Paco since the Miracle of Saratoga. Perfect timing, thought Jimmy, fighting off another smile. The horse-whisperer was wearing a colorful new outfit topped by a smart new straw stingy-brim which he did not remove, and in his eye was an new spark, something close to a swagger. McGoohey thought he was looking entirely too sharp for a man whose duties included hefting sacks and mucking out stalls. He found the new Paco inappropriate and irritating, but something told him to back off again. Jimmy saw the electricity flickering between them, no longer a target himself and beginning to enjoy this phase of the hangover.

"So where you take little girl now, Mister McGoohey?" asked Paco.

His tone further annoyed McGoohey, but he quelled his irritation, smiled a mysterious senior-management smile, and took the high road, flicking his eye at the bartender in a way that led to the appearance of his private bottle on the bar. Well aware that this undistinguished group had ventured East and returned as local heroes, the bartender was hoping for a clue to the mysteriously born-again Arabiche. He produced the bottle with a respectfully subdued flourish, along with three of the small tumblers McGoohey favored. Outnumbered by his men, the owner regrouped, moving the party to a table. Seated and smiling, he spoke

"Everybody ain't here, but after what we done up there in Saratoga I got confidence. No reason not to drink to the future, and especially to Len."

Wherever the hell he is, hopefully not in the hands of the authorities.

They lifted their tumblers and sipped the very fine and costly whisky. McGoohey preferred the old, subservient Paco, but you had to cut your people a little slack once in a while, and Len said he was the key guy in Saratoga. The men in front of him knew that they'd been successful; only he knew of his failure to cash in on that success. With this reflection, a better mood came over him, a mellow mood, as if things were back to normal, but on a higher level. They were on a mission, and getting it done would be mostly up to Len. Going into his third drink he initiated discourse on the great Seattle Slew, followed by a general discussion of horses of the very highest class. McGoohey abandoned Slew and held out for Citation on the basis of his father's detailed recall and incorruptible judgment.

"But *Secretariat* – " said Jimmy, amazed.

"Abnormal size of heart, but thees kind of horse, they all the same," announced Paco. "Ruffian same level. They in another place, look down on everything, laugh at people. I give anything to work with horse like that, help him out when people, you know – bad decision, horse needs friend, I am there."

"I'm gonna get you that kinda horse, Paco, and I'm gonna see Jimmy up on him winnin' big stakes like Sunday. Derby quality horse. We got a damn good team here an' 'Biche has got the right stuff to give us that horse. I gotta plan goin'. Take a little while, can't talk about it yet."

The names and addresses of the Louisville relatives were on an old but carefully preserved sheet of his mother's stationery, in her precise hand, each name with a note. (Head Custodian at King Street School; clerk at millinery shop on Graves Street; laborer; farmer; works at race track.) For sentimental reasons, Len had kept this list since his army years, never thinking he'd meet any of these relatives. Now he wanted to, but as he drove slowly through the muggy morning it wasn't looking good. Not a single Thomas relative was reachable by phone, so he drove around through the humid heat asking directions to various streets. By noon it seemed clear that yesterday's luck had not spilled over into this day. The King Street School was gone, and an entire block that had housed relatives. Looking at the people and houses as he drove slowly through the black section, he guessed family ties would help, but money would do the real talking. If he could only find an appropriate relative. Any relative.

A promising building full of cousins had become part of a tired-looking brick Project, and another was on a street that felt like a movie set – warped tar, potholes, and broken windows, whores on one corner, dealers on another, each in a little patch of shade. Len disqualified Lamond S. Duncan. By noon the heat outside the car was overwhelming whenever he left it to knock on a door. His elation of the previous day was long gone, and despite skipping breakfast, he felt no hunger. All he felt was a desire to drive to the airport, but a plausible explanation of his presence in Kentucky was professionally required. Give the Devil his due, Pat had seen that right away.

At a table in an old-style corner luncheonette he sat thinking for a few minutes, looking out one of the many large old-fashioned windows. Then he ordered iced tea, toast and a soft-boiled egg from a heavy, respectful waitress, these being things very hard to spoil, unlike the coffee he craved, or an omelet. Coffee would wait for the airport Starbucks. Everyone in the luncheonette was sweating a little, himself included. The room had no air conditioning, but the food was delivered to his little table by the owner. A time-warp, he mused, eating slowly as the ceiling fan clicked and groaned, it's 1970. He checked his list again and confirmed that all but one of the Louisville Thomases were gone, and he didn't expect to find Farmer John Thomas of Elkins Road. No one in the luncheonette had heard of Elkins Road, or much of anything, Len suspected. All that stuff about the end of the middle-class family was true, and double for black ones. Those barber-shop Thomases would have been perfect, something about barber shops attracted people who understood a deal, but that had been sold to a gay couple.

He sat in the car afterward waiting for the AC to kick in, and as the cool air arrived, he drove slowly back into the modest ghetto until he spotted an old yellow man on a porch in a block of wooden firetraps. He approached respectfully, and the man was sharp.

"Elkins Road starts in the north end, but there ain't much there. Runs outta town past some farms and joins up with the highway fifteen or twenny miles out where the interstate's gonna be. Who you lookin' for? Ain't no well-dressed people out there for sure. Farmers."

"John Thomas. Man in his fifties."

The man was walking him back to his car. "Cain't help on that. Got a spare smoke, brotha?"

"Gave 'em up. But you been a real help – would you be offended if I offered you the price of a pack in exchange for that information which I been after all morning?"

The old yellow man laughed almost silently, leaning against the car.

"Not at all. Fair exchange no robbery."

Len gave him a McGoohey five dollar bill and the yellow man gave him clear directions.

Makin' friends everywhere I go, reflected Len. *All I got to do is make some relatives now.*

Following the yellow man's directions, he found John Thomas's neatly lettered name on the old roadside mailbox of his parched little farm. The man came out of the little white house at the sound of a car on the gravel driveway, a thin man, prematurely aged, looking like a sharecropper out of a photo from the Great Depression. If there was a company store, he'd be in debt to it, thought Len as he stepped out into the heat. But the man was civil as could be, soft-spoken   but clear.

"You're no bill collector."

"No, I'm a blood relative, Len Thomas, from Boston. Llewellyn Thomas."

The man changed before his eyes, a thin, bent smile working its way across his face.

"Lonnie's boy. We heard about you, got a letter when you was born. Step in, Llewellyn, it's hot out here in the sun, too hot to work this time of day."

They sat in the low-ceilinged sitting room with tall glasses of lemonade and ice cubes. Real lemonade, Len noted with sentimental pleasure. The house was clean and neat, and sad, threadbare, with not a single new or expensive item to be seen. A large fan sucked air from the shaded side of the house while another blew it out into the hellish afternoon. Len asked his cousin to please call him Len, and talked about losing his family roots in Boston. He described an imaginary job traveling for a New York import company that he'd once hoped to get, then briefly

114

described his search through Louisville. Touched by the man's innocence, he did not know how to proceed. In his experience, country people didn't lie well, and he put off broaching his request until they'd spent some time reviewing the small and scattered Thomas clan. Eventually he said he needed a favor.

His thin, worn-looking cousin looked at him so frankly puzzled that Len lost his game in the realization that he was looking at an honest man, for whom blood meant something, and definitely a man who had paid for his integrity. He'd surely have debts, but he wouldn't have a police record. The farmer went silent, as if considering other surprises that might be on the way, such as the real point of this visit. Len delivered a well-crafted fiction covering Boston, the Army and New York, not including California or horse racing.

"It's kind of complicated, John," said Len. "Work related. I need a reason to be in the area periodically, and indication that I was. If you could see your way clear to saying that I've worked for you from time to time off the books, that would be enough."

John Thomas looked at him as if the oddities of this statement were apparent. Trying to picture Llewellyn Thomas setting fence posts or cleaning the chicken coop distracted him enough that he smiled.

"*Hmm*. This is the damnedest thing, if you don't mind my saying so. You just like your daddy, you know that? He did magic tricks for us. Make a nickel into a dime, pull a silk scarf out of your ear. He was a talker, your dad – how he come to go north, you know. Talked to a white girl an' had to leave town. Your momma got her family to smuggle him out, then got him on the right track, brought out the best in him."

Thanks, thought Len uncomfortably. This old rube had some moves.

"I'm told I'm like him a lot of ways, but I never really knew him, he died in Korea when I was a little boy."

"Master Sergeant. Not a whole lot of decorated Negro Master Sergeants back then."

Stole them blind until he got killed, thought Len, with sudden emotion. *Sent it all home.*

"We lived well, but he was career army, a good provider

but always away somewhere, so really it was momma brought me up."

He wondered how long he could keep this kind of talk going, and how to go about dealing with an old-fashioned, honest, careful-thinking man like this one. A man so honest he was going broke while working hard. After a while Len remarked on the potential of this property, which he said was bound to rise in value when the interstate was finished.

"Worthwhile owning," he finished, starting his little agreeable nod and then cutting it off. It was a stretch, and while John Thomas did not quite stare at him, Len felt himself slipping lower and lower. He could not con this man and there was no point trying, so he had another draught of lemonade and sincerely complimented it. John Thomas acknowledged the gesture with an understanding smile and Len moved on to the missing relatives, and eventually back to his need for some sort of local connection.

"Only thing, it feels like there might be some trouble connected," said John Thomas after one of his thoughtful silences.

"You *in* trouble, cousin," said Len in the matter-of-fact voice of a man who has figured out solvency. "You got debts, and debts will catch up sooner or later. It's the interest."

Lower yet, thought Len, feeling like a snake as he saw shadows pass his cousin's homely old face.

"That's true," replied Thomas after a pause. "But I still got my good name and credit."

Damn the man. McGoohey's money offered a path to safety here for him and his wife. It would be totally safe and secure owing to Len's forethought, and the man was avoiding it.

"And you got this land you need to hang on to," added Len firmly, returning to an honest theme. "I been doin' well, and I need a place to go from time to time,. If you got a spare room, that would help."

"That I got." The man paused to gather himself. "Well, here's the story, cousin. Few years ago my wife Nell got sick. She's on the mend now, but I ran up doctor bills the insurance didn't cover. They lie, but I guess you know that."

"How much?"

"Thousands."

Len nodded, reflecting on his own good luck in life, and how little all of John Thomas's hard work and good character had brought him. Mainly because he was black.

"How many thousand?"

"What do I have to do?"

The sudden, honest, matter-of-fact desperation got to Len. *Poor sonofabitch doesn't know how to lie. Gotta teach him his lines. That old yellow man gave me directions, he'd be no problem.*

"Give me a job."

John Thomas had a sense of humor. He chuckled and the air lightened a bit.

"Ain't had a hand since Nell got sick, and that was two years ago."

"Sure you did. Me. I just didn't show up on a regualr basis."

"I really – well, this is a *deal*, Len, and it's not on the up-and-up. I got no employment records, for one thing."

The up-and-up. Len smiled gently.

"No matter. What you've got is bills you can't pay and a sick wife, John," said Len in his formal voice. "And blood kin who can help. It is not strictly on the 'up-and-up,' as you say, but neither are the insurance and the government and the banks and white people in general. Waste of time to deal with them as if they were. What I need is an informal confirmation that I've worked for you off and on the last couple of years, staying in your spare room. Few slips of paper with dates. Week here, week there. As a family member I come under different rules, and the pay would be nominal. Meals, place to stay, twenty dollars a day."

Another farmerly silence as John Thomas surveyed the hard place his habit of honesty and hard work had put him in, and the immovable rock of obligations.

"I'm going to excuse myself and speak with Nellie. I'd introduce you, but this first time it's easier if I speak with her myself. Less of a strain. She's on the mend, but she sets back easy."

Len nodded.

"I owe over eight thousand dollars, Len."

He left the room and Len worked it out. There couldn't be any obvious, traceable financial changes in this man's life, assuming the sick wife didn't stop everything right now and start praying for his soul. John Thomas would be fine by just making slightly larger and more regular payments to the people he owed. That wouldn't draw attention. But the story had to have some body to it. He had to know what people like this did every day.

His cousin was back before he'd gone further than that, and he looked much happier.

"Nell remembers your momma real well," he said warmly. "She says whatever it is you're up to don't really matter, we gonna lose the place anyway if nothing happens, and you happened, and so be it. Nell gets right to the point, not like me."

Len nodded. "Good. I hope to meet her when she's up to it, John. Now I want to know exactly what I'd have been doin' if I was around here helping out."

They talked for close to half an hour about farm work, which began early and seemed to involve many tasks, an endless range of skills, and no shortcuts. John Thomas refilled their lemonades and Len explained about doling the money out little by little.

"Let it show, taxman be here like a shot. That's one thing I learned from white people. Rich ones. You got a secure place for cash?" John Thomas nodded. "I'm gonna give you three thousand dollars today, fifty dollar bills. Another three if and when things work out. You don't have to do any more than say that I come and go as I please and that you're glad for the help with your wife bein' sick. I drink too much and chase women. Basically, you're fed up with me and my drinking and I probably belong in jail – little character assassination'll protect you."

"It's criminal, though, isn't it; I'm your alibi now."

"Definitely not an alibi, because you needn't say I was here any time in particular – you don't bother to keep track of my comings and goings. It's not like I'm sticking up a bank some Friday afternoon and you have to say I was here. I just need to be able to say I spend time down here on some kind of basis. Anyone asks, you haven't seen me for a week or two. They don't expect an informal family thing like that to be written down. Anyone calls you, you haven't seen me for weeks, probably lost in a bottle of Four Roses or lookin' for other work."

"I'll do it. It's a lie, but when I saw Nellie's face light up at the thought of catching up on those bills it changed my mind real quick. I need for her to feel good. You may be doing the Devil's work, Len, but you're doing some good along the way."

"Ain't *hurtin'* no one, John. That much I can say in perfect honesty. I'm not that kind."

"Nell had an idea we ought to have a drink on it. I have Four Roses or something a friend of mine makes which might be an interesting change."

"Like to try that. A short one, though – I'm on the road for another hour or two."

John Thomas nodded, and gave him a smile Len could not quite understand. Nothing like family, he thought, lifting his glass. Makes you human.

In the car he could feel that very pale home-made whisky, along with a general relief. John Thomas would be discreet and prepared. But there was another kind of problem, brought on by his cousin's straight-arrow character and loyalty. A big one seething down there in his belly as he headed for the airport. He was after a classy woman who deserved a better type of man than one that doped horses, duped friends, and took advantage of his family in support of a criminal enterprise.

I hate it, he thought. It's low. But stop now and I'm out of a job. Job that could become a career if we get us a good horse likes to run and has some fight in him.

"Ain't *got* a plan yet," said Len, tired after his flight and his Kentucky experience. "Didn't call 'cause it'd be stupid. Things go wrong, they pull up phone records first thing. Specially that little one you gave me – it shows where you're at on a map. All the new ones do. Handy for the government."

It was a quiet Monday afternoon in the Dead Heat and Len was speaking his mind, wanting to go home and relax.

"Huh. Bought 'em 'cause I liked how they looked," admitted McGoohey. "Small."

As usual his trainer made sense. Money in hand didn't change his personality – very unusual in a black man. And Len was calm; he could feel Len's calm and envied it. A good thing, they didn't need two hotheads like himself. In turmoil since

119

Saratoga, McGoohey had sharply curtailed his drinking for reasons he didn't fully understand, but he knew now that there was no easy path to real social acceptance, which he now saw as his goal. It was full of confusing situations and fierce obstacles, like that Dixon bitch who had the shit kicked out of him in that restaurant. But it was the one point where he and his wife really came together. She liked rooms full of smiling, well dressed people with style, and now he shared her desire. Getting there was job one, but now there was another problem – Jasmine's abrupt morphing from chilly JAP to some kind of nympho. Just when he couldn't care less.

Thinking about it all he went silent, and his trainer waited him out.

"Tough week here," McGoohey said finally. "Everyone thinks we did real well up there, but you and me know better." A pause. "Only one thing. Right at the end there 'Biche looked like she lost her momentum."

"Black Ice no quitter, Pat," said Len in a slow, puzzled-sounding voice. "Come-from-behind horse, Eclipse candidate."

"He held her, didn't he – "

"Jimmy held her you say? You talk to him?"

"Christ, you're the only one can talk to the crazy bastard. You know he ain't right, Len. But he give her a perfect ride, it looked to me, right up to the end."

"Me too. You said you wanted third, no mixed signals there. He done what you said."

After a moment McGoohey spoke again, in a different voice.

"I just keep thinkin' we shoulda had second," he said. "Might of done the trick – good enough to beat Black Ice, good enough for Missile Man."

Len looked attentive and said nothing.

"That woman actually said we fouled her! You believe that?"

"Well sure, anything to save face. Any doubt whatever and you know how the vote'd go. States-rights Supreme Court do a one-eighty, appoint theirselves a President, you think stewards gonna favor a California man over Bluegrass people? 'Biche even breathe on Dark Lady, oligarchy throw the book at us, beat us to death with their tennis racquets."

McGoohey smiled. Then he chuckled and waved for the Bushmills.

"Okay, Len, what'n hell's this *oligarchy*?"

No time for books, but not ashamed to ask, thought Len. His irritation vanished, and he was relieved to be home. Pat was better company than most. Smart, big-picture man.

"Just a big word for high-end cronies – family an' friends runnin' things. Eat, sleep, shit t'gether, vote t'gether. Like Wash'ton."

"Oligarchy," said McGoohey, seeing himself as a member one day.

"You got any idea yet how yer gonna do it?" he asked casually.

"A little. First step, someone take the tour. Got this Lee Farms tour, anyone can take it. Check out security, find out if they got computerized alarms – black boxes an' all that. I got someone in mind. Computer student who needs money. Maybe twelve hundred total."

"Yeah, that's good. You got a kind of criminal mind."

"No kind-of about it."

How I make a living lately. Mainly because of you, big guy.

His face showed nothing, and the owner was distracted by the TV. A rapt expression came over his features.

"Know who that is?"

Len looked up at the screen. A very large straw-haired golfer who looked like a McGoohey blood relative was addressing the tiny ball.

"Ain't Tiger Woods."

Through the half-audible voices of the announcers, McGoohey lovingly explained.

"John Daly. Won the Open as a complete unknown. Bad drinking problem, in and out of rehab. On the comeback trail, climbing back up."

Daly hooked a long drive into the rough and McGoohey sighed. "Sonofabitch. Guy can't catch a break." He had a thoughtful sip of Bushmills. Len waved to the waitress, who strolled over.

The waitresses all liked Len and saw him as a good influence on his employer.

"Like t'try some of what Mr. McGoohey's drinking."

McGoohey smiled, green eyes twinkling, then turned to the waitress. "Pour him a nice double, water back." There was a roar from the TV and joy leaped in his eyes as Daly's ball rose from deep in the rough, trailed by a chunk of turf and a spray of dirt, rising in a high arc to descend miraculously within several feet of the cup, exciting the commentators enough that their hushed murmurings became audible. Daly holed out and moved up to fourth on the leader-board. Len smiled. He felt nothing in common with Tiger Woods other than skin color, but it was fun watching the White Hopes come and go. McGoohey bellowed with quiet joy as Daly hit a huge drive setting up a birdie.

"Runnin' up bills, Pat. That local-residence alibi's gonna cost – got me over a barrel."

"Oh, I already figured that. One load of that juice will go far, it's worth it."

Len flashed on the option of simply disappearing with that load, and just as quickly killed the idea. However many foals came into being from that bag of sperm, his interest would be limited to the one born to Arabiche. Unfair, but McGoo was fond of announcing that he didn't *have* to be fair, making it clear that this was both fact and guiding principle, not to mention a special satisfaction. No question – lack of greed was a weakness. *Greedy man automatically sees opportunity*, he thought. *Wakes up that way, doesn't let himself get distracted.*

Still on East Coast time, Len was restless in the early evening as he thought about his job, looking for things to do. Checking his messages, he was displeased to hear the old Charlotte call. Than another and another, leading to an ultimatum with deadline. Which had passed.

He stood in the doorway with a sense of relief, looking with satisfaction into his front room and its floor-to-ceiling bookcases. He couldn't read though, still too unsettled. Finally he went to his LPs and pulled *Wheatley at the Wasp.* The name always brought a half-smile to his face, the only thing WASP about Wheatley being his rich wife. Len wanted to hear it loud and full, too loud for his neighbors, so he put on headphones. Then he put enough Canadian Sticky in his pipe for one hit. Designer weed created by those fishbelly-white Europeans, too strong, but it got him back to the G-Spot. Eyes closed, he saw himself dancing face to face with the first woman he'd taken seriously in years. Then her face at the Blue Lantern as she opened the little beaded purse with the gold horse to give him her card.

Smitten, he thought, that's what this is. Corny old word, got some real meaning. Gotta think about something else.

Then he carefully dressed, a stud on the prowl, thinking he could afford a nice new ride on his winnings. Social asset, but money in the bank beat it. Left you with options. Finally he peeled off some fifties from the mother lode and strolled, talking to himself: Repeat three times: 'You are not a new-car nigger, you are a bookish black man who can score without one.'

Then he burst into a dry laugh and forgot about being smitten.

14

After the elaborately catered and well received dinner (choice of beef Wellington, seared tuna, or duck *a l'orange*), Dixie's guests moved to another room. A special, newly reopened room where a choice of desserts waited, buffet style. One tray was piled with delicacies of many colors, another offered a new Tasmanian coffee or traditional espresso, and a third had liqueurs and brandies. Except for the dashing Sheikh Lakham, unofficial guest of honor, the guests were old local-gentry racing friends. Absent from dinner but presiding over this phase, definitely not in any usual servant role, was Holly St. Cyr, appearing discreetly as the well-oiled group drifted in, everyone having put away at least two glasses of wine with dinner, which had been preceded by drinks.

"Most of you know Holly, since we're inseparable and Ah positively could not *exist* without her," said Dixie in a voice meant to be understood. "But for those who don't, she is the person responsible for the décor of this lovely room, and she curates our art, about half of which turned out to be fake."

The laughs that followed established Holly's special status beyond doubt, much to the horror of an émigré South African trainer who liked the South because of its racist tradition. She was immediately engaged by the Sheikh in conversation, and joined by him for coffee on a sofa. This did not please Daphne de Lesseps-Fournier, owner of Trotzky, runner-up for three-year-old of the year. She was the mindless widow of a rich Frenchman, the former Daphne Jepson of Louisville, currently being serviced by Trotzky's jockey, the studly cockney Teddy Phillips. Getting Phillips out of Daphne's bed was an item in Dixie's agenda, and the Sheikh struck her as the perfect candidate in a damn funny game. Having washed down her duck with plenty of wine, the widow Fournier longed for the exotic. She deeply desired to watch films with the Sheikh in his enormous airplane.

Unexpectedly, old Major Carruthers joined them. Like Dixie's father, now asleep in his chair, the Major was pleased to think of this evening as integrated. *Tastefully* integrated, by virtue of Holly joining them for coffee rather than dinner. And the Sheikh, of course.

All nice people, Holly was thinking, watching them mill about smiling and finding places to sit compatibly. As nice as they could possibly be, really, given who they were. With Tom Lee asleep, the room was permeated by conservative sentiment, socially imprinted by the ageless spirit of the Gentlemen's C and the taste of finishing schools in educational drag. Several financiers gravitated to a corner for an intense discussion of what these oil cowboys were doing to the market, while their wives more quietly discussed mature male celebrities. It will all be fine, thought Holly, if only Dixie doesn't decide to play Ella Fitzgerald or Mahalia Jackson. She smiled at Major Carruthers without actually turning away from the Sheikh, and inquired after the elderly Bombsaway's well-being. Both men found her footwork and presentation very acceptable.

"*Wonderful!*" replied the Major from his heart, amazed yet again at what education could do for certain Negroes. "We have an apple together just about every morning. You remember him, eh?"

"Yes, I do. I thought Dixie must be pulling my leg when she said he'd just turned sixteen. Sweet sixteen, she called him."

"And, umm, still taking care of business, solid as a rock in his obligations. Which provides a wonderful revenue stream, going on ten years now."

Holly nodded seriously. Drink having obliterated the socioeconomic chasm, the old goat was twinkling, flirting her up in his cumbersome way, as if his horse's priapic capacities ran in the family, equine and human. In her peripheral vision Holly saw a change in Dixie's body language. A kind of tensing that often preceded a wild burst of laughter, which would sometimes trigger one in herself. The Sheikh picked this up, and changed the subject.

"That fifth Sunday race at Saratoga," he said. "That little California horse, I liked her. She will not breed with Missile Man, but she looked so – good, I thought. Very good. There is in my barns appropriate blood."

In her nearby chair Dixie went from the edge of laughter to close, cold attention. Before Carruthers could recommend

Bombsaway, she cut in.

"Of course, Space Commander still has the best record at stud of any active sire," she remarked with alcoholic firmness, surrounded by supporters. The Sheikh smiled and replied with respect.

"True. Actually I think she was a bit too good that day, that little mare. One of my trainers looked up her record, and it was very ordinary. Too often the middle of the field. Some horses are too smart, that is how I think of it. I looked at her walking after the race, and in her stall. She was fine, but that could be a very strong animal that received an injection. Just a feeling, not an accusation, of course. Any horse can have a good day."

Everyone listened. The Sheikh's Oxbridge accent had been Americanized by a long succession of mistresses, and he spoke with casual assurance, Dixie getting every word. Losing to Margiedaw in a slow race was not terrible, but having a no-account California horse take Black Ice to a photo had been humiliating.

"Didn't show up in the tests, though," observed Carruthers blindly.

The Sheikh shrugged. "There is always something new that the small owner will try. People who cannot afford to play by the rules. And Saratoga itself – the graveyard of champions, it's said. I wager that little mare won't appear in the Go For Wand, where No Lie should make it a different kind of race."

A small grim smile remained on Dixie's face.

"But still, a very good little horse," finished the Sheikh. "She should be bred to some very hot blood. Her foals would be good, I think, much better than her record would suggest."

Dixie mulled this and the Sheikh returned to Holly, whom he'd met before.

"Your room," he said, with a small, incisive gesture that took in the room, a subliminal gesture of command cloaked in congratulation. She nodded with the barest of smiles, mind far away. Had that quiet well-mannered Llewellyn Thomas actually done a number like that and got away with it?

"In a sense; I found the furniture," she replied with professional detachment. "But it grows from what this house is and has been, going far back in our history. The Lees have been here since

126

the early colonial period, of course. Dixie and I worked on it together, finding things that would create historical harmony."

It went on. The Sheikh was mildly astounded at the instructional tone of this upstart black wench, but still amused. He knew exactly what he would do with this bitch, given the opportunity. Oblivious to this undertow, Dixie was loving her assistant to death. Just the kind of conversation she imagined they'd have in those Parisian salons where you got some quality long-hair intellectuals and artists mixed in with the right people over drinks in a room full of historical harmony and somebody playing a harpsichord. She was sure no one in the State of Kentucky had a better dinner party going. An increasingly drunk Daphne de Lesseps-Fournier now broke free of the Dixie group to join the Sheikh set, kneeling in a pose that reminded Dixie of a sorority girl at a pre-prom gathering. Approaching forty, the widow still had that body and mind, oblivious as ever, and her posture suggested supplication, as if she might be applying for a position on the Sheikh's entertainment staff.

"Youah airplane is just *magnificent*, Sheikh Lakham. Mah little jet is so cramped, it has barely room for a few friends."

She spoke the timeless and universal language of steamy Southern women. The Sheikh smiled faintly, nodded pleasantly. Another Christian volunteer. Studly Teddy stood thoughtfully aside with his goblet of tinted mineral water, a realist. If the Sheikh was going to take Daphne, he'd like to be part of the deal. Lakham raced extensively in Europe and was known to favor British employees, but the Sheikh did not speak with jockeys in social situations. Dead loss, he decided, and took aim on old Carruthers.

Happily exhausted by the success of her party, Dixie toppled quickly into a deep sleep while her father was attended by old Frank. Holly was glad it was over, pleased that Dixie had had this very definite success, which would work itself through her circle by word of mouth and small regional publications, making it known that Lee Farms had brought together the major blue-grass players and the nifty Sheikh. The opening of the new room would be prominently mentioned, along with herself as *auteur* under Dixie's sponsorship. Dixie's position in the Confederate Dames would be enhanced by various references, with her own Creole presence somehow worked in as another instance of the Lee's enlightened, forward-looking social views.

All water under Holly's bridge, but her extended cameo as the right kind of black girl left her slightly manic. Sleep was out of the question, and at 4:00 A.M. she was in her pajamas at her laptop to see how her investments were faring. Very damn well, she noted, and after some research, she made two trades. Then she had a look at that information on the Lee trusts that she could access. It was fantasy, but after several drinks, playing with the Sheikh just a little and almost laughing at Daphne de Lesseps panting desire to *go foah a rahd and watch films in youah simply magnificent aeroplane,* Holly was feeling devilish.

And who exactly was Len Thomas?

A computer search yielded nothing; McGoohey was in construction and didn't even have a website. Those "Farms" would have damn little greenery. Another search revealed Arabiche as either a chronic underachiever or a fraud, and left her respecting the Sheikh's shrewd guess. With no particular interest in the race, he had sensed things no one else noticed. She surfed onward to Lakham Racing, which had endless information on its tastefully understated website, including a very long and distinguished record in European and UK racing. She was still wide awake, brain buzzing with thoughts of her future. *What should she do with the rest of her life?* Since Saratoga, she had been trying to imagine life as something other than a spiffy satellite to Planet Dixie. Picking Ronnie Pitt's limited brain made it clear that "investment advisor" was a field with unlimited potential, becoming prominent in TV ads and programs. It was something she could handle with one hand tied behind her back. But her business minor was getting stale, and it hadn't been the right school for that. Nor would Dixie help. Pretty much anything was okay but leaving the plantation.

The house was silent. Across the hall from her office was another, for Ronnie Pitt's convenience. The Lees were his major client, and the families had been close for generations. Sleepless and driven, she crossed the hall. The door to his office was always open, and the computer was on standby as usual. She knew what was in his files, having set them up for him, and she sat down without hesitation to see if he was still selling off tech stocks across the board. At least he'd stopped that idiocy and was following her suggestions. Unable to stop herself, she started looking for what she really wanted: a crib-sheet file of passwords to the inner sanctum of trusts set up by an earlier, brighter Pitts. Fingers flying, she spent an intense twenty minutes on various kinds of searches and decided the information wasn't there. Ronnie came to her with his tech problems, and she knew that the more sophisticated means of hiding information were beyond him. Given his druthers, Ronnie would revert to large file cards, a lifelong affinity. The handsome roll-top desk was littered with them. She started from the top down, being careful to disturb things as little as possible. In ten minutes she had ransacked the big desk and found nothing.

She stopped to think in the silence. Those passwords might be in his office, his home, or even his wallet, where they would be safe, useless to anyone who didn't know what they were and how to use them. She'd helped him reorganize a few years ago and knew how he thought. He had a memory like a sieve and would definitely need that information when working here, which he did often. She kept going, in what quickly became a half-controlled frenzy, imagining places a teenager would hide something. In one of those tomes on the shelf over the desk, for example. Another few minutes revealed nothing. His paper files were few, and perfectly organized. Nothing there.

Something *corny*, she thought suddenly, some old-fashioned cliché from one of those black and white films that were his secret passion. She got down on her knees and began sliding out drawers, examining their undersides with her fingers. It was a file card, of course, under the middle drawer. He'd taped a very oversized card to the bottom of the drawer, creating a pocket, with a small section cut away that allowed a moistened finger to slip out the smaller card with the passwords. He used it often – that was evident from the thumb smudge. Card in hand, she stopped and listened carefully before copying them. His system was so childlike that she had to smile. He had used the names of his relatives, and alongside each of these was a number, the number of a trust that might have anywhere from under five to over fifteen million. Seeing these keys to the Lee kingdom stopped her short.

I'm off the rails, she thought. *I just crossed the line.*

She'd think about that later. Meanwhile, she copied everything on yet another file card, wiped down his card and everything around it. Only then, with the original back in its pocket and the computer as it had been when she went in, was she finally nervous. Fearful, breathless and shaky, she was barely able to get down the hall and back into her wing of the house.

15

"Jazz, are you gonna tell me what this is all about? You ain't usually up at this hour."

It's about being ignored! screamed a voice inside the former Jasmine Felter. She wasn't quite awake, it being barely dawn, several hours before her usual wake-up time.

McGoohey endured the silence, which was still echoing her injured tone. Woke up special to give me the silent treatment, he thought. Peculiar – she hated mornings. Then he saw it. He'd been all over her since they met – just look at her a minute or so and there it was – but he knew she wasn't crazy about it. Not really, not like some women. And suddenly she had to have it, right away, right off the plane, while he was still digesting his humiliation. Right, *humiliation*, his face on the fucking floor. But he was damned if she was going to know the truth of *that*. He returned the silence and swallowed some coffee. The screened area where they ate seemed enormous and pointless. Empty. He hadn't spared the money on this place. It was a big, conservative, good-looking brick house, impressive inside and out. Double corner lot, well back from the quiet street. Beverly Hills. As attractive and convenient and comfortable and classy as Jasmine had been able to arrange, an event for which she'd been in training since childhood. Best house in either of their incompatible families. The scale of it emphasized his isolation. Flowers, trees, grass, fine big pool. Big empty house, and his life tasted like dirt.

"I don't know what happened in Saratoga," she said unexpectedly, in a quiet, thoughtful voice, "and I know you're not going to tell me, because you're such a – " Peasant was the word that came to mind, but she kept it inside. Likewise goy.

" – because you're the kind of man you are, and don't share. But I feel like you're not the same man any more. The man I loved and married."

Man. She just had to use that word, triple up on it for emphasis. Might as well say not a man at all. A week without it and all of a sudden it was everything. And he'd thought she wasn't noticing. She noticed everything. Then she'd go college on him and interpret his behavior.

"I experienced a reversal," he said in a slow, heavy voice, wondering where that word had come from. She let him know.

"You sound like my cousin Allen,"

"But without the fuckin' degrees, right? And who's gay." His voice rose blindly. "Well fuck you, Jazz! Make me chase you around like a virgin for three years unless you've got a load of Margaritas on, and now – now, when I got my ass on the line six ways to Sunday, y'gotta have it for breakfast. What the hell is that?"

She certainly wasn't about to accept that tone or say she'd decided to secure the marriage by having a baby, and silence was working better than words. *Reversal* she understood, but *ass on the line six ways to Sunday*? In Irish that would mean major reversal, business problems on an order he hadn't experienced since they married. Her husband was in a risky business, which he made more risky because that was his way. And those smelly horses – what did they cost? Reckless Pat running wild, pushing his luck, blowing it with the Commissioner, house of cards flying off in a gust of wind. Herself losing her husband, cars, house, family standing, everything all at once. Thirty, divorced, skin loosening, this marriage to a crazy goy hanging from her neck like the Ancient Mariner's albatross, haunting the rest of her life. Who would have her now? She'd been leading him around by his eager uncut member, her prize bull, and now that member didn't seem to matter to him any more. Acting his age? She was struck by a new impulse, wanting to help, and realized she had no idea how.

I know how to spend money tastefully, she thought, that was my job. She began to cry at the thought of losing her job, soundless tears.

"Oh, Jesus – I didn't mean that how it sounded, Jasmine."

"Let me alone," she whimpered, in a small wounded-bird voice, hiding her face in her hands. "You don't love me anymore, don't you think I can see that?"

"No," he said soberly, achieving real gravitas. "It's not that. I love you as much as ever. More, in some ways. It's just other stuff

132

going on."

"Like some woman up there who didn't make you chase her around like a virgin."

"Christ, *no*."

But it was a woman, all right, he thought. A tiger-woman with a big army and powerful allies, an opponent requiring his total focus. And he'd been chasing her, all right, chasing her around Saratoga like a goddamn clown. Chased her right up to the no-net trapeze and fell on his kisser. Then that silent restaurant, and then talk starting up again as if he didn't exist. A disgrace to his beautiful little horse.

"Nothin' t'do with Saratoga," he said, lying automatically.

"I am not a stupid person, Pat McGoohey."

It amazed him how she had put herself back together in just seconds, and it didn't occur to him that his lie was completely transparent.

"No, you're not. I wouldn't marry a stupid woman no matter how good she looked – "

Before he could finish saying she was both beautiful and smart, she was in tears again.

"It's my breasts, you want a woman with larger breasts."

"It's *me*," he said desperately. "It ain't you, you're fine, it's *me*. I got a real problem."

"You could get help. And there are pills now – "

"Not that kind of problem," he said coldly. Then he was alarmed, a sudden dull, delayed panic. Maybe it was *exactly* that kind of problem!

"I gotta go. Lookin' at a horse this morning."

He lumbered off in a daze, inarticulate and afraid. Annabelle Dixon had hit him where he lived, hit him in his dream. As soon as the car left the driveway he felt himself losing control, seething up into a rage the way he used to as a kid who'd get into bar fights on payday back when he was poor, like all the guys he knew. He remembered the pure simple satisfaction of landing a good one, and taking one without showing anything. Him and Mike Neal.

Maybe the track would cool him down. Cruising at a sedate seventy on the San Diego Freeway, he got out his flask, opened it with one hand, and had a solid snort. By now Len should have something to say.

"Yer not sayin' a word," observed McGoohey. The swift but frail Tokyo Tamari was breezing out in the middle of the track while other horses close to the rail worked with watches on them. Tamari was a beautiful runner, but his warmups and distances were calibrated to how much work Paco and Len thought this victim of thoroughbred incest could take.

"Better not talkin' much. Job gets done is what counts," replied Len.

"Just keep laying out the cash and don't ask questions, huh?"

Len knew a dangerous mood when he saw it and moved to change it.

"Ain't really like that, Pat," he said in a mildly injured tone.

On the phone McGoo had been easy and cooperative. Now that damn stare. No obvious reason. Len considered what he'd risked in Saratoga for his boss, and how the man had botched it. Just a rich ignorant honky who paid him monthly and acted like he owned him. Reminded him of a white boy back in high school who bought a horn thinking it gave him musical entree.

"Paco say you got a big job in Pasadena."

"Third crew's more trouble than it's worth, but Alice can just about run it herself with a good crew chief. But I'll tell you something I ain't really told no one else, which is that I am fucking bored with the construction business. Wanna get out of it, for Jasmine."

Len listened, nodding, felt a break point. His speech was measured.

"This operation we thinkin' about. You got money at risk, but you a rich man," said Len in a slow, reflective, for-the-record. "How Ah'm doin it, you isolated. Ah got real skin in this game, Pat. Kentucky bein' the South, don't favor dark-complected people. An' that family *own* the town. Police, mayor, DA. Piece of the governor, congressman, whatever. Isolation's a plus. Less you know, Pat, better you do on polygraph. This ain't shopliftin', an' the boys ain't professionals."

There was a very long pause as these facts forced themselves on McGoohey, who began to feel less comfortable.

"Yeah, I got the red-ass this morning. Wife ain't barely talkin' to me, Len. And there ain't no pre-nup, she can clean me out, everything I got's here in L.A."

Len didn't want to know about this and moved quickly.

"Sorry to hear that, Pat. Don' know much about all that, ain't never been married or owned much. Mebbe jes' a bad day."

Yeah, maybe it was, thought McGoohey. Len had good sense. Got it done in Saratoga, where he himself had screwed the pooch. In the worst-case scenario, he guessed Len would take a reasonable rap and keep him out of it. Say, half a year actual time, good-faith money to his account, balloon payment on release. He smiled painfully. Damn small balloon if Jasmine split. At least two lawyers in her immediate family. He looked at his flask, shaking it reflectively. Nearly full, he noticed; he hadn't been drinking at all. Then he had a strong belt.

"She doesn't bother puttin' out my special water now. And crying – crying about what?"

"Women," said Len diplomatically. McGoohey stared into space and pondered what was behind it. Not getting laid? Not likely. Maybe it was all smoke, and *she* was the one who'd changed! What if *Jasmine* was not to be trusted, and *that* was the problem! Watching the fragile Tamari and waiting for a wheel to come off, McGoohey focused.

Okay, he thought: *Find out who she's fucking.* Shouldn't be hard, useful information if they split. Call his attorney, who would recommend a private detective and add five hundred to his bill for being called at 6:00 A.M.

A serious Paco watched his bosses from a distance, busy with resentments about his young cousin Mike, who was family, more like a brother, and very special. Mike was as important to him as anyone in his life. Paco had been watching him like a hawk since childhood, when his looks and natural style set him apart, not only from the family, but from the neighborhood, and the whole second-class-citizen thing. He'd been pleased when Len asked if he might be able to help with a tech problem, and agreed without a thought. The next day Mike was on a plane across the country. Shaken by the scale and speed of the move, Paco had been very upset, convinced he'd put Mike in harm's way because of these two at the rail. He was still upset. He should have said *no*, but it went by too fast and Mike wanted to do it. Unable to deal with his irritation, he'd gone to see DJ, angry with himself because he hadn't stood up to Len. When it finally burst out of him, Pete Suarez reminded him that there was no trust outside *La Raza*, what did he expect?

And he couldn't even call Mike, because Len had made him leave his cell phone at home! That had further disrupted and frightened Paco, who was used to speaking with his favorite relative almost every day. Mike said this phone thing had a logical reason, that it protected him, but it didn't feel right. If this game wasn't supposed to be dangerous, why did they have to be so careful? And Mike wasn't even supposed to call him from a pay-phone! Len as his daytime boss was one thing; Len in the middle of his family was out of line. He, Paco, number one guy in the family since his stepfather's stroke, couldn't talk to his own *cousin*?

It had pissed him off more and more, until he went to the strongbox with his Saratoga winnings and bought a rock of uncut cocaine the size of a child's fist, which he'd begun pecking at to lift his spirits. Now he felt like a ticking bomb. Until this latest plan, whatever it was, went down, his life and his family's would be bent out of shape by these two. Paranoia was one fancy word that Paco felt he understood – it was those crazy little waves of fear that came when he was doing something wrong and knew he might get caught. And obsession was when you couldn't let something alone, like the rock.

He was getting so worked up that he had to walk away. When he heard Carlos coming around a corner, he stuck out his foot, and Carlos went flying, landing on the feed sack he was carrying. They looked at each other, and Carlos saw something that made him wish he was at a checkout register or packing groceries – his mentor and cousin Paco looking at him like rat shit.

Jasmine did not move for a long time after her husband left. She was too bewildered and depressed to do anything until eight, when the chickadee in the bird-call clock sounded its song and something clicked. *Her husband had guessed about Ron!* She was instantly convinced, and she was petrified. His physical dominance over other men had captivated her, and now this hulking *shagitz* might beat her and/or her lover to a pulp. And have the Commissioner fix the judge if she tried to fight back. Or just have them encased together Italian-style in one of those concrete highway things. Very deliberately she went to the toaster and placed a slice of oatmeal bread in it, pressing the lever slowly as her mind raced. And there it was – the gentle forgiving mother she'd never had, the one person she could open up to. Alice Smith. Kind, clever, funny, gentile Alice Smith, who understood her husband for the rowdy hellion he was, including that brutal and unpredictable intelligence. Construction, like horse-training, started early in the day, and Pat would be at the track or the new site now, never the office.

The toast popped, she applied a thin layer of apple preserve, then ate half slowly, like a sleepwalker. The other half went down the disposall. Then she called Alice.

"Jasmine! How *are* you? I've been meaning to call but this new site's driving me crazy."

The relief was so enormous Jasmine couldn't bear it. She was alive again!

"I've been terrible! I'm going to kill your employer!"

"Can I help?" asked Alice. "He's out at the track, naturally. What's he done this time?"

"I'll tell you in a minute. Were you really going to call me?"

"Yeah. I decided it's time to see your Dr. Ron. Jack is away someplace I can't know about and I thought I'd get a light lift."

"I can get it for you wholesale."

They laughed, enjoying themselves and the endless conspiracy to save men from themselves and direct their efforts to better use.

"So what is it that gets you on the phone at this ungodly hour?"

"Something happened with Pat in Saratoga, Alice, and he's – I don't know, I'm just concerned. Naturally he won't say anything. First I thought he, you know, got involved with some tootsie and felt guilty. But I don't think so anymore. He seems more like – distant?"

"Yeah, he's off on a tangent. Spending more time with the horses and over at that place they hang out. The Lineup, Dugout whatever it's called. I might as well be running that new site."

Jasmine felt herself returning to normal, as if the law of gravity had been restored after a period of entropy. If her fears were real, Alice would know and find a way to tell her. A plan was forming, a plan to bring her husband back to his normal self. It started with dropping Dr. Ron Steele this very morning, calling from a pay phone, so that if Pat sneaked a look at her phone bill there would be nothing recent. Ron was nice, but he was just a naughty game. Her marriage was her life, and Padraic McGoohey III was going to see that she knew it.

II

16

Vaughan Willetts was the name Len had appropriated for his new self, the ID expedited by an old friend in the documents business who provided the papers and a credit card which would stay alive if charges were paid. Virtual Vaughan had a legal and financial life that checked out as long as the plastic was maintained and there was no close scrutiny. It had worked for airfare (out of Oakland, for general misdirection) and renting a car. The real Assistant Professor Willetts taught English at Halprin-Birmingham, a school that had employed him for five years according to its poorly protected computer records, searched from a Wi-Fi café. He was on an exchange program in west-central Africa, and not easily reached.

A Vaughan Willetts was never seen with people like Paco and Carlos, who appeared typical of the millions of immigrants, more or less invisible until seen out of social context. With the punctilious virtual Vaughan they would be very noticeable, so Len sat alone among white civilians, drinking coffee and eating blueberry IHOP pancakes on a too-bright early September morning and recovering from the red-eye flight with his crew. He was getting edgy about their lack of cohesion, and pondering how to handle the foot-square insulated box required to preserve 'the specimen,' as the woman in Newark had called it. His stomach was sending early warning stress signals and he ate slowly.

Two tables away, Paco was disliking IHOP, or being awake, or eating with a kid like Carlos. Since Cousin Mike's involvement, he hadn't liked much of anything, though nothing had gone wrong, and this morning a complete stranger had appeared in Len's skin. He watched from the corner of his eye, clueless. Len was no longer the cool guy who got him his job. His strange unnatural morphing into a black Mister Clean tight-ass was too close to magic, unmooring Paco. Physical pain was nothing for him, but family issues, and loyalty conflicts tore at him. Since Saratoga there was lack of appropriate respect. Him, the guy with the knowledge, the dream, the one who really knew the horses, the connection that put them in the bigtime! Smooth, perfect injection just the right place.

"I be glad when is over, Len making me crazy," he said to the shy, quiet Carlos, who had just graduated high school. American-born Carlos was too young to really get it. In the gang, when you did something, you did it together, usually not far from home. This didn't have that together feeling, and the travel made it much worse.

"Len has to do it, I think," said Carlos. "It's all planned out and he has to, like, be this other guy for a while. Big stress for him."

"Big stress all around. I gotta be myself, man – my mother always say that. 'Don't be afraid to be yourself.'"

Carlos agreed in principle and planned to be himself some day when he knew more about it, but right now he was a nervous boy caught between two bosses. Two tables away, Vaughan Willetts-Thomas read the *New York Times*, checking on Israel. A conservative Democrat, Vaughan backed the President in these trying post-9/11 times, but had problems with Israel and those no-bid Halliburton contracts, especially with those mercenaries earning more than he did. As played by Len, he was an adman's dream, a model for educated African-Americans. Intelligent, professional, reliable, discreet, and well-spoken, he had informed positions on all current issues. Vaughan Willetts, B.A., M.A., and solid citizen. Better cover could not be found.

This prim and irritating academic didn't completely disappear when they returned to the car. Like a Method actor stuck in his role, Len was having difficulty getting back to his usual self. He did know for sure that something was amiss with their horse-whisperer, though.

"Who wants to drive?" asked Len when they reached the car.

"Me," said Paco. Len tossed him the keys as if everything was fine, then sat down in the back seat to observe, hoping for a clue. The drive would be a marathon, but it would give him time to figure out Paco's problem before it blew up in their faces. Silence being classic gang behavior when unsure, he decided to recognize

Paco's attitude by offering nothing more than road directions when requested. When they hit a rest stop he might be able to get Carlos alone.

Paco took the wheel and Len settled himself below the window line in the back, two Hispanics being less suspicious than two Hispanics with a black man.

"Better I be out of sight," he said, then withdrew into a kind of home-made yoga that calmed his stomach and cleared his mind. Soon he was asleep.

The dull whine of fast, dense Jersey Turnpike rush hour traffic greeted Len as he came out of his rest period, and his mind went straight to Paco. Paco's resentment, the shrugs, and the lurking, guilty expression on his normally open face. It was gone for the moment, but only because he enjoyed the challenge of driving in this different kind of traffic. Normally they closed ranks under pressure, as in Saratoga. Unable to figure it out, Len was silent. It was late afternoon and they were moving south, navigating rush-hour traffic smoothly. Len was relieved to find himself free of Vaughan Willetts, but with a stiff back and a fear that he was approaching fifty faster than he wanted to.

"Where we at now, navigator?"

"Past Baltimore, near Washington," said careful Carlos, keeper of the maps.

"Les' get off this interstate first chance, find us someplace t'stay. Wash'ton good place un-white people to chill."

"Okay," said Carlos, for whom Washington was a mythical entity of great interest to social studies teachers. Visiting Washington would be something to tell his family about.

Len leaned forward between the seats and Carlos handed him a Coke from a cooler they'd picked up while he was asleep. Focused now, he started explaining the plan. Tired very interested, they listened carefully while Len talked, studying Paco as he spoke, knowing knew he'd have to get to the bottom of his problem for the plan to work. He cast the situation as Saratoga all over again, with Paco again the key man, and began detailing.

"There's about a two-mile stretch of road front of the stables with a turnaround each end," said Len. "Stable's close to the road. No big rush, main thing is, gotta make sure we put out the security. Job one, I cut off little box like Mike showed me. Then back to the car, an' you get out. Then I cruise back and forth that two miles while you inside. Give you twenty-five minutes, then I swing by slow, lights off. You see me, blink your flash. Lot of bushes, good cover. You ain't there, I be comin' by for you every ten, twelve minutes, lights off, real slow.

"Goin' in, Paco, first thing find the guard an' take him out. Carlos, you do whatever Paco says, but don't forget to hit the guard's butt with a needle. Got three needles 'cause there could be more guys – groom get up to piss, whatever. Take your time, go in slow an' careful. No noise, top priority."

Carlos was sucked into the draft of the older men, as they felt the lift and edge that came with finally talking about it. No one went into a gig like this comfortable, and the word *security* had triggered Paco's lingering resentment about Mike. Living alone, Len might forget about family, he surmised; Len didn't mean any harm, but that didn't make his actions okay, because Mike was the one Gonzalez who could make the family stand out, with himself in the background, head of the clan. This was a sacred, unchanging dream, requiring much respect, and Len had failed the test.

"Ah'll drive now, been on these roads before."

Paco pulled over and climbed out to continue his thinking in the back seat. The plan made sense, like everything Len did, but this did not spare him from being an object of resentment.

"Steal the horse just as easy," he said after a while.

Len felt Carlos react, but replied as if this was worth discussion.

"*Problemo.* Even if you get out of state, you still got Lost Horse Registry after you."

"What this Lost Horse Registry? You shitting me, right?"

"Nope. Worldwide outfit. Real quiet. They hooked up to the owners, tracks, associations, FBI, Interpol. Rich horse people behind it, cost no object."

"Yeah, okay. They in Mexico?"

"They everywhere."

"Mexico they got problems for sure, but yeah, why look for trouble," said Paco, snapping out of it. "Plan is good, low risk, we stick with it."

Len bypassed the Washington known to schoolteachers and found an endless motel strip of upscale accommodations. Having decided to end the plastic trail in Newark, Len wanted a low-end place that would accept cash.

"*Tired*, man," said Paco, who never complained. "Gotta find place to crash."

A fair statement, but when he added something about napping, Len knew it wasn't over. If he didn't defuse Paco, it could be him and Sam Gwynn all over again, only worse. And he'd be finished with McGoohey, whose crews never got out of control.

I am prejudiced, he thought. Outside of his gift with horses, Paco's big gift is making me crazy. Being a typical beaner, he's doing it now, worst possible time. *Patient*, he told himself. Gotta be patient. Not himself lately. Gotta show love, I need the man, he needs me.

As they rolled on in heavy traffic, the motels older motels appeared with dead bulbs in the signs. But the endless No Vacancy signs continued.

"Kentucky Fry," said Carlos hopefully. "On left."

"*Yeah!*" said Paco, who had eaten nothing since boarding the plane and was getting dizzy. "Pit stop, fresh grease."

A mood change, thought Len. Weird. Maybe something to work with. And across from the KFC was exactly the funky motel he was looking for.

"There's our crash," he said. "You guys get take-out an' I get rooms."

The Cajun Moon Motel was run by an extremely old woman who mumbled thickly and could have been of any dark-skinned genetic blend involving Amerind, African-American and/or mestizo. Inside the dark little entryway-office, he realized why rooms were still available. The smell of a drainage problem. Nasty, but there was no problem about plate numbers, cash payment, or anything else, and there was a suite available at the end of the building. One big and one small room, three beds, one bath. Inspecting it, he was relieved that the odor was less evident, then set the air conditioners on high with open air intakes. Outside again, he noticed a light wind blowing fresh air toward that end of the building, which would help.

Back in the office, he paid with tens and twenties and asked where he could buy some beer. Peering at Len through thick granny-glasses, the crone replied.

"Downa road a mile otha side fo' legal. Illegal right here. Fridge unner counta, save drivin'."

"I'm a illegal-type person, but if I tip I bet that make it legal."

"Wayu fum, missa? You funny."

"Up north. You got any Coronas?"

"Got Heinies. Six-pack tweldollah."

He put out another ten and five singles, leaving the change.

"Nice doin' business."

"You too, sonny."

Paco and Carlos arrived with buckets of food as he paid. And they walked to the end of the building. Entering the suite, Paco seemed to rear slightly, raising his head and sniffing like a spooky horse.

"Yeah, I know. No choice this late," said the trainer, wondering at this reaction. Just how close was Paco's thinking to that of a horse?

"South wind clearin' it," he added. "Turn on AC, air be okay in a while."

Paco lowered his head with a half-accepting shrug, accepted a beer and sat down, watching intently as Carlos opened a bucket of chicken and set out the food on the table-desk. Then came fast, no-talk eating as two giant buckets of chicken and assorted side dishes disappeared, washed down with Heinekens as they sat at the table in the large room. Len ate sparingly, and as blood drained from brains to bellies, his crew entered a calm zone. They were ready, he decided, and Paco was as rational as he was likely to get. He waited for silence and spoke deliberately.

"Somethin' Ah been meanin' t'say when we settled down."

His lock-and-load manner ended the rest period. Smooth and serious, he emphasized the gravity of the moment by pulling the black book out of his right rear pocket and referring to it as if every detail was not set in his mind.

"Talkin' 'bout *future*, first of all. We all workin' for McGoo, and now we all runnin' risk while he back home in his big house. His house his castle, he earn it an' own it, but he ain't got it by sharin'. No benefits or insurance in case somethin' fall on you – not unless you first-crew union white. But I done somethin' when this idea come up. Tole McGoo it bein' my skin, I wanna a piece of that Missile Man foal or ain't worth the risk."

This got their full attention and understanding: inescapable fealty to the brutal and all-powerful McGoohey. Point two was implicit – himself as authorized straw-boss, having a special relationship with that same brute which enabled him to cut such a deal. He let a moment go by and spoke modestly.

"End up I get a little ride, little percentage. Ten percent of winnins from any foal outta 'Biche, and however else money come out of that foal, like stud fees. Gross winnins – before his Jew accountant get his hands on the numbers."

In fact Alice did the numbers, as Len knew, but the room was quiet and sober, bonded now against the brutal Irish and their perfidious Hebrew numbers-men. Paco was resentfully impressed but still suspicious, waiting for the other shoe to drop. Carlos was assimilating the fact of this remarkable agreement. Unlike Paco, he grasped that Len's point was sharing, and that he wasn't finished.

"McGoo and Len Thomas two different-thinkin' kind of people, and Len Thomas know he ain't alone in the risk. Ev'body in this room, we sharin' that risk. So what Ah'm sayin' is, you got to be in on this too. This thing go down right, you guys each get a piece of what I get. I keep seven points, Paco two, one for you, Carlos. Don't sound like much, but it is, cause those big races ain't cheap. Fifty thousan', hundred fifty on up. Ordinary hundred thousan' dollar race, we split up eight thou. Plus stud fees later, an' Missile jism gonna be magic. I look it up, where he come from, there's a book has it all. Sound, healthy Commander foal earn four, five hundred thousand by third year, minimum. Just a average one. Good one earn five, ten times that. We know Commander is Double-M's daddy, an' 'Biche born to breed. Your percent of that up to third year maybe ten thousand for Paco, five for Carlos. We get a good one, more like fifty/twenny-five. Horse be racin' five years, that's money. An' you know, Paco. You there when the Sheikh come over with his man. He know 'Biche a natural breeder."

This time there was no pause.

"This you put in writing, what we get?" asked a haggard and sleepless Paco.

"Yeh. I got paper, signed an' notarized. Can't have it on us when we do the job, but once we clear you get it, and I ain't known for lyin' to people I work with."

Just bend the truth a little when required, he thought. Then he opened his case, took out an envelope, and handed them a draft copy, watching them work through the words, Carlos tactfully leading the way. Len saw no need for them to know he was in for 12% plus $20K, half of which he already had. They needed to know they were being cut in for once, and he needed to know he could count on them. But even with Dr. Willetts gone, his belly full and being cut in for once, Paco was not happy. Len waited in silence, feeling the resistance re-form itself inside his main man. Then he ripped up the draft and had Carlos flush it.

"Signed one is home, eh?" Is *peligroso*, this job," said Paco thoughtfully. "Big danger for us, we inside."

Len, who would be in the car after killing the alarm, nodded, as if something new and important had been revealed. Paco reached in his shirt to remove a large knife from its sheath.

"My protection."

Len reached for the knife, which was a beauty, a Special Forces item with a big heavy blade and black composite handle, useful for many tasks but primarily intended to kill people. It was the first serial-numbered knife Len had ever seen. He balanced it and Paco smiled.

"Yeah, you can throw too. I been practicin'."

Their eyes met, and everything came together for Len. The unnatural spark in Paco's eye, the attitude, and the weight loss. Saratoga had sent Paco over the top into a snow bank. Simple as that, and he'd missed it. Paco had bet all he could borrow, and now his beloved Step Program, his moral compass for years, was blown away. No more inspiring stories of men who sold wives and wives who sold babies. Two weeks of *perico* and Paco had reverted to Clantonista. No point discussing it.

"Got to have protection," added Paco, unsure now, looking in Len's face.

148

"Ain't no protection in this," said Len easily, flipping the knife and catching it. "This an *escalator*. Send things upstairs. Man see this, ain't no more break-an'-enter. Armed robbery, scare the man, put him in shoot-to-kill mode. Knife quick, bullet quicker."

He nodded slowly for emphasis, then improvised some laws for the sovereign state of Kentucky, including inevitable deportation to his native Mexican village for Paco, following the mandatory no-parole eight-to-ten that trespassing gangbangers with criminal records all got.

"*Tica de Gualpa*," muttered Paco, lost for a moment in squalid old memories of life without running water, memories enhanced and kept fresh by his mother.

"Like that, huh?" asked Carlos, U.S. born, in no danger of exile.

"Jes' like that," said Len. "I ain't bringin' nothin' but my hands, eyes an' brain. Po-lice all over, troopers worse than Texas."

He nodded for emphasis, and paused. "Pipe time?" he finished.

"Yeah," said Paco. "Whuchu got in there this time, Len?"

"Jes good herb and relaxers. Yag'nahde," he improvised. "African friend tole me 'bout it. Help neuron flow."

He went deliberately through the ritual of removing a wide, flat pipe made to fit under the false bottom of a large, old-fashioned Dopp toilet-kit inherited from his father, killing time and thinking about Paco. Paco's deal with his Higher Power had been simple – show up for work, drink beer and smoke reefer. But no more cocaine. Now he had this skinny, paranoid Paco whose pants didn't fit. Definitely on the blow, but Len sensed this was not the only problem.

The pipe went around and worked its alchemy and Len told the story of the big old toilet kit. How all his father's belongings had been spotless, but the interior of this kit was caked with soap and lotion residues. He'd cleaned it out himself, and much later, old enough to shave, he'd come across the secret compartment in which, prior to his death by enemy fire, Master Sergeant Lionel Thomas had neatly stashed a number of personal possessions, including thick stacks of rubber-banded fifty-dollar bills, this pipe, and a quantity of Asian herb in a flat bottle, everything sprinkled in Tide to kill the smell. The soap residues had concealed the seams. Carlos was wide-eyed with youthful wonder, but the story struck Paco much harder. The dead father hit him where he lived. By the time the pipe made a second circuit, bonding was under way.

"Mike," he said. "I worry about Mike, is like my brother. He is the special one for us."

Unscathed and happy, Mike was home free, and would never have occurred to Len as the problem. He thought about it and nodded slowly, his most serious and simpatico nod. Icon Mike, symbol of success, family passport to a better world. Hard-coded gut fact, like his mom.

"Ah knew it was somethin' family botherin' you. Mike special all right, Ah seen that."

Len touched his right temple respectfully with two fingers and Paco nodded.

"In his heart, too. He never forget where he from, know what I'm saying?"

Len nodded, remembering the daredevil French source of Michael's specialness. Paco's tired face opened into a smile and he went into his bag for his black lizard dress boots. In a toe was a rock that resembled a white hockey-puck, wrapped in glaring green cling-wrap. Len concealed his true reactions of rage, horror, and fear. Knife and drugs on a plane. The insanity of it.

"Damn," he said lightly. "I sure hope you ain't *smokin'* this!"

"No-no-no! That for crazy people – no pipe, never! This grade of product, not necessary. Only for nose."

"Beautiful," pronounced Len. "Problem is, I do this, I ain't sleepin' for a long time, and we still got a job to do."

"Yeah, he need rest," said Carlos respectfully, an intelligent boy addressing an unstable man who had become dangerous.

"Yeah, I doin' a little each day," said Paco pleasantly. "Keep me going."

Every few hours, thought Len, recalling Paco's toilet stall disappearances.

"How about party after we fill the Ziploc and get out?" asked Carlos, leading Paco as-carefully as he used to lead Popsicle.

"What about pipe?" asked Paco, conceding gracefully. "Little more yag'nahde, I prob'ly forget about it an' fall asleep."

"This pipe ready to go, mah friend, just need a little more beer with it."

He was happy to note that his stomach was finally relaxing.

17

Pat McGoohey felt like a king. He couldn't move, but he felt like a king, like the night he'd knocked Mike Neal over the Dead Heat bar. Handsome, quiet, ladies-man Golden Gloves Mike. What a shot – in years of brawling he'd never landed one like, and hadn't understood that miracle any more than he understood this unbelievable afternoon. He did remember his startled feeling as Mike's arms flew out and he went sailing across the bar and slid over the top. Then his fear for Mike, who was out cold but fine. And the faces around them – his gang, right then, no mistake. Then the cops, and getting booked, no big deal after clocking Mike, who held no grudge and ran his top crew.

And now, in this quilted silken paradise, his wife's mouth dripping with his sperm, eyes glazed with what felt like love. He saw her throat move as she swallowed, looking into his eyes, all respect, her eyes slightly crossed. Going at it like teenagers. No, he didn't understand, and he didn't care. He was a king. The King of Beasts.

"You got a little drip on your chin, hon."

Her breasts wobbled deliciously as she dragged the back of her hand across her mouth.

"I love you, Pat. I wanna give you a son as good as yourself."

Dazed on weed and sex, they rearranged themselves on the huge bed, side by side now, his testicles nestled affectionately in her small, soft hand.

"You're an animal," she said. "I never let it all out before, I was always afraid of you. And now it all feels good. I just wanna make you happy, Patsy. Make you feel so good you don't want to go anywhere else for it. You can fuck me any way you want, Eskimo, Mexican, Greek, Martian – "

Her hand was moving, just barely. It was delicious.

"I never knew you could fuck like this, baby."

"I couldn't. I read a book and took a course on the Internet."

A huge chuckle began deep down in McGoohey's weighty abdomen and brimmed up through the barrel chest.

"I guess I gotta stop bitchin' about technology, huh Jazz? And weed, too. I didn't think you liked it. Where'd you get it?"

"My mother. Would you believe? She said, 'Loosen up, Jasmine.' She was a hippy back in those days."

In his triumphant euphoria McGoohey would have believed anything, and she loved him for it. His little green eyes were round and warm.

"This is a fresh start, baby," he said, his hand reaching down to the hot, wet, luxuriously plangent area that had come alive so dramatically and generously. Without premeditation he up-ended her, spread her legs and began kissing that magic place every way he could think of, the little area where Dr. Steele would normally apply a vibrator at the end to ensure complete satisfaction. This was different, old fashioned – a big rough tongue – and she was hot again. Crazy hot.

"Inside, Pat," she said in a husky voice. "I need penetration today, a bang."

The heat in her voice brought him right back. Boy, did she want it!

And knew what to do with it, open wide and squirming.

"Side to side," she muttered. "Oh God! Fuck me, Pat – fuck me so hard I can't talk."

And then she pulled his head down and kissed him so sweetly he felt it right down his spine. For the first time in a month he completely forgot his sacred quest for the perfect foal, the Derby-quality horse and social acceptance. Full of cannabis and love, he ejaculated again after the long leisurely effort she preferred, and collapsed on his equally dazed wife. Afterward, propped up naked on fine silk pillows, he looked at his crude, pink, heavy body with its freckles and blemishes, comparing it with the pale, subtle splendor of his wife's. Perplexing. She had done all this for him, this least expected thing, given him the gift of this beautiful dreamlike Sunday afternoon. Gave up that thing she'd been hanging onto forever, her . . . her independence-cherry, that's what it was. Made him a gift of what he'd always thought of as having a price. First she'd driven him completely batshit since Saratoga, and now – what would you call this? What would be the words for a beauty like her giving it up completely to an animal such as himself? And the wonderful mood that went with it, neither of them wanting to go out to a movie or turn on the TV. Just peaceful.

"You asleep, Jazz?"

"I dunno, Pat. Kind of. I mean, I can't think or anything."

"You just done somethin' for me, whatever it was, whatever happens, I can't never forget it. I didn't know you had it in you, babe. I married you 'cause you were the prettiest woman I ever got near, and now you're the hottest on top of it."

"Good, now you're my sex slave."

"I'll take it."

"You better. You like a beer or something?"

"You can move?"

"Oh, sure. I just got all your precious bodily fluids. I'm digesting them now. You sure you don't want anything, 'cause I think I've gotta get up and pee."

"Mineral water. I'll have some mineral water, Beautiful. Say, how come an ugly old sonofabitch like me gets the top woman in LA? I know everyone says it's money, but it ain't really money, you coulda had all kinds of guys with money."

Waiting for an answer, he forgot his question. A few minutes later he realized his wife had fallen asleep, and he rolled over to do the same.

"McGoohey Construction."

"Is he there?"

"He was in and out. He'll be at the Dead Heat for lunch with Mike Neal, his new best friend," said Alice. "Call me on the land-line, Jazz, the battery's going on this thing."

A minute later they picked up where they'd left off.

"What'd you do to the man, Jasmine? If I didn't recognize the clothes I'd swear it was someone else."

"I did what you said. That stuff was awesome. I mean, back in school we used to smoke sometimes, but *that* stuff – "

154

"I heard. I don't smoke since I've been with Jack, but before an action they take something the government invented, and when it's over they smoke. All but Jack, he quit after Nam. But he needs to be close to his men, so he goes presidential – doesn't inhale."

They burst into a tiny laugh that included all things male.

"Now that he's back I can joke about it, but anyway the guys in his unit gave it to him, and he's superstitious about presents, especially from people he's close to, so he couldn't refuse it or throw it away. They had a good mission, no losses or badly wounded, and of course no one inspects them going in and out; they could smuggle the Taj Mahal for all anyone cares."

"Well, it's a real aphrodisiac when you're all bottled up. If we didn't make an Irish-Jew baby Sunday afternoon my middle name isn't Bubby. I'm really glad. He's been on this campaign, like he's all tied up in important matters, but he wants a kid, as you know. I tell you things no one else ever hears about. So I just pop out this cigar and light it and we have a great time, but later he asks where did I get it, right? And I tell him my mother! Just to say something, a joke, and he believes it! My mother the Hadassah Queen has a secret life, right? Because Jews have mysterious ways? Her wild and crazy hippy years. When I got my mind back I expected him to bring it up but he never mentioned it."

"Plenty more in the garage. But I've gotta ask you a question, Jasmine. Do you know what's going on with Len and the boys? Pat can't get through a day without some horse talk to take his mind off business, and suddenly there's no Len. It's happened twice since that Saratoga trip."

"No idea. But you're right, he's not talking about the horses. About a week ago he went into the safe where we keep special keys and papers and my jewelry, and I think it was his deposit box keys, because he went back again that night when he thought I wouldn't notice."

"So we've got a mystery here. Missing persons, people I never heard of taking care of the horses. His whole little gang is on a mission. I mean it. That's why he had the time to spend with you. Don't take that wrong, it didn't come out right. I'm just used to knowing what's going on, it's my hobby. I know you're really happy and I'm glad for you, but when Pat leaves the

Commissioner hanging overnight you have to wonder what he's thinking about."

"Not me. I'm just a wife now, Alice, I only think about babies."

Traffic rumble and bright sun told Len that he'd overslept. Rising from the saggy bed he felt a sudden rush as he remembered Paco's rock. Had he? With company-man Carlos around to rat him out? He stood naked looking at the black lizard boots, which were exactly as remembered.

In the other room he found both sleeping peacefully, Paco in his clothes. He woke Carlos and stayed until he was sitting up, eyes in focus.

"Quick shower now. You gotta get Paco movin,' we slep' too long."

Carlos tried to look sharp, but there was a childlike fog in his eyes.

"Get Paco up an movin'," Len said, with business in his voice. "Now."

"Right, right – wake Paco, I understand."

After his shower, he found Carlos packing his bag. Paco was sitting up in yesterday's clothes with a blank expression, and Carlos saw from Len's eye that Paco was his ongoing assignment.

"Goin' for coffee," said Len deliberately. "We got a schedule. You ain't got Paco ready, we off schedule, an' McGoo want to know why."

From him, of course. A gang captain might leave Paco there to wake up and find his way home, thought Len, teach him a lesson. Fun idea, and as he went out the door, he found himself smiling. Next to Kentucky Fried was a Dunkin' Donuts, and when he returned, Paco was exiting the shower in a towel, still very slow. Even with the Mike problem straightened out there was still the rock. Len no more wanted to be invading Lee Farms with this crew than the Kamikazes had wanted to dive their planes into American ships back in World War II. Except that they apparently had, like suicide bombers on their way to Allah and the Virgins.

Packed and ready, he lit his daily cigarette and blew smoke around to offset the stench. Then he sat sipping coffee at a table stacked with coffees. A few minutes later Carlos appeared, crisp in a pink golf shirt and jeans, leading a bushy-haired Paco looking rumpled in loose chinos, deep black eyes radiating confusion. It was obvious he'd lost twelve or fifteen pounds since Saratoga.

"*My man!*" said Len warmly. "How you doin' this mornin'? Got us some coffee."

"Yeah, okay," said Paco in a voice that said last night's re-bonding had been weakened by memory loss and the need for a wake up hit. He moved the rock from boot to pocket looking embarrassed and resentful.

Gotta build the damn bridge all over, thought Len. Any which way he could, because he needed this peasant mystic in that stall full of stud horse or they had nothing. Never get near Cinnamon Lady again.

It surprised him that he hadn't thought of her a single time since they got on the plane. She'd been in and out of his thoughts all through the preceding week. He recognized mission focus, old military habit taking over, and it told him what he had to do to get Paco's confidence.

"Yeah," he said. "Might could use a little piece of the rock myself this mornin', help get us on down the road."

Paco brightened like a child, smiling as he emptied sugar bags into his cup.

"Be right back."

When he reappeared he was holding a hand-hammered silver box with a very decent replica of the old Texaco horse on it. In the box was a device made of transparent blue plastic, popular with young stockbrokers. It allowed a measured amount of cocaine into a kind of staging area, which was then accessed by a little pop-up tube for inhaling. Paco explained it to Len, who took a hit for each nostril. Then he smiled and wished he had never met Paco Gonzalez. The rush had him jumpy as a teenager on the way to his first convenience-store job. Carlos was explaining to Paco that he was forbidden by his religion from partaking. His religion, Len suspected, was his mother.

Nerves jumping, Len knew that the only cure was his pipe, and another ten minutes were lost. The stage was set now, and Len reached in the bag for the very important gloves, unbelievably thin, soft, luxurious black Italian leather. Perforated, they resembled driving gloves, light and flexible as a second skin.

"*Sheet!*" cried Paco, in ecstasy. "For fingerprint, eh?"

"Right. They'd claim that jism-factory is interstate commerce. Case go federal, FBI lab get in there. But we okay with the gloves. We get close, Ah pull over quiet spot off the main road. Change clothes, put on gloves, wipe down the car. Gloves stay on 'til we out of Kentucky."

"Yeah," whispered Carlos. Paco nodded, a born-again criminal coming alive.

"Worried about that knife, Paco. Quality product. Notice it got a serial number, and I bet you bought it new after Saratoga. What it cost?"

"Almos' a hundred with tax."

Len went to his wallet, extracting two fifties.

"You could mail it to yourself, but the way they handlin' mail these days – "

"Yeah, you right. Homelan' Security."

The knife went into a black K-Mart evidence bag. Then a quiet professional moment as Paco and Carlos tried the gloves, switched, and flexed their fingers.

"Fantastic – perfect," said a subdued Carlos.

"Yeah, fit like made for me," said Paco. How much these cost, Len?"

"Like your knife, each pair. The best."

Len reached into his bag again, this time producing a large professional blackjack. He passed it to Paco, who hefted it thoughtfully and massaged it, feeling the lead shot inside.

"Case you never used one, they tricky. You a strong guy, Paco. Guard got a thin skull, lights out, we goin' capital, dig? Don't – y'know – "

"Gotchu, Len – go easy. No capital crime. He still movin', I hold him for duct tape. Position of choke, not too hard."

"Right."

He glanced at Carlos, who nodded.

"Bring us to this."

He reached into the bag again and removed a large old-fashioned eyeglass case. Inside were three pre-loaded hypodermic needles in plastic.

"Couple extra in case two guards, somebody wake up an' take a whiz. Stick it in butt and press here, slow. An' use plenty of this."

He handed a big roll of black duct tape to Carlos.

"An' keep this stuff with you, on you person, all of it. We got cargo pants, lotta pockets. Drop everything in trash later outside state – everything we use."

Both nodded.

Then he handed each man a sealed flash, taped to allow a narrow beam.

"Yeah," said Paco. "Moon tonight?"

"Almost full, but probably some clouds."

Paco nodded. When he spoke, Len expected a last-minute booster request, but Paco was under control. In his gang, he had seen plans that always fell apart but he was getting a good feeling about this one, reminding him of Saratoga.

"Organized," he announced. "In gang we always talking organized-organized, but then jus' go out and do same thing. You know what, Len? Now I really understan' why McGoo trus' you with everything. Saratoga, impossible deal, goes down like honey. We like Green Beret team, Special Ops."

"Yeah, military. Good experience used to be no women, no gays, no distraction. Poker. That was it. Get drunk onna weekend. Fuck up an' you stuck on base a long time, never see a woman. Jes' guard duty, garbage pails, grease pits."

He paused.

"Thing about crime – one mistake ride offense up from minor to major. Too much choke hold snap the neck, end of story. What we doin' now, it ain't no super-crime, and no need of us gettin' caught if we stay with the plan."

He paused again. Two sets of eyes on full alert faced him.

"Open mind. You got any questions, now's the time."

Paco shook his head, appropriately serious, willing to be led.

"Good, les' find some food. Soon as Ah passed that chicken, hungry again."

By the time they pulled out, Paco felt very well. Len was

recalling the Saratoga tattoo inspection, when he was suddenly fed up with horse racing and his life, thinking he'd rather work for himself and be a thief. Well, now he was a sperm thief, and still reporting to Pat.

"Hey!" cried Paco, "Look, over there!"

Over there was a little Mexican diner, open for breakfast. Len's heart lifted. Always alert to signs, Paco would be reassured.

18

For Holly St. Cyr, the period leading to the Breeders Cup was a little worse each time around. Dixie drank more and had little daytime hangovers, but she didn't nap them away like her father, just attacked anyone handy. This particular afternoon had been saved by the arrival of a magazine containing an extensive piece on the rise of Lee Farms and an interview by Dick Dodge, an aging queen related to half the thoroughbred upper crust. Missile Man's syndication was featured, but the story centered on the Margiedaw/Black Ice rivalry, which for Dodge was right up there with Affirmed/Alydar and Seabiscuit/War Admiral. ("In this undeniable Century of the Woman, the rivalry of these two incomparable mares epitomizes the new realities. Trading places and vying for dominance like their 20th Century predecessors, Gloria Steinem and Kate Millet...")

A small unflattering black-and-white shot of Eleanor St. James with Margiedaw was spitefully included, but the photographer had done brilliant work with Dixie, removing many pounds through choice of lenses and angles. The article was a great distraction, generating many calls, but Holly was near her limit, and she had emergencies of her own and needed to escape Dixie's suffocating demands before she lost control. The magazine piece was a godsend, distracting Dixie and allowing Holly to steal an entire day to visit an aunt in grave but fictitious danger of leaving this world via St. Louis. This was Cousin Gentian, still going strong in her eighties, and the trip enabled Holly to deal with a real emergency – replenishment of the compote additive. Cousin Gentian had seen her through the Little Isaac catastrophe, but was now a very strange old lady devoted to augury, witchcraft and powerful herbs. She existed at the extreme periphery of the clan, bluntly referred to by some New Orleans family members as a witch or juju woman, but Holly felt a troubling debt to this woman who had as much as saved her life in the aftermath of Little Isaac.

As Lee Farms disappeared behind her in the six o'clock mist, Holly felt a strong general heady sense of lightness. She was a natural driver, and Dixie's little Mercedes coupe would really move. It had a radar detector, and she was holding close to eighty, skipping parts of the interstate for more interesting roads, enjoying an airborne sense of freedom. Many hours of it, until the mood broke on the outskirts of East St. Louis, home of many talented car thieves who would fully appreciate this set of wheels. It was a mostly black town, with the poverty and general hopelessness plain to be seen in the way people dressed and moved. Tens of thousands were struggling with recession and the wave of immigrants was cutting into traditionally black domestic work. *And clean little me in this clean little car*. But it would be safe – there was a parking space in Tremaine Court.

The Court was a strange old relic, a U-shaped building that surrounded what had been a large garden, now paved over and full of cars. Its colors were strange, too – faded purple, orange, and indigo, baked in the sun for decades, dating from days when well-to-do people lived in this near-slum. She sat for a moment and geared down to get social with Cousin Gentian. Toothless now, but important history. A younger, very different Gentian had got into Holly's head as a young child, when she visited on vacation. Around age twelve she'd realized that the woman was of the "old religion," a believer in magic and a creator of potions. Gentian had explained some of these to the girl, how they were made, and when they were used, It was fascinating and nervous-making, but resolved for Holly by her mother in simple terms:

"Cousin Gentian has her path and you have yours. A girl who scores around ninetieth percentile in every single subject doesn't need magic to succeed."

Bingo. Except that it was Gentian that Holly went to after Little Isaac, and somehow she had made that horrible episode all right in Holly's stunned high-school mind, isolated it like an encapsulated virus, separate from her everyday life. Then she'd made it right with Holly's mother, a miracle Holly never understood. Gentian had been a healer then. But when Holly graduated college and showed up to tell her about her great new job, she found a caster of spells in the unchanged apartment with its ancient furniture and complex smells.

"Go good or go bad," Gentian had said in her quiet, half-mumbled but direct way. "You needa take over."

"A black girl doesn't just take over a rich old southern family, Cousin Gentian," she'd replied, amazed.

"They got they 'vantage, you gotta have you 'vantage. They gotta love you. Somebody gotta love you a lot, p'tec' you. Ah give you a potion, but it cost you. 'Spensive 'gredients."

Whatever the hell it was, she'd accepted it, paid for it, used it as directed, and damned if the Lees didn't love her. But as the Lees opened up to her, these rare meetings disturbed Holly more and more. As she climbed several flights of stairs, she no longer enjoyed the fine old marble walls and hand-carved wood banister ornaments that used to please her eye. Conscious of her mood, she stopped on the landing and collected herself before knocking. Then the usual wait.

"Holly girl come t'see Gentian right on time," said the crone, opening the door with a thin half-smile. She made no move to embrace Holly, who smiled back, wondering what "on time" meant. Gentian had no phone, and Holly had not written, knowing she'd be there. There was a weird formality, and she sensed that Gentian had become even more secretive and distant.

"Looking well, Cousin," she replied, taking a chair that had not moved in many years.

"Look same," said Gentian. "Take special things. You don't need 'em yet, girl. Not yet."

They drank herb tea in the dark little sitting room and talked family, or tried to. Who was alive and who had passed was the only topic, Gentian's sole interests being magic and those who practiced it. It became clear to Holly that the herb tea was strong stuff, and that Gentian had become bored with her. This afternoon it was apparent that she was basically a customer, and she found herself becoming claustrophobic, watering a dead plant with much of her tea. She waited until they ran out of talk, then asked some questions about the potion she was buying. The old woman's toothless argot was dodgy on the subject of the brown powder, and Holly gleaned only that the many ingredients were difficult to obtain, some from Gentian's associate, the down-river swamp witch. This was one recipe she was keeping to herself.

"All natch'l 'gredients," she proudly noted.

This woman saved my life, and now we have nothing in common, nothing to talk about. It cut through the spell of the tea, and she found herself feeling strangely empty. She looked at her watch.

"I've got to go, Cousin. Gotta drive back this afternoon."

"Drove in a cah?"

"It's down there. I'm keeping an eye on it from the window."

The old woman giggled. "Good idea," she said, and didn't press her to stay.

"Drive careful now," she added absently, and Holly left with nothing except the powder and Gentian's observation that a little extra would help on a bad day. The relief of her dawn joy-ride was long gone, replaced by guilt and shame. Facing this as she walked out to the baking field of cars, packet in her bra, she felt dirty and niggerish, with a head full of uneasy thoughts. The old woman had repeated the phrase *jes' li'l bit more* twice, convincing Holly that the stuff was more dangerous than previously acknowledged.

She sat very still in the hot car as she waited for the AC to cut in, unable to think clearly, feeling endangered and concerned with her future. She'd planned to hit the road directly, but she was at half speed, feeling the midday heat and that tea. Why had Gentian done that to her? Except for the Little Isaac episode, Holly had never used drugs, and feared them. She sat thinking until the AC came on, then crossed over into St. Louis for no particular reason, driving slowly until she saw a small, safe-looking park. Out of the car, she walked deliberately toward a group of shaded benches with one clear thought: No more potion for Dixie. That had to be. A little less every other day for a couple of weeks, and then let the chips fall where they might.

Feeling cleaner with this decision, she selected a bench and sat down to deal with the larger question of how in hell she'd ever escape the passionate clutches of Dixie Dixon. Other than Horny Howard Budney, no one else would offer her anything like the life she'd become accustomed to. And that was addiction, too. Around her was a hot, heavy, *fin du siècle* St. Louis afternoon. Inside was general revulsion. In Saratoga she had experienced an insane desire to lock her teeth into Dixie's mound like a pit bull and make her beg for release. She wanted to see that plump peaches-and-cream smile streaked with tears of humiliation, fear, and mascara. Wanted to hear her beg. Wanted freedom from the endless sense of entrapment and control that infected even her most private thinking. Today her thinking was very simple, calm, and a little desperate. She'd always been able to figure out where she wanted to be, and some way to get there. Where did she want to be now? What did she *want*? Just money?

It was slow coming, and it wasn't an elevated, educated wish: she wanted to be having a drink in some cool clean place with some cool smooth man with a head on his shoulders. A man. And that would be the warm, quiet, considerate Len Thomas, who still hadn't called. He'd got under her skin, no denying it. The way he'd walked right into Howard's turf. The way he danced, the way he half-smiled and didn't say too much, and the way his little bay mare had nearly given Dixie a stroke in Saratoga. And then at the yearling sales he had just half-smiled when she'd caught his eye and practically thrown him a kiss. Since the Blue Lantern she was hot for the man.

Why did she keep avoiding that? Especially since he might be the path to freedom. Since invading Ronnie Pitt's office and getting those passwords, her ideas about the future were sometimes wild and criminal. A job in asset management wouldn't be easy to find and would take years to really pay off. Skimming a couple of million from the trusts and relocating to some no-extradition place where they spoke French was a much more exciting idea. But she didn't really want to do that. There had to be a way to change her life that didn't leave her feeling guilty, and she didn't have forever. And Llewellyn Thomas wasn't calling. Of course not. Must have women after him, all types, sizes and colors.

No longer exhausted and sleepy, Holly went with the flow. So okay – what would Llewellyn Thomas be doing out in La-La land at noon Wednesday morning? Showering after working his horses prior to some afternoon sex, probably. And Jesus, now I'm *horny!* I want to fuck that man so he doesn't forget it, because he may be experienced but he's not invulnerable, and I do have a hot streak. Give it up and then let him know what me and my smarts can do for him and his life. What to do with his money, and how to escape that freckled gorilla he works for.

No time like the present. She found his card, dialed, and heard his smooth, warm voice.

This is Len's machine. Leave him a message and I'll pass it on to him, word for word.

She didn't leave a message, but she did smile her first real smile of the afternoon, a smile that wouldn't go away. Friendly, she thought again. Nice dry sense of humor.

She called again. "You know who this is, Len, and in case you lost my card, the number is . . . "

After that she sat some more, amazed at herself. Damn! Totally out of character.

Finally she called Dixie.

"Oh Holly, I'm so glad you called! Everyone wants to talk about that silly article and all I could think of was you. Is your friend going to be all right?"

Holly allowed an awkward pause.

"They don't know exactly what it is, but it's probably not – not what I was afraid of, and she's feeling better. But it took something out of me. She's my favorite cousin."

"Of course. You know, that's an awful drive. You should just find a nice room and come home tomorrow, hon."

"Oh, Dixie, you are *so* nice. But really, I can do it, I'm not tired and I'm a good driver."

Holly felt perfectly fine now, and very contrite about her resentments. Getting Dixie off the potion would be rough, but getting Dixie off her – that was the real problem.

There was enough moon that when their eyes adjusted they didn't need flashlights. Len parked off a dirt road that he'd noticed on his first trip, and quickly laid two stacks of gear on the car top. While Paco and Carlos changed, he put on gloves and wiped the car down twice, as carefully as he knew how. When he stopped he noticed light, lacy clouds far above, darkening the moonlight from time to time. But it was going all right so far, he thought. A crazy scheme, and this night had a mood to match. Did McGoo really grasp what he was putting at stake using these two, or did he think he led a charmed life? Or was he just *poco loco*? Whatever. As usual, it was all up to him. He allowed himself a rare second cigarette while the other two bagged their street clothes and felt himself beginning to tighten up just a little, but he saw that Paco was at ease, at home in the night with skills that went back to that childhood border crossing and his gang days.

Paco felt fine. Adventures naturally took place in the dark, and it would be the same tonight as that crossing – close calls, friendly umpire. Falling back on his natural gifts of sight, hearing and instinct, he dropped into gear and went game-face quiet, feeling confident in Carlos, who could always follow his thinking. Full of assurance, his thoughts roamed free and optimistic. He recalled their last meal, eaten in a booth in a funky diner well outside the rich zone. They'd examined the photos Len had taken, his hand-drawn map, and a similar map on a card his cousin had picked up on the tour through Lee Farms. The maps were almost the same, except for two small buildings, storage sheds built since the postcard was printed, or deemed of no importance. One of these little buildings had a view of the long main barn and the smaller one flanking it – a perfect place to take a little nap, because when you woke up, you could see everything at a glance from the doorway. He'd circled it, and Len had nodded.

"Figure he hangs out there?" Len had asked across the table.

"Little nap maybe."

Then Len had made them each draw the map on a napkin from memory, and they both had it perfect. Len had nodded and smiled, and Paco had smiled back.

Looking at Len across the top of the car now, Paco smiled again as he slipped into a light silk ski mask, folding it up into a hat before pulling on the gloves. When everything was in the evidence bag they drove off in the warm night, filmed with sweat, windows open to the sweet country air, all of them gloved now, and slightly crazed, with time dragging. Len broke out the freshly packed pipe and they smoked by rank. When they were finished, he carefully wiped the pipe and tossed it out the window far into the brush. His father's pipe. Well, he'd have understood. Still almost half an hour to go.

"Okay, Pooko, I know you got that slick little toot-box somewheres. We pretty close to zero hour, like t'try that device one more time if you don't mind."

"Sheet, no – try three times, my treat. I need some re-up myself. Ees called Snow-blower, new thing. Self-contain'."

He passed it to Len, who faked two hits, then doubled that for himself.

"Lemme see that thing again," said Len. He wiped it clean one-handed, and flung it out the window as far as he could before his horse-whisperer could react. A cry of anguish leaped from Paco.

"Evidence, man. Find that in a pocket an' we in ten times more trouble."

"Si, si, I know, was wrong. But is nice thing. They got in silver too."

"We pull this off an' I get you a gold one."

"Clellon town line," said Carlos.

"Pull over, I take the wheel. One more thing, gotta go in the trunk."

He came back with the dry-ice box in a large, awkward backpack. Vapor rose as he opened the metal container inside. Paco was irritated but Len ignored it.

"Yeah, like I said before, gotta bring it in. Jism in bag, bag in container, container in this compartment, no delay. An' like I said before, don't touch stuff in there. Dry ice, burn you bad."

"I ain't carry this – no way, man."

"I say anything about you carryin' it? You in charge, Carlos carry the box. Carlos, what I just say?"

"Jism in bag, bag in container, container in compartment, get burned without gloves, I carry box."

"Is focking *trouble,* go in with this thing," interjected Paco. "Evidence."

"Is okay." said Carlos, "Scientific necessity. No problem, not so heavy."

"I be driving past every ten-twelve minutes real slow, lights out. You flash me down. Like we talked about."

Holly St. Cyr, Tom Lee, Dixie Dixon, and Security Head

Arpell Donner were all quite drunk, all by themselves. In his seventies, Tom Lee had only the occasional carnal moment, but he wanted Holly's company. Wonderful company, got every joke, and truthfully told him the Lees had changed her life more than school or anything else. Except for that rotten Little Isaac, whom she didn't mention. She did say to him without lying, "I like spending this time with you. It's fun, and I learn things I'd never have known."

Ready to retire, Tom Lee was lonely, pouring another small tot of bourbon and debating sleep or a new JFK conspiracy book. He wasn't going to wake Frank at this hour, but felt dependent on him at this stage of the evening to get himself to bed properly. Dressed in loose white cotton slacks and shirt, he was very comfortable in his big calf-leather club chair, custom-made with concealed buttons activating electric motors that made this handsome chair a regal recliner. Sipping his bourbon, he considered another possibility. Suppose he went to sleep right here?

He drank off the bourbon with measured grace and closed his eyes in the silence. He'd sleep fine, he decided, but it was always nicer with Holly or Frank around for a while. They just understood. So simple – they understood and forgave, and he slept better.

Dixie's evening was ending on a rougher note. Bottle on the bedside table, she had foreseen her condition and got into brightly flowered silk pajamas while reasonably sober, then got in bed feeling deserted, and started writing notes to friends. Social formulas dissolved and the primal Dixie took over as she struggled to write Eleanor St. James, with whom she damn sure didn't want to talk. And Holly – God knew where she was, probably getting laid just when she really *needed* her!

No, it was a sick friend. Relative. And *damn* Eleanor St. James anyway. Skinny bitch, homely horse. What to write.

Thanks for calling, we're gonna kick your ass in the Breeders...

So nice of you to call, but I can't help you get in a magazine. Dick's gay, so your usual approach won't work...

Thanks so much for calling, your horse is so ugly I can't tell one end from the other...

It was great seeing you in Saratoga, I guess you had to see that magazine before you called...

So nice to hear from you. You probably wonder why they write about us when your horse won. Being from Texas, you think it's all about oil and money. What you <u>could</u> do is fuck a Sheikh, that would really get Dick going and we've got the perfect candidate...

She had another swallow of bourbon, but it wasn't having any effect. Why the *hell* did she always get this way leading up to the big ones? And what the hell *had* happened at Saratoga? But then she remembered the Sheik's remarks and McGoohey's humiliation, and felt much better. A burping chuckle emerged as she closed her eyes and recalled him on all fours, which had been just about perfect. Must have ruined his lovely white loafers.

In the guest house, where she'd gone to avoid Dixie, Holly was drinking straight Absolut from the freezer, where it lived in a block of ice. Unbelievably, she was still obsessing on her empty, sold-out, squandered life, and how she'd stopped dead in her academic tracks at the thought of writing a thesis. Just *didn't like writing.*

Or couldn't do it? She thought about that as she removed her clothes in slow motion, placing them slowly and carefully on the back of a chair so as not to wrinkle them. Her slowness struck her.

"You *drunk*, bitch," she announced, looking up at herself in the ceiling mirror that Tom Lee had installed forty years before at the behest of a mistress. "You drunk, but you *fine.*"

It was the voice of Little Isaac, more or less.

19

Arpell Donner was about to be vertically asleep in a disciplined manner as befit a retired MP staff sergeant in charge of security at Lee Farms. One minute he'd be looking out over the brightly lit barn area. Some minutes later, appearing exactly the same, he'd be asleep. Little nap, no big deal. Thieves avoided Lee Farms, it being well known that the Lees always had someone qualified for security work, someone like himself, instead of some low-rent night watchman. Large and fit, with extensive sidearm experience, but not trigger happy, Donner was martial by nature. He knew when to crunch gravel warningly or slip up like a hunter, and he was in excellent shape. Good little workout almost every day. Drifting pleasantly courtesy several shots of good bourbon whisky, he planned the rest of his night. The alarm would wake him and he'd begin a quiet reverse-order tour of the grounds. Standing in the doorway of this little shed in the at-ease position while viewing the barns always put him in a good solid mood, a command-post kind of feeling, and not much could happen around the barns that he would not pick up on with his excellent vision and the night-vision monocular.

An experienced alcoholic, he kept himself sharp by doing a lot of things that weren't really necessary. Thought control was everything. Donner had learned this from a man named Templeton, a Master Sergeant at Bragg, a man of great self control who could sleep on his feet even in daytime and shared the secret: *thought control.* Now, at forty-six, Donner had pretty well mastered the technique, and enjoyed the feeling of coming awake on his feet without a giveaway twitch, which he usually managed to do. You needed the right percentage of blood alcohol, and he still didn't seem to have it, so he went back to the grain bin and had another. Straight, no chaser, to leave the taste in his mouth. Best whiskey in the state, and one *hell* of a discount. No profit, no tax, straight from Lee's own distillery, though he kept his name off it.

He checked the alarm clock on the bucket shelf and set it

for forty minutes.

"What's he doing?" whispered Carlos, turning to Paco. They had been observing Donner from a distance as he stood in the doorway swaying slightly.

Paco shook his head. A large half-asleep guard inside a doorway was a tricky target; you needed to be behind him for the blackjack. And a .45 on his hip, it looked like. If he came outside, fine, but as he was – *Coño!* This big fool was taking up valuable time. What would Len do?

"Okay. I go around through trees, come alongside of building behind him. I wave my arm, you walk up from here, loose, like you drunk, an' tell him you are drunk and lost. Not till I wave, right? Guy steps up to throw you out, I get him from behind, *bop*, get the gun, we pull him inside."

Working his way to the side of the shack in a long arc through the brush, the big pants and loaded pockets irritated him. This should be smooth and quiet, a special night pleasure. He circled silently into the orchard, around to the side of the shack, and no problem. Just get him out of the doorway. He waved at Carlos, who started walking toward the shed, looking perfectly sober. Carlos had never been drunk, and hadn't seen it often enough to fake it.

Estupido! He sees you are sober, too much time to think.

Carlos continued forward and nothing happened. He was halfway there, walking right up to Donner in the bright moonlight. Paco had never seen anything stranger – his skin was prickling and chilling. He crossed himself. Finally Carlos was standing in front of the guard.

"I am loss," he announced to Donner, trying for illiterate. The man made a sound that wasn't a word. Paco almost laughed. Lousy criminal, lousy cop.

Coming awake with a jerk, Donner almost fell backward, lurched forward, recovered, reached for his .45, and stepped back. Then he started forward again, towering over Carlos and speaking in a thick voice.

"It's a lot worse than that – you're on your way to jail, my little *amigo*."

With the gun out and pointing at Carlos, Paco stopped smiling. Not funny any more.

172

"Jail? Why jail?" asked Carlos. "I jus' want to find way to the road." He paused and added, "I have been over-drinking."

Over-drinking. Suppressing an impulse to laugh, Donner was looking forward to some kind of benefit from this windfall if he could figure how to play it. He holstered the .45, setting up for some hard-ass army-style talk as he slipped a pair of plastic cuffs out of his pocket. As he stepped forward in a deliberate, John Wayne manner, Paco was in synch behind him, blackjack in hand, reaching high, and Donner was felled with a heavier shot than planned, slumping silently as Paco put him in the standard cop choke-hold and took the pistol with his free hand. Then they dragged him backward into the shed. Paco was feeling great. Donner was gagged, wearing his own cuffs, thoroughly trussed up in duct tape within seconds. Then Paco leaned forward and listened carefully, ear to Donner's face. He saw Carlos waiting, hypodermic in hand.

"Wait."

They waited almost a minute before Paco spoke again.

"Okay, breathing good, trying to move, start to wake up."

Donner grunted, said *fuck!* and was neatly sedated through his chinos by Carlos. After the shot he continued waking up for a minute or so, then subsided. They rolled him out of sight under a workbench, tossed empty sacks over him, and went on to the other shed. When they found no guard, Paco called a break and peeled an oversized band-aid from his inner arm, revealing a folded piece of paper full of crushed cocaine. Making the paper into a crude funnel, he tilted his head back and inhaled. One nostril burning, he dumped the remainder into the other and felt himself taking off. Then he was zooming. He didn't move until he felt stable in overdrive, ready for anything. Then he trotted to the main barn without a word, feet dancing, Carlos at his heels with the clumsy dry-ice pack bouncing heavily.

The tall barn door slid open without a sound. *Everything work perfect here*, thought Paco as he entered, .45 in hand, exactly as in a Clint Eastwood film he had seen several times. Carlos crouched in a shadow outside as lookout. Peeling back the duct tape that narrowed the beam of his flash, instead of the double row of stalls he was expecting, Paco saw a long single row, with the other side of the building devoted to an orderly array of vehicles, a giant lawnmower, a tractor, and two shiny trailers, the smaller hooked up to a new Hummer in the Lee colors, maroon and yellow. Minimum three thousand dollar custom paint, he estimated. The barn was vast, with a good clean horse smell and huge padded stalls. Perfection. He moved in further, talking to the horses as they woke up, making their quiet night-noises. Instead of stall numbers, he found names carved on big varnished wood plaques, names anyone in racing would recognize. Then he began to tighten up: there were lots of stalls, but not enough for all the Lee horses here in this single row. There would be others in the smaller barn, but he had no idea how they were divided. Where was Black Ice? Maybe they had the mares together in the other barn. Or the super-horses, which would include both her and Missile Man. If he was there, more time would be lost, and Len, trolling back and forth, would be further exposed. A rich police department would have at least one car out roaming around the clock. Why didn't they have *radios*?

He was almost at the end, up to Space Commander, and still no Missile Man.

Something in Paco started to come loose. Get to barn, ten minutes, then guard, lose fifteen, easy. Check other shed, go to barn, search for horse – another ten or twelve. And Len out there getting pissed, waiting and worrying. Whack off horse – another ten?

Anything goes wrong, he just drive away. Len's safety was irritating, too much like boss Pat.

But there it was! The last stall. No, the first, looking in from trackside! *Numero uno.* The stalls had plenty of space for a horse to put his head through, which several others were doing, but not Missile Man, who remained inside.

"How you doin' in there, man? Whuchu up to, big boy? You wonder 'bout Paco, eh?"

Missile Man whickered quietly in response. Nice mellow sound, thought Paco, sound of classy horse. No fear. The horse's head now appeared, good big eyes in a dark gold background, and the well-known zigzag blaze.

"See you in a minute, big guy."

He turned to see Carlos entering the barn, index finger to

his lips, beckoning with the other hand. At the door, he pointed silently to a groom in white underpants about to relieve himself against a tree. Paco slipped up behind him to apply the choke-hold again while jamming the .45 into his ribs. The groom froze, and Carlos injected him. Rapidly duct-taped, he was rolled out of sight in the bushes. More time lost. Paco thrust the .45 into his belt and went back to Missile Man's stall, followed by Carlos. He opened the door without hesitation, secure in having seen his eyes and heard his balanced, mature *Hello.* In front of him was the super-sire, a tall red-gold stallion. Smiling. Worth so much, thought Paco, but a pretty friendly horse with an easygoing, approachable look. A confident look that Paco recognized as the sign of a horse that didn't freak out at post time or get crazy over nothing.

He reached in a pocket for a baggie containing the *chef d'oeuvre*, a double-bagged handkerchief that had swabbed Arabiche's genitalia when she went in season. It was very fresh, and the stallion responded immediately, his easy night mood swiftly replaced by a kind of general electrical warm-up.

"Hold to his nose."

Carlos did, and in seconds they had a randy young stud at the ready, snuffle-snorting as he breathed in Arabiche's vital juices taken as she entered her cycle, and his member began sliding out.

"I don' do this for no one but you, big guy. Come on, you know what to do – close your eyes, think *Arabiche*, right? She fine as they come, boy."

It worked better than he'd dared to hope. Further aroused by Paco's gloved hand, Missile Man's posture changed, muscles tensing and bulging as he started shifting foot to foot in a little dance to the beautiful music in that handkerchief. Paco kept a hand on his neck and the handkerchief at the horse's muzzle. The erection became a majestic sight.

"Carlos, hold shank one hand, keep focking handkerchief in his nose."

Then he addressed the horse.

"Yeah, good, some day you meet her, you forget all about Paco, man. Nothing like real thing."

Carlos lost his carefully schooled English. "Wow – look ot hees *theeng*!"

He was giggling, and Paco understood. It was a pretty crazy scene, all right. Unembarrassed and feeling useful in a good cause, Paco grasped the enormous penis. Almost ready, he guessed. Quick side-trip into the anus to get that prostate turning over per Len's directions. The danger in such close quarters was obvious, but he was sure it would be okay. He reached into another pocket for a container of petroleum jelly, scooped a gob into the glove, and went back to work. Missile Man stabilized, sensed relief on the way, and accepted the situation as Paco kept the glove working. The horse was getting a little crazy now, vibrating, bouncing around and scaring Carlos, but Paco was unafraid – horses didn't hurt their friends.

"*Handkerchief! Keep it there!*" he barked at Carlos in a whisper, then addressed the horse.

"Yeah, *good* boy! Come on, you feel better in a minute."

It was going faster than he expected and he saw Carlos falling behind, forgetting the Ziploc.

"*Bag!* Focking *bag, estupido!*"

It broke Carlos's paralysis, and there was the mother of all Ziplocs.

Then *Whammo!* into the bag just as Carlos got it there, a great priceless gooey glob fired from that cannon, followed by some snorting, as if this had been an interesting warm-up and maybe he was ready for more. No more craziness though, as Carlos closed the Ziploc and Paco opened the chill-box. Then bag in cylinder, top closed, job done.

Or was it? With the makings of the foal now safely in the box, they backed out of the stall and Paco took a moment to admire this fine world. He noticed the Hummer again and shined his light inside admiringly, noting how it was laid out with respect. In the old days he'd have stolen it in a heartbeat, just for bragging rights. Paco sighed at his decline as a man and had a bad moment. What had happened to his *cojones*? Step Program! He snarled at Carlos for no reason, hating himself, his fear, and his whole life. Missile Man had his head out of the stall now, watching them with interest and catching Paco's eye.

Sacred Mother of God, what a horse!

He drew himself back from the mood and ignored his inner

madman – perfect plan, perfect job. Big step up for everyone. This foal would be a super-horse, and he owned part. Down from his excitement, Missile Man looked directly at Paco and whinnied quietly. Paco returned his look and talked to the horse. Derby winner, champion horse, triple crown except for fucking jockey. Just like Slew and Secretariat. He slipped into a confused, wrenching, drug-enhanced sadness signaling some lack in himself, evidence of his decline.

It didn't *matter* that they had the foal in the box! What was he, Paco Gonzales, supposed to do with such bad feelings? Time was everything, but a familiar storm was rising in him, and he could only stand there in the grip of this force welling up in his Aztec heart. It rose out of his basic understanding of himself as a creature of earth and sky, fired by an energy he could not ignore. He closed his eyes, silent, waiting, unmoving as a rock. In these moments he became blind to the world as this breathtaking force roared up from his depths, gathering strength with every moment, and he could only wait for the vision that would follow. Carlos stood back, frozen, silent and fearful, only Christian prayer defending his soul as this mad pagan thing occurred.

Our Father who art in Heaven, hallowed be thy name...

Energy radiated from the silent motionless Paco in palpable waves, and the horses began to stir restlessly. A couple whinnied nervously, hooves shifting with contagious anxiety. Carlos was afraid. He had seen these dream-trances before, but this one was lasting too long, with Paco more statue than man, his eyes open but blind.

Then he was back, clear and refreshed, knowing exactly what he had to do, giving Carlos quick orders. The horses relaxed and quieted down. Their friend Paco was okay, they saw, though changed, leading Missile Man into the trailer.

Len had stopped counting his passes by the gate. He knew exactly how the white fencing would show up each time, coming from either direction. He rounded the bend, dropped the lights, and slowed down as he crept along the far side of the road. If there was ever a totally suspicious vehicle for this county it would be a cheap little blue rental driving lights-out with a black man at the wheel. The boys had gone red zone, no question. *El Chaparrito's* relation to clock time made your average unemployed Brother a walking chronometer, and there was the distraction of that barn full of great horses. Len knew the drill: time out to introduce himself, first of all. Paco Gonzalez, Equine Rights Advocate. Brief dialogs to find out how everyone was feeling and what their concerns might be.

Or Paco in a metal chair, being worked over like a terrorist. Paco the old Clantonista would lose his English and become a lost migrant half-wit, very tough nut to crack. But not Carlos. So why was he still here, waiting to get himself arrested? Because they were his guys, and he had to wait for them. What was the worst that could happen? It would be total. If a cop stopped him, he'd find some excuse to go into the trunk, find the evidence bag, and sayonara. Local rules, they'd get away with it, always did. So get rid of the evidence bag on the next turnaround, pick it up on the way out. Should've thought of that before.

Still no light! Eighteen minutes past bug-out time. He'd counted on Paco to at least get them out of there if they couldn't pull it off, and he'd counted wrong. A cloud passed over the moon and he lost his bearings, slowing down and keeping the wheel straight. The cloud passed and there was the fence again. Still no one in sight. And *another* cloud! Crawling along through total darkness, he strained to see the blink of a flashlight. Nothing.

Then a roar, a snapping-crackling sound and a huge crashing *thud* as a giant blow T-boned the little car, rolling it over into the ditch like a toy and knocking him out cold.

Minutes later, heavily stunned, he found himself hanging upside down in the belts with no sense of what had happened or how much time had passed, and he began struggling to free himself. Fumbling for the release, he realized that his eyes weren't focusing. Double vision. He kept fumbling and the belt let go, dropping him on his head and shoulders. No pain, just dizzy, but part of his mind was clear. *Concussion*, it said. The evidence bag had to disappear, and his bag with it. The belt had saved him, but he had no idea what had happened.

Car's clean an' I ain't bleedin', he thought. Unable to think beyond that, he struggled through the open window, crawled to the back of the car and found both bags conveniently in the ditch. *Trunk popped, lucky thing.* He left the scene still seeing double, stopping to drop his own little bag into the evidence bag, then heading up the hillside into the pines on pure instinct, counting his steps, slipping and sliding. No sign of any activity thank God, and despite the ringing in his ears and the headache that was building with magisterial power as he struggled up the slippery hillside. The inactivity was more luck, giving him time to hide the bag. But what the hell had happened?

About a hundred feet into the woods, he stopped to look back and remembered a piece of his emergency plan. Shiftless hanger-on cousin of his dirt-farmer cousin, he was prone to drunkenness. Cousin Jim on – what road? No not Jim. Jack? *John.* Elkins Road. And he might as well have a swallow from the pint of Four Roses, miraculously intact. He stopped and cracked the seal. Still out of it, he spilled some on his shirt, and that seemed lucky too. Drunks did that. Two good long pulls, one to luck, the other to a stronger immigration policy. He'd be tested for alcohol if they picked him up, and he wanted a major positive. Another pull. Looking down the hill through blurred eyes sending information to a blurred brain, he knew he was a city boy who could easily get lost. He saw lights far off, two sets moving around, his eyes refusing to join them, but everything was wonderfully peaceful. He feared getting lost, but decided that if he just went downhill he'd get to the road. What to do next, though, he had no idea. After a blank moment he decided this would come to him once he got rid of the evidence and this motherfucking *headache* eased up a little.

Stumbling and slipping up through the pine needles, he put it together. The thunderbolt that nearly killed him was Paco of course. Had to be, and the crackly sound had been that pretty white gate flying to pieces. Paco had had a vision in there, gone back to his gang roots and stolen a vehicle, a really big one.

And the horse!

Drove through the fence flat out while that cloud was passing over the moon. Right. And now he, Len, had to pick up the pieces, get rid of anything connecting them to this disaster, to horse racing, to California, and to Pat McGoohey. Who was going to fire him after this fiasco, if he didn't kill him, because those two would never make it back with that priceless canister of sperm, which needed fresh dry ice every day and a half. It came to Len in bits over a period of several minutes as he stood panting in the pine needles, figuring out the next step. It was going to be messy and involve hard physical effort, but he had to be rid of the bag, and the adrenaline was still pumping.

Then he slowly and painfully climbed up into a pine tree, bag hanging on his shoulder, high enough that the tree was swaying and he was invisible, hidden by the lower branches and the other trees. Then he carefully taped the bag to the trunk, thinking through the pain. Black duct tape, thank God

Use some of that booze to clean up the hands. Dead giveaway. With luck he might make it to the next town before dawn and sleep in the woods 'til dark. What he'd do then without wallet and ID, he had no idea, but he had a very clear idea what would happen if he was picked up.

20

"We jus' kill Len," said Carlos in a small bewildered voice, dazed by the impact.

"*Silencio, maricón!* God, He will take care of Len. Was accident, si? No opportunity for priest. Where we go now with horse? State border? You been looking at maps – where we go?" He too was dazed. Unbelted, his barrel chest had slammed into the wheel and he knew he had at least one cracked rib, unlike the belted Carlos. Except for the Hummer's momentum and the angle of impact, the collision would have brought them to a dead stop, but when the rental Ford rolled, he'd wrestled the wheel around on instinct, regained control, and kept going.

"Straight to highway, then west – right turn. The maps are all in the black bag. Paco, I like to get out when we get in next state an' go look for farm job, okay? This is not possible to do, we got no money for gas even."

"*You* got no money. Paco has money. Plenty."

"No, pockets were all empty, remember, no wallet."

"No rock either, right? *Wrong!* I got my *perico* an' I got what we need. Len gets popped, what we do without money? I think ahead."

"He popped all right."

"*Accident!*"

"You think horse is okay?"

There was a pause.

"This is first thing you say worth anything. We check after cross state line."

"Is getting light pretty soon, Paco. Vehicle is damaged – "

"Military vehicle, made for this."

"But the *paint* – custom paint, alarm goes out, people will notice."

The Hummer came to a gentle stop and both got out. Paco opened the doors and stared in shock. Inside the trailer was twenty or thirty million dollars worth of stud horse, dead of a snapped neck. The horse's bowels and bladder had voided, destroying all beauty and dignity. Time stretched out for him as it took hold and he looked away, tears pouring down his cheeks in the silent country night. He had killed the fine, trusting Missile Man, and probably Len, his best friend outside *La Raza*. He closed the doors without a word and there was total silence as they drove. When he spotted a side road he backed in and unhitched the trailer, unable to talk. Then the bent-nose Hummer continued up the road. Leaving behind the trailer and the remains of a racing legend, another Paco spoke, in his old gang voice.

"Easy case for Lost Horse Registry, no identification problem. Dead horse, hot car. Got maybe two, three hours. What you think, little Carlos?"

"Ice. Horse blankets in back, I wrap the pack in blankets with icebags all around it. Hot weather, we got maybe fifteen hours before re-up dry ice."

"Yeah, or no foal."

Then more silence, tears streaming down Paco's face.

"We did a great sin," said Paco after a while with calm dignity, including Carlos. "There was no other such horse, Carlos. Greatest of his time. He trust me and I betray him. And Len, another bad sin. *Sheet!* Fucking guard throw everything off."

They both spotted the big motel at the same time.

"Ice," said Carlos. "Around back, out of sight."

Paco swung into the rear, very aware that that it was getting close to dawn and the Hummer was instantly recognizable. When Carlos returned, the vehicle was empty. He stopped in his tracks, bags of ice in each hand, very afraid of the next surprise.

"Over here," said Paco from under the dash of a sparkling vintage Monte Carlo in midnight blue, a classic untamed emissions-exempt V-8 tiger. GM, his favorite marque. Two minutes later both vehicles exited, Carlos following the Monte Carlo until Paco spotted a dirt road and waved him in ahead. Out of sight of the highway, he honked his horn once. Carlos stopped dead and ran back with pack, blankets and ice bags.

With the pack on the rear floor blanketed and packed in ice, Carlos waited for orders. The silence lasted long enough for Paco to became aware that he was suddenly very tired. Carlos was wide awake.

"Where we going?" he asked.

"West. We going *west*, Carlos. California. You driving, I gotta rest. Find a gas station."

"Got no money or card."

Paco revived himself irritably, noting light coming up on the horizon.

"Carlos, you are like a little baby. I *told* you – *you* got no money. Paco got money, got money in condom, in rectum, you *peon*. How you keep money in jail. You think I go anywhere without money?"

Still irritated as they drove off, he twisted around, lowered his jeans, and removed the condom, amused at his assistant's distaste.

"Good smell – sweet smell of success. Gonna save your life, don't make face."

As he moved as if to dangle it in his cousin's face, Carlos twisted his head away, further amusing Paco as he removed the money with fastidious care and tossed the condom out the window.

"Sorry, man. Little crazy today, lotta stress. I kill greatest horse in world, and my good friend Len, too."

Close to tears again, he went silent and tried to regain control.

"Glove too, Paco. Dangerous germs."

"Only Len find gloves like this, rich guy gloves," he said, carefully removing them and tossing them to the roadside, looking at his hands with distaste and amusement. Then he soberly displayed a tight, fat roll of fifty dollar bills, which he stuffed deep in a pants pocket.

He stopped, and his voice changed.

"Len – I don't say nothing because nothing to say. We probably kill a real good guy, best black guy I ever meet, but is all luck, Carlos. He jus' happen to come by when we come out – couple seconds either way, no harm. I change the plan, but no chance to tell Len. If we have radios, no problem. I hope was quick. Jus' when I have such good feelings for him, too."

He pictured the little blue car tossed like an unlucky matador. "Too bad, last thing I'm thinking can happen. Vision came from the Devil this time, possible explanation". He looked back down at hands with thoughtful distaste.

"Gotta wash. Hey – look! *Exxon!* Gas and clean-up! Corona!"

Carlos ignored him and drove on.

"I jus' tell you buy gas!"

"Wrong place," said Carlos. "Remember how Len pick that motel and the places we ate? We stick out here, two Mexicans, rich person's car, no sign of migrant work. Tank is half full, Paco. Later we'll see a little place for low-profile people."

"You getting better, Carlos. Wake me up when you find some place feels right. Or water, any kind water, river, stream, whatever. I got to wash."

"Yeah man, you really got to do that. Smell better if you sleep in back, okay?"

Paco slipped between the seats and remembered the band-aids securing other coke stashes. His abdomen was festooned with them, and the thought cheered him enough that he was able to doze until Carlos found the right kind of station. The sky was bright between the hills, but they were out of Kentucky.

Befuddled on awakening, Paco sat for a moment in the parked car, eyes slitted against the early sun until Carlos came over with a key. In the bathroom, he washed his hands for several minutes, lathering extensively, and with will-power that surprised him, he resisted going into one of his stashes, saving them for when he took the wheel again. When he emerged, the Monte Carlo was gassed up and standing at the phone booth. Paco stopped and took a long look. Metallic midnight blue, original paint, no rust, fresh wax. Cherry ride, somebody's special baby. Somebody calling the cops right now unless his girlfriend was keeping him busy. Time to cross another state line and find a Latino scene where they could sell it and steal something else. As he walked up, Carlos reported.

"I got a chest and some cokes an' cakes. Map, too, and more ice."

Carlos doing good, thought Paco. Sensible things. Never make it in a gang, but good assistant. He felt so good about Carlos's growth as a man that he remained in the front seat to

184

admire the countryside in the clean morning light until he remembered the sin he had committed and crawled into the back, silent and ashamed. *Two* sins, he thought, reclining on the soft dark blue leather. Why I keep leaving Len out?

McGoohey was unnerved by the extended silence. Len's phone phobia, he reminded himself, and drove off for a surprise visit to the Palo Alto site. The next day he threw himself into some things at the office that he'd been ignoring for weeks. The third day began at 2:00 A.M. rather than the usual 4:30, with a gripping fear in his chest. They'd blown it, and of course they'd talk. *Never trust a nigger or a Mexican.* He could hear his father's voice. He lay with eyes closed, not moving, but the energy coming off him by four o'clock was intense enough to wake Jasmine. The new, loving Jasmine distracted him so effectively that he staggered out of the house an hour late, knowing with certainty he was soon to hit fifty.

In the Porsche for a change, McGoohey reflected that there wasn't a damn thing he could do. It was growing on him that any one of three men, none bound to him by blood or any special cause to love him, could destroy his life. This unrelenting fact was cutting deep. at the office, Alice Smith detected fear in a routinely courageous man. Jasmine, obsessed with pregnancy, didn't notice. Her world was the baby and its father, the benign, passionate, newly considerate Paddykins. She required two consultations with Alice that day, forcing her to agree that impending fatherhood had changed McGoohey. Alice said nothing, but knew the long absence of Len's crew was a very bad sign.

Strangest of all, McGoohey began following a routine, two site visits each day, and even looking at papers before he signed them. She was increasingly afraid of the next surprise, mainly on Jasmine's behalf. When the other shoe dropped, she thought it would be a big steel-toe brogan that might find its way up hubby's butt.

Cousin John was not very surprised to get the extremely early call and was fully prepared. Phlegmatic and methodical, he had the money deeply buried in sealed metal army-surplus boxes where no one would ever find them, in triple heavy-duty plastic bags. Being a thoughtful man, he had worked out a very plausible tale of Llewellyn the Lifetime Loser.

"Not at all, officer. I haven't had my coffee yet and may be a little slow in my answers. Can you tell me what this is about? I can't recall my last contact with the police."

A thin, cool, old plainclothes cop stood holding his phone with a slightly pained expression. Ed Finn had a bad leg, and some days it was easier to stand. His soft voice was not southern – this Chief Detective job in Leesville was a kind of semi-retirement from Boston, where he had got tired of arresting black people who couldn't find jobs. Overqualified and over-age, he lived with a niece and was happy with his little job. He fit in surprisingly well with his quiet manner, careful speech, and his Celtic ability to appreciate and control the excellent local bourbon like a gentleman.

"We have a man in custody who claims to be your cousin," he said in a neutral, almost kindly voice. "He calls himself Len Thomas, and he was under the influence when we picked him up."

"I'm not surprised. I was wondering what became of him. Can you tell me what he's charged with?"

"So far, vagrancy, but he was picked up in the vicinity of an estate where a major crime had been committed during the same time period."

"Vagrancy has been the curse of Len Thomas's life, but I'd find it hard to connect him with a major crime," droned John Thomas. "What happened, officer?"

"I'm not free to divulge that. Property valued in the millions."

"That's – that just doesn't sound like Len Thomas at all. Is this man black, in his early forties, thin, short hair, about five-nine or ten?"

"He is. Would you mind coming down to identify him?"

John Thomas had been waiting for this and was ready. He did not want to be in a room with Len Thomas and the Law if he could possibly avoid it, and he was already wary of the soft-spoken Finn.

"My wife is on her sick bed, officer. She is seriously ill, and I take care of her needs. I would have to find someone to stay with her if I came over, she can't be left alone. A trained nurse is very expensive. I don't suppose Len had a bottle of Four Roses when you picked him up?"

"No comment, but I see your predicament. It may not be necessary for you to come over; I'll give you ample notice if it is. Do you have any idea what he might have been doing here?"

"He used to work summers in the area when he was young, and when he's drunk he talks about it. He might know a woman out that way, that's his other weakness. But that's only a guess."

Ed Finn thanked John Thomas for his cooperation, broke the connection, and stood there expressionless for a full minute. Then he went down the hall to the Chief's office. Chief Oxland, Fred to anyone not under arrest, was a large, slow, middle-aged native, politically adroit, and used to a crime-free county. Extremely disturbed by this case, he was expecting that he'd have to place the blame for failure on Ed Finn if it wasn't solved fairly quickly, but he was very relieved to have Finn around meanwhile because he was so smart.

"He's who he says he is, Fred," said Finn. "I just talked to his cousin, where he works, when he does work. Even knew what he drinks. He sounds like just another one of these useless – "

" – niggers, Ed. I know you don't like the word but it has its meaning. Like white trash. I imagine this cousin sounded embarrassed."

"Now that you mention it."

"Cause the cousin isn't a nigger. Can't embarrass a nigger."

The thin cop nodded as if conceding to local wisdom, not pleased with himself about it, or anything about the situation. He was conceding a prejudice he did not share, engaged in a war of wits with an itinerant black alcoholic, and getting nowhere. Probably because he had the wrong man.

"I know how you feel, Ed, believe it or not. They can lead you down the garden path. That's why Clinton didn't fight the anti-welfare people too hard, he's a Southerner, he understands about these things. This Len Thomas doesn't sound like our perpetrator, does he?"

"Not so far. When are the owners getting here?"

"Soon. They're in shock. If you're not a horseman, you can't know how they'll feel. Like losing a child. And the financial loss – twenty million at least."

Finn hesitated, then gave him a calculated but natural-sounding pause. "They wouldn't want to hang it on someone?"

The Chief controlled his reaction. Ed Finn was his one man with major crime experience. He didn't know the Lees and couldn't be expected to understand people like the Lees or restrain that nasty Northern way of thinking.

"Not the Lees, Ed." He paused. "This isn't Boston, and the Lees are some of the best people you'll ever meet. Liberal Democrats, in case that's of interest. I'll let you know when they get here. Keep working on him if you think it's worth it."

Finn walked out covering his limp. He was clearly the go-to guy, and now he couldn't even raise the insurance issue! People were killing horses for insurance all the time lately, it was a growth industry. And what was it about Len Thomas that bothered him? That black leather book, for one thing. More like something an old Back Bay gent would use to keep track of his affairs. But anyone could steal something like that, or buy it on impulse. The problem was that the notes didn't make sense, and Len Thomas probably wouldn't be much different sober. Somewhere he'd got the idea of a diary, but couldn't quite figure how to do it, or even spell. Finn went to his desk, and wrote on the legal pad he was using to keep notes:

Tuesday 0730:

Cousin John Thomas, farmer in Louisville area, confirms identity and general small-time profile. Len Thomas apparently borderline alcoholic but John Thomas doubts significant criminal history or capacity for major crime.

A buxom middle-aged blonde woman appeared in the door full of suppressed excitement, eager to be of assistance to Detective Finn, on whom she had a terrible crush, gimpy leg and all.

"Lieutenant Sir?"

Finn nodded. Her eager eyes were sparkling.

"What've you got, Evelyn?"

A paper appeared silently under his nose. A fingerprint report, when no one had expected anything. Llewellyn Kenyatta Thomas, a.k.a. Len Thomas, had been arrested for heroin possession twenty-four years ago. In Boston. The faxed picture was about right, too, if you cut the Afro and added the years. Distinctive nose.

After graciously thanking her, he found the Chief in the corridor.

"I'm not through with this man. He's not quite a virgin. Let's check his urine, might find something there."

"This black book you were found with – it makes reference to Lee Farms."

Finn's no-pressure voice was quiet and civil.

"Does," replied Len. Need a job. Other places too, lista places somewhere."

"Your cousin says you work for him."

"No real job, jes mah cousin he'p me out. Gotta sick wife an' no money."

Len observed his captors. One McGoo-size brute and this old guy with a bad leg who should be retired by now. Len wished he was, because he had a quiet natural patience that would wait and wait, looking for some inconsistency. Anything to hook into. *Lost and hitchhiking* had not raised his eyebrows, but this old white gimp was too interested in where he hailed from. He'd explained: Georgia mama, Louisville daddy, part Boston-raised, currently going wherever he could get work. He mentioned Farmer John again as if he'd forgotten the earlier session. This got no response, and they took a break to have him urinate in a bottle. Len guessed that John must have played okay. Nor would John lead them to the money, making himself complicit. It would be well hidden, buried, probably. John would be okay unless they brought him in and pressured him. Speed was John's problem, couldn't make tempos. Take away his think-time and he'd slip. Then John would give him up. He had to get himself clear because of his sick wife. That was only right, and Len knew that whatever happened, the money wouldn't pop up in a bank account.

Finn kept on and on, reshuffling his original questions, and for each line Len had a reasonable explanation.

"We know about your heroin addiction."

Len gave him an incredulous look, undisturbed.

"Thas why I gotta pissinna bottle? I was a kid, I ain't done that for twenny years. Jes a little smoke once inna while. Rather drink."

But he avoided explaining the initial H. in the notebook.

"*Pers'n'l*," he announced, with alcoholic dignity.

The old cop let it go, but the big young one tried to keep it going.

"Your own diary, right?"

"Not no diary, jes a book he'p me r'member." He paused before delivering his next statement.

"Ah'm a *veteran*, I got rights."

"You want a lawyer?" asked the young cop, and Finn shot him an icy glance.

"Don't *need* no lawyer, ain't done nothin' but get drunk."

Still under the influence of that pint, Len was aware of his fear and amused at himself. *Trivialize*, he was thinking – trivialize yourself down to a drunk and disorderly pain in the butt.

"Okay, a *book*," said the old cop. "But who is this 'H'? We can't just ignore that."

"Cain't talk 'bout that, issa woman got nuthin t'do with this. Ah know they was somethin lef' in that bottle, off'cer. Help settle mah nerves – "

"This is no time for jokes, Thomas. Do you know you're in serious trouble?"

"In a police station, ain't I? Course Ah'm in trouble. Cain't hold my likker, never could. But I ain't *hurt* nobody or stole nuthin'. Jes' needa sleep it off."

The old cop kept watching, but to Len's eye he was at a dead end. And drunks fell asleep on people all the time. The door opened before Len closed his eyes and his insides jumped. The young blond cop who'd profiled him the day he checked out Lee Farms had walked in to ask the detectives if they needed coffee. He looked at Len without interest, smelling the whiskey. Len decided to fall asleep while they talked.

"I think I might've seen this man somewhere before."

"Where's that, Dan?" The old detective's voice had the beginning of an edge, like he wanted him the hell out of there, and it seemed to jam the younger man's circuits.

"Not sure, Ed. I'll try to bring it back."

"You do that, Dan. Large black, no sugar."

"Me too," said the second interrogator.

"Him too?"

"More like medium-small black," said the old cop in his gentle whispery voice, and it struck Len as very funny. Having his eyes closed felt better. Except for the blond kid-cop, it was going as well as he could hope for, and Len doubted Finn would place much faith in him. Didn't like him. It was beginning to feel like soccer, which could go on forever to a scoreless tie. Finn would feel that, too, and it would be making him irritable.

There was a quiet sound of feet shuffling as the narrow booth behind the one-way glass filled up. Finn stopped his assistant from waking Len, then left to see what was going on. On a hunch, he went the long way round and ran into the Chief, who gave him a cautionary look.

"On my way to tell you the family's in there," he said, as if at a funeral. "Go easy. Tom Lee, father; Annabelle Dixon, daughter; Holly St. Cyr, colored, daughter's personal assistant." Touch of emphasis there, noted Finn, and then the Chief's voice tightened. "Security guard named Donner, retired Army. They got his gun and drugged him."

And brought this down on us in an election year.

He turned and walked back to his office, quietly seething. Finn waited a moment before entering the dark, badly ventilated little room. Crowded together facing the one-way glass stood the people that mattered, and the sheepish Donner. Finn didn't know the Lees, but he knew Brahmins, whatever the lighting and location, and introduced himself respectfully.

"I'm Lieutenant Ed Finn, sir, and this case has been assigned to me."

Tom Lee extended his hand, then introduced everyone in his courtly antebellum manner, impressing Finn considerably as he felt his hands being gently tied. The old gentleman's civil rights position being known and Fred Oxland being a political animal, this hiatus eliminated the surprise transition from civilized officers of the law to the gloves-off racist cops routine that he'd been building toward. Roughing up the suspect was the only point of his moronic assistant, but now Len Thomas would be treated like gentry. Hilarious.

"So far this man is our only suspect," he said in his soft, polite voice. "He was drunk when we picked him up a couple of hours ago, and I'm letting him have a few minutes' rest. I'll wake him up and get him talking so you can have a better look at him and hear his voice, and then I'll rejoin you."

Lee's views made things harder, but as a long-term Kennedy man, Finn sensed the man's enlightened spirit and appreciated the fine packaging. He looked something like the picture of FDR that Finn's father had left to him, and he doubted this classic Southern gentleman had ever experienced anything quite as seedy as this little world. Back In the interrogation room, he woke Len gently and asked the same questions he'd started with, leaving space for Len to ramble, letting those in the booth get a sense of his look, voice, and manner. Len's answers were impeccably illiterate, delivered in his slurred half-drunk speech, but consistent with the first go-round. On the other side of the glass, Tom Lee remarked that Len didn't look smart enough to get in serious trouble. None of them recognized Len except Holly, whose reaction was delayed, then perfectly suppressed.

"The gang was Hispanics," blurted Donner. "Knives, accents, cigar smell. I would say Cuban."

Keep thinking that way, thought Holly. She felt a nightmarish fear for Len Thomas, admiring this remarkable acting performance and very aware that any connection with horse racing would doom him. She also remembered the Hispanic groundlings in the McGoohey camp, guessed almost exactly what had happened, and was determined that Llewellyn Thomas should not go to jail for a damned horse. *Any* damned horse. She was clear on that, but how to prevent it wasn't clear at all. The police machine would grind away, and given time, even these local cops might eventually make his connection with that redneck owner. But since those perfect meetings at the G-Spot, Saratoga, and the Lantern, she'd been thinking that Llewellyn Thomas was somehow her man, or going to be, and these damned white cops weren't going to take him away.

192

In the Chief's office, chairs had been assembled by two young cops at the ready in the presence of Royalty. Not until everyone was seated did Ed Finn ask if anyone recognized the suspect.

"Just looks like some unemployed itinerant to me," said old Tom Lee, sick at heart with the loss of his splendid stallion. The other three nodded, and the party left, escorted now by the blond kid-cop who had questioned Len at roadside.

Alone with the family in the gravel parking area, Twombly couldn't hold it in.

"I'm Officer Daniel Twombly," he said, removing his western-style uniform hat. "I – I want you to know that I think I may have seen the suspect in the vicinity of Lee Farms last month."

Through their fatigue, all four looked at him with surprise verging on amazement.

"I haven't said so yet because I can't be sure," he added, suddenly confused.

Why was he saying this to them, when he hadn't reported it to his superiors and wasn't sure?

"The problem is, it could have been another Negro entirely. The man I saw was well dressed and sober, and he spoke differently, like he was educated. I haven't said anything to anyone else yet."

"If you're *quite* sure it's the same man," began Tom Lee with gentle firmness, feeling very old. "But if you're *not* sure, son, if you have any doubt at all in your mind – "

The last part was spoken with grave, unnerving judge-like emphasis.

"I thought I might have seen him once, but I can't think where," said Dixie suddenly. "You see something familiar about him, Holly?"

"I don't know – I don't think so, Dixie."

"I'm so damn upset I'm probably imagining it," said Dixie, at the edge of tears. "He really doesn't look like anyone in particular. Just some poor sonofabitch lost his job to some Mexican."

Lacking Holly's confirmation, it was settled for the moment, all parties accepting implicitly that black people saw each other more clearly than whites.

Now I've lied for him, she thought, walking through the

193

afternoon heat to old Tom's big Benz. Why? Chances are, it will come out, and when it does, I'll be out of a job, because this is horse business, and family business on top of it. Out of a job and no references, black and turning thirty. It had felt manageable until that suck-ass blond cop showed up, but now she felt fear.

"Dixie, you drive, I shouldn't be at the wheel," said Tom Lee as Twombly's boots crunched across the parking area. "I'm just so broken up I can't think. So damned sad."

"Holly, would you sit with daddy?" said Dixie. "It's lonely losing something you love, and Double-M was part of the family. Damn if I don't feel like crying myself." Then in a different voice: "Get in front, Donner."

Donner climbed in alongside Dixie wondering if he might possibly still have a job, or at least some decent severance. One incident in four years – that wasn't so bad, only just that the incident was on the big side. Probably never see the new maid without her clothes on again, either. Dixie drove quickly and smoothly back to Lee Farms, and Holly took the old man's hand with no sense of hypocrisy, liking him and feeling deeply for him in his pain. After a while it struck her that a black man involved in something so heinous as the kidnapping and death of a legendary horse, a Derby winner in the Bluegrass State would get a hellish sentence. Twenty years of bad food and confinement and Len Thomas would look and feel about like Tom Lee did now.

"It'll come to me," said Dixie. "If I *did* see that man somewhere, I'll remember. But he was so *ordinary*. Someone like that – it just doesn't fit. I wouldn't want him around my horses, no one would. What do you think, Holly?"

"Dixie, I wish I could help."

"Well, you are, Holly," said Tom Lee. "You're like family."

I'm a damn witch, thought Holly St. Cyr as she watched the rich greens of the countryside flow by. Picked it up from Cousin Gentian. I'm saying good-bye to my life, which I like more than I ever thought I could, including these really decent white people.

She gently squeezed Tom Lee's hand, and he smiled and nodded. Inside was a ever-growing fear as she tried to figure out some way to cover for Len Thomas. Get him out of it, somehow. God, but he was a smooth sonofabitch! What an actor. What a *man.*

194

Hundred and forty pounds of stress-tested balls. She remembered that funny message on his phone. Then she remembered leaving him that message in St. Louis, a call that could be traced to her, and eventually would be, if that soft-spoken big-city detective was as smart as he sounded. She'd be guilty by association, and it would look like an inside job. Both of them being black would seal the deal. But she felt safe for the moment with her hand warm in Tom Lee's, and she stopped trying to think practically. These people had changed her life, but hard as the Queen loved, she could hate harder.

Then it hit her. Once Dixie remembered where she saw Len, he'd be gone, and she was too. Dixie and that cute Princeton lawyer would send the pair of them up the river. Why not? They'd sure look guilty, which Len probably was.

As they drove up the pink, blue and yellow flower-lined drive she was calm, seeing it all as if for the last time, sharing a sad silence with Tom Lee. Then she saw that she could still come out smelling like a rose. All it would take was remembering Len Thomas from Saratoga before Dixie did.

21

The most significant moments of Paco's adult life had been his visions, many of them lost, leaving only a privileged, sacred feeling behind. Half awake in the rough purr of the Monte Carlo, he had another one, a very calm one this time. Very clear, almost a set of instructions, which was unusual. It was a magnificent vision of riches, revenge, and salvation. He would be his own man again. Pat McGoohey would never hear from Paco Gonzalez, because this new vision did not require him. What was in the container was priceless, and with Len gone, he was on his own. God wanted that jism follow a certain path, and that was up to him. Carlos was hardly a man yet, but he was book-smart, got things done, and he was a brother in *La Raza*. Good enough. And Texas was Mexican-friendly if you knew how to keep your head down. Dehydrated, crashing from drug deprivation, he was ecstatic, filled with this clear, pure, simple vision, so different from that one at Lee Farms. He slipped off, then woke in a little while, half delirious, suddenly so thirsty and hungry that he simply forgot about his band-aid stashes. Right now he wanted beer, several bottles of beer, and the kind of salty-greasy food that comes in plastic wrappers off convenience store racks. And a phone. Most of all he needed a phone.

"Stop next exit, Carlos, find a store and get a six-pack and some chips. Two six-pack, lotta chips, whatever. Find a place with a phone and get a lot of quarters. You still okay?"

"Yeah, for a while. What kind beer and chips?"

"Dos Equis, Corona, Heinies, just no Bud, different kind of chips, all kinds, like a party, right? And some sweets. Little cheese-cakes, pies, guava if they got it."

"Okay. But we gonna have to stop and rest pretty soon. I'm beat."

"Okay, I take over after we eat, you sleep. Two coffees."

He climbed into the front seat and rubbed his eyes, mind clearing, knowing exactly what he had to do for his gorgeous vision to become real. He sat silent for a while and another part of the vision appeared – a wild, simple, daring and dangerous idea to complete the dream. Make it absolutely, completely perfect! He scanned the searing afternoon with eyes that had never been weakened by reading.

"Up there – see sign? Gotta be stores, we get off highway, gas up again, check oil. An' get quarters – gotta be a phone there, too."

Exactly as he had foreseen! Opposite the ritzy Mobil station was a generic poor-people's station. He handed Carlos two twenties, got out and stretched. A few minutes later, pocket full of quarters, he went to the outdoor booth. His luck was still running, and his old gang-buddy Pete Suarez answered on the second ring.

"Hey Pete, it's Paco – "

Pete Suarez made a weary noise that lacked enthusiasm. Paco had crapped out as a protégé, and by gang law they should not be in communication. But that hadn't stopped Pete from selling him the rock, because Pete loved money and was family.

"Pretty early for me."

"Yeah, I know, man, I know, and not s'posed to speak with Clanton guys, but my wife is your wife's cousin, her bes' friend, right?"

This got an assenting grunt, laced with doubt. Pete's wife was a fearless hellion. If it got back that he'd let Paco down, he was in trouble. The grunts continued as Paco developed the plan.

"This 'bout me bein' in trouble because a stupid guy made a mistake, but is really about money. Six large –

"Like this, simple – you steal a horse and get it to Tijuana –

"Yeah, from my boss, who else? The little mare, Arabiche –

"I don't *care* how, and it got to be total secret from everyone where she goin'. *Total*. And *fast*. Like *tomorrow*. All you do, I call you couple times a day about nothing and when you got her there, you say 'let's get a drink,' an' set a time. Then we meet in Tijuana at the Golden Bowling Ball. But *Fast*. Fast as possible. You get horse in trailer and roll. Take a guy you trust, pay him good, make sure plenty of water –

"Sure I know Golden is queer place – perfect, they never look for us there –

"Six big ones. Half on delivery, half in six weeks – three and three –

"*Big* trouble, Pete – got to leave States kind of trouble, but big potential, too, very big . . . chance to score huge, *gigante*. Like Saratoga but bigger –

"Okay, then – four up front. But man, just don't talk to *no one*, right? No one ever know you even *hear* from me. Our secret, your money. I'm out of the gang – like what? Ten years? Amnesty, okay? When you hear the story you gonna shit from laughing, except maybe I got a manslaughter rap if this guy dies an' they figure out what happened. Accident, no intent, jus' bad luck. Hey, an' don' talk to my wife, my brothers, anyone. *Period*. Nobody, right? Just you and me. High stakes, amigo. Time is biggest thing. Every hour counts – I explain at the Golden."

Paco hung up feeling much better. Of the people he knew, Pete was the only one he trusted to get anything done, because he was so greedy. Six grand for a little job like this! But just a little more luck and he'd have the jism and Arabiche together, both outside the U.S., *and she would be in season*! The timing was perfect. He couldn't really afford the money, but the dream demanded it, and it gave him joy to obey it. As he was standing there in the sun, really satisfied with the call, he turned and felt the pain from his cracked rib, and had a sharp recall of the collision – bouncing off the little Ford, slamming against the wheel, the wind knocked out of him, the incredible stabbing pain that would not let him get air, somehow twisting the wheel and flooring it. Then came the slow, overwhelming sense of sin, as he remembered the great red-gold horse. The horse had trusted him, and from his, Paco's, stupidity, he had died. And just when his new career was opening up, just when he would be tooling the finest mares you could find. *Tragedy!* He would have to pray a lot, starting tonight. Only one thing to do, find a church, make prayers official. Donation and candles. Confession later, in Mexico.

In a daze of grief and guilt, he approached the Monte Carlo, which was rolling toward him from the pumps. When it pulled up he saw two six-packs of Dos Equis and a big box with more junk food, including half a dozen of his favorite little cheesecakes, plus ice.

198

"You got everything, you doing good. How long take us get to Texas? The border, El Paso."

"Wow. I dunno, twenty hours maybe. No license or registration, got to take it easy. Cop sees car like this, two Latinos – "

"Yeah, okay. Paint this baby, get fresh plates. Is *Classic*, previous owner going nuts by now. Grand theft auto plus interstate. Federal, Carlos, on top original charge – big rap for little beaners, eh? Lost Horse Register after us for sure."

In the large, clean, pale gray drunk tank were a teen-age white boy caught with a trunk full of white lightning, an old black alcoholic drying out after appearing naked on his front porch to relieve himself, two well-dressed white car thieves from Florida, and a young black groom from Windhaven Stables being held on a traffic violation. Each had been offered a clean walk by Finn if he could get Len talking. Len had guessed why they were all there, since suspects in major crimes and well-dressed car thieves don't go to the drunk tank. He lay on an upper bunk, stone sober, stomach griping, reviewing the hours since his capture. The one big plus was a heavy rain, which would have washed away his track from the wrecked Ford into the pines and his tree-top stash. He tried to recall exactly everything he had said, knowing the old dope conviction was meaningless and that his incarceration was being extended beyond normal limits, but he hadn't asked for a lawyer, preferring to appear ignorant or eccentric. When none of his cell mates suggested it, he knew the fix was in. The afternoon passed and the attempted conversations continued, some more than once. They were obvious and perfunctory in their probing, except for those of the senior car thief, a white college-educated thirty-year-old man who didn't like work.

Len accepted a cigarette from the car thief, thanking him profusely, and the man proposed going into business together when they were out, a ridiculous idea given Len's appearance and manner. Len nodded agreeably, looking doubtful.

"Don' wanna get mix up ennathin' lahk that, fella. 'Fraid to. Not born lucky, Ah'd get us all caught. Got a cousin he knows Ah'm here an he ain't done *nothin'*."

He carried on for a minute or two on the un-caring Cousin

John to whom he'd been a good friend and helper over the years.

"Maybe you got a future you don't know about," said the younger college-dropout car thief.

"Awready got that kinda fewcha. Cousin ain't said *nothin'*. Told 'em he knew me is all. You think they not lettin' him see me?"

Finn was following this on the speakers in his office as he went about his work, and recording it. Solely responsible for solving this crime, his hands tied behind his back by the Lees. Chief Fred handled only client relations. It was irritating, and so were Len's borderline moronic responses.

So was young Dan Twombly, standing in front of him now after finally working himself up to it.

"The individual is also physically identical to the individual of my report A4464 of that date," finished Twombly after an endless preamble in cop-speak.

"You can't accurately say that, of course, especially after the delay," said Finn in a deadly near-whisper touched with malevolence, regarding Twombly as an athletic-scholarship idiot. "There's no photograph, and you didn't measure the man or weigh him or print him. What you *can* say is, *closely resembles*."

"Very closely."

Finn looked at him with more focus, interested in the kid's feisty persistence. He was local and middle class, which gave him a certain unearned confidence, and he was ambitious.

"Very close resemblance you say. Despite which it took you forty hours to notice this resemblance. Are you sure they don't all look the same to you?"

The boy slowly reddened.

"I am not that kind of person. I played ball with blacks on our team, and we drank together."

"Smoke together?"

The big blond cop hesitated. "Once. When they made me a starter."

"Long as you didn't inhale – "

Humor was lost on Twombly.

"I did, sir, and I got real disturbed. Maybe it was being the only white person and not turned twenty-one yet. I got real disturbed, and they understood, and then I saw why it should be illegal."

"For white folks, anyhow."

"No kidding, Detective Finn, I wouldn't be here without this strong feeling."

"I hope not."

He paused and began in a less acerbic tone. "Well, there's something about this Len Thomas that gets under my skin, too, and I still don't know what it is."

"How he speaks and dresses and carries himself, it's all different, but I – "

"I'm not spending this time with you thinking it's wasted, Twombly. We're both suspicious of the man without any evidence to go on. But I've been listening to everything that comes out of his mouth, and it's very consistent. I've got your description of the incident, read it very carefully. Your report describes a very different kind of man. Clean, educated and well-spoken, papers in order. This man's wallet had nothing, as if he'd been rolled. Takes a professional actor to be two completely different kinds of person convincingly over any period of time. We've held him going on two days and he's the same now as he was when he got picked up at the crossroads. Nothing to connect him to that car, either.

"I also checked out the registration you recorded that afternoon," he continued, "and the credit card was phony. There was some serious planning here, and then that accident and the horse being killed – "

"That's right," said Finn softly. "Possible insurance case. Or sperm not motile, possible erectile dysfunction."

Or the horse was gay, he wanted to add, but this wasn't Boston and Twombly was the wrong audience. "But you being so sure now that you saw this man, that could be useful. I can't hold him much longer otherwise. Any lawyer – "

Bursting with insight, Twombly appeared about to levitate. "He never asked for a lawyer, and *anyone* knows the court has to give you one!"

"Or he's waiting for his cousin to step in and fix it. Probably been helping him out of scrapes for years. So you write me a new report dated 0800 today, carefully stating your belief that this is the man you saw, why you think so, and that while his speech is different, it could be the same voice."

"Well – just barely, Detective."

"How old are you, Twombly? I need grounds to hold the man. I want to see what kind of lawyer shows up if his cousin gets tired of this. But time is on our side as long as he's in custody. It could be argued with merit that he should be released, so let me see a draft of that before you submit it. I know what it needs to say. Patriot Act gives us more latitude."

"Boy – this is just like *Law and Order!*" exclaimed Twombly reverently. It burst out of him with complete sincerity, as if life was finally measuring up to the dream. Finn's smile developed slowly as Twombly was exiting, a difficult smile to control, diverting him completely from his leg and taking him close to a stifled laugh. Len Thomas was not kosher, and that should come out, given time. By bending the truth, Twombly would give him more time.

Ah got to lie down an' res' mah stomach, whined the voice from the speaker. *Cain't do nothin' with this food.*

Alone again and looking up at the ceiling, Len thought about those two clowns he'd sent to get a pint of cream who ended up killing the cow. No one had informed him of Missile Man's death, but it was all around the jail. Was it possible Paco had had the foresight to milk the cow *first*, and if so, would that priceless sperm be kept on dry ice? Maybe yes, with conscientious Carlos. And Paco would probably have some money and a fresh car. Fine. But Pat McGoohey would eventually find out what happened and might send a lawyer, which would be the worst possible thing. He'd do it out of Irish honor or he'd do it to keep him from talking, but unless he was thinking clearly, he might do it. Which would be disaster.

"*Thomas!*"

"Yeh, up heah," called Len from his bunk in a weak voice.

"Detective Finn wants you."

It was the heavy stupid voice of the second interrogator.

Mouth slightly ajar, looking as decrepit as possible, Len climbed down and followed him, admiring the jail as they walked. Fresh paint everywhere, didn't even *smell* like a jail. As they approached Finn's office, he heard faint echoey voices talking about wild cards. Voices from the drunk tank, where a poker game was starting up. The voices disappeared as they passed into a pale green corridor. Was Finn late at the switch, or was that calculated? Len had expected a mike, but the confirmation got to him. He was under a microscope, running out of time.

The detective was at an old oak desk, and did not speak to his fellow officer, simply nodding at a gray metal chair for Len while he filled out a form. The big cop left, and Len sat looking at the floor for several minutes thinking about the computer keypad, sitting like a deadly weapon on a slide-out panel originally intended for a typewriter.

"Paperwork," said Finn in that quiet, focused voice. "That's my downside. I notice you kept notes on things."

There was something about the way Finn kept going back over the obvious that led told Len every word was being taped. Just one inconsistency could do it. Or his little black book. His one big mistake, not putting it in the evidence bag.

"On'y way I can remember stuff," he said, laboriously methodical. "Taught me in school, on'y thing any use mah life. Fum school Ah mean."

Finn's reply was almost openly amused.

"We checked you out, working back from that drug conviction. Nothing since then we can find so far. You did well in school, Thomas. I'm from Boston myself, and I know that was a good school."

Len shook his head wearily, as if at a hopeless misunderstanding.

"Yeh, well, not much racial stuff in the halls. Mah record not so good as it looks. Hadda get us through, black kids – you could read, they puttin' you in good classes an' give you a break. Tutorin'. Good example for others. Ev'body knew. Ah like readin', no trouble readin' mah whole life, officer, enjoy it. Mother taught me at home. Cereal boxes."

Finn smiled, noting the subtle adjustment to fit new information.

"You never went to jail for that possession, although it was upheld."

"That school again. English teacher was nice man. Gay but

okay. He come down an' talk for me, see. Always gave me good grades but nevah laid hand on me. Mistah – cain't r'member his name. Mus' be gone now. Wrote pomes."

But as the machinery ground forward, eventually there would be his military record. Quick promotions, more bad news.

"I don't think you're anything near as dumb as you act, Thomas. I've got a deal for you, and I think you'll be interested. Whoever stole that horse, I think they picked you up along the way and made you some kind of lookout. We combed the area for a cell phone or walkie-talkie, but no luck so far. Next we'll check service-provider records, which we can do under the new laws."

Way ahead of you there, detective.

"You know what I'm saying, Thomas. You're very clean, except for that old conviction, but this good high school transcript makes me think you're hiding something. Like a good mind. You were different when you came in."

"Was drunk. My cousin ain't called, I guess?"

"No, and we aren't going to disturb a man with a sick wife for no reason. He confirmed your identity and employment to our satisfaction, even knew what you drink. Why haven't you asked for a lawyer, Thomas? It's free, and you've been here two days now."

"Ain't *done* nothin'! You think Ah trus' some lawyer y'all find for me, all these rich white people lookin' t'lynch someone? Y'all cain't prove I done what I ain't done – Ah don' need some crooked court-lawyer."

He expelled air and righteous indignation before continuing more calmly.

"What this *deal* you talkin' 'bout?"

"You weren't a player in this caper, and that's who we want. Turn them in and you walk, no legal proceedings, no record, gone. Think about it."

He paused and continued in a different tone.

I Have to wonder how you got mixed up with a bunch of Hispanics, Thomas. They can't be migrants, the job was too slick. Got to the security system."

"Ain't mixed *up* with no Hispanics, don't know any Hispanics person'ly. Got drunk and got lost is all."

" Well, what about this "H" in your book? Comes and goes. First turns up when you were visiting 'Sara' about a month ago, right?"

Sara. Saratoga.

"Thought Ah tole you, but issa a lady, a good lady. Don't need none of this any more than me. Ain't doin' that to her."

"We'd just want to talk to her briefly."

"That be the end of her rep'*tation*. Rep'tation all a woman got."

It was a very stony wall, backed by an angry stare and vigorous nod. Finn gave him a long, quiet look.

"Thomas, you just don't sound like any Boston black man I ever heard – "

"Ain't *from* Boston, mother from Georgia, Ah tole y'that. Move to Boston an' then come back summers. Already tole you all that. Mama talk country an' it rub off. Taught me to read, though. Cereal boxes. Not stupid."

"Oh, I don't think you're stupid, Thomas, but I don't believe that line. I'm keeping you a while longer to see what else comes up. Computers find everything, just takes time."

"Ah don' nec'sarily b'lieve *you*, off'sah. You got all these rich peoples on your case an' your boss want results, so Ah'm your result, don't matter what Ah done or didn't do. What about these Hispanics – how come you ain't talk to *them*?"

"What Hispanics are those?" half-whispered Ed Finn.

"Ones you jes' said was behind it all."

Furious with his slip, Finn felt his face tighten.

"Just a theory. You make yourself comfortable here with us, Thomas," he said in a friendly voice full of jailhouse irony. "You'll be getting your own cell; you're a material witness as far as I'm concerned."

"Got to be some law, false arrest or somethin'. Drunk and disorderly all I did. No 'resistin arrest' or ennathin. Overnight, thas' one thing, three days – "

"You are free to ask for an attorney at any time," said Finn, cutting him off and speaking with slightly more firmness. "Do you want to call your cousin?"

"No thanks, he prob'ly thinkin' bout *his* rep'tation. Sick

wife enough, don' need mah bad luck. He wanna he'p me, he do it his way."

Then an idea, a real one, his first since the crash.

"Maybe he findin' a *good* lawyer fum a *org'n'zation*. *Cullud* org'n'zation. Mah cousin John *intelligent*. Very intelligent man. He maybe know some people he'p me out, jes take some time. Time he got, 'count of you, D'tective."

It made sense. Finn felt a power shift, and trouble on the way. He silently reviewed the elements of the situation without any change of expression. Nothing useful from the microphone, first of all. And not giving up the name of that woman – that had to be respected. Smart or dumb, Llewellyn Thomas had *character*. Most important, he was probably right about that quiet clear-speaking cousin. John Thomas could be letting this simmer, talking with like-minded friends and lawyers, burning up the phone lines. There were at least three powerful organizations that would see this bluegrass horse theft the way he did himself – not the work of an itinerant black laborer. Too big. More likely an inside game. Insurance. Attracted to Dixie, Finn thought her capable of anything.

He sent Len to a single cell, getting less comfortable by the minute. Where the hell was Dan Twombly? How long could drafting one short paragraph take? He'd end up having to rewrite it himself anyway, and he might need it any time now. In Boston he'd known a judge he could discuss legalities with, but he was on his own here. It was barely lunch time and Finn wanted a drink.

She couldn't do it. She had to do it. She owed the Lees; they'd earned her loyalty. She was half in love with Len Thomas, and he had not. Hadn't even returned her call. She couldn't hurt Dixie like this; she had to speak out, because the Lees were what she had. And Dixie would remember where she'd seen Len sooner or later and put it together. She had to lie for him, because whatever had actually happened, he was going away for many years if she didn't. But she didn't owe him her life. She owed her present life to the Lees, and she was a person who paid her debts. And Dixie loved her as much as she could anyone but her father. And maybe a real special horse.

Would Dixie choose her over Missile Man? Holly was too shaken and desperate to chuckle aloud, but recognized her real self in the impulse. It settled her down and got her out of bed, but she was having to think through things that she'd do automatically every morning. Her face in the mirror was about as usual, but her composure was paper-thin as she wrestled with this decision and her eyes were tight. No question the compote would need to be strong this morning. Between the bourbon Dixie was getting down and the extra sleeping pill, Holly knew she'd be in terrible shape, talking about the effects of time on the female body before she was fully awake, and the pain for Daddy Tom. And her poor beautiful Missile Man, on ice now, yet to be buried. How it all began with Saratoga, every single bad thing. Then she'd talk about her exercise bike, and when she had herself together, she'd attack. That would take about an hour and a half and require more than a target of opportunity, but that didn't signify for Holly St. Cyr, because it wouldn't be her. Something had clarified and simplified her world. Len Thomas had engineered something *huge*, something that got out of control and went off the rails like the train in that old Richard Pryor movie, *Silver Streak*, plowing flat-out-Whammo into the station, people running in all directions. Careful as he might be, they'd find a crack if they held him long enough, which they would, and that quiet Detective Finn would be prying him open by any available means. Then a Soviet show trial, Southern style. But if he had an *alibi*, a really solid, unshakable alibi, they'd be out of luck. If, for example, he'd responded to her phone call and had miraculously appeared to fuck her brains out – well, that would leave her out of work and in bed with the suspect. Who fascinated her.

Bottom line, Dixie owned Fred Oxland, but that wasn't enough. She had to use that power, and Holly had no idea what might happen, because she was considering betrayal. The worst kind, because their periodic bed-togethers were a major element of that woman's tight-wound life, the only times she ever really let her hair down. Little Isaac had told Holly this act was normal, a routine feature of The Life – how the ladies relaxed. It wasn't unpleasant, and she'd been off men since Isaac, so she'd let it happen a couple of times at school, and she'd seen Dixie coming from day one. *Who's zoomin' who?* That had been the only question.

At compote time, her employer looked like grim death, eyes haunted, flesh sagging, each of her fifty years making its statement in a sketch of wrinkles-to-be as she lay corpse-like in the beautiful room they'd put together. Neither said a word. When Holly arrived with the coffee, she felt something. No change in protocol, pure intuition.

Boy, does she ever know me, thought Holly, and a great tide of fear passed through her as she poured the coffee. *And she's ready to kill.* Holly's rock-solid hand started to shake.

"What is it, Holly."

"I can't – "

She put down the coffee, suddenly unafraid but sad beyond belief to be leaving this behind, this life where she'd learned so much and been treated better than anywhere else except for her own home. Then she poured the coffee.

"Tell me honey. You're in worse shape than I am, and that's unbelievable. What've you done, girl?"

Holly nodded, the coffee ignored after the first sips, both of them wide awake. The kindness made it worse, and she began to tear up, something that never happened.

"Holly, don't cry. You can't have done anything that bad."

"I've done something so disgraceful I would never tell anyone on this earth, except that someone else will suffer terribly for it if I don't."

"I can take it. After what happened the other night, I can take damn near anything."

Dixie paused.

"You're not saying a word – well, it's got to be a man. You haven't got yourself pregnant?"

"No. It's about that man they've got, that they picked up after those people broke in. I know who he is and where he was, and he had nothing to do with it."

Another Dixie appeared, ice forming despite her attempt to maintain.

"Well, who *is* he, Holly? He doesn't exactly look your type."

208

"This is really, really – embarrassing."

"He's a relative, I suppose. We've all got them, Cinnamon – you should see some of the Lesser Lees, as Daddy calls them."

Holly's head, which had been gradually dropping, lifted with an effort.

"Worse. That night I went out and got drunk. This Len Thomas – he's just an ordinary person, practically an illiterate, but after a couple of men tried the usual number, he sat down and said I looked pretty sad. He said he'd like to buy me a drink but it would have to be just one, because his boss owed him back pay. I felt sorry for him, thinking what it must take for someone like him to approach me at *all*, and then I saw that it hadn't been hard for him, because those weren't his motives. He just – felt sorry for me."

"But Holly, even allowing for the situation, the man could barely make himself *understood*."

"He was still drunk, didn't you see that? I lied to you – my cousin has cancer. I was drinking my way through the news, and he was really sympathetic. Quiet. He understood how I felt and got it all out of me."

She paused and sighed.

"I'll be gone this morning, Dixie. But you might as well know I also brought him here, to the guest cottage, and when I sobered up I saw what I'd done and sent him away."

"Does he mean that much?"

Dixie paused, about to come down hard. Holly stepped inside and hooked deep to the body.

"His rotting in jail does."

Her voice was thoughtful and measured, and it was the first time Annabelle Lee Dixon had ever heard the real, straight-on voice of Holly St. Cyr. It was in no way impolite, but detached and impersonal, and very solid. It was convincing in a way that left the older woman without a response. Then she rose to it.

"That doesn't have to happen," she said, smelling something unrevealed. Furious but cunning, she was controlling herself and conveying what felt like human warmth. This apparent compassion nearly undid Holly, who again found herself close to tears.

"It's over," she managed. "I know. You were the biggest thing that ever happened to me, you and your father, but it's over.

I know that, and I'm so sorry."

The truth of that didn't come to her until after she'd spoken. The Lees had given her love, let her really know them, done more for her than anyone but her own mother.

Annabelle Lee Dixon lost track of her suspicions and took pity for a moment.

"Honey, I know you can't do anything about it and I know you never meant harm. Hell, I married a fag. I'll notify the police; they shouldn't be holding him."

She paused again, and suddenly her voice exploded into a roaring firestorm.

"You made a *terrible* mistake that night, broke a *written agreement* and a code of *honor*. You lowered yourself and disgraced your kind. Stupid, Holly, *stupid!*"

Holly's utter lack of reaction stopped her. *Your kind* – how had she let *that* out? Something flickered in Holly's eyes but she didn't respond. A hot screed of domineering aristocratic contempt was fighting to get past Dixie's throat, her famous word-whipping, but she mastered herself and spoke with deadly calm, as if washing away some dreadful filth. Then her voice rose again, soaring out of control.

"I can't even look at you! Can't stand the *sight* of you! I don't know *what* I'll tell Daddy."

With the thought of her father's pain, she was ready to release the full screaming rage, but again Holly was a step ahead, standing now, contrite, composed, rock-calm. Detached and immovable. Dixie saw it when their eyes finally met, anthracite and blue ice.

"I'm packed, Dixie. I'll drive down to the police station and answer their questions. I have to."

This shut her opponent down instantly, because it involved Lee Farms and her father. Dixie thought quickly, her eyes sharpening. Enough bad had happened. To Holly, her eyes were a pair of blued-steel ball bearings with a clear message: She was absolutely, totally finished anywhere this woman's reach extended.

"It's best if I call first," said Dixie in a cool business-bitch voice. "I'll do it right now. Stay here. I know how I sound, but we did put *so* much into you, Holly." Her voice was shaking now, as if

210

things could go any direction at all. "I'll be *damned* if I know how you could've done it. I could rip your eyes out but I still – damnit, I can't *trust* you now."

Before she completely lost it and began weeping she picked up the phone and dialed. There was a long chasm of waiting silence during which they did not look at each other.

"This is Annabelle Dixon, and I need to speak to Chief Oxland right away.

"Good."

Another pause.

"Brace yourself, Fred, because now you're down to no suspects at all. My Holly was in bed with that fool that night. She's coming down, and I'd appreciate it if you didn't take a lot of her time. She's goddamned embarrassed already, and doesn't need your boys around watching –

"Right, of *course*. But she's *not* lying, and what would be the point – she just confessed to *me*, for Christ's sake, lost the best position she'll ever have –

"Use your *head*, Fred. Another day or two and that cousin of his will show up with a for-real ACLU lawyer. SPLC gets involved, N-double-ACP, and next thing the county is sued for false arrest, unlawfully extended incarceration, civil rights violations. This county will look like some kind of Jim Crow paradise, which Daddy Tom will just *love*, being a member of two of those groups.

"You want to kill my Daddy? After what he's done for you?

"Yes! Of *course* you should let him go, you brainless townie! He's a *time bomb*! You don't think that cousin is just sitting there with a jug, do you? You've had the man going on three days for nothing but drunk and disorderly and supposedly resisting arrest, which I doubt. The delay is giving the lawyers time to get coordinated –

"What we *want*, Fred, and I am *really* losing my *patience*, is for this to *go away* in about as long as it takes Holly to get there –

"Do the damn paperwork *yourself* if you have to! I've got enough on my mind without having to defend backing you for Sheriff again when we've got that bright fellow from Boston and young Dan Twombly right there, who both could do the job –

"*No!* You've had the man too damn long. And no evidence at all, any kid lawyer could rip you to *pieces* –

"No, I'm not angry, just *busy*. You don't want to see me angry, Fred – you'd know the difference right away. Think about the consequences. Think of your boys.

"Right. Right. She'll be down in half an hour to pick him up, and it better not take more than five minutes."

Holly sat in silence as her employer hung up the phone, reached into a bedside table drawer, past her revolver to her checkbook.

"You don't have to do that, Dixie, I'm really – "

"Yes, I do. You're going to have a really bad time thinking about how nice it was here, and this will help you time to get through that. I know you, and I know you appreciated everything. They were some great times. So now get the fuck out, because I'm about to start crying. I still love you Holly, but it's over."

Jail, bank, gas, out of state, thought Holly. And hope to hell I get it all done before that detective turns something up on his computer.

22

In Chief Oxland's office were Holly, Len, and Twombly, with Twombly looking at Len hard, arms hanging, long neck exposed. Finn had opted out. The Chief was announcing his unconditional release, but Len was looking at Twombly, dreaming. Between Boston race fights, MP training, and necessity, Len knew how to seriously injure a larger man, and now he felt his right hand forming into a peculiar flat fist, taught him by a Korean in a bar. Single accurate shot to the throat and Whitebread would be injured and helpless long enough for Len to bring his knee into play, and then the elbow when the head came down...

Unfinished business. He hated the kid and couldn't let it go, almost vibrating with fury. What was Twombly doing in the room, anyway? But there was the Chief, affably signing papers and apologizing, with Holly standing there projecting cool sanity.

"Our mistake. No hard feelings, Mr. Thomas. Wrong place, wrong time. If you'd accepted a lawyer it would have been quicker. And congratulations on leaving that addiction behind."

The man was a whipped dog, but he had to drop that one.

"Not'tall," responded Len graciously. "Ah knew mah innocence would come out. Y'all jes' doin' y'job."

And they left, Len still choking down his rage, now against Oxland as well as Twombly. *White men, cops,* he thought: *Pricks with ears. Pigs.* Although it *had* been a completely criminal enterprise with him in charge. But then outside and free, he felt the sun charging his batteries, and it seemed as if the weather was encouraging sanity. As they got in the car, his murderous mood was gone.

"We've got to go back," he said quietly from the passenger seat, as if Holly showing up and getting him out in nothing flat was all part of a plan to which he'd had previous access.

It's him, all right, she thought, picking up on him. Back to the scene of the crime like something out of a book! I ought to stop the car and get out or drop him at the bus stop. I've just thrown away the best job I could ever hope for, and he's a criminal, pure and simple. I've been a fool.

"You're sure we really have to do this?"

"I am, Holly. I left something very important there."

"Do I get to know?"

"Better not. Something goes wrong, you just got involved with a bad man and didn't have any idea. No need to know, that's what it's about. Protects you.

He paused. "That addiction he wanted you to know about – I'm no addict, Holly. They found cannibanol in a hair sample. Can you imagine that? Should have had a haircut. That was the next diversion if I lawyered up."

There was a brief silence before the words came out of her mouth, very clear and quiet.

"Tell me something, Len – do you *like* me, or am I just another stroke of luck? I just threw away a nice life. I mean – you sound so goddamned *impersonal*."

He opened the sun roof before replying.

"I not only *like* you, Holly Sincere, I'm totally crazy about you. None of this could have ever happened if I hadn't met you. I'd've never run risks like that."

"Not that you're admitting anything specific."

"You were so cool and sexy on the dance floor that night I thought I might have a brain hemorrhage or something. Saw you that next morning and I just knew I had to change my life in a hurry. I like everything about you, even your little Kraut-green car."

She knew it was true, and a great weight lifted.

"Okay – now we have to go by the gate where the accident was. You can drop me off a little before it."

"This is really pretty crazy, Llewellyn. Shouldn't we just get out of this town before they find some rope?"

"We will. Isn't this a beautiful morning, Holly? Nothin' gonna go wrong this morning, weather's too nice. Okay now, before we get to the gate you stop and I jump out, and I want you to go up to that turnaround spot about two miles up the road. You can back up in there on the dirt road and be out of sight, this little car will blend right in. Just wait there twenty minutes. Then come back, and slow down right here, and I'll come out. I put in my bag in back, climb in, and we skedaddle. If I'm not here, just keep going, turn around again and come back in ten minutes. It may take a while to locate my belongings."

"I still have to go into town, Len. I have to cash this check. I set it up by phone, won't take ten minutes. I can move my accounts later." She hesitated before the kicker, delivered with a kind of suppressed giggle. "I got ten thousand dollars hush money to get out of town."

"Mighty white of her, considering the type of low-life you be hangin' with. Okay, we're here. I'll be as quick as I can."

In the darkness of the pines he lost his sense of direction immediately, climbing through the slippery needles on dead reckoning in a zigzag pattern, slipping and sliding, looking up the trunk of each tree. It had been night, he'd had a concussion, and nothing was coming back. Only that he'd taken one hundred stumbling steps up the incline before climbing the tree. He worked his way back down, his neck stiffening from holding it tilted back so long. Rattled and sweating in the humidity, he started back up the hill. Nothing. The duffel bag was definitive evidence and he had to have it, but there was almost no light at all in the dense-packed pines. Ten thousand identical clusterfucking conifers. Okay, start again. Probably been here half an hour already.

And there it was, closer to the road than it ought ot be, a strange, unnatural black bulge midway up the trunk, barely visible, looking like some ugly sci-fi thing about to release android babies. His heart leaped, and he struggled up to painfully rip away the layers of duct tape with his ungloved fingers, an endless process that finished with the bag bouncing off his head on its way down to the pine needles, where it slid halfway to the road. Back on the ground, he opened it, stripped to his shorts, then slipped into his khakis, a blue sport shirt and loafers. Then he shoved the old clothes in the bag and made his slippery way down to wait behind a tree, fingers numb and sore from ripping at the tape, hangnails everywhere. *How had he made it up that tree with this heavy bag?*

He stood there with it for a few minutes, slightly back from the road, invisible man enjoying the smell of the pines, feeling restored, sweat drying, sun beating down through a gap in the pines and charging his batteries. Then he saw the khaki-green Beetle and stepped out. He emerged, hands grimy but otherwise completely respectable as he slipped smiling into the passenger seat.

"You got really good timing, Holly Sincere."

"St. Cyr, it's Creole. In the glove box there's a bottle of something that will cut that resin on your hands, and some little towels. The big bottle is lotion."

Texas was full of dry ice, bull semen being always in demand. The teenage Hispanic phone operator liked Carlos's polite young voice and his earnest, innocent California civility. When he told her it was an emergency, she looked up the nearest supplier for him, hoping he'd ask her for a date.

"This one is right off the Interstate," she added. "About twenty miles." It was a sleepy mid-afternoon and she really felt like flirting.

"Thank you," said Carlos formally. "Is there a distributor in El Paso too?"

"Six," she said playfully. "Is that enough?"

Then she gave him all six numbers, which he wrote on a pad, virginal, and oblivious. He told her she had been very helpful, and drove on to the distributor with Paco still asleep, took some money from his pocket, and had the box refilled.

"You just about made it," said the attendant. "You don't wanna push it like that. That'll be forty dollars even."

When it was all taken care of, he woke Paco, who placidly accepted a Coke.

"We in Texas yet?"

"Yeah, little way in."

"Gotta re-up dry ice."

"I just did, you were sleeping."

"Still asleep. How far to El Paso?"

"Lotta hours. Plenty of dry ice in El Paso, too."

"But then Mexico," observed Paco. "Means we got two days max if we don't find dry ice down there. I gotta call Pete again, remind me later. *Importante.*"

216

Then he waited for a question about why McGoohey's jism-jug was going to Mexico, but none came. After a while he became curious. Had the kid's mind had been damaged by so much school, or did he understand exactly what was going on?

"I got to sleep pretty soon, Paco."

"Right. I'm feeling okay now, I drive through the night. Doin' good, Carlos."

With his assistant asleep, Paco stopped to call Pete, who was in bed with a girlfriend, trying to get her to play Russian roulette to distract her from his ongoing case of coke-dick.

"Good timing, Paco," he said. "You got something new? Still same deal?"

"Right. I jus' take a minute now, but is super-important, maximum importance: Get the horse there fast as you can. I don't have a cell phone yet, but I stay in touch 'til the Golden."

"I got two cells, you got pencil and paper?"

"No, man, not in my office right now. Gimme one, and *get to the Golden*. You gotta to stay over, I pick up tab. Horse is only thing that matters. And time. You miss it, big problems. An' remember, *plenty water*."

"Gotchu. Four when I get there, right – plus expenses?"

"*Si, si*. Jus' get horse there. You can get her tonight, easy. Probably Stall 38. Dark bay, little star on her forehead. Arabiche her name, she look up if you say it."

"You don' change, Paco. Okay, gonna do it tonight, I need to get out anyhow. Maria's brother next door gets in, he can help me. You pay all expenses, two guys, call it three hundred a day. You don't show, you better stay in Mexico about ten years 'cause you twisting my life, bitch."

"Is no game, Pete, an' I grow up, not your bitch. You think I call you I don't have the bread? I got it. Big situation, can't explain now. Jus' get her there an' meet me at the Golden soon as you can. I'm with my cousin Carlos. You remember him?"

"Yeah, skinny kid, big ears. Fucked his sister in eighth grade."

"Like butter," announced Paco, returning from the sale of the Monte Carlo, feeling invisible among El Paso's Mexicans.

Carlos saw the light in his eyes as they sat in a crowded little bar. Not painting the car had been high risk, but clinched the sale for the buyer, who had raised the money via his extended family. It would be all through the *barrio* in a few hours and someone would smitch, but they would already be part of a stream of laborers starting funneling across the border into Ciudad Juarez, where he would find someone to drive them to Tijuana very fast.

"*Corona!*" he called to the bartender, who responded quickly to the big juice coming out of those crazed orbs. The last two bandage-stashes had celebrated the deal, and Paco was on top of the world. Then his mood changed.

"You know something Carlos – high now, feels good, but I never do what I done that night except for blow. Cocaine work with Devil, set you up to do crazy things. No blow in Mexico, Carlos. I do that again, you pull my coat, kid."

A little later, standing in line and waiting to cross with the priceless pack on his back, he felt satisfaction and pride in having followed this new vision exactly as it came to him. The car money meant that he could pay Pete's first installment in cash, but the bills, mostly fifties and twenties, were an enormous wad. Most of it went under their insoles, and they walked strangely, but Paco was untroubled. They could arrest him, and he would go peacefully in the knowledge that when called, he had answered the vision loud and clear, no hesitation. With Len gone, the link to McGoohey was severed, the day was perfect, and the crossing blessed, because no one gave a damn about Mexican labor going home for the night. And Pete would not insist on the whole four thousand. Saratoga had raised Paco's status, making his *compadres* more respectful and cooperative. Maybe three grand, plus an interest in the foal. Pete would see things his way when he heard what he had, which would leave them with plenty by rural Mexican standards. Enough for the winter, easy.

Day max to get there, he thought. *'Biche still in season few more days, got turkey baster.*

Finn entered Oxland's office silently, closed the door quietly behind him, and leaned against a wall to ease his throbbing leg as he watched his boss filling out a report on an old electric typewriter. Sensing another major event coming at him, the Chief took time to collect himself. When he looked up, Finn's eyes were radiating a cold blue anger, and there was no professional respect in his quiet voice.

"Told you to stall 'em, Fred," he said in his half whisper, causing the Chief to lean forward very slightly. "Here's your smoking gun."

He placed a fax alongside the typewriter.

"That *Negro* has been in California for years according to his driver's license. Semi-fake name, took a while to find. Next thing, we're going to find out he's in the horse game. Count on it."

The Chief listened silently, not moving, still recovering from Dixie. Finn seemed to be looking both at and through him. Oxland did not want him to resign, which looked possible. The fax machine started up again while he read the one in his hands, still silent.

"And we will eventually get it all," resumed Finn, "because my nephew out there is a good cop and knows how to find things out. Phone records, bank accounts, credit cards, and so forth. But Thomas will be gone. The only thing might be the airlines. That nose of his is a giveaway. Black couple, easy to spot if they're dumb enough to travel together."

There was another little silence while Fred perspired in his icy office.

He tore the original fax in half, and then repeated the process until the stack was too thick to continue. Then he put the pieces in an envelope, which he sealed, and put in the breast pocket of his sand-colored uniform jacket. Finally he spoke.

"*You* are a big city detective with big city experience. *I* am a County Sheriff, which means I'm a politician, and a longtime friendly acquaintance of the plaintiffs. I'm also a family man with no place else to go, and what's in that envelope might could blow my clothes off and leave me stark naked with a real bad burn like those people at Hiroshima. Can't have that."

Finn looked at him silently, deadlocked between contempt and something more humane.

"That woman finds out we had the perpetrator, and that he arranged the theft of her priceless stud horse *and* her little brown girl – well, she might just walk in and shoot me, and get away with it probably. Or she might rather hold me up to public ridicule, or have me fired, or just have my kids cut out of the lives they have now, causing my wife to leave me. No end to what that blonde bitch would do. Only child, Daddy spoiled her."

Ed Finn nodded equably. He had not done well as a family man; it was his weak point, the one thing he'd failed at that bothered him. And Oxland had done well in this most basic test of a man. Was he being a politician now, or a desperate man trying to be as honest as he could? Oxland's voice was calm and firm.

"My thinking is that this Len Thomas is about the smartest man we've ever had to deal with here, and he's goin' to evaporate with that girl. Probably on a plane to Canada by now, or Mexico or France, but not California, from what your fax said. We'd be chasing our tails, making headlines and looking like fools."

He shifted in his chair for a more extended talk. "Tell me, Ed, you've had a year now. Do you like it here?"

Definitely a loaded question, and after half a minute Finn thought he got it.

"You mean, do I want to be Chief if anything further goes wrong?"

"Uh-huh. That's what she'd do. Invite you to cocktails, and if you do okay, then try you at dinner. Then find some super-specialist to fix your leg, price no object. She's gonna be bored without that Holly, and she likes intelligent people."

"Felonious Finn, the Boston Lapdog. I don't think so, Fred. That Donner had it right – Cuban terrorists undermining the American thoroughbred establishment. Good man, that Donner. Anything from Miami?"

"No. Or should I say *nada*?"

With the suggestion of a smile in Finn's eyes, the Chief swiveled his chair to open a cabinet in which stood a half quart of Tom Lee's hand-labeled bourbon, along with several glasses and a large bottle of Saratoga Springs mineral water.

"No ice, Ah'm afraid."

"Just spoil it," came Finn's whispery reply.

As they sipped, the Chief relaxed by degrees, realizing in retrospect how frightened he'd been, and what a relief it was to

220

know he could trust Ed Finn. Tearing up the fax, he'd been seeing the pieces circling the bowl faster and faster, pieces of his life swirling down the tubes. Out of habit, he now pulled out the new fax, which contained further dangerous information. He folded it up, thinking that the fax machine was his enemy now.

"How'd you know?"

"Dan said he thought it was the same man he talked to at the roadside last month, and he wouldn't let it go. Dan Twombly's your problem now. Ambitious, got his family behind him."

"He'll let it go now. But you knew anyway, I could see you worrying at it."

"That beautiful woman go to bed with drunken trash? Not likely. And those guys I put in to get him talking never got to first base. He was as patient as – he was *abnormal*. With them, with me. Never asked for a lawyer, even Dan noticed that."

Oxland paused, and Finn's voice finally was up in the fully audible range.

"Even blind drunk that's one smart educated woman. Naturally refined. But that wasn't him, of course, it was an act. Best I've ever seen."

He paused again. "I see you just got another fax and put it away. Let's just make sure whatever else comes in, it doesn't get into young Dan's hands. He'd *love* to be Chief, that I can tell you. Went right around us to the family that first day."

"That so? Well, I've got an urgent need for a man down in Belleville right away. Field office, local part-time deputy assistant will report to him, help track down people growin' marijuana down there, other than his family of course. It's a real emergency, this marijuana business, I'll get him moved tomorrow."

He paused. "I ain't said so, but I'm much obliged, Ed. You're a real member now, I'll vouch for that. I'll get Joanie to sew you up a sheet and you can join us in the Ceremonies down Georgia. My cousins say us police officers make the best members – starch their hoods to keep 'em straight, hold up in court when things go wrong."

Finn finally smiled openly.

"Sure had us chasing our tails, didn't he? It's only been a couple of hours – they're gonna disappear, you know. Sure you don't want to put out an APB?"

"Not with that Holly involved. Dixie was real sweet on that girl, kind of an open secret. Disappear is exactly what I want them to do, and my two boys getting the kind of education that gets you out of law enforcement, and Joanie not crying cause her friends cut her dead. Just a god-damned horse for Christ's sake. Offer you another?"

"Thank you, I will."

"I'm going to have Mama Coolidge send some chicken and yams, which I hope you'll be joining me for."

"You bet, Fred. Wasn't he something, though? Just sat on his cards, never blinked once. He's right up there with those fellas did that Brinks job, and that was a big professional group with time and resources."

"Well, he had those Cuban masterminds to direct him, of course," said the Chief thoughtfully.

"Or Nuyoricans or freelance Mexicans or your Columbian drug lords – "

"I believe that Donner fellow had it right. Cuban Cartel."

23

Alice walked right in while McGoohey was on with the Commissioner, picked up some papers on his desk and glanced at him as if he were some kind of canine excrement. It had been nearly a week since the boys disappeared, and they both knew it, and he was still pretending nothing had happened. Before she ever met her fiancé, Alice Smith knew that you don't leave your wounded behind. She'd been born knowing it, which was one reason Major Jack couldn't get enough of her. It was completely logical to Alice that McGoohey's favorite horse had been stolen. Payback from the Man Upstairs.

As she walked out, McGoohey felt a delayed impact. Something definitely disrespectful about her presence and attitude, walking in like that on a private conversation. First 'Biche, now this, from his *secretary*. As if he was on notice. He felt it in his guts. Just a little bad luck could end his new life as an upwardly mobile citizen and father-to-be. No initiation into the upper money-eyed class, no induction into the community. No becoming a member, respected rather than feared. Alice's contemptuous departure brought fear on a whole new scale. His entire world could implode, doing irreparable harm to his loved ones, along with his own rotten conniving self. All because of a silly game. And Alice, knew everything. Closer to Jasmine than her mother.

The Commissioner was still talking into his ear. McGoohey had no idea what he was saying, except that it seemed to go on indefinitely and require no immediate response. Then he realized that the man hadn't heard about the theft of Arabiche and wanted back into McGoohey's box for her next start. He didn't bother to explain; it would be in the papers next day.

"Fine, glad to have you."

Len warned me, but I fuckin' had to do it! What a fool!

Somehow he got through the call with the Commissioner before another unexpected thought hit him: *God forgive me.* If he got out of this one, no more stupid games. Be a father, act his age. Be a father and hope to God he was better at it than his own. He closed his eyes and tried to right himself. After he'd pushed some more paper and was feeling normal, Alice was back, with the same bad-smell expression. *Rats from a sinking ship.* But this rat wasn't darting down a hawser or leaping into the sea. Alice Smith was impaling him with her gaze like a note on the out-spike. He put down the phone and she spoke, openly observing him, unafraid.

"Well, they got Len."

In the silence he realized that it was really happening, everything he'd feared. They looked at each other and she watched his eyes squirm. He took it, unable to speak or settle himself. She let some time pass before continuing in a clear, deliberate way, as if for the record.

"They *had* Len, that is, when a woman came and sprang him, about an hour before they traced him here. Now they're both gone."

She watched his reaction. His thinking was slow and fuzzy like after he got sapped at Spuyten Duyvil. He felt like a fighter on one knee trying to guess how long to the end of the round. She was doing this deliberately, he realized dully. So used to jerking people around he'd forgotten what it was like to be on the other end.

And I was worried about a fucking horse –

"Who told you this?"

He tried to sound irritable and dominant. Her smile was borderline insulting.

"A little bird that sounded like a cop whispered it in my ear. I could just barely hear him. He didn't want to talk to you. Just pass the word. No number to call back, caller ID was blocked. They just want you to know that *Llewellyn Thomas is no longer a person of interest.* Those were the exact words, I wrote them down. I said I was sure I didn't know what he was talking about. Then he said something about friends on the force. Not to call them. Then he hung up."

She paused and looked at him squarely, like an old-fashioned parochial school principal regarding a thick-witted delinquent. Then she explained it, in case his shocked state might interfere with his understanding.

224

"You're supposed to make it history. There was no question he knew who sent them."

This was true, but the reference to his friends on the force was a lie to shut him down before he did more harm. McGoohey's blank, cornered stare confirmed her suspicions.

"Somebody fixed it," he said, sounding very dull. "Nothing about Paco?"

"No. Just to shut up, basically."

Telling him to shut up in his own office, ready to walk if he called her on it.

"How do you know all this, Alice?"

She gave him a variant on the dog-shit look, and his voice became quiet and deferential.

"Alice, I may really need your help and advice. The boys went out East – "

Her eyes stopped him like a wall of ice. It was as if McGoohey Construction was suddenly a union shop and she was the shop steward. His fears metastasized.

You sent them to do your dirty work, you sneaky overgrown Mick bastard, said Alice's fearless eyes. *Now you want to lie about it when you should be down on your knees thanking God.*

She turned away sharply and gracefully, leaving him with his brain stuttering.

At her desk thinking about it, Alice realized that Padraic McGoohey III was no longer fun or interesting. He'd crossed the line. But this ugly-slimy-lying-bullying Pat McGoohey had managed to get her close friend Jasmine with child, and Jazz would be needing her support. McGoohey Construction would continue to be her base of operation.

Right. And exactly what the hell *had* Patsy got himself into? Was the theft of his favorite horse some kind of godfather revenge thing? Another mystery. Disgusting, yes, but the man was not boring. And it was time to talk to her best friend again. Childless herself, she was deeply caught up in Jasmine's happiness, which now entailed saving her contemptible spouse.

Holly woke up looking through the windshield into a starry night, Kentucky far behind, feeling comfortable and protected by the big white Lincoln he'd rented. They'd been on the empty Interstate holding a steady seventy for many hours, music just audible on the radio. Old R&B. She'd curled up and fallen asleep by sunset, exhausted by her day. By what she'd actually gone and done. She noticed a faint warm odor and felt safe in the quiet hum of the big Lincoln. The night had gone chilly, and rather than close the windows, Len had spread his jacket over her. With his smell, which she liked. Tough-minded as she usually was, this thoughtful gesture undid her. She saw that it was ten-thirty, and that she had a perfect angle to study Len Thomas at the wheel in shirt sleeves and suede vest, relaxed, remote, driven and preoccupied, all at once. He'd looked the same before she fell asleep. What was he thinking? Wrong time to ask.

What Len Thomas was thinking was that he might very well be some kind of psychopath. Not a nasty one, no urge to kill or torture, but with the benchmark chill. His lack of emotion all those hours in custody had come too naturally. Likewise his non-reactions to Finn's little surprises. With a little practice, he might be the type to beat a polygraph. His only emotion had been that violent desire to severely injure kid-cop Dan Twombly. When he'd read about this condition years ago, he'd had plenty of lively fears and other emotions. All over the place emotionally, but then he'd turned a corner somewhere. And while his chill was indispensable, a long-cultivated thing, he didn't like it – it was too automatic lately. Where did that come from? Could a single act tip you over into that world? Like Saratoga, for example. Dirty, Jimmy had called it. True, but an act of love. His jailbreak, his shot at the big-sky world outside that little window in the wall.

The reward for that wild act was curled up next to him, silent miles rolling by while she slept her way into his world. The one good result of McGoohey's relentless campaign to breed his mare with the perfect stud. McGoo had left him no time to think. Followed by lots of think-time, as Finn acquainted him with a new level of fear. He functioned well enough, the new Len, but he was a mystery to himself. How did he rate Holly St. Cyr showing up to save his sorry ass, for example? Hadn't been too careful what he wished for up there in Saratoga, other than this woman. And change – he'd really wanted change that afternoon before they met.

226

Got plenty of that. He could barely remember his life before Saratoga.

"I'm awake, Len. You must be exhausted."

Emotion, he thought happily, feeling it surge through him. Lots of emotion, nice and warm. Liberating.

"I'm fine, Holly. I got enough rest in that *facility* to last me a long while. There's coffee, bought it while you were sleeping – it's in the caddy."

Black, the way she drank it, in an insulated cup, hot enough to enjoy. She sipped, then passed it to him, and he had a swallow.

Time to open up a little, man. Woman just saved your life.

"I was working with fools," he began. "No choice in the matter. And I had nothing to do with the death of that fine horse, by the way. But I keep thinking that's all history, and how wonderful it is to be in civilized company at last."

It struck him that he was going to have to break another of his rules.

"You saved my life, lady, and you gave up a whole lot to do it. A good life. Those were very nice people. I've got some idea what that must have taken, and I'll never forget it. Changed my way of seeing things."

"Speech after long silence," she said quietly.

"Yeats, I believe."

It was *unbearably* romantic. She went wet and then thought she might actually *cry*, feeling so alive she could hardly stand it.

"I'd offer to drive a while, but I'm not sure I'd do a very good job," she said unevenly, remembering how quickly they'd picked up on each other while dancing. "We should find a place to stay," she added, hoping he'd get the point.

"Nice to be with someone who has some common sense," he replied.

Common sense. She laughed to hrsolf, knowing she was completely out of control, capable of anything, her life in the hands of this suave, considerate criminal.

"Most people would say what I did was stark raving mad, Llewellyn."

"No, it was class. I never did that much for anyone. They had me, Holly. I've got a clean record, haven't been in trouble since my teens, but once the computer put me in California and the horse game – end of the road. That Detective Finn was gonna hook it up."

Clean record. Her heart danced. Dixie wanted this all to go away, and Fred Oxland was Finn's boss, so it would go away, and Len's record would stay clean. But she said nothing, and the silence stretched.

I've got to talk to her, thought Len uneasily, accustomed to women who talked too much. I'm being impolite. And she's got to know the truth, because otherwise this thing will turn ordinary, just another game, and that's exactly what I need to get away from.

"Some things you need to know," he said in a calm, level voice.

"Why?"

A lot packed into that one.

"You earned it, and I don't want to hide things from you, which is my natural way. I'd rather tell you now, with this fine night all around us."

"I didn't do anything I didn't want to do," she said. Then she got it.

"You want to start fresh."

"Need to."

She said nothing, so he continued. "Cousin lied for me when I was in there and took a big chance, might have lost his farm. And has a sick wife. They talked it over, and decided in favor. When I saw how *truthful* it was between them, I stopped feeling superior. I was envious."

In the background was the maroon murmur of Baby Face Willette's Hammond and the deep indigo guitar lines of the young Grant Green. Another good man gone too soon. The tune ended and he was ready to talk, but he couldn't bring himself to the heart of the matter, which was his dream. What he wanted and believed in.

"What happened in Saratoga – I couldn't take it anymore, how my career was going. Something about that place made me see it – my life, and what I could accomplish with the guy I worked for. That morning at the training track before you came, I was a million miles away, thinkin' about Europe. I was there a long time with the Army. Color wasn't so big over there – lot of expats. The

French – history stays around there, it's kind of in the air – Josephine Baker, Louis Armstrong, Chester Himes. Lotta great musicians. Lot of black Americans just happier there. First day in Saratoga I was thinking about going back – making a break and getting back there with my savings. Why I ever came home at all, I'm not sure. Just wanted more excitement. Money, nice ride, nice crib, big stereo. Big Apple action."

I am dancing around and talking shit. I've just got to go against my nature and come out with it.

"So next morning in this state of mind, standing there with McGoohey, the both of us see the both of you. Owner is thinkin' if 'Biche pulls third in this big Handicap, he can break into the line waiting for Missile Man's services and get us a super-foal. Very smart man, but doesn't get some things at all. My part was for 'Biche to finish third. McGoohey then, with his unique personal charm, speak with your boss. Except that our pony was never going to finish third in that field unless you bought every horse, which couldn't be done."

Holly smiled, thinking about the scene at Spuyten Duyvil.

"Boss lookin' at Blondie and seein' his triple-crown foal, Ah'm lookin' at Blondie's executive assistant. You and Blondie side by side – both head up, straight back. Made me feel like an indentured servant. My life didn't fit any more, felt like a strait-jacket. No future. Man buys horses with problems, I'm supposed to fix them. Point is, *you* were *marvelous*, just like the night before, and I was gonna get your attention."

She felt it coming, had a sip of coffee.

Just say Jimmy used a machine! No!

"I doped our horse up there in Saratoga, Holly."

Okay, got it out, take a deep breath.

"Hadn't ever even thought of doing such a thing before. Terrible act, could've cost us everything, risked a good friend and a horse I really love."

He paused, not noticing her silence and unable to see her shocked face.

"I had to break out. So I did it, made my little mark, became this trainer who wasn't completely unknown. Paco knew, but I kept it secret from the others, including the jockey. Good friend

Jimmy. He didn't know until it was too late to pull out. I told him because he might have to hold her, because a no-name beating the Dark Lady was gonna bring the sky down on Chicken Little and his boys.

He paused and gathered his thoughts.

"You did that partly because of me?"

"I'm not gonna lie. Just might have been fired if we didn't get that third place, but – yes, I wanted your attention, lady."

"I'm not easily shocked, but you just did it, Len. I'll get over it, but I don't like it. And it's ugly to say, but I can't help thinking that your employer hired you knowing you'd be in love with the job, and he could get you to do things a white trainer wouldn't."

She paused to think. Len was silent, absorbing the blows, and started again.

"I guess. We're both risk-takers though, it's just in us, Holly, and Pat's not all bad. But whatever Blondie did to him, she fractured his ego and made him crazy. One day I made a joke about a Special Ops raid – just steal some sperm if she wouldn't take our money. He picked up on it and wouldn't let it alone. We ended up talking numbers, because if I refused I could be out of a job, as you suggested. Lot of other trainers available. And you know what – the best part – "

"I was getting tired of my job, too. And just so you know, I've done a few things in my life that nobody knows about," she added gently. "Not that I'd ever think about doing them again."

"Or telling me what they were. So now you know all about me, and I've got nothing on you."

"Way it's supposed to be," she replied, with a smile in her voice. She was extremely pleased with his confession, flattered that she'd been part of that crazy Saratoga equation and completely possessed by the wild, hot, insanely romantic fact of what she was doing with this man, how tight they were already. Minutes passed, and she found herself almost shivering in anticipation.

Out of nowhere the music was suddenly replaced by a hair-treatment ad, and then a preacher program. *Saturday night?* thought Len, amazed. Must be midnight, Sunday morning in the provinces. And this preacher is moronic, got to be the dumbest nigger ever make a buck on religion. God gonna save listener and make him rich if he just send this idiot some money. But he was said nothing. Women could be strange on religion. After a blank half minute Holly broke the silence.

"I don't know about this station," she said, in a demure but hilarious and intimate way that he found attractive in all sorts of ways, starting with sexy. Yeah, she was sexy, and it was all going to happen in a new dialect.

The minister burst into song. Trashy romantic for-profit gospel.

"And this music just isn't very *religious*," she added. "The man sounds like Howard Budney making a move on the Virgin Mary. I'm afraid I just don't like commercial music."

She paused. "But I do like money."

It made him laugh, his real unrestrained laugh, heard only by intimates with whom he felt very safe. He changed the station, and after another few minutes Holly spoke again.

"Llewellyn Thomas, I'm a high-strung woman. If you don't get us out of this car and into a bed I might be going into convulsions on you, mister."

Spoken lightly, but it seemed to Len that the top of his skull might lift off with sheer lustful joy. The heat in her voice was very clear, the words popping out with an uneven urgency he knew and relished.

"You *horny*, girl," he said lightly, as if dreams came true for him all the time. She moved closer and placed a gentle hand on his thigh as a sign appeared:

Food Lodging Gas

"*Praise the Lord!* Should I let you alone so you can drive?"

"I can handle it. Jesus that feels good! Yeah, you better stop. Sure you don't want to pick up some eats?"

"Don't be funny," she said, removing her hand, overcome again with that heady sense of being borderline irrational. And beautiful. That was it – he made her feel beautiful. Beautiful enough to do anything and get away with it. In a Motel 6 if fate so ordained. Len demurred until he saw the Luxor, off by itself on a little knoll. He neatly parked the big white Lincoln by the entrance, visible from the desk.

"When this unruly thing here go down, I can walk to the desk without embarrassment. I'm gonna putter 'round the trunk till I subside, get the bags out."

"I'm gonna fuck you cross-eyed, Len Thomas."

"Don't talk like that, just makes it worse," he said, popping the trunk and walking back to rummage around in its new-car aroma. Some minutes later they entered the lobby with such assurance and composure that the manager was actually very pleased to see these obviously respectable and well to do persons of color. Only one night, but in a very expensive and usually vacant suite. A teenage white boy ran out for their bags.

In the immaculate cream and beige suite, a more composed Holly showered at length, steaming the room thoroughly for her pleasure. Then she flipped on the exhaust fan and reappeared in a turquoise robe to briskly announce that it was his turn now, and that he would find a surprise waiting in bed if he was quick about it.

"Yeah, Ah'm not so musky as you think, mainly it's that special jail soap, smell makes it easier for the dogs if you break out."

"It's *terrible*."

"You think I don't know that?"

His voice was civil, and at the same time faintly condescending, as if it ought to be obvious he'd intended to rid himself of that strange stink, had done everything right so far, and was not to be called out for no reason. She found his directness very attractive, and he smiled wickedly, as if he knew. As he entered the bathroom she tossed her robe over the chair next to the bed and climbed in, as ready as she'd ever be, but feeling a little strange and shaky. She'd had little real experience with the opposite sex, and was feeling hot and shy at the same time. When he walked into the room stark naked and unabashed with an easy smile, her mind cleared, and she saw Llewellyn Thomas as God made him. Good shoulders, tapered body, smoothly muscled, with a confident, straight-spine posture. Hung.

"I'm not really queer, in case you were wondering," she said with a smile.

"Me neither, far as I know."

She let herself laugh as he slipped between the sheets and lay beside her in an unhurried way.

"I do like enjoy oral sex as an entrée, though," he said, running a warm and thoughtful hand the length of her body. "Ease the transition."

"You're terrible. *I* like to *kiss*, Llewellyn," she said primly, slipping a hand gently under his testicles as she kissed him, causing the blood to rush down from his brain as if escaping an evil place and setting out for Mecca. Then she spoke in the hot, tight voice that said *ready*. Ready, but not incoherent.

"Here's what we're gonna do, Len," she said softly: "I'm gonna roll on my back and you're gonna climb on top like a good missionary. Then you're gonna fuck me every which way you can, like I've been thinking about ever since we danced that night."

"Good plan," he said in a voice that melted her.

Now I'm his woman, she thought afterward, wide awake while he slept with a faint purring sound. *It's a done deal, and if I lose him I won't be able to bear it.*

III

24

Arriving mysteriously in the dusty little town one morning in a shiny silver SUV towing a trailer containing a very good-looking horse, the immaculate Americanized Paco was welcomed as a prodigal son. Well dressed, accompanied by a rich, smiling ally and a neat young assistant, he was impressive to the simple farmers of Tica de Gualpa. Old people remembered his mother's courage after his father's untimely death. His cousins were proud to know him, and a legendary party followed their arrival. By late afternoon the town's one cantina was packed and roaring, with shouts, toasts, earthy laughter, and local music racketing off its blue-tiled walls. It was selling more cerveza, tequila and food than it did in a normal month. The town's leading citizens surrounded Paco and Pete at the bar, densely flanked by lesser parties. As Pete bought endless rounds, Carlos was settling Arabiche in a little shed that opened onto pasture. Unable to gain entrance when he returned to the jammed cantina, he sat patiently on a small bag in the street, observing from a distance and trying to make sense of his last week. Paco had launched him into adult life on a path his mother would never approve, and the longer he put off calling home, the more he feared calling.

Inside the incredibly hot bar, everyone avoided the busy open-flame kitchen in one corner and toasts flew freely at. Countries, flags, presidents, governor, and mayor were toasted, along with Paco, Pete, leading landowners, the cantina's owner and other worthy people, places, and principles. Slim, dapper Pete, dressed in the latest baggy-but-tailored all-black gang gear, his gold on neck, wrists, fingers, and left ear, cut a swathe. There was a potentially awkward moment when, expecting to exercise his *droit du seigneur*, Pete quietly propositioned the mayor's daughter. She smiled, disappeared into the raucous mob, got in her father's old Beetle, and drove to the next town to stay with her sister.

At the bar, Paco was holding up his fist for all to see, along with Paco's, both with the signature tattoo-dots on three knuckles. He was in no rush, assuming that the woman who had caught his eye was off to relieve herself and prepare for him. By now he had broken out a large bag of cocaine and was introducing the leading citizens to this wonderful new thing. A blue tile was placed on the bar, and the lumpy substance was crushed by Paco, breaking his pledge to Carlos and availing himself generously while trying to think of a way to get some for personal use when Pete left. By five the women were gone, and the sixty or seventy village men had been eating and drinking for half a day, going outside to relieve themselves, vomit. and return, driven on by this remarkable substance, drinking with renewed energy, everyone talking, sweating, and laughing, crowding around the suave and sociable Pete, who topped off the festivities gang-style.

Having identified the leading local criminal, a fat, smiling bully, eager to be recognized, Pete had smilingly and generously fed both nostrils of this very large thug four or five times, then jammed his black nine millimeter into the fat neck. The room went dead silent while Pete made an announcement in a loud new voice, looking into the man's face at very close range, but glancing deliberately into the crowd as he asserted Clantonian dominance.

"Thees guy, my frien' Paco, he is under the Protection," he explained slowly and clearly to the frozen Pedro. "Unnerstan'? Clanton protection.

"Your name is Pedro, I know what you look like. Small eyes, fat belly, big nose, black tooth, big guy. Bigger they come, right?"

Eyes staring, the man produced a tiny nod.

"You say something?"

"Si, si."

Pete paused again, enjoying himself and displaying his shining, perfectly capped teeth.

"Anything happen to these guys or the horse, *anything at all*, I come look for you with automatic weapon, and I don't come alone. Horse belongs to rich American, I am responsible, Pete Suarez, captain of Clantons."

As the gun appeared, those near the doors had already begun to make themselves small and melt away, and by the end of his statement, the remaining crowd was watching from a safe distance. Those who stayed were treated to more tequila and cerveza, and the remarkable white substance that had these stolid farmers lively as yearlings on a snappy morning. When no shots were fired, the others reappeared to partake.

Paco could not remember the end of the party, but he was clear on a few things. The disappearance of the Mayor's daughter, never identified, had put Pete in an evil mood. His final words to Paco had announced his intent to collect the balance "soon," and like a complete snake he had failed to slip him a little something to help him through his hangover. It was going to be a bad time, because Pete had insisted on the four thousand plus expenses, leaving Paco nearly broke.

The cool sunless air was damp with fog, confirming Len's suspicion that northern California was overrated, Henry Miller notwithstanding. Holly had wanted to see the wine country, but as they approached it another kind of fog was rising between them, increasing Len's sun-craving. The day was turning into everything he had always feared about domesticity, and he felt himself being infiltrated by sinister black male attitudes regarding women, or *bitches* as they were called by its advocates. He felt this nasty version of the eternal man–woman standoff setting up shop like an evil asteroid hiding behind an innocent, romantic moon. *Can't live with 'em, can't kill 'em... Be a bounty on 'em if they didn't have the pussy...*

Just a mood, he told himself. Stupid rap-think. The white whale drank gas and put miles behind them and Len turned his thoughts to McGoohey, who was probably in the dark about everything other than the death of Missile Man. He'd be going nuts by now, running scared, since everyone involved worked for him. Scared and unpredictable. Not contacting him was bad politics. Suspicious. But Len doubted he'd be given credit for standing off Ed Finn or for the risk he'd run. He could maybe just catch Pat unawares and do some kind of act, but he didn't feel like tomming the bastard. Not since that jail. And he was damned if he'd return the $10K advance or the remaining expense money. Reengaging with Pat would be dangerous, with both of them on short fuses. So stay away from Pat for now. At least until he knew what happened to Paco and the jug.

Still need a plan, he thought, staring at the road. His previous evening had produced no information. He'd dropped Holly at the stylish and pricey Chateau Marmont, where she'd watched celebrity revelers from a balcony overlooking the pool while drinking Tequila Sunrises. It left her in a bad, jealous mood, with a real but undiscussed hangover. While she was drinking herself into a bad mood, Len had begun the night by slipping into his apartment and burgling it, packing two large suitcases with essential items. His favorite clothes, true ID, books, a brick of hundred dollar bills sheetrocked into a bathroom wall behind an Elaine de Kooning sketch of Thelonious Monk, his favorite CDs, and the Jimmy Winkfield photo. Hot, endless work in barefooted silence, stripped to his underwear, unable to use the A/C or lights, which would reveal his presence. He did not want it known that he was back. After sweating in silence for several hours, working by flashlight, he'd sponged off with cold water and dressed himself for a Saturday night. His cell phones he left in the shoes where he'd stashed them, still fearful of an electronic trail. After getting his bags into the trunk unobserved, he'd dropped in on several unhappy bookies who owed him for Saratoga. Then the Friday poker game, where he intentionally lost about a hundred dollars while listening to gossip and relating a plausible tale of Big Apple activities to cover his absence. These were old friends who didn't know his employer or ask questions or talk much.

Then Crazy Pete Suarez had showed up, completely lit, handsome and paranoid, celebrating some secret event, making everyone nervous with his glittering eyes. It was clear that Pete had an appointment with disaster sometime soon, and everyone knew he never left home without his *nine*, as he called his Glock, which might come out any time he was hit by a spell of paranoia. The cocaine would come out regardless, and to refuse it would be taken as an insult. Like Dutch Schultz and King Lear toward the end of their reigns, Pete was big trouble, and no one wanted to be around him. Listening to him brag about Clanton growth that would soon eclipse Bloods, Crips, M-13, et al., Len was careful not to win and endured Pete's repeated compliments on Saratoga until they began to verge on insult.

"Ah rely on your friend Paco," he replied with respect. "Number one guy, comes to horses."

Pete smiled broadly and agreed, and Len left wondering what Pete knew that he didn't.

On the way to the Central Avenue crap game he had his one idea: *Call Alice*. If anyone could read the situation it was Alice Smith, who tracked more or less everything in McGoo world. Whether the boys had showed up, or if anyone was asking after Len Thomas, for example. In his black book he anagrammed her name and wrote *Licea call soon she hot*. But McGoo might be in the office and pick up the call, and he had a dangerous intuition, often knowing who was calling without benefit of Caller ID. A pay-phone call followed by a hang-up would make him suspicious, since these antiques were used mainly to conceal identity. And he couldn't call Alice at home because he didn't have the number, and there could be a thousand Alice Smiths in the greater Los Angeles area.

"Are we hungry?" Len asked cautiously, eyes on the road ahead, peering into patchy fog.

"It's almost two – let's see what we can find."

Her tone suggested that no harm was intended by her silence. Maybe just homesick, premenstrual stress, constipated, or bang-bladder from the nonstop action. Ought to give that a rest. Maybe just noticing who he was and what she'd got herself into. The stately Lincoln continued along smooth winding blacktop toward Wines of the Native Peoples, and they drove into a pretty little town with a good looking restaurant. High Ground. It smiled at them, yellow umbrellas over white tables on a tile patio. Just down the same very clean street, a Cell City sign caught his eye. Paving his escape with apologies, Len placed Holly at a table and asked her to choose a wine while he took care of some urgent busi-ness. Then he was gone, with his first idea of the day. Holly accept-ed his abrupt departure, glad to see his energy back.

He returned soon with a pair of throwaway cell phones, making his amends with a pair of not inexpensive silver and turquoise earrings. She smiled at him over a glass of Merlot.

240

"I didn't like leaving you alone last night, but I just couldn't expose you to the risk," he said. "And that was impolite just now, running off like that. I saw a way to clear up something important." He paused to check her expression, which was fine. "Thinking about it, I see that I maybe could use your help to pull it off."

"Well of course, Llewellyn, I'd be delighted. It's a big change, the Bonnie-and-Clyde lifestyle, but of course I want to help. What do you need me to do?"

"McGoo's office manager is a close friend, someone I really trust – Alice Smith, middle-aged white sweetie. I hesitate to call the office because – this is pure intuition – if she's out and McGoo picks up, well, the man is pretty intuitive. He doesn't exactly think like a white man. Or a black man, or any kind I know of. Extremely sharp where his interests are concerned, that's the best way I can put it. Whole thing last night was to check things out and stay off his radar."

Ball in her court, he picked up his glass and had a sip to cover his expression.

"So let me guess: If he should pick up and hear *my* voice saying I seem to have a wrong number, it wouldn't register, and it wouldn't be a suspicious hang-up. And if *she* answers, I ask if it would be a good time to talk to an old friend she hasn't seen for a while?"

"Your slave," he said. "From day one."

"Good to know. Is this call to Alice immediate or does it come later?"

"Wine first, definitely, and food. If you click with Alice, the two of you might want to talk a while. She gets the word on McGoo from her very close friend Mrs. McGoo. Alice is smart and cool. Good person, the best. I trust her."

"What don't I say?"

"Where we are. That's the beauty of the cell phone. But you should let her know you're placing the call to, umm, spare possible awkwardness. She'll get it. I think Alice gonna want to get t'know you. You could even be calling *for* me because – of a situation I got caught up in."

"I know what to do. I used to do this stuff for Chubby all

the time. Second thing, you should be out of sight, baby-cakes, no distraction. Maybe in the bar."

"Sounds good to me. I was running flat out last night, and this wine is putting me away. You could call from right here and just nip away at this nice wine while I nap in the car."

About twenty-five minutes later there was a tap on the car window, and Holly climbed in the passenger side with two large cups of coffee and a burrito, looking tipsy and serious.

"Okay. You're gonna love this. Your ex-boss has no idea where you are, and just suffered the loss of his favorite horse, the notorious Arabiche, stolen right out of the stable. He had what Alice called a 'strange reaction, almost no reaction.' Seems his wife's expecting, and that's the big deal in his life now. Meanwhile, some gangbanger named 'Pete' has been talking a lot, and every-one at the barns knows he did it. She got that back-channel from a friend of Paco's, and the boss doesn't know anything about it.

Len nodded and his mouth tightened.

"Remember what you said about no more mysteries?

"This Pete is Paco's old gang buddy. Showed up at a card game I dropped in on. Riding high, and it wasn't just the blow. Hardly looking at his cards, and definitely checkin' me out. Just stole the horse that made my reputation – my meal ticket, how he'd see it – and then playin' voyeur, dyin' to know how I'm takin' it. Pleased with himself, real gangster. Lucky they die young."

He went silent for a long stretch, sipping coffee while he thought.

"Horse gotta be in Mexico," he said with finality, as if talk-ing to himself. "Pretty big country," he added after a while.

"Well if this Pete stole her for Paco, and Paco is like most peasants, he'll go for family."

"Paco's not like *anybody*, believe me. But you're right, fami-ly first, and I know the town he came from. He's got the horse, and I bet he planted the seed. Carlos not dumb, we lucky Carlos with him. Ah'm wakin' up now. Little more burrito, and then back on that nice road. Paco's crazy, by the way. That accident at Lee Farms – typical Paco. Higher Power said take the horse. He has visions. Sometimes knows what's going to happen, or what has to happen. Sometimes not."

He started the car and drove onto the road before continuing.

"Crazy, but also a horse genius. Sound like I'm jokin' but I ain't. All kinds of genius, right? Math genius, musical genius, word genius, physics. There's a mule genius in Faulkner, one of his easier-reading books. I'm real good with horses, but Paco's *magic*. Never wrong. Very pure soul, not like me – why we need each other. Paco is an Indian, and that signifies. He's all from the heart, and the horses know. "So tell me more about Alice and McGoo and let me steal your coffee."

"Fine. Alice didn't exactly say McGoohey was baffled about the missing horse, but that's how it sounded. Or muffled. No big bang, like she'd expect."

"Nobody at Patch Stables gonna tell McGoo a thing especially with Pete involved. Everyone afraid of Pete, with good reason. Too bad, 'cause I'd prefer boss-man chasin' Pete to thinkin' *I'm* the thief, which might occur to him."

"That's right, lover."

"Nah – he knows me better. Lotta people interested in 'Biche since Saratoga. By the way, Pete Suarez is real nasty. I doubt you ever had contact with people like him. Vicious, bad to the bone, a killer. Very sick man lookin' for trouble, insult people for no reason, hurt women for fun, hard drug aficionado – "

He glanced over and saw her face. "That wine put you *away*, babe."

"Well, I was hung over and hiding it. I'm okay though, Len – I learned to drink with the Lees. I'm feeling better now. And I think the Native Peoples are gonna have to wait, 'cause I've done my wine for the day. But tell me something – that little run last night – how can you be so sure it won't get back to your former employer? You keep telling me the man is no fool."

"All those people I saw were old friends, except for Pete. No connection to McGoo, and they wouldn't do that. I've never done anything worse than beat 'em at poker when they insisted on it. If Pete stole the horse he's gonna stay away in case someone ratted him out."

"You know this cracker better than I do, but I saw a very nasty animal. Low. Took on three men and sent one to the hospital."

"Okay, agreed, but he's not all bad. Gave me a very decent salary and a *real* big break. 'Case you hadn't noticed, I'm black, but he made me trainer, right? And stuck with me."

"Yes, I noticed. I noticed how he used you, too. But I see it. The Lees aren't bigots, far from it, but I doubt they'd consider a black trainer."

"Or a black jockey, even though a black jockey won the Derby two years running back in the old days. Jim Crow union put him out of business."

"Really. People don't talk about him."

"Right, they wouldn't. Winkfield, Jimmy Winkfield, a.k.a. the Black Maestro. Successful trainer, too."

And I've gotta live up to that, thought Len Thomas.

"Winkfield was a hundred years ago, and all we've done since then is go backward. But Pat McGoohey came along and gave Llewellyn Thomas a break. I can't fault the man too hard."

"Yes, I see that." She paused. "Something I left out from drinking that bottle of wine, Len: Detective Finn talked to Alice. Not to McGoo, just her. He did his homework, knew all about your boss. Explicitly said for him to stay out of it, let it die. By the way, Alice was pretty happy to get my call. She figures he sent you guys on this mission, which she hasn't figured out yet, assuming you'd take the hit if things went wrong, and he could deny everything."

"Plausible deniability, right? Man reads the papers."

"Not very well, or he'd know about RICO. Conspiracy law says he's in it up to his little pink pecker if it ever comes out."

"Know what, Holly – I haven't smoked anything since I left that jail. I miss it and I don't. Just as soon have a glass of wine. Strange."

"It's me, I'm your good influence. You're supposed to notice. Len."

"Definite influence. Pervading. Military call it infiltration."

Respect for Paco diminished sharply when he rented a cheap little adobe house without plumbing. Like most of the people, animals, and chickens of Tica de Gualpa, he and Carlos were thin and hungry, but English-speakers were needed at the sneaker factory in the next town, and they were hired immediately. Under a corrugated iron roof in a half-acre shed so hot that people passed out, women did piece-work while Carlos read packing slips and Paco trundled loads over the packed-earth floor. Everyone worked ten-hour days, and drank a mandated two quarts of water each shift. The work was not hard, but it was not manly, with the women at the machines free to say anything, which they did. Paco was still crashing the first two days, and Carlos's virginity was clearly at risk. On their fifth morning, there was a very loud hammering-chattering noise, and a big army-surplus helicopter delivered a cadre of corporate suit-soldiers from across the border who went roamed the factory like Dobermans, recording production, examining records, checking for theft, and tapping notes into little electronic devices. With them were a *Federale* and a government official. Paco was too depressed to care, but the following morning Carlos had gone home to his mother.

Alone in the adobe hut, flat broke and deeply shaken by this defection, Paco was out of dreams, his days melting into a serial nightmare, each episode ending as he fell into a nightly torpor. The hut was soon filthy because Paco could not afford a servant, and doing work that women had always done for him was out of the question. Instead of providing the final vision required to lift him from this dead end, his mind drifted. Carlos was forgiven and appreciated: Without him, that seed would never have made its way across the continent to fulfill its destiny. How many useful things he had done! Now that Paco had lost his assistant, his relatives ignored him, and he was smoking the worst weed he could remember in his entire life. All from the sin of killing a great horse. And Len – why did he keep forgetting that?

Sundays he rested on the straw mattress, smoked, and waited patiently for a brilliant *finale* to the magnificent vision that had come to him in the Monte Carlo, keeping the faith, lying very still, his eyes closed to encourage the final installment on this mother of all great dreams. Instead, he felt himself settling deeper into this cesspool of a birthplace, a man trapped in quicksand, trying to remain calm as he waited for Pete. The fear continued through his meal of goat, rice, and beans, along with the voice of Carlos:

We need Len, Paco. He's alive – we know from Pete, right?

Remembering this, he flinched inwardly. Pete had miserably failed the vision, in which he was intended to accept a stake in the foal as part payment. Would have changed *everything* – a thousand dollars was a fortune in Tica de Gualpa. He still couldn't believe Pete had casually turned him down between beers in the Golden Bowling Ball. Not even listening, no effort to understand. Maybe he'd been distracted by the queens, freaks, and transsexuals who made the place their home. Cleaned out, just like that, to the *crack!* of pins toppling in the endless lanes and the shouts and squeals of drunken gringo gays full of blow. Pete, his oldest friend, who had turned into a monster. And he'd be back for the rest. Only Arabiche was doing well. All his money and love went for her, and while it was too soon to be sure, he knew the sacred sperm had worked.

The Land Rover was sighted by young *Federale* Lieutenant Diego Hidalgo through his Nikon binoculars well before it approached the junction of paved highway and an unpaved road branching off to the south: Headed west at 1040 hours and duly noted. It was barren, deserted country, but this was a major checkpoint at a significant intersection on a popular smuggling route, hence a valuable source of bribes. Through his binoculars the slight, well turned-out young lieutenant could see these two were not involved in any of that. The vehicle was wrong, too expensive and conservative. Black tourists, apparently, an oddity. The woman looked excellent, worth raping for days on end, but that was for victim-type people, and these were not that. When they stopped, the woman said nothing, which he took as a sign of respect. Len alighted without being asked, showed his papers properly, and requested that his wife be allowed to remain seated. His calm, formal, almost military bearing, and air of worldly experience impressed Hidalgo.

"If she could step out for just a moment, and if you would both remove your sunglasses – it is required, a formality."

All done to his satisfaction, and the subsequent man-to-man procedure relaxed Hidalgo. He was American-educated and enjoyed speaking English, and he noticed that Dr. Willetts' speech was excellent.

"Yes, all in order. And what is your business here, Dr. Willetts?"

"I wish to locate a student, Carlos de Jesus, who is said to be in the province somewhere near Tica de Gualpa. He is probably with an older man, Paco Gonzalez."

The Lieutenant thought about it briefly. A failed law student, Diego Hidalgo came from an influential family and had been sent here from Guadalajara as punishment for an inappropriate affair. Young, inexperienced, new to the area, he had no interest in anything local except girls, and no idea who this Carlos de Jesus might be, or what to do next. But he wanted to help. He felt awkward in front of his squad, four young local privates and an old corporal.

"I was thinking that I should really have a guide," said Willetts-Thomas. "My Spanish is limited. I would be willing to pay decently, of course; it would be an expensible item."

Expensible. Obviously there was no point searching these people with their excellent vehicle and respectful understanding of how things were properly done. He was bored, and wished there was an excuse for a more extended dialog. Looking at his men, he addressed them sharply in Spanish.

"You know this 'Tica de Gualpa'?"

The youngest and smallest nodded, puzzled. People in Land Rovers did not go to that place.

"Yes, sir, I know it – it is off the road, small, not easy to find, but I can take them there."

"What would be an appropriate fee?" asked Len, looking at Hidalgo.

"I would say – a full day, overnight – thousand pesos?"

It was outrageous, a month's pay for the private, chosen as the starting point of a negotiation, but the black man nodded agreeably, unconcerned.

"That is fair, and you have solved my problem, Lieutenant. I am obliged. Do you mind taking American dollars? I think that would be about a hundred – "

The Lieutenant managed not to smile as he agreed, and Len removed five twenties from his black snakeskin wallet. Part of Hidalgo's punishment for the indiscreet affair had been the loss of his allowance, and this was great luck. They exchanged cell-phone numbers, and the very thin teen-age private climbed into the rear seat with his Kalashnikov.

"This Tica de Gualpa – you do not know what you will find there, Señor Willetts," said Hidalgo. "The back country – well, it can be dangerous. The boy is a very good shot, and quick, but as a matter of precaution, you should also be armed."

Len agreed, and observed that crossing borders with firearms these days was no small thing.

"Luckily, there are no borders involved here. Come with me for a few moments, please."

Hidalgo led him to a collapsible table with two chairs and disappeared, leaving Len to consider the situation. *Bored*, he thought. *Rich kid, used to doing what he feels like. Thinks we're interesting, wants to be friends. Love to get his hands on Holly.*

His new friend reappeared with a well-used old Colt .45.

"This is a personal item. You have had some experience with small arms?"

"I was trained on this model in the Army."

The Lieutenant smiled. Willetts was his kind of man, no matter about the color – quick, sharp, well-spoken, and with an excellent woman under good control. He snapped his fingers, the corporal appeared with a box of official stationery, and Hidalgo jotted a note on official stationery to the effect that Dr. Willets was authorized by himself, Lieutenant Diego V.J. Hidalgo, to carry a firearm for the duration of his stay. His signature was enormous.

"You are more than kind. It gives a sense of security."

"And let it be seen, Doctor. There is no holster, but the waistband is good. The trigger-pull is hard, by the way. With uniformed escort, you will be fine."

They shook hands cordially, and before the Rover drove off, the Lieutenant spoke at the private in rapid-fire Spanish, telling him to mind his manners, and not to steal, take bribes or talk to girls, or he'd face court-martial. Satisfied with his performance, he watched them drive off.

The Rover rolled along the dirt road trailing a little cloud of golden dust, with open sun roof and windows creating a pleasant breeze. Private Pablo was having a wonderful morning. He would love to smoke some of the Michoacán in his pocket, but that was out of the question. After a while he settled back to an early siesta in the fine leather seat. They were going to the wrong town of course, no one intentionally visited Tica de Gualpa, but then they would have to find the right one. And it was all completely correct, approved by the lieutenant – his first real assignment. He smiled. The others would be furious with jealousy, especially Corporal Hinojosa.

Behind the wheel, Len Thomas wondered why he detested everything about Lieutenant Hidalgo, right down to his cologne. It went beyond hereditary privilege in a corrupt oligarchy. *Cruel* – that was it. He would enjoy inflicting pain. But Hidalgo was from a rich family, Len could smell it, and he wanted to be friends. He was worth thinking about. Len was confident they'd find Paco and Arabiche with the help of Private Pablo, a likable boy. Then he would shock and frighten Paco so he never forgot it, for which a *Federale* with Kalashnikov would be the perfect prop. Straighten him out, then settle on a plan. Paco would know how to get things done cheaply down here. If 'Biche was with foal, which he figured at better than 50/50, they had an endless project ahead, and limited funds.

25

Being at the Dead Heat with a woman was unprecedented and unnatural. Who could have predicted Jasmine's curiosity about this of all places? With two women it was unthinkable. McGoohey saw it coming, and his first instinct on entering was escape. Suddenly the room felt warm, and he was perspiring. But he couldn't be seen as running away. Not here, with Jasmine on his arm and the bold new Alice there at the bar with Jimmy, looking right at him.

Jimmy sensed what the off-balance owner could not: *Setup.* No accident – too weird. Good at quick decisions, he was already sliding off his stool, saying a brief, apologetic good-bye to Alice ("Gotta go, Alice, can't stand bein' around him."), taking care of the tab with a quick nod at the bartender. Burning a hole in his pocket was a short unsigned note from Len, just delivered by Alice. Darned interesting note.

Something happening down here, looks pretty
interesting.
Come on down, I'll cover expenses. Will call
soon.

Mexico, of course. Len was always good for a surprise, and Jimmy loved secrecy. What the hell, why not? The thought sparked a big smile, and he left it turned on as he walked up to the McGooheys for an obligatory hello. He was slipping away as the ladies embraced, and with a last smile for the delicious Jasmine he was on his way.

Don't Go! cried a voice inside McGoohey, but the jockey was gone, and now he had two women on his hands. He stood flat-footed among the many empty tables, smiling benignly as his wife said something in her kind new motherly voice. As the women sat down, he adjusted their chairs, feeling even more peculiar. He never did things like that in this dark old room full of male memories. *Close to Happy Hour,* he thought, noting the angle of the heavy, smog-tinted orange light as the women chatted. What the hell – maybe this could be painless, melt some of those icicles Alice had been sticking him with lately. Get a drink into her. For once she was smiling, and he was pleased to think that they were an outstanding table. The blissfully pregnant Jasmine spoke to his taste and virility, and Alice, as always in the company of men, created a vague general sense of alliance. He settled down. He was Pat McGoohey. He could buy and sell any man in the house, and take out most with one shot. The smiling Alice showed no hostility, he lumbered genially forward.

"What we generally drink here is always this special Irish whisky," he rumbled bear-like and friendly. "But they got all kinds of wines, of course, and different beers naturally."

Then another pleasant surprise: instead of Jasmine punishing the wine list with something bordering an amused sneer, she spoke in an offhand way.

"I'd like a glass of the Cabernet, Pat," she said, smiling at her husband. "I doubt a glass of wine is going to disturb any child of yours," she finished, warming his heart. Alice, with no baby to think of, would have a real drink.

"I'll have what you're having, Pat," she said pleasantly. "I've been wondering for years what you keep in that flask."

"The good stuff," he said, hoping the old Alice was really back. "Straight from the ould sod, although I'm told it's made by Orangemen. I guess they've gotta be good at somethin', and we're not shootin' at each other for the moment."

But what the hell are the three of us doin' here? Odd, peculiar coincidence. As the women moved on to babies, he took in the old room, luckily free of hot ladies, and found himself deep in history. A great little place, the Dead Heat, the perfect escape.

Except I don't really belong here anymore.

The women stopped talking as the waitress arrived to deal with this unprecedented social situation. After he'd ordered for everyone, something unusual came over Pat McGoohey: a powerful impulse to real honesty. It delivered itself spontaneously, with a thoughtful *gravitas*. As the waitress left, he began.

"Sold one horse, a killer; had one stolen, my favorite."

It came out as a kind of declamation, in someone else's

voice. He stopped, very aware of the women's eyes on him. The waitress stopped moving. Who in hell was this solid citizen posing as Pat McGoohey? Had his doctor put him on one of those new drugs like her mom?

McGoohey glanced at her sharply and she scurried off.

"Handwriting on the wall," he continued. "Plus more writing, you could say, thanks to Jazz, who writes a beautiful hand."

This little touch focused all parties, creating silence and anticipation for those at the bar. The waitress returned with their drinks quickly, and he had a last look at his old world, leaving him sad, resigned to an unexpected fate. And yet, as seconds passed, he was pleased with himself, as if he'd been invited to speak at a Stanford Commencement like that Greed-is-Good guy who went to jail and found God. Looking at the skinny barflies, the dark, greasy-looking wooden walls with their endless pictures of great horses and the sneaky bartender, he remembered knocking Mike Neal over the bar that crazy night fifteen years back, and he felt old.

They drank, both ladies thirsty, he noted. Reassured, he resumed.

"Getting out of the horse game."

He announced this without premeditation, surprising himself and feeling something in the air as strong as the smell of raw earth at a grave. Heartfelt and resonant, it was heard by all. Did he mean it? He wasn't drunk; it was time for it.

"I seen in Saratoga that I really didn't like those people at the top. Kind of people, out here they'd own the Commissioner."

He meant that, all right, but he hadn't meant it to come out of his mouth.

"You're right, Pat, it's an oligarchy," said Jasmine, who had, after long restraint, quaffed her wine in three barely separate swallows. "But you know what, hon? Give them time to think about it and they'd rather have you than cousin Jed."

Oligarchy, thought McGoohey pleased with her and the ambience of civility. *Asshole buddies in suits and ties*. Learned that from Len. Hope he's okay, poor bastard will lose his job when I get out of the game. Find a place for him somewhere maybe, except horses are all he knows and he's got that accent. Glad I ain't black...

"You two are gonna love this," continued Jasmine in a mischievous voice. "The only reason I was with Jed when we met was because his ten-year fiancée finally had photographic proof that Jed's gay. Well, *bi* – but too gay for Justine."

"Holy shinola – no kidding!" said the old McGoohey, with a grunting *gottcha!* cackle at this useful information. And everyone thinking Jed was the big cocksman. Then he shrugged as if it were unimportant, relegating his competitor to business hours and picking up where he'd left off.

"I tried something I shouldn't have," he stated, in a quiet thoughtful voice.

Where the hell was this coming from?

"Got the boys in a situation," he said even more quietly. "Learned a lesson – I miss 'em. But while that was going on and driving me half crazy, somethin' happens so much bigger that the only thing I cared about was no one gettin' in trouble. Once Jasmine told me she's definitely having this baby – I thought, well, McGoohey Farms took a great horse to a photo. Black Ice, Eclipse Award candidate. Havin' an oil painting made off it to look at when I wonder what happened to all that money.

"Then later I thought, 'That's enough for me, that one big moment.' No more'a this throwing money at the king a' sports, not when you're a father and you got a kid's goin' to Harvard on his mother's brains.' That's where I'm breakin' with the family tradition. Fresh start."

Bullshit. He still craved a great horse. But with the jug on the table and Alice to be placated, the richly blarneyed cadences of his little speech took over, resonating easily to the bar, where all had gone silent in the effort of catching every amazing word. Thirsty again, he topped up the drinks, saw Jasmine's empty glass and waved for the waitress.

"I hope we're eventually gonna drink to the baby, Pat," said Alice, causing Jasmine to giggle.

"*Too-shay*, Alice," smiled McGoohey. "And then to the boys."

A kind of smile came over Alice's handsome and generous face, a smile of great depth and irony, so full of meaning that it stopped McGoohey in mid flight.

"Penny for your thoughts, Alice – "

"Not on your life, big guy."

He was damned if he could figure out which Alice this was, or what the hell was going on. The waitress appeared with the wine bottle, pouring Jasmine another glass and standing the bottle next to the Bushmills. Alice turned to the expectant mother with a smile.

"You're doing great work here, Jazz," she said. "I first met your hubby, he just knocked a Golden Gloves medalist I had a crush on right over that bar – "

"Why am I not surprised?" asked the mother-to-be after another swallow.

McGoohey was thinking it had been pretty unbelievable, when you thought about it. One of them was gonna be boss, there was no one else. One lucky punch! On a guy who could give him twenty pounds and tattoo his ass six ways to Sunday. Plus looked like a movie star. And himself rubbing it in all these years? With the boys gone, he needed company. Well, maybe not gone *forever*, but Mike Neal could use a break.

He topped up his drink. Whatever happened with the boys, he'd find out sooner or later. He could always start fresh with a couple of horses. Just a couple, and good ones. His thoughts turned back to business and he smiled. Mike wouldn't know whether to shit or go blind when he heard about his promotion and the money that went with it. And his wife Colleen, who hated him with undying devotion – Colleen would have to put a sock in it for once. He noticed the jug in front of him and poured another for Alice and one for himself, then topped up Jasmine's wine.

"A round for the house, my good man!" he roared at the bartender, his voice filling the room. "We're drinkin' to the good luck of Len Thomas! More guts and brains than the President of the United States."

It was a basically Democratic room, but there were a couple of men who didn't like that one at all. They all liked Len and feared McGoohey, though, and it was a free drink. They drank to John F. Kennedy McGoohey, then Jasmine, Paco, and Jimmy.

254

"Well first of all I like t'know who I'm talkin' to," rumbled McGoohey coldly through his hangover. "Second, I'm kinda busy, so let's get to the point – what is it you know that you think I oughta know?"

"Your horse."

There was a small conversational gap. Cryptic Hispanic hard guys ranked low with McGoohey, but he was vulnerable to the word horse. Nastiness was replaced by roguish cunning.

"That's it? *'My horse'*? Which horse? I got a number of horses."

Pete was raging, unconsciously palming his Glock. Was the man stupid? Last couple years people didn't take attitudes with Pete Suarez. But a little wave of calm chilled his rage. There was money involved, and what did the guy know? Stranger calls him up –

"You lose a horse, right?"

"Yeah, was inna papers, so what?"

"Maybe you like to have your horse back? Good horse, I heard."

McGoohey's innards convulsed, but his voice was unchanged.

"Sure, good horse. Insured. So what do you know that I don't?"

His bland, unimpressed voice totally disrupted Pete. The gringo was *bored!*

"I know you ain't find your horse in this country, mister, but not so far away you can't get her easy."

"Yeah, so?"

McGoohey had been doing this to tough, experienced, men for years, opening them like oysters. Pete's stomach erupted acid and he cursed himself for revealing so much. He had started the conversation convinced that Paco would never come up with the rest of the money in time for an investment opportunity he'd been offered. Now he was confused, a bull being worked over by an expert picador, not sure where to attack. And Paco might do anything – that was his big thing, surprises. Pull one out of his asshole like that Saratoga race.

And because of his own accent, this white guy would

already be thinking *Latino perpetrator* – a.k.a. Paco Gonzalez, already involved with the horse. And that was *extremely* dangerous, because sure as hell his wife would find out somehow, and this was family. What the fuck to do?

But there it was! Perfect!

"Tell you one thing – you don't find this guy too easy at night, right? An' I got more. Where horse is now. We got to meet, settle on price, I sell you information, full detail. Half in front, half when you got the horse, reasonable number – "

"I don't think so. Plenty insurance on that horse, and she was getting old."

"Getting *old*? Paper say she five, has big future – you shitting me, man!"

"Nope." McGoohey was serene. "This don't sound like my kind of deal. I could show up and who knows what happens, right? Thanks anyway."

The line went dead, so Pete did the only thing, which was to smash his cousin's telephone hard several times.

Fuck it, time to re-up. He got out his silver Sno-blower, tooting twice, then shaking and tapping the device. Empty again. He held it up, waved it at his younger brother, and pulled a baggie from another pocket. Win some, lose some. He'd find the investment cash – couple grand, no big deal. Then he addressed his brother.

"Know what? I have two of these, you could keep one loaded for me. After you load up, go buy a couple. Get one for yourself too, impress the girls at lunch time when you go to your locker an' get your Clanton jacket, right?"

Back at his desk an hour later, McGoohey was almost trembling with rage, a giant mushroom cloud beginning its majestic rise from backbrain to frontal lobe. *Don't find too easy at night.* So that was what Llewellyn Thomas, his good friend Len, had been up to. Why he never showed up after being released from that jail. Person of interest again, this time to Pat McGoohey.

That was one piece of information, but his Heimlich Maneuver had popped something else out of that Chicano sleaze: 'Biche was close by. Knowing how guys in his Latino crews expressed things, "get her easy" would mean not too far from the border. Probably not far from Tijuana, a day's drive at most. Paco was from down there. The map of California on his wall included northwest Mexico – everything in a long day's driving distance. He didn't know that territory, but he did business in Mexico, spoke some Spanish, and felt he understood Mexicans pretty well. Easily bluffed, low literacy, but very sharp eyes. ID from a photo better than most Americans, and very responsive to dollars.

Bottom line, his boys had ganged up against him. And he, stupid trusting bastard, never got it. That Spic would think it was a *great* story for the shitkickers at Patch! Didn't get his name, dammit. But he'd be tight with Paco, who was tight with Len. Right. And the way Jimmy had slipped out of the Heat the other day. Him and Alice having a drink? What'd *they* have in common? Out to get even, that's what! After all he'd done for them. As part of his mind was calmly calculating, a poisonous black rage was bubbling, driving out other thoughts.

Outfoxed by a goddamn nigger! Because Len was the leader. The old man was right again! He could hear his voice from the grave: *Toasted the black bastard in front of thirty people at least – when're ye gonna learn, Pat? Ye trusted the man! Gave him his big break, and it all came out the way it was bound to, boy-o, it's just how they are.*

Right! And soon it would be common knowledge.

What thick Irish impulse had driven him to play with that guy's head? For a thousand he'd have had all the details and saved time. Impulsive. Act now, think later.

Invisible, he thought then, suddenly calm. Take a couple days, fake business trip, handle it on his own, forget the cost, buy whoever had to be bought. Leave Len Thomas wishing he hadn't crossed Pat McGoohey. And maybe – just *maybe* – come back with a mare that had a Derby horse in her belly. No reason to *expect* that, but with Len and Paco involved, a pretty good chance. Definitely no need for Jasmine to know about any of this. Or anybody. It was his secret shame.

The setting sun bathed Tica de Gualpa in deep orange-red, and the street was as empty as Paco's mind, which contained two desires, one for a cold beer, the other that someone would shoot

Pete Suarez. Then the soft sound of a slow-moving vehicle pulling up behind him. Instinct froze him. He turned cautiously to see a spotless, expressionless Len in fresh khakis stepping out of the Rover, a .45 under his belt. Behind him was a *Federale*, automatic weapon at port arms.

"Len." He could barely get it out, and Len did not reply.

"Sheikh give me this," he said, fumbling in his wallet and quaking.

The engraved card he held out was simple and well worn: *Lakham Racing*, with the Sheikh's endless name, phone, fax, and e-mail address. Len was too pleased to smile and too deeply irritated to express relief, so he drilled his slowest, most skeptical look into his friend's eyes. Paco was terrified, his belly an icy knot, surrounded by the gazes of Len, the boy soldier with the Kalashnikov. And now the beautiful, expressionless Holly who had joined them. They stood together on the dusty main street in front of the cantina. It was the end of a very hot day, and the Rover had attracted interest. Now people were stepping back from windows as Len and the *Federale* were visible, hardware in plain sight, bad intentions obvious.

"You been sittin' on this card how long?" drawled Len.

"From Saratoga race day. I forget, an' then I get the rock – you know – "

"Oh, I know," said Len in a deadly calm, dry voice. "Remember that rock well. Got you real crazy, got a great stud horse killed, damn near killed me as well, put me in jail, made us all fugitives. Remember that rock real well."

Maybe got us a pregnant horse, too, said a voice in his head, but he ignored it, locking eyes with Paco long enough to let him see the disaster from his point of view and to compare their relative estates. The Rover and the *Federale* had already unmanned Paco, and Holly, abducted from the heart of Kentucky, was final proof of Len's amazing powers. In the gang, Paco had seen a man die for less than he had done that night, and Len would do what he had to. Dope a horse in venue of Tiffany and get away with it, good example. He watched Len hold the card up again as he considered it, and resisted falling to his knees.

"Good thing you remembered, Rocky. Don't suppose you

happened to *call* the man?"

"Oh, no, ees for you call Sheikh."

"If I happen to have his number."

Len almost allowed himself a sardonic laugh, then was struck by a thought.

"McGoo know anything about this?"

Paco shook his head.

"Don't talk to McGoo. McGoo no give *chaparrito* piece of action. No one see card but you an' Carlos. We discuss, an' we agree only you can do this. No way to contact you."

"Right. I'm in the slam an' you just sit here an' wait for me to show up. So where *is* Carlos?"

"Went home after few days, scared. You want see 'Biche? She pregnant, very happy. I taking good care. She give us nice foal, Len, we talk about it, me an 'Biche."

"Hope she doin' better than you, Rocky, you lookin' *thin*. I didn't track you down, you be in a real mess. Les' go see the horse get you in all this trouble."

There was silence in the Rover as Len thought about the Sheikh's card and how to play it. Paco sat tense with fear in the back seat with Private Pablo, who was having the time of his life. Five minutes later Len was pleasantly surprised. Paco had found a section of lush pasture and rebuilt the shed with care. Aside from being a bit thin, the horse in the field looked fine, and came trotting over followed by a nondescript pony-size friend. Paco's face registered confusion as Len casually reached in his pocket for sugar cubes and 'Biche came to lip them from his palm. Len's pockets never contained anything extraneous. Paco had been explaining about his factory job when he saw this.

"Chu *knew*!" he said in awe. "*Everything* – where I am, jism is, where she have to be."

"Love this horse," said Len. "All-time favorite horse."

Then he slipped into the corral to talk to 'Biche, rubbing her neck and massaging around her ears, enjoying himself. Paco smiled inwardly, knowing he was forgiven. The vision was correct and the new order was going to be fantastic. He could tell by the look on Len's face as he slipped through the corral rails.

"'Course I knew. You think I got stupid, Paco? 'Biche disap-

pears, I gotta wonder where she went? Pete should carry a sign –
'Clantonista Horse Thief.' Anyhow, I got special feed and vitamins
and a lot of other stuff which maybe you could get outta the car.
And money of course, which you look a little short on."

"*Sheet!*" said Paco ecstatically, looking at a sheaf of pesos.
Then he excused himself to Holly, who nodded in a way she'd
learned from her former employer, a little distant, but not dismissive or unfriendly. Out of habit Paco crossed himself to thank God
for his luck, and resolved on a full church confession, plus a lot of
money for the poor to pay for his vision.

"Yeah, I feed her now," he said. "Is time anyway."

"Okay," said Len, cool and reassuring. "You need some
company, Paco. Wash up an' change, we all go have a beer and get
you a good meal, my man, if they got such a thing here. See if you
can find out about some place I could take a lady to stay. After that
we talk about Pete."

Paco's good cheer disappeared and he stiffened as Len
watched from behind dark glasses.

"Got to tell you – owe him two large, very soon, for get
'Biche cross border," confessed Paco. "Paid all I had. He *dangerous*
now, man. Big man in gang, doing lot of blow, don't take no for
answer. Like we don' know each other anymore, didn't grow up
next door marry my cousin. Pete make the local tough guy look
real bad – Pedro, big fat guy. Pedro like to take it out on me, but he
afraid of Pete. This town, man – I know why my mother get out of
here. Curse on this town, you ask me."

"Couple days you outa here too, man. Forget that factory,
too. We got some thinkin' t'do."

Afterward Holly waited in the Rover until he was about to
start it.

"Kind of hard on him, weren't you? I mean, he's pretty low
after all this – "

He dropped his hand from the key and gathered his
thoughts.

"With Paco, first of all gotta get his *attention*."

"You did that in about half a second."

"Yes and no. He's also gotta take it all in and think about it,
which is not his natural way. Shock is easy, but changin' behavior,

260

that's hard. Hidden Paco agenda, always lookin' t'let the vision take over. Meanwhile got a manpower problem."

Holly sat thinking about this and he spoke again.

"Don't misunderstand. I love the guy, we work together real well, but when he's alone he gets unstable. Carlos leaving – big hole in his life, not used to bein' alone. Family ignorin' him, so Carlos being there was important. Kid got scared, made a gringo-type business decision. Doesn't have the guts of a gerbil, but he wasn't lazy, and we're short a man, 'cause Paco needs a sidekick. Can't be me – playin' on my dime puts me in Pat's role."

"So you need Paco comfortable, and Paco needs support."

"And it's gotta be someone equally – someone who understands him and respects his genius for horses. Someone who gets that, not some kid wants to be an accountant when he grows up. I've got a candidate, think Paco be cool with it."

"Think Paco be cool with it,'" reflected Holly aloud in his voice.

"OK. work my way up from exercise boy, right? Talk like that sometime."

She giggled and they both began laughing as if the air was a cloud of ganja.

Adapting quickly to the uses of an executive assistant, Len had Holly call Jimmy at the Dead Heat so the bartender wouldn't hear his voice. In a minute the jockey was on the line.

"You alone, Jimmy? I don't want people hearin' our business."

"Yep, everyone's watchin' us lose the ball game. Good to know you're okay, Len. You wouldn't be down south somewheres I suppose?"

"Why would you think that?"

"Just a guess. Alice guess. Case you ain't heard, somebody up and stole 'Biche-girl, an' everyone but McGoo knows it was this Pete Suarez, used to be Paco's asshole buddy in that gang. If it was me, I'd get her across the line pronto."

"Well, I ain't turned horse thief yet, Jimmy, an' I sure wouldn't go near that Pete dude. But you and me, I think we can do some more business. For the record, what we're sayin' now is

261

just for us, you and me, startin' with the fact you ain't even heard from me, okay?"

"Same as Saratoga, Len."

"I'm where you think, an' there's some real opportunities down here, but I need someone I can trust who knows horses an' understands Paco. You wanna come down an' stay while on my nickel? You might could be gettin' in on somethin' real good. Come in on ground floor, piece of the action."

"Sure was good last time, just a little *risky*. Only thing is, I got some rides, all of 'em pigs. Good news is, I got new brakes and tranny offa my winnings, an' everythin' else, too. So this trip is all on your tab – I got that right, Len?"

"Gas, eats, room, little entertainment. Get receipts."

"Okay, deal. Alice got me your note but it didn't say much, and of course *she* don't say much, but you guys bein' gone, it came across for her like the Mick took advantage again – "

"Take advantage? Pat McGoohey? I must've misunderstood you, mister."

Jimmy fell into a snuffly half-suppressed cornball guffaw that reminded Len of his country summers as a boy.

"I got my pad an' pencil, you wanna give me directions where I'm goin'?"

"Right. First thing, write down this number. Temporary cell phone. Private. Not even Alice. Prob'ly good idea to pick up a used extra wheel and tire and bring your tools. Facilities down here on the primitive side. An' a throwaway phone that works in Mexico with some hours on it. I'll cover all that."

"Lucky I still got the Jeep. Sounds like you're in the outback."

"I guess you gotta come down an' see for yourself. Figure a good twelve, fourteen hours drivin'. Sooner the better."

Afterward Jimmy felt very peaceful. You could always count on Len to come up with something, he reflected, sipping a light beer in celebration of this surprise call and waiting to see what girls would show up for happy hour. A loner born, he felt closer to Len and Paco than anyone except his sister in New York. McGoohey had been his bread and butter, and he was getting out of the game. Plus his favorite Tijuana girl had quit to marry a customer, and he didn't know what to do with himself. Not a reader, didn't understand most movies, and you could only watch just so much TV.

Whatever Len needed, it wasn't a jockey. This was about 'Biche. He could smell hard work coming, but he'd never been afraid of work and he could always come back if it didn't pan out. But shit – why wouldn't it, with Len in there? Only bad thing with steady labor, you had to *eat*, which made muscle weight, very hard to lose. But he could scout up local rides and he'd be a star by Mex standards 'cause of that picture in the *Times*, him and 'Biche-girl just *barely* losin' to Black Ice. Local guys wouldn't like him horning in, but him an' Ramon Ortiz was on good terms since Saratoga, talked once on the phone, so *no problemo*.

Call Len tomorrow. Prob'ly best thing happen since – Saratoga, of course, what else? Good idea to make some calls now and get out of his rides.

26

McGoohey got the early start he wanted, but the rented Cavalier was a dog. Any rental would feel that way after what he was used to, but an hour after crossing the border the AC quit, sending him into a mood so evil that he seriously wondered if he shouldn't just turn around and go back. Jasmine and Alice talked every day, though, and they'd figure he was up to something and how to stop him from settling the score. And did that black wiseass motherfucker ever need settling up! No way he could get away clean after stealing him blind. First the advance, then the jism. And a shit-load of expense money plus his best horse...

He's fucking laughing at me! he raged inwardly, a large pink object in the hot dry air swirling through the car. It had seemed like a good idea to rent a low-profile car rather than take his own, but the Cavalier looked *cheesy,* and Mexicans worshipped appearances. Should have sprung for a better ride, Caddy'd been sitting right there. But all those fifties had been a good idea. Cleaned out the box, well over seventy thousand in a bulky pair of manila envelopes. Overkill, but maybe useful, like the .38 that happened to be in the deposit box. In his experience, there wasn't a whole lot of real Mexican law, and what there was, he'd buy. Worse came to worst, the .38 would come in handy; get it out of the trunk into the glove box.

Len kept popping up in his thoughts, bringing on the same crazy-mad feeling each time he got himself under control. *Set me up, and now he's laughing at me!* Over and over, the same furious inner voice... fuckin' books won't help when it's just the two of us in a room. Gonna kick Llewellyn Thomas's black ass, blow his mind, and spoil his looks, like Ali did with Patterson. Take my time, keep talking to him while I do it, explain it so he don't ever forget.

And fuckin' Alice! Not just betrayal, *alienation of affections!* Playin' kissy-face with my wife, finding out private stuff, *personal* stuff, like I've gotta smoke weed to get it up. To the moon, Alice, no severance. 'Cause she knew all along. Had one too many at the Heat, let her face slip. Little smile when I toasted the boys. Shoulda seen it earlier.

Okay, beat the crap out of Len, fire Alice, get 'Biche back in her old stall, keep Paco, and step up to a real trainer.

My whole crew's down here with my horse! But these beaners will talk. Just a question of price, and this is a no-limit game.

These recirculating thoughts drove him hard until he approached the first little town and saw that he was in the middle of Mexicali Nowhere, sweating like pig, no idea where to begin, no friggin' AC. He pulled alongside a burro cart with a load of manure, driven by a very old man who could not understand his Spanish.

"Where's the police station?"

The man said he didn't understand twice in a thin rusty voice, staring in fear at this huge angry American, cringing and shrugging helplessly. McGoohey gave it up and continued to the little cluster of houses and shops baking in the sun. Adobe, cinder-block, wood, all with corrugated metal roofs. He got out of the car and stood in the sun, asking a group of three men about the police station and scaring them all except one, who spoke some English. There was no police station, he said, just a constable working off in the fields.

"We have no crime," the English-speaker added by way of explanation.

McGoohey reached into his shirt pocket and showed him pictures of Len, Paco, and his horse, watching his face carefully. His staring scrutiny alarmed the man, who said he had seen none of them. When he walked into a tiny lane and suddenly disappeared, McGoohey was sure he'd recognized at least one, which would mean he was close. By sundown he might luck out. Looking around for other people to talk to then, he wished he'd remembered to bring a hat to keep the sun off his head. Through its ruthless glare, he spotted the town's restaurant across the deserted street, and went in. It lacked air conditioning, but it did have a huge fan and cold beer. He sat in front of the fan and downed two Coronas, sitting quietly as men drifted in for lunch, moving slowly in the heat. They were all men whose wives worked in the local sneaker factory. Check that out, too, he thought. Thirst quenched and afraid to eat local food, he went up to the bar with his photos and got the same reaction as he'd seen in the man who disappeared down the lane.

I'm too big, I'm scaring the fuckers, he decided, putting on his dark glasses as he walked back out into the blazing mid-day sun. He had an absent-minded desire for the company of Len and Paco and grunted a laugh at his fried thought processes, lowerin his body onto the searing plastic. Then he drove on and tried again in two more dusty little towns, seeing that the photos really meant nothing to anyone, and looking for a new angle. The Mexicans' expressions were so blank that he saw no point in flashing his pocket wad, and he felt as though he'd been across the border for days.

In the next town was a police station, where he was not unexpected. The special aggressiveness of certain American males being a general red flag, people in his network had called ahead. Both calls had identified him as a dangerous criminal type, possible assassin, bounty hunter, or drug mercenary-enforcer. The horse photo had irritated everyone as a new kind of Yankee insult, bracketing a Mexican with a black man and a horse. Chief Garcia was ready when this barrel-chested American strode in with his false smile full of large, irregular teeth. The Chief, who spoke good English, had responded to the heads-up calls by stationing two conspicuously armed deputies in the big room. McGoohey paid them no mind, overwhelmed by the relief of entering an air-conditioned space. Looking at him, the Chief agreed with the callers, but sensed that McGoohey was not a small player, and that he was on his best behavior.

"Please sit down, Señor."

"Gracias," said McGoohey in his mellowest tone, settling himself.

"We can speak English, sir."

"Good, my Spanish is terrible. I don't think my business should take much of your time. I'm looking for these friends of mine, came down here on vacation and I'm supposed to join them."

He spoke casually, unaware of the insulting falseness of his statement. Every American had a cell phone, so either his "friends" had met with a problem or they were avoiding his calls. But the Chief nodded. Then he prepared to take notes on the appropriate form. He wanted to observe McGoohey as long as possible and get a sense of the man which did not take long: Fearless, dangerous, tricky, bad liar. His tale of the two friends remained sketchy and smelled of careless fiction. McGoohey didn't seem sure exactly when they had begun their 'vacation' or what it was that drew them to the area. The Chief smiled genially, thinking that these particular vacationers might need protection. McGoohey understood the smile, which was as insincere as his own. In towns where he did business, he was accorded a respect evident in everything, including smiles. The Chief's effort to conceal his character reading fell short, but it provoked an unexpected response.

"It'd be a real mess if anything *happened* to these men," said McGoohey importantly, as if representing his country.

"We are a law-abiding people," said the Chief with suave dignity, "and I have had no reports of violence or kidnapping. I don't see how I can help you without more information on your friends and their location, I am sorry to say."

"Me too," replied McGoohey, trying to mask his irritation. As a token of respect, the Chief had one of his men Xerox the photographs while he made notes.

"I have your phone number if I learn something," he added, sensing slippage in the civilities and hoping to restore them as he handed back the photographs.

"And I have your name from the sign on your desk, Chief Garcia. Could I have your number as well?"

The Chief pointed with satisfaction to a grotesque plastic device holding a stack of cards. Taking one, McGoohey rose, white shirt clinging icily to his body. Forcing another smile, he bid Garcia a good afternoon.

When he was safely gone, the Chief glanced at the muddy copies and made several calls about this dangerous American, accurately describing the photos of Len and Paco, saving the horse for comic effect. In ten minutes, authorities in the area were alerted, along with a number of restaurants and cantinas.

"Be careful with this man," he told them. "He does not need to be armed to be dangerous. If you see him, note his direction and call me immediately."

Thirty miles from Tica de Gualpa, in an air-conditioned resort hotel, Holly St. Cyr looked out at the afternoon sun, fresh from her shower, cool with air conditioning and touched with a light cologne. Then she stood in front of a tall mirror admiring her body, which usually put her in a good mood. After that, she slipped into her jeans and a fuchsia blouse and sat down to consider the new situation. Promising but problematic, she thought. Seeing Len take control and then seeing that pretty mare on her way to foaling a horse that would make their fortunes – all that had felt very good. But she saw that legitimizing the foal could be a serious problem. Mexican papers would be okay here, but Mexican papers on a super-horse with a black owner would be an issue at U.S. tracks when it did well in big races. And if it looked anything like Missile Man, God help them. Knowing the peril Paco had put Len in, something in her wanted to blame it all on him, but of course it was this same horse-genius who had put them in business. She was irritable when Len finally emerged from the shower with an untroubled light-hearted air, a white towel wrapped around his waist. As he changed into his shorty-pajamas, she spoke in a no-nonsense tone that curbed his mood.

"I'm still bothered about your midnight LA ride. The exposure. Crazy Pete has it in for you.

"Okay, we can talk, but stop scolding me before you know the facts: Fact One, no guarantees in this line of work. Fact Two, in LA, the Pats don't talk to the Petes. Fact Three, I own the moral high ground 'cause I didn't steal the horse. Fact Four, I really own that high ground 'cause I didn't rat him out, if you will. Drop a dime on Pat and I was home free, maybe get a lifetime stipend from your former employer. He owes me, and Alice will let him know that when she has the facts."

He went on, words slowing down for effect.

"But the really important thing is that Pat McGoohey is a changed man now that he's gonna be a father. Any number of witnesses heard him carrying on about it at the Dead Heat. Now that his wife's got one in the oven, that seems to be the only thing he really cares about. That's from Alice, eye witness, and she knows him like a book. He's not stupid – he wants Kentucky to go away like everyone else."

Holly settled herself into a corner of the couch with her glass of wine, and when she spoke again, her voice was calm, cool and indelible.

"I half-buy it. But I need to know *everything*, Len Thomas, every damn thing, because sometime you're going to need me and my experience again, and I think better when I know what the fuck's going on. You're *secretive*, and I don't appreciate being locked out."

"Okay, just don't talk dirty," he replied, rocked but maintaining. "Lifetime habit, bein' discreet. It's why that detective never got to me before you drove up and saved my life, Holly."

"That nasty word was to help you remember. We've got a job ahead of us, Len. Getting that foal on the books to run in the States with you as owner – you can bet your cute little butt that if we show up with a winner that looks anything like Double-M, Dixie's gonna be right on us, lawyers and doctors and intent to kill."

Len smiled, hearing his own voice in her words.

"I know. That Sheikh who came to look at her in Saratoga, whose card Paco was holding onto like a complete halfwit – that's the man who could do it and not be challenged. You talked to him – where's he at? You said he hit on you?"

"Only once. He's a Royal, a Prince of the blood. Distant, but in the line. They do what they want. Having danced with you and seen your horse blow Dixie's mind, I was unresponsive."

"Naturally. But this is business, so I have to give it a shot. That's a project where I look to you. Man like the Sheikh doesn't just take calls."

"Nor do you, Llewellyn" she said deliberately. "Because an important man such as yourself has a very capable hard-ass multilingual administrative assistant, which is *me*."

"Then there's the approach shot – "

"Are you thinking about a call? I was looking at the Sheikh's card again," she said, relaxing on the couch. "That was his personal card he gave Paco to pass on, didn't have his trainer handle it. That could be promising. We could certainly write him a nice letter about this soon-to-be-discovered gold mine in scenic Tica de Gualpa. With e-mail there's no physical address, which is a plus."

"Moving target my normal style, but it feels shifty here. I'm not hiding from the man. I'm just not sure yet. Certified snail-mail kind of classy. Maybe courier."

"So why are you set on a call, which you seem to be?"

"Don't know that I am. Lot of things I do, I'm not sure about the reason."

"Well this is one time when it's worth some thought."

Len looked at the ceiling. *Who she think she talkin' to?*

"Maybe good time to back off, too, lady. I ain't holdin' out on you an' my brain don't work better in a schoolroom."

"Suit yourself. But I wouldn't sit on it too long. He's a quick decider."

Len's eyes came down from the ceiling and he looked at her.

"Hey, when was the last time you ran the show? I work how I work. There's a right way to do it, and I'll take as long as I feel like to find it. Ain't no one called Len Thomas *slow* recently."

"That's not what I said or meant. You have to get mean when you think, be my guest."

He looked at the mountain through the open French doors, holding back.

"Okay," he said. "Time out. Least said, soonest mended – old northeast saying. Guess it never caught on down south."

Holly's mind was exploding with replies, and swallowing them could give her indigestion or a headache. She was dying to challenge him just a little more, but that could send everything down the toilet.

"Do it your way, Len, it's your show," she said quietly, facing him. "But I'm not wild about your tone."

"How about we just take that time out before you go ballistic?"

How about admitting you're stuck and can't make up your mind?

But it was time to chill, whatever she thought about the condition of his synapses. She'd seen rage in every black man she

270

got to knows, and she didn't want to see his.

And I'm crazy in love with the man, she thought, walking to the door.

"Okay, me and my missiles are going for a little walk."

He nodded and said nothing, working it out as she left. He lay on the couch and closed his eyes, and when he opened them she was at the table with her laptop. He spoke thoughtfully.

"Figured out what's wrong with e-mail, Holly. I don't know jack about technology, but I *do* read, and seems like e-mail's an open book to governments and probably anyone with real deep pockets. With a terrorist in his family, Sheikh's gotta be monitored by all kinds of agencies – phones, faxes, e-mail. Nowhere to run, nowhere to hide. Whereas voice analysis, which I'm also not expert on, we'd pass that test easy, 'cause any halfway intelligent person gonna know that this really is just two horsemen talkin' horse business."

What he didn't say was that a steady diet of Holly St. Cyr had increased his confidence in the voice that was at times Dr. Vaughan Willetts and other well-spoken virtual people, to a point where he felt it would be acceptable to the Sheikh.

"Okay – mister high-school diploma wins again."

"Autodidact last time, wasn't it? No need to get chippy, girl – I'm feelin' good about this call. Which I need to be, for it to work."

She took that, and he held her eyes as her features screwed themselves into an expression he hadn't seen before. Embarrassed confusion.

"It's just nerves, Len."

"Mmm. So then there's the content of this call, and his reaction. You *do* know what I'm asking the man to do?"

"Marry the girl and give the child a name. It's in the interest of all parties."

"And then we have the special problem. Aside from a local skank he fancied, 'Biche got the only load of Missile-jism on the planet. Bein' my impulsive associate killed the sire, creating an international scandal, how do I *tell* the man?"

"You don't. You suggest a meeting since he's already expressed interest by leaving his personal card."

"Yeh, you right. But what I'm asking for is a little out of the ordinary. Covering up a crime is only part. I also want his backing for my own operation. It's not the Lakham business model, and they're used to doing things their way."

"Royals are different, Len. Short of sedition, conversion, or regicide, this man can do whatever he wants, which is hard for us to get our deprived democratic minds around. He makes the rules, and he breaks them when he feels like it. When you let him know what you've got here, I doubt that Judeo-Christian ethics are going to be a factor. He guessed 'Biche was juiced for that race, by the way, and it didn't seem to bother him. He's been dealing with sanctimonious oil-Christians all his life, and I'm sure he's up to here with it. He wants to do on the track what we've been doing to his people any place there's oil under the sand."

"Mmm. This is some tricky stuff, Holly-girl. And I kind of stand out in these circles of course. Only thing fits is my nose."

"You're pretty tricky too, Llewellyn, and well spoken when you feel like it. You, 'Biche, the foal, Paco, Jimmy – nice package, and he won't want anyone else to get it. Like Godolphin."

"Y'right, babe."

He let the better part of a minute go by, thinking about that, and the fight they'd avoided, and how she'd snapped right back, no hard feelings.

"Got a little testy there, didn't I. Sorry about that."

"Alpha males are all the same. Howard Budney damn near raped me on the front lawn in Saratoga 'til I bit his ear half off."

Alone on a steep tourist trail climbing a scrub-covered mountain in the heat of early afternoon, Holly held a steady pace. Cell phone reception at the hotel was poor, and this call had to be made. *Just keep on chooglin'*, she told herself, not enjoying the climb, but knowing the trails were well guarded, and that eventually she'd find a place where the phone worked. Shy on melanin, she was no sun-worshipper, and even with Len's Panama, she felt unprotected. Every few minutes she tried the phone with no success. Almost halfway up the parched little mountain, it occurred to her she must be on the wrong side, and turned off to the left despite a sign warning against this. Then she walked another fifteen minutes, stressed, grumpy, and sweating now, nothing like the beautiful woman she let Len see. It was the ugly side of the mountain, with fewer, scrawnier trees offering less shelter from the sun. Why did people come to this arid, ugly place?

Resting in the shade of a gnarled dwarf pine and drinking from her container of water, she suddenly and passionately hated Llewellyn Thomas, and knew that her secret desire to have a baby with him was a *terrible* idea, even though it would inevitably be the coolest offspring since Miles Davis. Irritation brought her second wind, and she tested the phone, successfully this time, warming up on her delighted half-sister LaVerne, who could not stop asking questions.

"I'm having a baby," said Holly, to reboot the conversation.

"*You're having a baby?!* Not with that jail guy, I hope! Are you *married*?"

"No, and I'm not having a baby, either. But I like California a lot."

This set LaVerne off again, causing Holly to appreciate Len's natural quiet.

"I'll tell you more later, sis – I'm running out of juice and I need to make a business call. I'll call you again when this thing is recharged."

Calculating the approximate time in Saudi Arabia, it struck her that talking to LaVerne had made her stupid. The Sheikh could be anywhere. Placing her handkerchief on the dusty grass she sat carefully in the patch of shade and willed herself to be the Holly St. Cyr who had studied so hard and successfully. Then she dialed and waited while the phone emitted the sound of a call being forwarded. Finally came a sleepy British-sounding receptionist voice.

"This is Holly St. Cyr of St. Thomas Racing, calling for Llewellyn Thomas, Managing Director," she began. "I'd like to arrange a call with the Sheikh for Mr. Thomas later in the week."

"This is the Sheikh's personal number, and he's not available. If this is a business call I can refer you to another number. Perhaps Mr. Thomas could speak with Mr. Purtees?"

B-team Brit, thought Holly, and added a dash of vinegar.

"I would not be calling this number if it were a matter for Mr. Purtees."

"Oh. Can you tell me what this would be in connection with?"

"No, I'm afraid I can't, but it will be quite clear to the Sheikh if you reference *Saratoga*."

"Oh. May I have a number to call back?"

"We won't be reachable for thirty to forty hours. We're installing new phones, and I'm not sure this number will be operative. But we will definitely call again in that time range. Again, *Holly St. Cyr*. The Sheikh will remember me."

"And you will call back in approximately thirty to forty hours. Someone else may answer, but I will leave these details: Holly St. Cyr, calling on behalf of Llewellyn Thomas, Managing Director, St. Thomas Racing."

"Referencing Saratoga."

"Yes, Saratoga. I'll give Alberto the information. The Sheikh has a busy week, but I'll make sure he gets the information."

"Thank you."

Alberto. Who would that be?

She stood up several minutes after placing the call, and realized that she was spent and unsteady. She didn't like carrying so much weight, or situations where chance and risk were so prominent and you needed eyes in the back of your head. But this was Len's game, and it was chance that had brought them together. Plus the risk he'd taken with Howard to meet her. And the terrible risk he'd taken at Saratoga with his horse. It was his style – light stake, long odds, steel balls.

The man owns my ass, she thought. And I own his, long as I'm reasonable.

McGoohey saw the checkpoint from afar and hoped it would be a source of information, for which he was prepared to pay generously. An officer stepped out of the brush as he pulled up.

"Step out of the car, sir."

There was no *please*, and the man was wired. What the hell for?

The attitude took him by surprise, but he controlled his tongue. He didn't know what the problem was, but he recognized the uniforms and the weapons and the overly excited look of the young enlisted men. He resolved never to travel second-class again, then stepped out of the car, hot, tired, and wooden-faced. He stood beside the open door and said nothing. To the alerted Hidalgo this enormous American bristled with danger, and he addressed him in English, in a neutral tone.

"There has been much narcotics traffic recently, sir, and we have standing orders to obtain personal identification documents and examine all suspicious vehicles."

"Since when is a Chevy Cavalier a suspicious vehicle?" asked McGoohey.

"Since drug traffickers began renting them to avoid having their personal cars impounded," replied Lieutenant Hidalgo in cold, flawless English. McGoohey, who had stopped sweating during the late afternoon, felt a fresh wave engulf his torso. One Private patted him down while another held an automatic rifle on him. Being searched for no reason by a jerk kid lieutenant struck him as insulting, but he was glad he hadn't moved the .38 to the glove box. He stood without moving. This moronic little squad looked trigger-happy.

"Look, ah, if I could make a suggestion – this ain't really a good way to treat your tourists. My name's Pat McGoohey, I'm in the construction business in Los Angeles, and if you was to look me up in your computer, you'd find I am the owner of a large company that does business with Mexican contractors, the State of California, and so forth."

"And to me, you do not give the appearance of being a tourist. You are alone, in an empty car without visible bags, not even a briefcase. And if you are the owner of a large U.S. company, I question why you travel in a cheap rented car. As you might imagine, no computer is available at a field station of this type. In any case the delay should not be long. Would you like to tell me the real purpose of your presence in this area?"

"Yeah, okay, maybe you can help me out. I'm lookin' for some people I was supposed to meet, and not havin' much success. It's a private matter. I have pictures of the parties in question."

"Perhaps I could have a look at them, and also your license, registration, passport, and whatever else you may have that would verify your identity."

McGoohey stifled himself and turned impatiently to reach into the car. Hidalgo stepped behind him and placed a hand on the grip of his sidearm while the corporal released the safety of his Kalashnikov with an audible click, causing McGoohey to freeze.

"Move slowly, please, Señor McGoohey," said Hidalgo. "There have been incidents, and my men are quick to react."

"Right. I hope that guy of yours knows what he's doin,' because he's got dead aim on my gut and we're nowheres near a hospital."

"He does as he is trained and ordered. Weapons sometimes appear in place of papers."

"Yeah, I suppose."

"We are very careful about our guns in Mexico. Only government-authorized persons and landholders may carry them."

Sure, you fuckin' spic-lizard, you got yourselves a real great country here, I can see that right off. Drug cartels running the place and everyone else running north to work for guys like me.

One of the enlisted men slid under the car to examine the undercarriage, rmoinding McGoohey of the manila envelopes full of fifties and the .38 in the trunk, which would come next. In sudden desperation he produced his best smile, along with his passport, wallet, and the envelope of photographs.

Hidalgo looked the passport over carefully, then handed it to his Corporal rather than returning it. He noted the credit cards and handed them over as well, along with the wallet, finally arriving at the envelope of snapshots to find his new friend Dr. Willetts looking at him in tweed jacket and turtleneck. He paled, but maintained his composure and said nothing until coming to the shot of Arabiche.

"And the horse?"

"A thoroughbred I own. One of my string."

"You are concerned with the man in the first picture? The dark one?"

McGoohey's answer got stuck in his throat.

"The horse is missing, then?"

"Oh no, nothing like that. Just happened to be in the envelope."

276

His confusion resolved all doubt for Hidalgo. The man was lying, obviously dangerous, violent by nature, as Garcia had said. And a threat to Dr. Willetts.

"We must completely search the vehicle – it is routine."

"Okay if I make a call?"

"No. Hand me your phone, slowly."

McGoohey reached into his pocket and did so, shaking his head in feigned amazement. Hidalgo nodded at another private, who began a slow, thorough search of the interior. Then the other private emerged from under the car and dusted himself off.

Fucked! thought McGoohey, unable to think. *Screwed, blued, and tattooed.* As the rear seat was removed, he spoke quietly to Hidalgo.

"Maybe a good idea to have a private conversation."

To his relief, Hidalgo walked away from his squad, positioning himself carefully, making sure a Kalashnikov was trained on the American, and thinking. This crude thug meant harm to his new friend, a man of interesting possibilities, but hardly capable of dealing with an animal like this.

Paying full attention to the man in front of him, he was considering alternatives. Simply disappearing McGoohey was a possibility, but that was sure to further exasperate his influential uncle. According to the experienced Chief Garcia, this brute was probably a bounty hunter, enforcer, drug merchant or an angry man chasing down some people on an illegal matter. He let the silence stretch as they looked at each other. He wanted Padraic McGoohey III under control and off his hands, but he hadn't actually broken the law.

Then he did.

"I'd like to come to an arrangement here and be free to go about my business without being harassed. Would that be possible?"

"This is not harassment – it is all perfectly routine."

"Well, okay, say it is. It's worth real money to me to know I'm free to do my business."

A gift!

Under McGoohey's powerful green-eyed stare, Hidalgo was glad to have his experienced Corporal holding the automatic weapon aimed on the American's midsection. Hidalgo was expressionless. This was a serious situation, beyond anything he'd ever had to deal with. It was his clear obligation to report this attempted bribe, which bribe would have to be more than he'd ever received before. Tempting, and McGoohey's patient stare was bowel-loosening. Hidalgo rallied and took the opportunity to express his distaste and social contempt, returning the stare with all the power of the government in his eye. He said nothing for a long moment though his decision was made. McGoohey was silent.

"I'm afraid you have made a very serious mistake. I am required to report all such attempts to corrupt our law enforcement system. The U.S. has similar regulations, I believe."

Going numb, his breathing constrained, McGoohey doubled down.

"I'm not talking about a couple of thousand dollars, Lieutenant."

They heard the trunk open.

"Five figures US dollars. I'm a person of some influence – "

"And I am a mere lieutenant junior grade in the army of a second-rate – "

They were cut off by the excited voice of an underling who had struck gold.

"Lieutenant, if you could come here for a minute, sir!"

"Name your number," said McGoohey quietly.

"I have no number," said Hidalgo proudly, believing it for the moment. "Mexico is not for sale, Señor. *You* will have a number. A case number, and possibly a number of years, depending on what my men have found. Put your hands behind your back. The corporal is going to put handcuffs on you as a precaution."

Head swimming with satisfaction, he held his .45 on McGoohey while he was cuffed. With a determined attempt at self-control, he went to the rear of the car to see the evidence spread out in the trunk. His men had even worn the gloves mandated by regulations. A loaded revolver and a huge pile of U.S. currency. An open and shut case – his uncle would be more than pleased, and he might be forgiven his indiscretion with the young wife of the ancient Secretary of Defense. This incident was big enough to merit his uncle's attention, and would would benefit the family, whose name would appear favorably in the media. Most of the money would disappear, and this punitive assignment might end. And on top of all that, he had probably saved Willetts's life. What a day!

"Corporal Sanchez," he said as if in a dream, "you will assume command until I return. I am taking the prisoner to jail."

Turning to McGoohey, he ordered him into the seat alongside the driver and had Sanchez connect the safety belt. Then his feet were cuffed. Hidalgo sat diagonally behind McGoohey, sidearm in hand, because this big angry man struck him as capable of anything.

"The safety on my pistol is off," he said, for McGoohey's benefit. "It has a sensitive pull, but I will avoid vital organs if I must fire. The authorities will expect a live suspect for questioning."

Before leaving for the jail, he handed the .45 to Sanchez and walked off into the little grove of scrub trees to urinate. He had rarely experienced a more exciting and enjoyable afternoon, not even with the Secretary's wife.

27

Paco's afternoon séance with his favorite companion was long and detailed that day, including hard to find apples and a lengthy massage with big strong hands. He addressed her in English, her native language, to encourage a classy attitude.

"Len ees hard, 'Biche, but at top mus' always be hard man. Also hard man with good heart – Len love his little 'Biche-girl jus' like Paco. All these nice food come from Len, whatever you need – vitamin shot, papers, nice clean place to stay, big stall, special trailer with name for you and little boy – "

While engrossed in this incantational discourse and massaging the place where back and haunches joined, he heard a voice closely resembling his own:

"Also is providing Kif, Lamb's Breath, Chocolate, Stenamina – "

He turned to see a pukka-sahib Len in khaki shorts and shirt, smiling the full smile, perfect white teeth shining. He was wearing a white Panama.

"See, 'Biche – speak of Devil and he is here."

He slapped her rump and she trotted off, circling around to look at them before coming over for sugar cubes from Len and trotting away again to graze.

"Carlos didn't like the factory, eh?"

"He lack faith. Afraid. Pete – "

"Yeah. Lot of people same reaction to Pete. What's his connection?"

"Problem was, no Pete, we don't got horse. I bring him here for reason. Local guys steal like anyone. Jealous low-class Mexicans. Not much to steal here. They see big new SUV, gang tattoo, big gun, big wad, they get scare like Carlos. Pete explain to them what happens if they get smart. If I don't have old tattoo, they try steal 'Biche."

"They know about gang tattoos?"

"Better believe. We close to U.S. here. Pete secures investment, which I still owe two large. Gives cantina party, buys drinks in bar all afternoon, gets everyone high on blow, then picks head crook, Big Pedro, fills his nose few times, then sticks nine millimeter in his neck, tells him we are under the Clantonista Protection. Shows tattoo, everybody scared shit. But before you come, show disrespect."

"Too bad about Carlos. We missin' a man now."

"Yeah, an' Carlos very good on trip, good driver, keep dry ice re-up. Let me take time for rest and think. But yeah, we missing a man, and local guys no good."

"Workin' on it, Pook. Need someone knows horses, how to keep quiet, willing to work. Need some trust, too. Not easy to find. First thing, get rid of Pete."

"Easy, with cash. I call him, we meet Tijuana. He prob'ly kiss money good-bye and wonder now should he shoot me and sell horse."

"Call him. We drive to the beach, use a pay phone. Then we go for a swim in the ocean, have a couple beers, eat some nice fish, lay on the beach,."

There was a long pause while Paco adjusted to full reinstatement.

"Man, I thought maybe you *keel* me for what I done. Was a deer jump out of woods – impossible to stop, only way was step on gas – "

Len burst out laughing, and Paco's swarthy face turned deep red.

"You are one lousy liar, Paco, but that's all history an' you did good here. So – phone and beach tomorrow, call Pete, then Tijuana, get rid of him."

"All in dream. Dream tells Paco what to do. Everything great, but I still have bad feeling from how I kill great horse, keeps coming back. Is a curse, but maybe foal can make okay. You think? Bloodline does not die?"

"Yeah, your responsibility to fix that. But I'm gonna make sure 'Biche has everything. An' stay clean with Pete, Paco. You an' that rock near got me killed. Pretty close, *Chaparrito*."

"Out of control, man – crazy night. You see, got to move quick once horse is out of stall, set off mass-detector, so take to the max. You wearing seatbelt, eh?"

"Woke up hangin' upside down seein' double. They caught me walkin' down the road couple of miles away, had me in jail, but I got the evidence hid first. It was Holly got me out. Remembered me from Saratoga and lied for me."

"Yeah, she something. Serious woman."

"Right? So all we really need is papers." He paused to collect the thought. "Mexican papers not good enough where we goin'. Clean papers what I want. Squeaky-clean, Mercedes-Benz class. We all show up together an' colt maybe look like Double-M? That Dixie woman *connected* – lawyers, friends in high places. Blood test reveal paternity."

"An' I seen she sweet on Holly, too. *Sheet!*"

"Anyhow, I know you a U.S. citizen, but I bet you still got Mexican citizenship too – "

"Fifty dollars, Mayor sign anything. Anyhow, born here, got family."

"Easy doin' business down here. I been makin' friends with a rich kid *Federale,* he rented me my protection. Hooked-up family named Hidalgo. Seem like his uncle got major juice. Money talks down here, but it's gonna take a lot. Hidalgo backing – call that Plan B."

"So Plan A is what?"

"Still workin on that, man. Take some luck, Plan A. An' no more *dreamin'* for a while, right?"

"Si. I know what I done, Len. Was crazy from rock. Still see big gold horse every night, lie dead in trailer. He shit after he die – terrible to see. I wake up and cry at night, get on knees, light candle an' pray 'Biche foal save me. Only way my soul not burn in hell. Long time now I living with this thing.

"You left your phone here and it rang twice," said Holly from where she was seated at her laptop checking her investments. "How's our man in Tica-town?"

"Could be worse. Paco findin' himself again. Gotta be happy an' optimistic or he'll start missin' his family. Didn't tell him about Jimmy yet, but I think they gonna be fine with it. Both country-boy shitkickers, both crazy. Lemme check those calls. Gotta be our Lieutenant."

"*This is your friend Diego Hidalgo,*" said the message, the young voice on overload, vibrating with stress. "Call me soon as you have heard this – an extremely dangerous situation requires for us to speak immediately."

Then:

"Again it is I, Lieutenant Hidalgo. I hope you will reply quickly, as I have apprehended an armed and dangerous man, a criminal. This person was carrying pictures of you, with also a man of the local peasant type, and a horse. He is isolated, in custody, being handled carefully. His identity is Padraic McGoohey, of Los Angeles, about five feet eleven inch, gray hair, green eyes, powerfully built. In his bag we found a large amount of currency, very large, and a pistol, fully loaded."

Len sat stunned, his mind stopped dead.

"What is it, Len?" said Holly quietly. "You look like you just saw a ghost."

"Just about," said Len after a while. His voice sounded unfamiliar to him. "Guess who just got picked up with a gun and a lot of money not far from here."

"Pete Suarez."

"Worse. Padraic McGoohey III. Somebody spilled the beans and he reverted to type. Got himself busted at the checkpoint by our friend Diego few hours ago carryin' pictures of me, Paco, and 'Biche. Got him locked up."

"Well, I told you. I don't know why you have to play with people like that."

"Same thing made me juke out Mr. Budney, I guess. Damn if I know."

"What set him off?"

"Gotta be Pete. Who else? Sure am glad I didn't get all judgmental about our boy Diego an' had the sense to put some money in his hand."

He found Hidalgo's card and began dialing on the hotel phone while speaking to Holly. "Pull over a chair, I need your take on this."

Holly had a pen and some hotel stationary and was sitting next to him by the time the *Federale* answered.

"It is you!" cried Hidalgo. "Excellent! You speak on the hotel phone?"

"Cell-phone reception is poor, but messages work."

"Let us speak freely. If you are ready, I will summarize."

"Go."

"This McGoohey, he had been looking for you much of the day and drawing attention. The local police chief alerted me, and later the man appeared at the checkpoint. He was at first arrogant, pretending to be looking for friends. When I directed my men to search his car, he attempted to bribe me, which is of course a very serious crime. But with what? In the trunk was a cheap bag containing a large sum of U.S. currency and a loaded Smith and Wesson .38, medium barrel. I arrested him. He is in custody as a security risk."

Len listened without interrupting.

"Thank you, Diego," he said. "I cannot thank you enough. This man is mentally unstable, and some time ago he conceived a hostility toward me. I thought it was past."

"At this point I have much to say about what is done with him," said Hidalgo, "and I believe strongly that he can be a very dangerous man. For now is detained in a secure facility on multiple felony charges. He is not permitted a phone call and will remain there as long as we like. We have special rules for drug violators and national security cases, which is how I have indicated he should be treated. Caught red-handed with a large sum, and armed, and then an attempted bribe, yes? And perhaps further evidence with a more complete search – "

"I have no idea, but he is certainly dangerous. Our relationship – it was of a research nature and should have been finished, but he wants something further from me in connection with others I was interviewing, which he knows would violate a signed agreement. I need to speak with my attorney, who is unfortunately out of the country. Would it be possible to detain him for a day or two while I work that out? I would like to speak later, after I've had a chance to think about this."

"Certainly, take your time – "

"Also, can he be held incommunicado until I know my course of action?"

"He is, and he does not have access to his phone; I took it. Nor any phone. If another American appears, they will not meet."

"I will find some way to adequately express my gratitude. Words for now, but that is not enough. He is linked to some very bad people, which I did not know when we met, and he has an uncontrollable temper."

"There is no need to thank me further. He has – how to say it – thanked me already on your behalf, let us say. I have a replacement in mind for my car, a beautiful Porsche. But when your current business is finished, Len, I think that dinner with my uncle in Guadalajara would be a very good idea. He sits on the Judicial Committee, which is a wonderful group to have on your side."

"We will have that dinner, and I will act on this problem immediately, Diego. You'll hear from me quickly. Tomorrow."

After the click came a long silence as Len stared into space. McGoohey had replaced the Sheikh as the locus of his thinking, which bothered him more than the current situation, which was he knew was tightly contained, Mexican style. He sensed the hatred between the two men and knew his old boss was in deep trouble.

"Somebody up there likes you. No other explanation," said Holly, bemused but dead-serious.

"Somebody down here would like a stiff drink. Would somebody like to join him?"

"Yes, me. You run a very dry operation compared to my last employers."

"Glad I'm not going stateside for a while," he said, watching her prepare drinks and place them on a little tray. "Anyhow, he's got the same options as some Gitmo raghead – Mexican jail kind of like Abu Ghraib. I didn't like Diego right off, but I'm getting there."

"Gave me the creeps, too. But whatever it is you do, it was made to order for that boy."

"Rich kid, no focus, just needs something to get him going."

He had a sip of Bushmills and waited while she thought.

"Len, please listen to me. Really listen. We've got this one chance to hit Big Guy a real hard lick, and we'd better do it, because it won't come twice. Personally, I like the rot-in-jail option for anyone who comes after my man with a gun, but I know you won't do that. And while we're talking about gunslingers, why would Pete set him on you? What's in it for him?"

Len's face became unfamiliar to her. He spoke slowly, thinking aloud.

"First of all, money, he's greedy. And gangbangers don't need much *why*. Think like pimps – bored, twisted, looking for laughs. Plus Pete don't like black people at all – that's enough right there. But it looks like they didn't really connect, or McGoo would have come straight to Tica-town instead of running around like a fool and getting himself busted."

He walked to the French doors and opened them before lighting a cigarette while Holly sat waiting.

"Anyhow, it's all set up for Paco to pay off Pete, an' me to buy him out. Once that's done, Pete's gone. And just so you know, in Paco's thinking this is all hooked up with the horse god and the Virgin Mary and getting the curse lifted off him for getting Missile Man killed. If he ever gets on that stuff with you, be real nice and hear him out. He's not like you and me – he's old-style religious, Holly, and that's with him all the time."

"Okay. I listen as long as he needs to talk no matter how quaint and mystical things get. But what about your former employer, Len?"

"Couple nights in a Mexican jail bring him to his senes."

"I don't think so. Not that particular honky."

"Other factors here. His wife will be flipping, and he knows that. She's got no idea where he is, Holly. Guaranteed. She'd've stopped this in a heartbeat. This was a secret mission – that's how he'd go about something like this."

"I saw him in action, Len. He scares me, and I'm totally serious about getting him the message in his own language."

"*Damn* the man!" said Len after a long silence. "Everything he has to lose, and he *still* can't let it alone. Pete must've really got under his skin."

"No, Len, it's you. Pete got him thinking you made a fool of him."

Len looked at her and nodded slowly.

286

"You're right. Makes me eligible for just about anything. Pete sits back and waits to see how it plays out. Scorpions in a jar, one white, one black. Very creative gangbanger, Senor Suarez."

There was an irrational optimism in Jimmy Broughton that affected people around him pleasantly despite his many professed prejudices. Outsiders could feel superior and regard him as a borderline retard, but if they were horse people, they'd respect him as a professional, and know him as good company, which was why Ramon Ortiz, Paco, grooms, horses, and Len Thomas all accepted him and were protective of him. The closer they were with animals, especially thoroughbreds, the better Jimmy got along with them, and he kept his moods to himself. People like Padraic McGoohey III were triflers to him, ignoble and unworthy, like rich fans who bought ball clubs to be around guys they envied.

His disposition on this fine blue morning was excellent, because he knew that whatever was waiting for him, involved Len and Paco. And 'Biche obviously, with whom he shared the special bonding of creatures that have been through a miraculous experience together. As he drove, he took satisfaction in knowing that his faithful Jeep was ready for anything, with spare parts, a case of oil, a set of plugs, and various other items that might be needed. A ten-gallon container of gas was lashed down in a corner, just in case. The old Jeep's natural cruising speed was just about seventy, which is where he held the speedometer as he cruised south. He was feeling liberated to the point of euphoria. Things had gone stale after Saratoga, though he did set up a CD with the assistance of Alice Smith, who explained that the money would be safe from his partying for a year, growing on its own all the while. And he had this nifty trip, his gas, oil, spare parts and new cell phone all paid for now that he was a consultant providing expert advice and elbow grease. As a boy on that hardscrabble farm, no one had ever called him *lazy*. Just a little crazy.

Having set off just before dawn with a quart of strong coffee and two slices of dry toast, he was wild as a coot by noon, singing lugubrious bits and pieces of country and western classics, making up obscene new lyrics, sometimes singing along with the radio he'd bought at the last minute. He'd get tired of Mexican music fast enough, but not those incredibly hot and beautiful girls that went with it. As usual, he was hungry, this time for spaghetti, which he got to eat about once a year. The thought of it sent him back to boyhood, when his goal had been to outgrow his older brothers. He lacked for nothing, the morning was pure pleasure, especially the first long Mexican roadside piss that he put off for almost two hours because he felt that developing control of your body in all possible ways was a plus, except when you were letting it run wild, of course.

"*Yahoooooo!*" he howled, flipping a last few drops from his impressive penis in a near-desert landscape punctuated with small scrubs and cactus under the incredibly deep blue sky. That was one thing you never really saw back in LA – how *spread out* the universe was. Classy, all that space.

Having pissed and yowled, he stretched, then went to the cooler for a coke. Diet or Classic? Special day – he went with the Classic, sugar and all. He'd found a place that carried the little old-fashioned bottles, which tasted better and cost way too much, but were a trip expense, so what the hell. He stood sipping it in the sun in his Dodgers cap and speculating on what Len might have going down here. It had to be a little independent operation, easy enough to set up. With 'Biche for starters, to breed, though he had doubts about Mexican stallions. So there was your missing piece – the stud to cover their born breeder. Assuming, just assuming, this stud showed up quick, it would be years before the foal even got to start a race. But Len would have figured all that out, and what to do in the meantime. He got back in the Jeep, placed the little green half-empty bottle in the caddy, ran down the windows and turned off the AC to enjoy a nice free sauna.

Many carefree hours passed before he was snapped out of this mood around dusk at a road-block manned by a pair of antsy-looking *Federales* with automatic weapons. Jimmy noted their bugged-out eyes and wondered what they were so edgy about out in the middle of nowhere, and he conducted himself with care. Out of sight in the scrub, Hidalgo was reclining on his cot, exhausted by his day. The financial windfall and improved prospects did not off-set the shock and stress of contact with Pat McGoohey. But he roused himself, combing his hair and donning his cap before appearing to join his men.

Jimmy Broughton distracted him and put him in a better mood. He was so completely ordinary, smaller than himself and skinnier, laughably dressed, though clean and neat, and no threat – a perfect ending to this crazy day.

"If you would step from the vehicle, please."

Jimmy bounced out with a hillbilly smile, passport and wallet in hand. Hidalgo was extremely pleased at what appeared to be a cartoonist's creation from the past.

"The purpose of your trip?"

Run down fancy-pants fuckers like you if I can get 'em out in the open and fuck the bejabbers out of your women while I'm at it.

"Looking for a little town called Tica de Gualpa."

Hidalgo looked at him silently, digesting it. High strung by nature, the Lieutenant had had too many surprises and coincidences. Why was Tica de Gualpa suddenly the hub of all this mysterious activity?

"There is not much to be seen there," he said sourly. "It is not popular with Americans."

Jimmy sensed his condition and moved to ease it. "Got a friend in the area. Got his name and number if you like to check it out."

Automatic submission to authority was always pleasing. Hidalgo took the card and lowered his face as he read it. Len's number was another shock, which he tried to conceal. His young eyes tightened with the effort of focusing and reacting appropriately. Without a word he dialed the number and walked away. The connection was barely audible.

"Hello, Diego. I trust the situation is still contained?"

"Much improved, with your troublesome acquaintance behind bars. But a man has just appeared with your phone number "

"Oh, yes – that will be Jim Broughton, an equine consultant on my staff. I'm glad you called, because I'm no longer in that town, but I will meet him there at the cantina. Could you have one of your men direct him, perhaps draw a map? It's not really complicated."

"Soon it will be dark. I must remain at my post, but some-one can lead him there in our vehicle. It's easy to get lost in the dark and not very safe."

"Thank you, Lieutenant. Especially for your handling of Mr. McGoohey."

"Whom we should discuss as soon as I have reviewed the situation with the local police chief. We could request information from California, but this would reveal the prisoner's location. Meanwhile, I will make sure Mr. Broughton arrives."

"A very good point about the information – let's keep it to ourselves until we know more."

"That was my thought. Mr. Broughton will arrive in less than an hour."

After greeting Jimmy, Len rang off. Hidalgo was pleased, thinking that whatever enterprise Len was creating, and he guessed it to be serious, he himself was the inevitable choice as liai-son to the establishment, always critical in Mexico. It was sure to be more interesting than his military career, which hopefully would end soon. He had experienced his first adult *coup* and knew it.

"Big smile," said Holly, watching Len and sipping Bushmills.

"Jimmy's here and I'm going to meet him with Paco. Diego's not so dumb as I been thinkin'. He understood right away that requesting information on McGoo from the U.S. would be a trip-wire. He's definitely got the idea that I'm somebody who can make his life interesting and glamorous. We're on a roll here, babe, just gotta figure what to do with Patsy."

28

With a gun in his ear, McGoohey had been calm, under control and thinking clearly, and his sense of humor had returned by the time they arrived at the jail, which he recognized as Garcia's police station. Cost a bundle to fix, but no point thinking about that yet since no one stateside had any idea where he was yet. The one thing he'd done well was covering his tracks. Fearing his wife, he hadn't called home, but had left a vague message for Alice about being called out of town on business, knowing it would get to Jasmine. The message made no reference to Mexico. He'd called his lawyer the day before, but as usual the Jew bastard hadn't been available and he'd hung up on his secretary, and of course the SOB hadn't called, though he had his cell number. Phone, pistol, wallet, passport, money, all seized by Hidalgo. McGoohey figured they'd squeeze him for ten or twenty thousand, but the *Federales* weren't totally bent, and he guessed that after he'd signed something, they'd send him home minus the .38, and maybe seize the bad-luck Cavalier. But once they knew who he was, worst case he'd be dropped off at the border – embarrassing, but not the end of the world.

His composure was jerked out from under him in a back hallway of the jail/police-station, where he was ordered to strip. He did so in the glare of a single bulb, under the smiling eyes of Chief Garcia, two armed guards, six inmates, and a many roaches. Ethnic hostility was clear when he was denied even his underwear, dressing to the sound of whistles and lewd, demeaning remarks. The filthy old Made-in-Cuba fatigues repulsed him, unlaundered and complete with skid marks. It was late afternoon, and he was shaky, a very rare thing for him. Adrenaline had sucked all the sugar out of his system, and he needed food badly, but he was damned if he'd ask for anything but a phone call, and Hidalgo had emphatically repeated to the Chief that there could be no phone access under any circumstances *whatever*, for national security reasons. Being driven back to the checkpoint, Hidalgo noted the numbers each time the phone rang as they appeared on caller-ID, greatly relieved to getting McGoohey off his hands. Garcia was a seasoned professional looking forward to a payoff. Fine, all in order, twenty percent.

McGoohey pulled himself together quickly, making demands as he changed.

"What about some bottled water?" he asked in a loud voice, and the Chief explained that in this area everyone drank tap water, the water standards being very high. No one smiled.

"I have a sensitive stomach – how about I buy us all a beer?"

This was taken as somewhat offensive, but the guard tossed him his stripped wallet, which now contained twenty-one dollars. Then he was hustled into a large, dirty cell, its perimeter lined with tired mattresses and old army blankets. A hole in one corner emanated the usual stench. When the Chief left, one of the other inmates said his wife would be coming around to the barred window with his dinner. He could arrange a beer, if he also got one as a commission. The others jumped all over him and the room was full of cursing, insults, and accusations until it was negotiated that McGoohey would get three beers, and everyone else one. The price, negotiated through the bars of the window with his agent's wife in the alley, left him with a pair of singles. But the Coronas were cold, and the evening meal arrived after his first bottle: rice, beans, animal cartilage, and tortillas. He was too hungry not to eat, and after that they played poker for matchsticks, belching and farting sociably. Then McGoohey, who hadn't smoked since getting married, talked his beer connection out of a hand-rolled cigarette, pleased in spite of everything to be the obvious alpha male, the biggest, smartest and most dangerous man in the room.

This will be one damn good story once I'm out of here, he thought, digesting and sipping at the third beer. How Big Pat made every mistake in the book and ended up in a cell with a crew you wouldn't hire to clean the crappers. Slipping off exhausted after the card game, these musings morphed into a pleasant dream that continued until 2:00 A.M., when he woke with an uneasy feeling, swiftly followed by a mighty colonic convulsion that barely allowed time to reach the hole in the corner, where his body began firing salvos of unrecognizable semi-liquid matter from both ends, leaving him with one hand braced on the sink, the other against the wall, too weak to balance over the hole, spattered with vomit and feces like everything nearby. Dazed but still concerned with civilized decorum, he searched for something to clean up with. When it had been over for five or ten minutes, a guard offered to sell him a depleted roll of paper towels for a dollar plus the empty bottles, which he agreed to, bathed in a cold sweat and very weak.

When Holly woke up, the solution was as obvious as the sun peeping up the valley. If McGoohey would sign a document, he could go home and things would be fine with Len. Before coffee she was on her laptop, out on the Web looking at model agreements and legal documents, none of which covered the situation. Len slept as she worked, and by ten she had points for a document that needed to be written. Her mind stopped racing, she ate a graham cracker and put on water for coffee, feeling less secure than when she started. Cranking out polysyllabic art-hokum by the yard for an infatuated teacher was easy, but all she had now was essentially a laundry list with no connective tissue. After two cups of black coffee she made a second pass, skimming those model contracts for useful phrases. She knew exactly what she wanted: writing that was simple, severe, and paralytic, in the style of a bureaucrat who specialized in denying insurance claims. It was a black art with its own deadly wave-length, writing that sucked up oxygen, numbing the brain, killing hope and inducing surrender. If she could find that elusive and unnatural manner, the thing would write itself. There was plenty of evidence.

Freshly awake in the pale morning sun, Paco regarded Arabiche with a warm smile, totally involved in her welfare and his own related salvation. Then he went inside the little shed and scooped up some special maternity feed that would, as best as he could figure from the label, prevent weak lower leg-bones. He had rigged a trough near the fence that he could fill conveniently from inside, and she whinnied happily at the delicious smell. Then he came out and watched her eat, graceful and ladylike as always.

"Coming up roses for 'Biche-girl,'" he said in a voice full of affectionate respect. "What you got inside you, you gonna be in the books – dam of great champion, like Mary. You virgin too, look at it certain way."

Then he heard his name in an untroubled voice he was glad to hear. Much as he respected Len, Paco understood his new role and was a little uneasy in the proximity of all that will and wisdom, very happy to hear Jimmy's simple voice coming up the path, his homely face looking like a Grant Wood, the strange child familiar to all inbred dirt-farm families. Paco dropped the feed bag, stepped toward Jimmy, and embraced him. Despite serious drinking the night before, neither was hung over. Two crazy guys, Paco was thinking. But not too crazy to pull off that stunt in Saratoga. Who knew what else they might pull off? First thing, make sure Jimmy feeling at home. Visit a house soon.

"Man, what a difference, hear you voice! Couple weeks ago I lose Carlos – all by myself in this town, this *toilet*, broke and screwed, no one know shit – "

"Yeah, Len tol' me they drivin' you crazy. 'Biche lookin' good though, Packy. Maybe a little light, but her eyes an' how she moves around – got that happy little spring."

"Yeah, she thin, but she just start on special feed. Lotta vitamins, minerals, enzyme, everything. 'Til Len come, was down, man, broke, wait for tiny pay-check. An' Carlos. Kids jus' don' *know*. You down, they gone."

Jimmy was quiet and thoughtful as they looked at the horse and the assortment of feeds.

"Funny thing, Paco, just guessin', but 'Biche act like she got a secret, y'know?"

"Women, they all secrets. We finish up here, they got pretty good coffee at that cantina. I think 'Biche know you good enough she prob'ly wan' to share special secret. 'Bout 'macculate conception. No one else knows whole complete story, jus' Paco."

While he spoke, Jimmy was emptying the night's water and filling the trough from a fresh barrel, full of optimistic speculation and energy. It continued on the dusty walk to town and into the blue-tiled cantina. They were almost alone as men left for the fields, and they ate slowly, Paco enjoying a large breakfast and telling the entire tale of that wild Kentucky night, not omitting the guard who slept standing up. Then, with his soft eyes tearing up, he described the collision that killed Missile Man and left Len hanging upside down in the crushed rentacar, saved by a miracle.

"Rock, man. Rock did it. I bet everything an' all I can borrow, won most money ever have in life, even gang days. Bought my stepfather a scooter to get around, paid way ahead on rent, fix mom's car, cousin Mike tuition two semester, but *still* got money, so I buy this rock. Pure *perico*. Soon Carlos afraid of me, I'm pissing everyone off, 'specially Len. Night we do the deed I am lit. Take out guard, get jism, all set, an' this *thing* happens, crazy dream – Devil speaking from rock."

Jimmy nodded, matter of fact. It stood to reason that someone with Paco's talents would be strange in other ways, which short of murder would be incidental to his gift. Seeing himself understood, Paco continued his confession.

"Devil says 'forget Len plan, you are big man, Paco Gonzalez, got to take action like big man.' Tells me Double-M is my horse – take him. I obey. Minute later, big crash. God save Len but great horse is dead. Snap neck." He shook his head sadly. "So steal fresh car, still got jism, nowhere to go. But I got money up my butt, like old gang days. Steal beautiful old Monte Carlo, keep going, Carlos figure out where get dry ice. Smart boy, but no heart."

"So screw McGoo and steal 'Biche," finished Jimmy. "Nobody at Patch say a word to McGoo 'bout Pete. He just walks in with this guy, couple grooms standing around, takes her out the stall. They see that Nine in his belt, don't say anything, just want him to go far away, right? Fuck McGoo, 'cause it was only you guys made him okay with everyone. But I gotta think McGoo found out somehow, 'cause he split town just before I did, and Alice called me. You think maybe your friend Pete put the squeeze on McGoo?"

"You bet. Pete squeeze stone, he think it has money. Don't know me anymore, Captain Clanton, he fuck everyone equal now, family too, no prejudice."

He lowered his voice as the sun streaming in the doorway was cut off and shut down the conversation with a flick of his eyes as the giant lumbered to the bar, where he accepted a large tequila on the house and presented a filthy old Starbucks container, which was filled while he downed the tequila in one slug. He left with the container, ponderous   and silent.

"Local bad guy, Big Pedro," continued Paco. "He like to steal 'Biche, but Pete spot him right away an' scare him off – says to leave us alone or he come back with artillery. Then Len shows up with *Federale*, so now he *really* scared shit."

"Big guys are a pain in the ass," opined the jockey, which got no argument. "So what's Len thinkin' about doin' down here? I ain't got a clue, but it's gonna cost," he added hopefully. The country air was reminding Jimmy Broughton of his childhood on the farm, pleasant memories of long hard days, home cooking, and roughhousing with his brothers.

"No details so far, just get settled and wait for foal."

"Whatever he's up to, I'm in. I can always pick up local rides, get along until that foal is ready. But tell me – what about the señoritas down here?" he asked as he finished his soft-boiled egg and dry toast, eaten very slowly with full appreciation of the fresh, natural egg.

"Know what? This only place I ever know too cheap have a house. You believe? Women all locked up. But we out of here quick, Len workin' on it."

Holly had been shaking Len's shoulder for half a minute or so, and he was ignoring it, hung over after the obligatory night with his boys. Grumpy and defensive, he knew it would be a slow-brain day. Lured into late sex when he'd needed sleep, Len was not pleased with the woman shaking his shoulder.

"Stop shovin' me, Holly," he said in a thick voice, and she desisted, seeing that he could easily tip into a very bad mood. He raised himself to a sitting position and swung his legs over the mattress, still half asleep, looking at the wall. To himself, he admitted his fear. Jail was temporary, and McGoo was obsessed. He'd stay that way until he got even, and he could grind a man down with his resources and determination. He was the halfback no one wants to tackle.

He smelled coffee and remembered his night. *Tica-town.* How many grey cells had given up the ghost before he finally got to sleep? And why couldn't his woman just let   him sleep?

"Our problems ain't slowed you down much last night," he muttered, reaching for the cup in her hand. He was finding it difficult to remember his life in any kind of order.

"I just needed a little nap first," explained Holly primly. "You surprised me, Len. I'm putting a chain on your leg if I ever have to leave you alone."

"Chain on my heart is what you got, girl," he blurted out, gratifying her enormously.

"Don't say emotional things, we have thinking to do, Llewellyn. I've been working on it, and I think I have a way to get rid of that man permanently. But it depends on Diego."

"Not exactly a weight-bearing kind of guy," he said after a while. Then he lost track of what she was saying. Was the cup really empty? He tilted it slowly, still not waking   up. Empty.

"Isn't real coffee, need some more. And let's not talk so fast while I'm still wakin' up."

Then the unexpected satisfaction of seeing her walk to the little kitchen, holding her tongue, giving him some precious moments of peace. After an interval she spoke again.

"Hungry?" she asked, in a quiet little bell of a voice. Yes, she understood his condition.

"Afraid of the food."

"Me too, but I brought some things with us. It'll be good, Len. Safe."

He noted that she had slowed down without making him feel stupid or unreasonable. Classy, considerate woman. Sex maniac.

"I want to go through my book and think for a while," he said deliberately. "Maybe have a smoke for a change, feel like I'm in a Step Program. Do you think that *Federale* of ours – "

"Of course. You own his poor little adolescent behind. He'll give you anything he has and testify that you walk on water. Turn it into cerveza on request."

How to get the man to a condition where he could wake up, calm down, and think? And read what she'd put together. Feed him. Let him alone and stop fidgeting like an eighth grader waiting for her tits to grow. She almost sighed with relief when he left for his shower. When he returned she was finishing the best breakfast she could contrive.

"*Very* nice," he said, sitting down at the table.

"Pat really threw me off," he added. We can handle the man short-term, but he's dogged. Doesn't give up, enjoys a fight. Lotta resources."

He ate some more scrambled eggs and finished his thought. "I do know Diego really wants to be a player and thinks he can learn from me. *Oh my God – eggs! Mexican eggs!*"

"They're not – they're powdered American eggs. Just eat, Len, there's more. I'm still a little crazy myself since your boss showed up. Last night, it just kind of converted into sex."

"Yeah, didn't it, though?" He swallowed. "Really nice breakfast – don't know how you did it. Feel my strength coming back, like to hear about this idea of yours."

"It's simple," she said, refilling his cup. "After jail softens him up, we get the man to sign a paper admitting to his crimes, at the same time disinforming him, with Diego implicitly complicit, re the source of this document. Simple one-pager. I have some notes for a draft."

"Implicitly complicit, that's pretty neat. Kind of Presidential. But Padraic McGoohey ain't likely signing anything, babe. He'll sit it out, same as I did in Kentucky, because Alice will get his attorney on the case, and they'll eventually figure it out. Car rental, clue one. And there's the documents on the arrest, which legal pressure could turn up. Real problem is Jasmine – Jazz needs a husband, and *she* never did me any harm. Kid needs a father."

"You shitcanning my work without even reading it, Mister Thomas?"

"No, no, just thinking out loud. Read it for the eggs alone. But seriously, this guy is tough. Tough and *thick* – that's why he won't sign, even if it's in his interest."

Holly left without a word, and he read the draft document twice on his next cup of coffee. It left him fully awake, looking out at the mountain in silence as she withdrew to the kitchen. He called to her when his mind had settled down.

"Come back here, lady, explain a few things."

"Like who's it *from*?" he asked as she entered the room with his second breakfast. "And how can you have an agreement with one party to it? I only see one signatory – "

"Diego," she said, sitting down opposite him. "Ethnic hatred enabled by rich-kid entitlement. We're in Mexico, so basically there are no rules."

"How you plan to pull this off?"

"Something like this: Maybe Chief Garcia has a guard tell the prisoner there's someone from the U.S. wants to talk to him. No choice if he wants to get out, so he cooperates. He's brought to a room shackled hand and foot, armed guard. Walks into room and Diego's standing there. Tells him to wait and then he disappears. After he's had a chance to think about it, a Condi Rice type walks in like a cinnamon icicle.

"'Hello, Mr. McGoohey,' and that's it. I decline discussion – not authorized to discuss the matter, no name offered – I just say he's obviously guilty, give him the paper and say read it.

"Then I leave him with the guard to think about it. Come back, explain anything unclear to his honky brain and tell him he can either sign it or squat there indefinitely with his *compadres*. He signs or he belongs to Diego."

Len was wide awake and respectful, then he saw   the downside.

"I like it. But he's not a signer, and Diego – he'll throw away the key, Holly, which I don't like at all. I know they hated each other on sight. And there's still Alice and his lawyer and his wife's family lawyers – they'll find the records from when he crossed the border. Plus he might recognize you from Saratoga."

"He won't, though. I was just an employee he saw one time when he was totally focused on Dixie. You haven't seen me in dyke-bitch mode with the suit and cropped hair – high IQ establishment light-skinned female black woman out to improve herself by any available means. But say he *does* recognize me, which I'll give him time to do – then I play hired gun for the Rich Folks' Equine Mafia. He's guilty as sin under U.S. conspiracy law."

"Fill you in on the mythical Lost Horse Registry later, but don't stop now."

"Either way, he's up Hidalgo Creek. He'll ask who I represent, and I'll say him he can't have that information, which it goes since 9/11. Rendition – no rules outside the U.S. He just doesn't hold any cards, Len, and he'll see that."

Len nodded slowly as she paused.

"And when he sees Diego, he's gonna assume the worst," he mused. "Hate to have you for an enemy, lady. You dangerous."

"And there are lots of witnesses to his threatening Dixie at that restaurant," she added. "His voice carries."

"If he signs, we own him," said Len slowly. "Crossing the border with a concealed weapon and all that money, attempted bribery of a Federale. Missing horse? No one cares. All we need is a little editing," he added tactfully. "Get your points into some legal sounding paragraphs. I worked for a paralegal after the Army. First problem, keep Diego from drowning in the honey jar. Gotta be enough money left for Pat to smell bad."

Holly nodded.

"One signatory?" he asked. "Kind of irregular, wouldn't you say?"

"Not really – the police don't sign confessions. It would be a deposition."

"Yeah, y'right. Better than life with Diego. Well, first thing, gotta get it lookin' right. And with the presidents of these two countries about to sit down again, and all this flak about immigration – perfect timing. That's gonna be a serious meeting, big issues. Cheap labor, trade agreements, oil, union busting. Anyone gets in the way, he's gone. Which Pat will understand, 'cause he operates mainly on scab labor."

He looked at her with a mix of respect, awe, and some doubt.

"Impersonating a government – that's what you're planning, lady. Pretty outrageous."

He paused and thought while she watched.

"Worth a try. Diego's gotta go along, it all hangs on him. Might get scared, but luckily he's corruptible. Gotta get him in that Porsche right away. Kid stuff. I didn't mention it, but it's significant. Kid wants a hot ride, access to hot women."

Their eyes locked for a moment, and afterward he felt remarkably solid when he spoke with the *Federale*.

"I spoke with my attorney and some other involved parties,

and they agreed that for political reasons, this has to go away. I think I have a way to do that."

"The timing is good, Len. Our man becomes more realistic – this I am told by Chief Garcia, who has much experience with those who cross the border for criminal purposes. Our food does not agree with him."

"My attorney stresses that the amount of money McGoohey is allowed to continue to possess is critical."

After a micro-hesitation, Diego continued:

"He arrived with almost $74,000. Normally he might be left with twenty, but I see your point. What does your lawyer think would be acceptable?"

"Fifty."

"I suppose I must sacrifice the turbo feature," said Hidalgo, and both men burst into the special laugh of chicanery unfolding on a perfect victim.

"If McGoohey insists on being stupid, he can disappear. But he must have the option to walk away if he signs a document, essentially a confession," said Len. "It's being drafted."

Hidalgo was speechless for a moment.

"You propose allowing him to return to freedom then?! There is great risk for you, I am sure of it. This man does not forgive, I'm sure of that. He is like me in this."

"Minimal risk, really. The document will be airtight. It will bring him under control. Not to mention his wife when she finds out about this. "

Hidalgo did not laugh.

"It is your choice, of course. I will help any way I can."

"It can work only with your cooperation. I'll be in touch soon, Diego."

"That is assured."

Off the phone, Len nodded a *Yes* to Holly and closed his eyes to think. When he opened his eyes she was gone, and her notes were on the table where his breakfast had been, along with a legal pad, two sharp pencils, and a gum eraser. In his ear was Mr. Johnston's astringent teaching voice: *Respect for the phraseology of a calling.* Yes, it had to smell right. But the reader would be Pat McGoohey – Pat McGoohey alone in a Mexican jail with no lawyer at his elbow and no Alice Smith.

And no copy to show his lawyer afterward. That would be the trump card. If she could actually pull it off, which would depend largely on this little document he had to write. By noon he had finished a draft and he closed his eyes for a while. Then he read it again and made a few changes. The phone rang and Holly passed it to him. He listened briefly, hung up, and spoke to her.

"Well, we rid of Pete, anyhow," said Len, putting down the phone. "Jimmy and Paco gonna stay over in Tijuana and celebrate.

"Still need a Sheikh plan though," he added, "McGoo threw me off."

"I know," she said, "You need time to think, but Lakham isn't 'til tomorrow. I'm going for a swim now. There's fresh coffee."

He sat a while on the balcony enjoying the sun, sipping coffee and watching her swim. Then he went inside, made two more changes, and it smelled right.

Len was glad to be on the phone with Diego rather than face to face, not wanting Diego to see the boredom on his face.

"You continue to propose the possibility of setting him free then, this clearly dangerous man?" asked Hidalgo in a challenging spoiled-boy voice. Len settled himself into the couch and gave Hidalgo a few seconds to hear his own voice. When he ran out of words Len replied.

"Yes, I'm confident, for reasons I can't go into, unfortunately."

Then he slipped into a conspiratorial tone.

"Before proceeding, we should go completely off-record, Diego," he said. "Are you comfortable with that?"

"My lips are sealed. This is a Hidalgo trait, the thing my uncle values above everything."

"Good. Here are the facts, not to be discussed with anyone at all, including close family members. No one."

"Understood."

"My wife has certain connections from her employment. Consequently this document we want him to sign is being vetted not by ordinary lawyers, but by specialists, let's say, with an interest in the situation. I believe they want Mr. McGoohey free to move about in the U.S. so they can see where his activities lead. In any case, he will have to be extremely careful with the document on file."

"He is a very uncooperative man, and we have reliable alternatives."

"He's not stupid; he'll see it as preferable to the alternatives. He is a man of some means, and his assistant, who is effective and determined, would eventually make enough disturbance through his and his wife's lawyers that although his whereabouts are unknown, the car rental and border crossing would be traced, and then followed by media exposure. We should avoid that."

"I see, yes. Fortunately, we bypass routine procedures and when national security or drugs are involved, so there is no record of his arrest, or anything about him. But I would like to read this document."

Len hesitated a long moment to let Hidalgo know this was an awkward request. His voice was stiff when finally spoke.

"I suppose it could be argued that you represent your government, but it's not something I'd want to be known. I have seen a draft, and it is basically an admission of crimes against both our countries. No harm in your seeing it, Diego, but it is *extremely* important that my wife does not know you have seen it. Security is an issue – strings are being pulled, favors called in. It is all highly sensitive – the document, his actions, the timing. Everything about it has a political aspect..."

"I understand. Do not be concerned about my discretion, I understand these things. Mexico is implicitly a party to whatever is agreed. If it comes up, which will never happen, I can say that I read it and found it acceptable. My uncle will be there for me."

The words made sense, but Len was pleased to hear definite insecurity in the Lieutenant's voice. Fear of overstepping. The young Lieutenant began again, more respectfully.

"If I may, Len – I continue to wonder why this man is being allowed to keep any of this seized money he obviously planned to use for some illegal purpose – "

"That is not a question for us to be concerned about. I suppose they want to see what he does with it. Which reminds me of something personal. Do you know the term 'slush fund'?"

303

"Money that is maintained for emergencies under special accounting procedures, I believe."

"Exactly. A couple of days ago you mentioned being short on cash to complete purchase of your Porsche. He must leave with the sum I mentioned, but you should know that we have access to such a fund, and can probably arrange a long-term no-interest loan to bridge this gap. Remind me tonight when Holly leaves the table and we're alone. I may have it by then."

"That would be a beautiful favor – is only seven thousand dollars, and it would enable me to keep my family completely uninvolved."

This was from the heart. His mother hovered above him, clearly visible to Len, who saw his predicament. With her help, Diego could have the money through his trust fund, but that meant he would own this thing of beauty at her discretion, and this might involve the uncle, slowing the process. Too much delay and the car could be lost to his cousin. With this loan, the car would be his immediately, evidence of his first independent accomplishment as a man. McGoohey's arrest and this car together would mark a big step forward in life. His mother would think twice when he drove up the driveway, and his cousin would go mad.

"It is done," said the *Federale*. "When do you wish this meeting to occur?"

"Tonight, a couple of hours after lights out."

"2200 hours – a midnight meeting, then?"

"Or a little later. We should meet at eleven to finalize details. Is that cantina open then?"

"I'll make sure it is, and that we have secure privacy."

"My wife will want to freshen up when we arrive, which will give you a chance to read the document, which is simple and brief. Is time critical to our other transaction?

"Yes, very, but it should be a cashier's check, which takes time."

"If cash is acceptable, I think you could have it tonight."

"That would be perfect."

"It goes without saying that under no circumstances can McGoohey see me or know of my presence in the area, even by rumor, or I might never be rid of him."

"He will not."

"Also, Diego, if you show yourself briefly just before that meeting, it will remind him that he is not dealing with local police, but the Federal government. You should be in the room, say nothing, and leave when he enters."

Hidalgo chuckled nastily. "Yes, the 'silent treatment.' We meet at the cantina at 2300 hours?"

"*D'accord.* I must get off the line now. I look forward to our success and am very obliged to you."

Hidalgo was beyond joy. *What a week!* All in his twenty-first year, all owing to this new friend.

Arrangements in place, Len went downstairs to tell Private Pablo that they'd be returning.

"Get yourself a nice big meal and a bottle of wine," he said in bad Spanish. "Windows open when you smoke."

He'd been thinking about his own long-deferred smoke, but found himself focused on Plan A as if it were a chess problem. A problem where mate is do-able in several moves, but any mistake loses the match, and no draw is possible. The tricky part was a kind of role-reversal. Making the first move, he was playing white. But as soon as they engaged, he had to play black, follow the Sheikh's lead, defer and counter. By the time Holly reappeared and showered he was smiling.

"Well, you've got that look," she said. "Wanna talk about it?"

"Document's finished, you can type it up, two originals. Also got a handle on Plan A. You got kind of a look too, lady."

"Just irritated that I couldn't write that damn document. I was looking at your notes. Being jealous."

Len smiled. "Hey, I just did some editing – you did the heavy lifting, babe. Your idea."

29

Across the room was a manila envelope containing two copies of the agreement typed on heavy bond paper with an electric typewriter from the hotel office, as if to avoid computer record. Reading it again, Len knew that he'd nailed it. Then he listened to the air conditioner and looked out into the afternoon. Plan B was falling into place, with the Hidalgo uncle replacing McGoohey, but with majority ownership for himself. A deal with the Sheikh might be a Paco dream, but Plan B took the pressure off, and either way, he'd want entrée to the Hidalgo network. With the Sheikh as his ally, that entrée would be red carpet and the uncle would be under control. Nice long-shot. He imagined Hidalgo on his phone, happy as a clam, finalizing the deal for the Porsche. He smiled, chuckled, and then burst into a full laugh.

The stress began to reach Holly in late afternoon. Her eyes were no longer perfectly round, and she wanted a drink as she sat with Len at the table, the envelope between them.

"So you're cool with this?" she asked uneasily, knowing he was.

"I am since I talked with Diego," he said patiently. "With us letting McGoo keep fifty thou, he was gonna be seven grand short on that Porsche, which I'm gonna lend him so he can swing this dream ride without borrowing from mom. I like the idea of his being a little in debt to us, and he was real comfortable with it.

"Anyway, all set for midnight, and we'll tie up loose ends beforehand over a drink at a – *cantina securidad,* I guess you'd call it. You excuse yourself a few minutes to the ladies after we order, which gives him time to read this super-secret document. The meeting goes down like you wanted: Diego's there when they bring McGoo to the interrogation room, hand and leg cuffs, armed guard. Handcuffs off, Diego disappears an' you enter. You the Queen. Plus the hottest thing the boy ever saw outside a James Bond flick. Good for me, too, makes me special, future godfather like that uncle."

He saw her relaxing into a little smile and continued. "Truth is, I'm a little shady when I got to be, but you – you a born criminal, lady."

She smiled again, her eyes rounding out as she glanced at the envelope.

"You really made this thing, Len. It's seamless."

She heard her voice as solid again and wondered how much was bluff.

"I want to run the details by you, Len: I start by killing a minute going through some files, to see if he recognizes me. I think he'd say so, and assume that's grounds to say screw you. Then I explain his info went to the U.S. cop-to-cop, and he's connected with a big open case re which he's guilty under RICO. So sign it or retire in Mexico at government expense – "

"Yeah. Diego – death by a thousand bedbugs. And that's just too much, Holly. I *did* kind of steal his horse, y'know. Accidentally by proxy, no intent, no plan, but how would *he* know that? Pete set him up. I just can't stand by and see them destroy the man. And Jasmine and the kid – "

"So just get him in a support group for rich rageaholic Caucasians."

"Holly, you need to hear this part to understand my concern: Diego has a so-called 'black option.' A special beyond-the-law cage for alien threats and inconvenient people. That uncle's right in there – 'The Judicial Committee, a wonderful thing to have on your side.' It's their toy. Model prison, not usual pigpen, but no parole, no records, no good-behavior time. No gettin' out, either, 'cause accordin' to the records you ain't there to begin with."

Holly's face was cold but her eyes were smoking.

"He *asked* for it, Len." Her voice rose to a keening edge he hadn't heard before. "*Loaded pistol and a picture of my man?!*"

He saw the same blind rage he'd felt for the kid-cop in Kentucky. He nodded as if thinking, trying to bring things down.

"He was never going to shoot anyone, Holly, that was just insurance. Way to protect his seventy four K. Lot of money."

"Man's gotta sign," he added cautiously. Then he waited a while.

"You not gonna like this, but you gotta be his friend in court, Holly. I know you want him dead but you have to keep him from doing something stupid. He's the LA version of the Lees, if you can dig it. Where I was a year ago, Holly, life going nowhere – I really needed that job. Needed it *bad*. Responsibility, respect, income."

Her eyes reignited.

"Sometimes you really piss me off, Len Thomas! You keep referring to that one single act as if it justifies everything he's done. The Lees did a *lot* of things for me, all the time. He cut a deal that totally favored himself. He got you low-rent, totally loyal. You risked everything for him, including friends and good name. Even jail. Then he made you into a serious criminal."

She paused and looked into his eyes.

"What you don't seem to understand is *winning*, Len. Winning big, I mean. We're about to win real big – that man's in trouble up to his ears, and when I'm done, he'll know it. You wait and see, Llewellyn Thomas!"

"Stop raising your voice, girl. Don't you get it?! Pete set me up. Pat came after me 'cause he thinks I stole his horse and that jug of sperm! And forget hating him for a minute – I can't watch Jasmine and little Senator Freckles go down for an understandable mistake. What do you think I *am*?"

"How about me, Len? Everything blows up, you guess I'm smart enough to find my way?"

"I guess – I *know* – you're smart and classy enough to get him to sign so he can go home to his wife, nice woman who's goin' crazy by now."

"Your momma ever call you her little preacher-boy?"

"Imp from Hell for a while there."

"You got a visitor, gringo."

The rough voice was quiet and oddly respectful, like a mafia death kiss. McGoohey rose from his mattress verminous and unsteady, a pale, patient, wordless peasant caught in a vast corruption he understood and accepted. Blinded by the flashlight, his toughness undermined by fear for his family, he tried to guess what this rousting meant. Maybe open-ended interrogation, CIA-style. He'd never made a call, so the visitor couldn't be American. All he could do was humbly request that they keep the car and money and turn him loose at the border. Shuffling along in antique leg irons in front of the guard, he tried to think positively. Maybe some big *jefe* had found out and been in touch with the consul...

Maybe his prints had been identified! Hope burst free of his thoughts, which were slow and labored, mind and body weak from diarrhea. Please just one break. Some fellow Mick who'd respond to a tale of marital disaster and a two-day drunk.

No memory of crossing the border! Must happen all the time.

The old masonry caught his professional eye, and his thoughts drifted. When had this filthy excuse for a jail been built?

But in the interrogation room was Lieutenant Hidalgo, standing silent. More bad luck. But no:

"There is a new development in your case, and we have granted an interview. You will be joined by an American shortly. Sit down."

Saved!

He sat at the table as Hidalgo exited, suddenly awake, full of a general and frantic willingness to cooperate. A neatly dressed Mexican civilian entered without a word, then carefully cleaned the table and other chairs as the guard watched.

Jesus H. Christ, who is this mystery man?

The man left and soon a chilly-looking young woman in an expensive suit and tightly shingled hair walked in. Might be black, if you wanted to use that word, but just barely. Hard to tell in this light, and if so she seemed unaware of it, though her expression that reminded him of the National Security Advisor. All business, like he was some genocidal Serb. His fear shot up as he guessed that somehow he'd stumbled into something very big. A mistake, but could he get that across? He doubted himself as much as he had since he was a boy with lots of big brothers, and found himself almost trembling with fear for his wife and child-to-be. When she was seated, the woman placed her attaché case on the other chair and went silently through the files in her case as if he wasn't there. Finally she removed an envelope with two sheets of paper, which he recognized as the police and *Federale* reports.

"Mr. McGoohey, according to all accounts you were tracking down two men. Mexican Police, military security and civilian witnesses agree on your intent to locate them, and your apparent intent either to rob them or force them to cooperate in something, which I assume would probably be your taking possession of the horse in the picture. Is this generally correct?"

At bay, he found the strength to fight back

"Excuse me lady, but who in hell are *you*? I like to know who I'm talkin' to."

"I'm not authorized to tell you that. And we will conduct this interview with civility, or it will be terminated, which I don't think would be in your interest or that of your family."

His strength fled.

"Okay, sorry – I been in here for days, weeks it feels like. What I mean is, who do you represent? Not me for sure. Are you from the U.S. government?"

"I can't discuss that, but I can tell you that you have created a very awkward and embarrassing situation at a very bad time, and the discovery of a large sum of cash and a loaded firearm in your car gives Mexican authorities carte blanche.

"As you may be aware, the Presidents of Mexico and the U.S. are about to meet. Trade, exchange rates, immigration, drug traffic and so forth – these issues are very significant to both countries; you are not."

"So you're from the State Department, National Defense, CIA, some agency like that – "

"You can assume what you want. We have some facts here, though: three major crimes and more evidence than required for conviction in a court on either side of the border. In the U.S., your trial would take place secretly, under new rules applying to special circumstances involving national security, removing you as a possible distraction to the meeting I referred to. Mexican law is more stringent and would probably put you out of the way for at least ten to fifteen years. Your record of repeated brawling, including fairly recent incidents, will work against you, as would your company's repeated safety violations. So while you are a man of some means, your documented history is not that of a model citizen.

"Simply put, releasing you is all risk and no benefit for either government. Am I clear? No one gains from your release except you. The conscience of one scrupulous man is the only reason I am here speaking with you."

"Yeah, I get it. I've done some stupid things down here from drinking too much, but that won't happen ever again, and you can take that to the bank."

"You may be quite sincere, but there's no guarantee that you won't 'drink too much,' as you put it, again, and a lawyer might change your mind. I'll put this bluntly to save time: What is this all *about*, Mr. McGoohey? You are charged with very serious criminal activities by the Mexican government and there is plenty of evidence. These crimes are consistent with your record in the U.S., and they also represent a very troubling escalation, possibly linking the smuggling of Latin illegals and liaison with leftist governments unfriendly to the U.S.

"Most important, it could also involve non-Latin nationals – terrorists linked to sleeper cells. There is precedent for this, though it is not public. I am going to ask you again, and I suggest that you consider the outcome of lying or trying to mislead us: What were you doing here, and what were you planning to do?"

"Yeah, right. Well look, lady, you don't wanna hear my life story, but I can afford as many lawyers as it takes for me to get back home."

"You're sure that's where you want to be, then?"

McGoohey's little green eyes flashed briefly in confusion, and he had a sudden sense of being trapped, that he represented only inconvenience to this woman. Why would he stay in Mexico? Hidalgo hated him. How could she think he would possibly prefer being here?

"You've gotta be kidding – of *course* I wanna be home. Couple of nights here, you don't forget it."

The sound of his voice gave him courage again. Whoever sent this expensive whatever-she-was to this crummy jail, they hadn't sent her without good reason, and it wasn't 'One Scrupulous Man.' Those guys were long gone – gone since Nam. But his lawyer would figure it out, with associates, for a fucking fortune. As he was finding some confidence, she spoke in a flat near-monotone.

"Your recent criminal activities in the U.S. are of considerable magnitude as well. According to the Lost Horse Registry, you are the primary suspect in the death of an extremely valuable thoroughbred, Missile Man of Lee Farms, an Eclipse winner. Under U.S. conspiracy laws, you are as guilty as the employees you sent to steal that horse. Employees you may have intended to silence with that pistol."

She paused, raised her eyes, and spoke more slowly.

"There are witnesses to the restaurant confrontation in Saratoga between yourself and Missile Man's owner. Your words were, 'I'll get you for this, lady.' There were many witnesses, and the Lees would have a strong case that you made good on that threat."

Desperation engulfed McGoohey, a paralyzing sense of naked vulnerability.

"Okay. But that was never meant like it sounded, like a threat. I meant in business terms. I didn't send those guys to kill a horse, that would be crazy – "

"Nevertheless, the horse's death fulfills the threat. Your statement has no legal significance. You set a criminal conspiracy in motion, and under RICO law you are implicated in everything that followed from doing so."

"Okay – what do I have to do? This is the end of my . . . everything, if it comes out."

"Your crimes are not my real concern. The process leading to your release would begin with signing a document I'm about to show you. Read it carefully. I will explicate any unclear points when I return. Provided nothing further comes to light, you will be released when the Mexican authorities have signed off, which should be immediate.

"But bear in mind that you will remain in a very sensitive position. For a period of years, you will continue to be a person of interest. It would be convenient to leave you to your captors, but as stated earlier there are human values here that have drawn the attention of an influential person. That's all I can say."

As she spoke, the military and police reports went into her attaché case and were replaced on the table by two copies of the document. Then she left and McGoohey began reading a confession for a list of crimes accurately detailed, and a personal guarantee that he would never speak or write of them, or this episode, or this meeting, and never return to Mexico. If he did, both governments could be expected to prosecute for those crimes. Remand and deportation options were open upon arrest rather than indictment or conviction, and there was a list of rights and privileges waived should he break silence. It was the smell of National Security.

She returned quickly from her imaginary call, sat, and looked at him.

Finally he spoke in a small voice.

"That's it? Sign my own death warrant and then wait around and hope I get a ride to the border? What about my money?"

"That's not my concern, but my understanding is that your fifty thousand dollars will be returned. I'm prepared to sign off on this on the basis of this interview."

"Deal."

"When the other side signs off, you will be free, and you can count yourself a very lucky man. Your activities won't bear scrutiny, and any lawyer that leads you to think otherwise would be misleading you. Frankly, the secrecy clause protects you as much as the governments involved. A test case would tempt some lawyers, since under the Patriot Act certain constitutional guarantees no longer apply. You entered a conspiracy to commit a major crime for profit and revenge within the U.S., and the evidence suggests that you planned subsequent major crimes in a foreign country. When detected, you attempted to bribe a military officer of that country. Luckily for you, there is no indication of a political aspect to your actions."

McGoohey's defeated body sank into the chair.

"So – what's the plan, if I sign?"

"I can't speak for a foreign government, as I said earlier, but cooperation is assumed. The usual procedure is that when both sides have signed off, you will be taken to the border with your belongings tomorrow. Let me emphasize that because of time constraints you must make your decision quickly; I still have work to do to finalize this when I leave. There is no question of negotiation or altering the document. This whole procedure is a greater favor than you seem to understand. I must also strongly emphasize that if you discuss this with your lawyer, wife, or any third parties when you are released, you will violate Section Four, Privacy and Security, and end your protection under the document."

Listening through a microphone, Hidalgo, a failure in law school, was enormously impressed. Yes, there had been something remarkable about this woman from the beginning, and he had not missed it. He didn't bother trying to guess what her true role might be, or who she reported to – it was enough to be accepted in such circles. His friend Willetts was becoming even more remarkable in Hidalgo's eyes, almost magical.

"Yeah, okay," said McGoohey. He had a rare desire to speak for himself in a personal way about his predicament, and what had in fact occurred. "It was really just a private thing. I never wanted that stud-horse stolen or killed. That was some kind of freak accident never explained to me. And that pistol – I never shot anybody or planned to. That was protection."

When she did not reply or respond in any way at all, he was silent, and there was a pause.

"Okay – so do I get to speak to somebody?"

"You already have, Mr. McGoohey."

On a piece of Mexican government stationery she wrote:

Interviewed, acceptable.

HT

"This is for the Lieutenant.

He signed both copies and she whisked them into the envelope.

"I don't get a copy for myself?"

"One for the U.S. government, one for Mexico. You don't want one; it would be a danger to you."

She gave a sour half-smile, as if very bored with this grotty little assignment, stood up, and left.

30

It was almost noon, and she still couldn't come down from it. Up at dawn after a two hour nap full of horses and Mexican uniforms, she'd spent an hour on line tracking her investments and googling tech companies. Then she began testing her access to the Lee trusts. Had Ronnie by any chance forgotten to cut her off, as he forgot many things? Lazy, privileged and alcoholic, Ronnie Pitt was always dropping the ball. And he'd done it again. Signing in under his name, she tested the passwords taped under the drawer in his office. Still valid. Holly scooped up this fumble, and for the second time in two days she sensed what it was to really be a player. Ball in hand, red zone beckoning, she called a time out and went offline, feeling a strong urge for an early drink. She poured it at the sink and had the first taste standing there, McGoohey style, straight up, water back. A good belt, while gazing out over the peaceful green world as if she owned it. Finishing her drink, she fell into a nap on the couch.

When she woke up hours later, she walked around the suite, looked out the windows, then sat quietly in the living room feeling crazy, glad that her coach was sunning himself on the patio and dozing after many long hard days. It gave her time to get some perspective. Plan A – idea and horseflesh by Len, influence, and financing by Lakham. The great leap forward, but still Len working for someone else, whatever the papers said. Plan B-for-Bootstraps put Len nominally in charge but cash-poor in a foreign country, working with the Hidalgos. Hidalgo turf, Hidalgo backing, and again the difference between paper and power.

Plan C, funded by Lee money, had no drawbacks other than being illegal. As long as Ronnie Pitt was alive, there was zero risk. He could only lock the barn after the horse was stolen, because taking her down would mean taking himself down. And another Lee scandal. Dixie would suppress it at any cost to spare her father, and Ronnie was above suspicion – Pittses had been managing Lee money since his great-grandfather followed Joe Kennedy out of the market in 1929, just ahead of Black Friday. Plan C was purely criminal, and perfect, removing all bosses, senior partners, grey eminences, second guessers, and financial issues. Llewellyn Thomas knew how to handle money, and he was her man, which gave this plan a very special appeal. He was also the man who created that devilish document from her working points, and gambled on her, handing her the ball on a naked reverse, full of his contagious confidence. Plan C also made her the de facto senior partner, which she didn't especially want, knowing Len Thomas very well by now. The big sunny room was saturated with the kind of madness that comes over ad hoc corporate meetings where no notes are taken while a bright young partner-to-be lays out a new technique of white collar thievery for his seniors.

She poured another Bushmills, but had second thoughts after the first sip, and went back to the sink, where she managed to decant the remainder into the bottle without losing a drop. Bursting with her plan and riding her wild wave in silence, she made coffee, assembled a little tray of refreshments, and sashayed out to the little patio. Len was still dozing and sunning himself on the chaise lounge, restoring himself from the excitement, wearing only the scarlet briefs she'd bought him at the hotel gift shop in LA. Smiling, she passed a cup of coffee back and forth under his nose until he blinked. She envied his relaxation but he seemed a little slow to her edgy eye.

"Lookin' at the Lieutenant's card, occurred to me to check those phone books down the lobby," he said, California-casual. "That boy's *connected*. Solid fallback if he delivers his uncle, which I think he can. No problem about papers, Mexico so rotten you can fix anything. Plan B's alive and well, 'specially after Diego heard you work out on McGoo last night. You scared the boy. Tiny sliver of the pie, party invites and a little respect, that's all he wants. Point is, don't worry 'bout the Sheikh – he don't wanna play, we still fine. And before I leave it out, what you did last night – that was *clutch*, babe. One thing I can do, spot talent. You right up there with Paco."

She felt herself smiling at the Paco comparison and settled down. McGoohey had signed, but it was Len's voice bringing her gently down now. Standing inside the open French doors, out of the baking mid-day heat, she actually forgot Plan C for a long moment while contemplating her man of choice.

Home free, she thought, because whatever the legal value of that document under U.S. law, it was rock solid in Mexico, which was where they'd be for at least several years. And of which they could easily become citizens, which would be critical if Dixie attacked. Then, like someone recovering from a dizzy spell, she experienced a major epiphany.

Llewellyn Thomas, unlike most people, was really not in it for the money, it being life. He would want absolutely nothing to do with Plan C. It would seriously upset him, like doping his horse had. And it would lower her in his eyes, because Len didn't want to be a criminal. That was exactly what he *didn't* want. He knew exactly where he stood with that, and preferred going to work at dawn with the horses and earning the modest salary of an unproven trainer because he loved doing it. That part of him was everyday ordinary middle-class – he was satisfied to live well. It was all he asked, and he'd been willing to put up with Pat McGoohey to live that life until the man made it impossible. The doping in Saratoga had done more to his insides than that Spuyten Duyvil beating had done to McGoohey's ego, and he he knew from Detective Finn and that jail that he was out of free passes.

Len sipped coffee and she dug deeper, recalling what he'd said about 'Biche needing third place at Saratoga to be sure of his job, and his anger about the sperm theft. His crimes hadn't been for sport, like Little Isaac's. No wonder his eyes would get stuck out in the middle distance sometimes as he tried to work free of all that and focus on his personal dream, his innocent, untested belief that he was *good enough* – that with Paco behind him, he could play with Harry Armstrong and Fred Purtees. And Bob Baffert and Wayne Lucas. Simple dream of the winner's circle, and sticking it to those hard, smart, insolent, winning white men with a civil smile like Jimmy Winkfield would. A clean dream with no hate in it, just ardent desire.

Seeing it so clearly made her feel weak and dirty. And stupid, for having mistaken his sexy good looks for the man he was. Feeling unworthy, embarrassed and foolish, glad he couldn't see her face, she pulled herself together and consigned her nasty conniving to the past. How had she even *considered* cheating the Lees after all the affection and trust they'd put in her? And love, too.

I need this guy to keep me on the straight and narrow, thought Holly St. Cyr. *Keep me from being the horrible bitch Little Isaac had in mind, because Len's right about that criminal streak.*

She walked over and sat down on the other patio chair, so they could see each other.

"Len," she said in a reasonably normal voice, "I'm just about *dead*. I must've walked ten miles the day before yesterday, got all sweaty and bitchy until the phone worked. And then McGoohey last night. I haven't slept at all. I really need a bath and a book, and then could we just eat early in the room? Maybe watch some TV or a movie and come down off all the excitement?"

"Sure can, babe. Les' have a look at that menu an' see what might be safe."

"And a drink. We've been carrying that bottle around forever."

"Best in the world. Ask Pat next time you see him – he introduced me to it."

"We'll drink to Pat then. To the improvement of his soul."

"Baby, too – drink to that special baby of his. If I understand matrilineal descent, Padraic McGoohey III will be fathering an authentic, certifiable Jewish baby. Worst business enemy Jed Kline, gonna be *Uncle* Jed."

Then his voice softened.

"Just put the Sheikh out of your mind, babe. It's a long-shot and I know it, but there's always a way if a horse can really run, specially down here. Since I paid out Paco, 'Biche is my pony except a little slice. Cut a little taste for Jimmy, too, make sure he doesn't wander off. Once people see what we have here, I can deal. No real problem either way, 'cause we're hooked up. Diego's solid and Paco's known down here. For sure no beaner pony ever take Black Ice to a photo."

Naked in the sun except for the scarlet briefs, he looked divine, she thought. Composed, carnal, and maybe just a *little* bit criminal.

"Let's just have us a nice easy time, Holly. I'll see the boys in the morning."

318

She went inside, then reappeared in a wide straw hat, lowering herself delicately into the white mesh chair.

"We never talk money, Len, and we should. I know you have some, and I have a little, too. The Lees paid for everything and I just saved. We should lay our cards on the table, see what we've got and think about how to leverage it. No matter if I have more, this is your show on the basis of the livestock and sweat equity. And that business minor wasn't wasted on me – if we end up going with the Hidalgos, I can beat most guys at drop-the-soap."

"Oh, I saw that last night, lady."

Then he spoke gently in his most natural voice. "Holly, all this flim-flam you been seein' – just a phase. End of a phase. Up in Saratoga I thought I maybe wanted out of racing, but it's in my blood. I really want to be a big-league trainer with one boss horse and some other good ones to keep me busy. That's what you'd be putting your money into. Me and Paco and the foal. And you don't have to, you know. I wasn't thinkin' money when I decided to ask Flash Budney's date for a dance."

"Oh, what a sweet man you can be, Llewellyn Thomas."

"Nicest Negro ever want to meet, most the time. Y'know, now that I had some rest, I've got a godawful hunger for a real meal. Place like this, beef's pretty safe, if it's seared. Bacilli mainly on the outside, so definitely not ground beef. And potatoes okay if they're baked."

"Nothing green?"

"Not for this nigger."

"*Len!*" she cried in an outraged voice.

"You're right. I meant to say *Negro*. So did Richard Pryor, he just used to get high and forget."

She gave him a superior glance, and after a while he heard her snooty-flutey telephone voice.

"This is room 5-1-5. We'd like two filet mignon, medium rare. Cooked on a very high flame, so the outside is seared. They must be *seared*. Not well done, but the flame must touch the entire steak."

Looking over the hills, Len felt settled and rational. However much she contributed, it would help. He guessed that like himself, she'd be just breaking into the six-figure range, which would double his stake. Helpful with the Hidalgos, whom he saw as his real-world partners. And at the current burn rate he needed to make a move soon. A drink appeared on his tray and then a pair of soft hands was moving slowly down along his ribcage. Indescribable luxury.

"If you didn't have such a fine elegant body, I could never overlook your low side."

"Huh! I was thinkin' the exact same thing about you, lady. It's those plumpy nipples. Never saw such nipples in my life."

"They're imported. Creoles have special French luxury features." Then she pinched his ribs and walked around in front of him teasingly, slipping off her blouse.

"All yours, Llewellyn. You gave them complete amnesia about their previous lives. All yours until that call to the Sheikh."

"That's not for another day."

"Right! You are such a clever man."

"Mus' be. You ain't put up with stupid peoples, anyone see that."

A different voice answered the phone this time, a white American female office voice, handing her off nicely. Then came a young male exec with a chilly European accent.

"Yes. This is in reference to – ?"

"The Sheikh is aware of the purpose of the call, which I'm not free to discuss," she said. "As I told Ms. Fischer Tuesday, I am Holly St. Cyr, executive assistant to Llewellyn Thomas of St. Thomas Racing. We can set the call for another time if this is inconvenient for your employer."

Then it was the Sheikh-Prince, his voice hard and light.

"And you are the same Holly of that very pleasant evening at Lee Farms. You were dismissed for disrespect, I suppose?"

"No, of course not. I was tired of interior decorating."

He responded with a quiet laugh that sounded genuine.

"Yes, understandable, and I remember that charming room quite well. Mr. Thomas formerly of McGoohey Farms – that was the nice little mare that surprised everyone in Saratoga. Tell me about this."

320

"I think that would be more Mr. Thomas's department."

"He is with you now?"

"Yes."

"Good, we will penetrate this mystery. Very nice to hear from you, Holly. We should meet again."

Without responding to this, she nodded at Len and handed him the phone.

"Llewellyn Thomas," he said in a not quite flat voice. "Thank you for accommodating my schedule, Sheikh Lakham."

"I am always ready to discuss horses. Would I be correct that this is in connection with the little mare, and that you might wish to breed her?"

"Yes, to the first part, but the circumstances are a little complicated. Something more wisely discussed in private."

Long silence. Len slowly emptied his lungs, then took in a long slow breath of fresh mountain air, imagining the Sheikh as he considered this strange call and its unprepared request. Then he felt the man leap tiger-like to the heart of the matter.

"If she is not to be bred, can I assume that this has already occurred, and that it is an auspicious pairing?"

"Yes," said Len, without explanation.

"Missile Man," said the Sheikh with another deadly leap, voice quietly loaded. "Mr. McGoohey's first choice, I recall. A tragedy, his death."

"That was a very terrible thing," said Len, at his most serious. "I would not call if I were responsible for that, but I think I do know what happened there."

"I see. What can you tell me – we must be brief, I have obligations."

"The mare is with foal. It is promising – I would call it extremely promising, the bloodlines. But the situation is larger than I can arrange for properly myself."

"I think this is worth discussing."

As quick now as he had been doubtful before.

"Good, then. We can meet at your convenience. I have appointments tomorrow, but I could be on a plane any time after that," replied Len in the flat, businesslike tone. He slowly emptied his diaphragm, breathing deliberately, waiting.

The pause extended itself as if he had committed some gaffe and the Sheikh was considering a polite escape.

Wrong move. Damn. But they'd have to meet to do business. He felt himself age several years in a few seconds, saw his house of cards for what it was, forgot Plan B, and felt himself at the edge of that terrible slide down the classic black man's slippery slope. He stood pat.

"Yes," said the Sheikh. "Well, it seems I will be in Paris next weekend," he said cheerfully, as if he'd been consulting a calendar or assistant. "You can stay at our home. You will identify yourself under what name, then?"

"My own."

"You will be expected – you need only announce yourself on arriving. You will be alone?"

"Yes."

"I cannot be, as you will understand, but no trainer will be present, only those who preserve my existence under Allah, and probably some family members. I think what we are discussing is the – fathering would it be? – of that foal, by an unnamed sire?"

"Yes."

"Good! You must understand that I will ask for a substantial share and a voice in her future breeding. That is acceptable?"

"In principle, yes. But you will be unable to reach me at this number to cancel if necessary."

"Oh, I will definitely be there. The house is in Neuilly. Just ask for the Lakham house, it's on a lane of that name in the northern section. Anyone local will know where it is. A man named Alberto will meet you – you will recognize him. He is one of those whom Allah has favored in many ways, but not with the social graces. Don't be put off. And now I must leave. *Salaam Aleichem.*"

"*Aleichem salaam.*"

Another test, thought Len. A little series of tests, which he'd apparently passed. He felt weak, as if a nap would feel very good, or a nice taste of Humboldt Natural while reclining on his couch at home. Holly waited. After some seconds he drew a big breath. Then he was silent another few seconds, not moving.

"You did it, Holly," he said thoughtfully. "We meet in Paris on the tenth at his house. He guessed what's going on, and he's cool with it. The man is *quick*."

"He wants to kick Crusader butt real bad. When they retired Missile Man early on such a minor injury, he lost a chance to make some history. Two top horses of the new century."

"Exactly how he sounded. The only issue might be me getting to work my own show, which he's probably guessed already. It'd be nothing to set up a little operation down here. Dirt-cheap, inconspicuous, and 'Biche would be lost in the shuffle. Foal comes up a winner – well, just another Lakham success."

"And yours."

"And Paco's, babe. Me'n my crazy codependent horse magician who made all this happen. Gonna be interesting at Churchill if we make it. Us and the Sheikh – Dixie's gonna love it."

"Feel sorry for her, Len. I've got nothing against the woman, she did a lot for me. Had her life blown up 'cause Paco had a coke dream. Totally destroyed her life's work. And then me of course."

Seeing that he understood, she found herself admitting Paco's importance for the first time. If it happened, which instinct told her it was, Paco's idiot savant dream and blind faith would be the making of Len Thomas and all of them. Walking down the mountain in the dry, silent heat with their footsteps whispering in the gravel, she took her time, then spoke in what she hoped was a reasonable tone.

"You gonna fool around on me over there, Llewellyn?"

"Be serious, Holly, bad time for soap opera – Junior's happy, got no secret cravings, and I'm just now startin' to come down off that call. How he seemed to kind of know it all already. Man knows it ain't kosher for sure. That detective Finn – I'd hate to have him makin' the Sheikh knowledgeable. Set me up."

The paranoia was evident, a huge wave from nowhere. Her reply was light, almost casual.

"They just want it to be history, Len. They want it to go away. Finn works for Oxland, and Dixie owns Oxland, end of story. Those dish-vans and spy-mikes and reporters? Not how Daddy Tom wants Lee Farms to be seen."

"Yeah, that sounds right. I'm takin' a while to wind down from that little talk. Big jump from fugitive status. Gotta be real careful."

By the last phrase she heard that he was somewhere else, talking to himself, not winding down at all. She said nothing, waiting carefully, feeling the weirdness of a different and dangerous Len Thomas. Still walking in silence, he noticed the heavy stones in the dry earth bordering the path.

"Like this *phone*," he said in a cold tight voice. He left the path, selected a big stone, placed the phone on a small boulder, and began methodically smashing it in a half-controlled frenzy that Holly watched without a word. It didn't bother her as much as she'd have expected, but it set her wondering, not for the first time, if any black man ever really broke out without some of that madness in him. Maybe Colin Powell, but from the way he accepted his political humiliations, he might have less real freedom than the momentarily crazed Llewellyn Thomas. As she watched, the phone was reduced to a handful of crushed fragments which he carried along in his left hand, tossing bits here and there with his right hand.

Might be a psychopath after all, he was thinking as he tossed pieces right and left. She walked alongside and there were several minutes of silence.

"Oughta take the boys out to dinner tonight, all of us together," he said after a while in his usual voice. "Nothing about Paris or the Sheikh – just say I got some nibbles, goin' east for a couple days. But we gotta move 'em someplace decent right away. Invest in morale, celebrate with some good food."

"No problem, Chief, I'll get it done. And let's skip the tight-sphincter dining room – Laughing Goat Lounge, that's where this party of four belongs. So what is it? two days before you leave? I want to see what I can do on air-fares. I'm gonna make you a present of a first-class ticket, and arrange for you to get picked up. You need to come in on top, mister good-lookin'."

"Need a *pipe* is what I need. Paco says he found something worth smoking."

"You go right ahead and fry your synapses Len, I want all mine operating so I can take good care of my boys. But later there's ways we can prep for that meeting."

324

"How's that, Holly?"

"The web. Research the Lakhams and Arab culture. *Islam.*"

"Right. Islam. Proper technique of salaam, what not to say at the mosque. Actually used to know a few of the basics 'cause some of my friends back east were into it. Maybe I forget about pipin' for a while, do us a cram course. For a hot babe you pretty smart."

31

Len stood for a long moment taking in the half-deserted airport and pulling himself together as he looked for his woman, aware of his state, conserving energy. Not here. Peculiar.

"I didn't like the waiting," said Holly, appearing from nowhere at his shoulder. She didn't look as if she would be demanding, but she didn't look very happy. He faced her, foggy with lack of sleep, unable to remember the airport. It was the longest they'd been apart since she appeared to release him from jail, and he wasn't sure how it would go. Stupid to save money by returning coach, changing planes and missing connections, draining himself. Did she have a look in her eye? He was too tired to be sure. Would she be imagining jealous things and turn on him right there in public? He'd seen women do things like that.

Didn't happen – just a small, friendly kiss. She noticed that his breath was rank and sour, a first, but her sensibility ignored the affront.

"Shoulda done it your way, first class. Gonna forgive me?"

"I have to. I'm not used to that, of course."

"'Nothin' go right when your woman angry' – old underground railroad folk saying from Boston I just made up."

She smiled at him and her eyes softened as they walked through the empty airport.

"I'm not angry, Len, I'm recovering from my family. I don't know about the Lakhams, but *my* family was running a full-court press and I didn't enjoy it. They are damn nosy. Sheikh like that too?"

"Not at all. And I think I cut us a real good deal. Plus I get to call him Adji now, which is practically family. No lawyers either side, very simple deal. Handshake, hand-written one-pager. But his handshake good, and he takin' all the risk. Way better than – "

He stopped speaking and his voice changed as they ambled slowly through the big bright, empty space. "Y'know, Holly, I get luck sometimes I just can't believe. Like you. Can we get a drink? Us owners, we smoke less, drink more."

"The boys are parked outside, you know."

"This is Mexico, an' they good at waitin'. 'Specially Paco, Paco right out of Beckett. I feel like they our kids, but I need a little time with Mom."

Something told him to turn left, which he did.

"I see we found the bar somehow."

"Shall we sip then, you and I, while the sun sits like an omelet frying up there in the sky?"

Her eyes lit and she almost giggled. No men she knew had ever made literary jokes; the quality didn't matter.

The bar was quiet, half empty on Tuesday afternoon, the few patrons relaxed and casual, the way he wanted to feel himself. He slid his bag into a booth while appreciating the neat little way Holly got her bottom positioned. Woman like that spot a psychopath in a New York minute, he thought. Sheikh too, I must be okay. Just get angry at a cop or a cell phone sometimes.

She looked at him squarely, concern in her face.

"You really *are* tired. You've still got your sense of humor, but I never saw your eyes hang down like this before. Are you okay, Llewellyn?"

"I will be. This is one time I really do need a nice big drink. God, I hate flying. Cattle cars full of dirty air – you can taste it."

As he relaxed, he exhaled with a long sighing   sound, exhausted.

"This thing with the family was *bad*, Holly. Like gettin' in a game for serious money and not knowin' the rules. Playin' off the chords as they go by like a horn player fakin' a tune. Big strain, listen for cues every bar. Just keep smilin'."

He slipped into silence. When the waitress came by, Holly caught her eye and spoke quietly to save Len the bother.

"Large Bushmills, water back, glass of Chilean Merlot."

Pleased, he nodded and smiled, returning from another world. Just like that he'd been in Saratoga, 'Biche hot-walking head down with Carlos after the race, himself thinking how she must feel after that incredible effort.

"Take your time Len," said Holly.

Paris. Gotta get around to Paris before I pass out here.

"Driver knew right where to go. Big old stone house set back from the road behind a tall thick hedge. Fine hedges, really outstanding. His man Alberto answers the doorbell in about one second, lets me know I was bein' observed. Remembered him from Saratoga, Mister Security. Big Al, I think they did somethin' to his tongue. Painful to speak, only does so when necessary.

"*'I'm Mr. Thomas.' 'Please come in Mr. Thomas; I am Alberto.'* Door weighs a ton, probably take a tank rocket, and God knows how thick those stone walls would be. Like a bunker, but very nice décor. Not much stuff, but nice – got to see a Vermeer."

The drinks arrived, and each had a small sip. Len closed his eyes for a moment, still unable to organize   his thoughts.

"Gonna take a timeout here, babe. Back soon."

He closed his eyes and let the movie run. Alberto with his bag, leading him into a vast, warm, nearly empty room with beautiful rugs and an extra-long brown leather couch at one end. Alberto stopping to press a button without explanation. Little humming sound as a wood-slat screen at the far end rolled up to reveal a theater-size screen. *Clickety-Clickety-Clickety-Clickety.* Hint Number One – this is the hub, come back here after I clean up.

Then down a wide hall to his vast two-room suite with its big marble tub, which he filled with very hot water. Hung his blazer in the steamy room to get rid of the creases and then nearly fell asleep in the tub. Blazer restored, cold wake-up shower, back to the screening room and its endless couch. Real comfy, nothing to read except finance publications, but one long wall was solid with race videos, the other with horse paintings and photos. Reappearance of Alberto with a sort of grudging half-nod, half-bow, handing him a big leather book that matched the couch. Sommelier offering wine list – Mr. Thomas to select. Aggressive.

Settling into the big couch, he saw that he was holding the first of several volumes listing videos and containing extensive French, English, German and Arabic press clips. He took his time, Alberto at the ready. Too ready, let Al wait a while. The album was chronological, starting in 1919. He started with the first, Frigate-Almadine. Frigate, owned by some Brit, Almadine the Lakham entry. Len didn't know anything about European racing circa The Great War, but he did know the Arc de Triomphe was the top French race, and it would have been a great win for them after those years in the trenches, which he'd read about.

"I'll watch this one, Alberto."

In a businesslike tone, like Paco when dealing with a difficult horse. Then he walked to the left wall – paintings of Lakham horses going back to the early eighteen hundreds; the right wall had photographs of more recent ones.

In this game forever.

"If you are ready, Mr. Thomas?"

Old-fashioned standing start. Frigate, a small stallion with a lot of victories and balls was off like a shot, out to steal the race. Then a group of three led by the huge French champion chasing hard to stay in striking distance, but Frigate was flying. Beautiful dancing stride, holding several lengths well into the last turn, the French champion slowly gaining. And just as Frigate was smelling the finish out shot from behind the big French horse, fresh as a daisy, shooting past both to win by a neck. Beautiful piece of racing history from that single blurry black-and-white camera. *Very big upset* said the journals. Some said miraculous, since Almadine had done little that year. Len became absorbed in the commentary, remembering enough French to pick up the sense of it. One English writer suggested a pattern of lightly-raced Lakham horses peaking for classics. Another wrote of the "black cloak of invincibility" that Lakham seemed to wear on the biggest days. *Lose battles, win war.* Which could look like the plan with 'Biche in Saratoga. That would be living up to his nose.

Caught by surprise when the Sheikh appeared. Tall, slim, immaculate and smiling, with a neat, friendly little mustache to set off his bespoke tweed jacket and French flannel slacks. *Clean,* thought Len, standing to shake hands. Miles Davis without the attitude. Alberto disappeared and returned with three bottles of sherry on an antique silver tray, one of them hand-labeled.

"These are all good, this one extra-dry, the middle one a very nice medium amontillado, and then a heavier one that the English favor."

"I'll try the Amontillado."

"It's excellent for a day like this with a chill in the air. Your trip was not too bad, then? You look well."

"Not bad at all. I had a good book and a nice bottle of wine."

"What did you choose to view?" asked Lakham as Alberto filled the glasses and he seated himself at the other end of the couch with what felt like an egalitarian   spirit to Len.

"Frigate–Almadine."

"Oh yes – "the black cloak of invincibility." Our first big victory after that war, a surprise to the journalists, but not my great-uncle. He was quite young, with ideas of his own, included in his journals, which also contained the names of many girls. Lots of easy kilometers and no real efforts in the prep races, especially with Almadine. She would come alive late in a race, but recovered slowly. 'A creature of tremendous heart,' he wrote. Not to say pure speed, as you saw. I thought you might have prepared your Arabiche along those lines."

"Yes. She wasn't a fit animal when purchased – run down from too much racing. But then she got very strong, much better than expected. Paco, whom you met, saw it coming. We decided to keep our little secret."

Total fiction, but plausible. The Sheikh nodded, topping up their sherries with a small smile, Alberto having disappeared.

Thinks maybe we've got something in common now.

"Well, she gave them something to think about. I thought she had Black Ice, but that is a very fine horse, especially at the finish." The Sheikh went to the wall of videos and played DeQuincy at Saratoga under a deliberate, dominating ride that was over before the last pole. Then a shot of tough, swarthy, sneering-smiling Ramon Ortiz, who had never mentioned this ride to Len or Jimmy. Of course he hadn't cared about Novetta with that on his plate!

"We planned for him to meet Missile Man here, and again in the Breeders. A pity about that little hock injury – that could be expected to heal quickly, but he was injury prone, so an understandable decision in business terms."

Which were clearly not his terms. But his tone was forgiving, considering that a meeting of those particular horses would have been the most important of the new century, and centerpiece of Lakham's U.S. campaign. Len was about to have another sip of sherry when he saw 'Biche and the others entering the gate for her race. Len's heart gave a gentle *thump*. Saratoga had done so much to him that he'd avoided watching the tape. How much could be seen of those last   seconds?

Her usual perfect start, but quick, and she was working her way through the field as if they were making room for her, which some were. Flash of paranoia then. *Where's he going with this?*

But it made sense to look at the horse that brought them together. Fine, until the Sheikh slowed the action as 'Biche went into her picture-perfect final turn, gaining, gaining, *still* gaining, passing the three horse, then creeping up the unguarded rail until she was at Black Ice's neck. Then ever so gradually almost nose to nose, Jimmy going to the crop. On the far side, thank God. 'Biche ready to take the Queen. Definitely ready, not peaked out. But in using the crop, or appearing to, Jimmy also let his body slide back. Nothing obvious, almost not at all, but jarring the perfect bond. Neither man said anything, and then Len shook his head sadly.

"An opportunity lost, would you say?" inquired the Sheikh, his soft voice unreadable.

"The owner did. Several times. He blamed Broughton, the jockey. Broughton was angry with himself for not going earlier."

"Him I have not heard of, either. He could have been smoother at the end."

"Maybe so. We thought about someone else, but Broughton always did better with her."

"He had more horse than expected that day, perhaps? A little more Amontillado?"

"Please." Len wondered what might be showing on his face. "My fault, if anyone's. And you're right – we never expected that much of her. Beat Black Ice at her own   game… ?"

"I do not criticize – a marvelous effort for an unknown animal and rider. But then the owner undid all your work."

"I take it this will be a complete outcross, this foal?" he added, with no transition.

"Total," replied Len, blindsided but ready. "No shared ancestors for at least six generations."

"I believe in this," said Lakham with conviction, not asking the obvious question. "There are far too many overbred horses – they look good on paper and at a sale, sometimes very fast, but with so many problems. It is like raising orchids. The outcross, fresh blood, can produce hybrid vigor, the cure for this inbreeding when done with care. I picked it up from the old man at Claiborne, and he knew some science. He liked a healthy horse. Do you have her chart?"

Len nodded and reached into his jacket for a copy of the original, which the Sheikh removed from its envelope and scrutinized in silence for half a minute. Then he smiled, his finger tapping a name in the chart.

"*Charleymyboy,*" he said with satisfaction. "Another unknown with an unknown owner. I looked at him, visited, made a good offer. I wanted him, but the owner was unreasonable."

As they spoke, several men between twenty and forty quietly entered the room wearing white traditional Arab garb. Acting on some personal radar, Alberto was gone with the sherry tray and glasses as they entered.

"Some stomachs are upset by travel, but I hope you will join us for a meal, said the Sheikh."

"Thank you, I will."

Len rose to be introduced to the brothers, then sensed the focus of attention moving behind him. The Godfather had his own door. Very slowly, a thin old man with a cane proceeded into the room, head high, accompanied by his doctor, oxygen rig at the ready. With his entry, a great white cloth was spread by servants and a meal was appearing. Len recognized him; Holly had found the old devil on the Internet – Achmed-Ibn-Something-Lakham. Still a top royal advisor at an estimated eighty-five to ninety. Skin, bones, and balls, thought Len. And eyes that raked the group with what looked like bored irritation, ignoring Len. Then he made his way to what would obviously be the head of the table.

Suddenly back in the airport, Len looked at his empty glass and realized how long his trance had been.

"You look better now," said Holly.

"Yeah. Took a while. Well, the Sheikh: Sheikh very polite an' considerate, but he had these little *tests* for me. Saratoga tape, finish in slo-mo. Jimmy was pretty slick once he came to his senses, hell of an acting job. Adji thinks I'm smart 'cause he thinks we prepared her the Lakham way – low profile until the big race.

"It all came down to dinner – dinner the big test. Men only. Old Achmed Ibn Whatever at one end of this big white cloth spread on the floor, no one at other end – godfather chairing the committee and ignoring me. We all sitting cross-legged on the rug around this big white cloth. Meet the relatives but no introduction to godfather. After he's through ignoring me, he looks right at me like he's inspecting a slave, I guess. Tough old bastard.

"Food in waves. Not much I recognized, except lamb like you never tasted on this earth. But I dig in – everybody diggin' freely, enjoyin', passing me things to try, all with a smile. They got their own smile, hard for outsiders to read. They like the way I keep eatin' everything and expressin' my appreciation. No idea what they thinkin'. No clue what the hell to do or say, what's polite and what's insulting. English, French and Arabic flying around, Sheikh super-helpful, keepin' me up to speed on the conversation, passing me delicacies. I imitated this English teacher I used to have a lot of respect for. Mr. Johnston, very well bred, old Boston.

"Manners to burn – I kept seeing that about our guy. My brain was on such high rpms by then that my French started to come back. One guy asks in French, 'What's wrong with Purtees?' and our boy says in French – dig it – 'He doesn't fit with Americans, they are too quick and it upsets him. Europe is enough for him.'"

"Goes on to politics. Someone says it's those *Anglais* behind all the troubles, '*et les Juifs.*'"

"'*Oui, oui!*' says Llewellyn of Los Angeles, born-again bigot. Just came out. They so surprised an American speaks any French their eyes pop like in a cartoon, and of course they think I been following everything, including the observations and speculations on my nose, melanin count, politics, American policies, etc. So they figure they got a semi-seditious Black American Hebephobe. That broke the ice, and pretty soon they admit to knowing a little more English. Kept asking me questions about *America*, like I can explain us. They sure don't like that Iraq situation at all, can't figure out why the excitement when they pinned down every which way an' starvin'. Don't like Saddam either, of course – no religion, all those dangerous secular schools, women runnin' wild by their standards."

He went blank and sat waiting to find himself again. Holly had a sip of wine.

"What about our Sheikh?" she asked. "*En famille?*"

"Yeah, that's interesting. Big juice. He's the smart one. Bein' in charge of the horses is real big. Oil is like, very important, but it's just trade, routine business, whereas the horses are about honor. They're serious about that, as if Allah isn't sure if men or horses are preferable."

"Tell me the business part, Llewellyn. The money."

"Okay, in a little bit, but he can't know I share information like that, 'specially with a *woman*. He live in olden times when it come to women, and probably a lot of other things, too."

He stopped and she waited.

"They're thinking about Allah all the time, feel him all around them. They say his name a lot, which they enjoy doing. I kind of envied that. Like my mother and her church."

He picked up his empty glass and Holly got the waitress's eye.

"You're losing your accent, by the way, Llewellyn."

"Which one?"

A little laugh bubbled up between them in the relief of his good news, and there was a pleasant silence until the waitress reappeared. When she left, Holly sighed and said she really hoped he would take some time off and rest.

"Yeh, really. About the money, simple deal. We build a little low-rent rancho where I deem appropriate, subject to approval of his real estate advisor. He stakes the operation first three years, all expenses deductible, option to extend by mutual agreement. They've already got a hooked-up Mexican in place to front the deal. At some point I play the Hidalgo card, and he'll get it quick, like he gets everything. Anyhow, we find property somewhere between Guadalajara and Acapulco, and it's gotta be real pretty – suitable for development, in case yours truly step on his dick. Adji's idea of low-rent includes couple barns, big house with plenty of guest rooms, air strip, training track. I get that built, direct equine operations, run the show, hire-fire. He puts in more horses to provide cover for our little secret and keep the boys busy. I get twenty percent ownership overall, sweat equity. *You*, my dear, get to design how things look, he think your taste very classy. Nice little consulting deal, kind of de facto architect-consultant if you want it."

"And then live happily ever after in total isolation."

"Wrong again, girl, you thinkin' third world. Obviously this is a base, not a prison. *Airplane* comes along with that landing strip, little spare one he's got somewhere sitting around. Alberto-type pilot doubles as security, keep an eye on me too, probably."

"I don't know what's wrong with me, Len. I'm pissed off because you just cut the deal of our lives and I move from interior decorator to *faux* architect?"

"You a woman is all. Me, I'm a greedy uppity you-know-what, mistakenly let out of jail and obtained his own watermelon – "

"The foal?"

"Right, the foal. 50/50, and I get half ownership on subsequent 'Biche babies, no matter who the stud. He gets half of 'Biche, too – wasn't gonna work if I didn't go along with that. If we fall out, irreconcilable differences, one buys out the other. One gets 'Biche, other gets foal. Who gets option to buy out and who gets which horse is settled – check this – by the flip of a coin in the presence of a legal authority and witnesses. Price negotiated between us. Too high for one party, other party buys. Worst case, I come out with seven-digit assets and good ole 'Biche."

"Why does this sound more and more like a game of chance?"

"Cause it is. Horse racing ain't government bonds. What I like about it, not boring. So what'd I leave out? $500K Euros per annum to cover salaries. I plan to take half of that and you figure out how to hide it from the tax man. Adji covers all expenses. Bottom line, he doesn't really care about the money long as those Lakham silks are out front on U.S. soil.

"Oh, almost forgot, little hidden agenda here. In Arab racing circles, Godolphin is Godzilla. The Makhtoums of Dubai – tricontinental, *huge*. Biggest in the world. Some say dumb, but they won themselves a Derby, so Adji would like one of those and maybe a Belmont. No love lost, right? Anyhow, job one is triple-crown events, since we value them so much. 'Adolescent people, adolescent horses.' I wasn't supposed to hear that, of course."

He paused.

"He also knows a version of what happened that night I was nearly killed prior to being incarcerated. And he laughed. I mean, he *laughed*. He can get loose when the family's back in its cage. I think he was hip to Paco after about half a minute that day they talked in Saratoga."

"So what's he like? He didn't show much around Dixie's gang. Who's inside there?"

"Horseman, gentleman, cocksman. Polo. Social. I could really see it at dinner. Smooth, and friendly. Learned about as much at Cambridge as the Prez did at Yale, except he speaks English. No idea at *all* what makes that bad-ass cousin-by-marriage tick, and not even *interested*. Kill him on sight given the chance, though – rockin' the boat is not a Saudi option. No idea that boat's fulla holes, no idea the system's got a half-life maybe twelve years. Allah's system, you see. Kismetic system, can't fail."

He shook his head and paused as Holly waited.

"Follows finance, but no concept of the world outside that, except that he doesn't want it to change. He's America's Good Muslim – his idea of getting even with us for looking down on his world and turning it inside out is winning a horse race, right?! Or someone blowing up Israel of course, but no jihads, please. Basically it's all the will of Allah. He's rich because Allah wants it that way."

He shook his head, a faraway look in his eyes.

"The man got to me. I *liked* him. Good guy, personally. Being around him, watching tapes, working out our deal, I felt I could trust him. Not with you, though. I think you riled him some way, Holly. That architect thing feel like a little game."

"Well, he could see I wasn't interested in signing up for his harem, and being under Dixie's protection, I was kind of saucy. By his Royal standards."

"Never again, sweetie. Never again."

"Why don't you just say it one more time, Bwana, case I be missin' the first two?"

She stopped herself. "I'm really sorry about this nasty stuff jumping out of my mouth. You just did the deal of your life and I'm acting like Miss Black PMS."

He smiled.

"Anyhow, we set up bank accounts next week. I want you there for all that unless he shows up, in which case you prep me best you can. Maybe I bring attorney or accountant."

"Accountant. Attorney sets up a vibe, accountant's more a convenience, and they don't get into fights."

"Damn, I love brains. And the package – can't beat the packaging either."

"Would you still feel that way if I were pregnant?

Len looked at her with a mildly surprised half-smile, as if he had just heard a really good, subtle joke.

"But you're not. You're too smart."

"No, of course not, I've already been fired once this year, and you are one bad mother, Llewellyn Thomas. That poor cell phone. Sometimes you scare the brownies out of me. Those first hours you got out of jail, I was *petrified*. Going back for that bag and ordering me around like that. Then waking up in that nice big car under the stars."

She paused.

"And I do like to play with you sometimes. Like when you're exhausted and can't defend yourself properly. I need that edge. And me a St. Cyr, whose great-great grand-uncle played with Louis Armstrong."

"We can just about switch voices, know that? You imitate me for your family?"

"I imitated a nice well-bred college-educated black bitch living the dream, naturally. It was easy, just bein' myself."

The Rover appeared from nowhere, a spit-polished green Brit-built boom-box pumping an LA beat. As it approached, the sound fell respectfully away and it swooped up to where Len and Holly were standing with his carry-on and attaché case. Paco and Jimmy bounded out to greet Len with hopeful smiles and Paco threw his arms around him while Jimmy grabbed the bags.

"I see from your eyes, Len – the vision is correct, you got it!"

"We all got it, Paco," he said. "Long as Arabiche doin' okay. How she be?"

"Doin' *good*. She smart. Firs' day you gone, she trot around, look for you, no eat right, don't move bowels regular time. I no sleep good, so sleep in her stall next night. Morning she say, 'Fuck Len – I got Paco!' Eat good, shit good, everything fine."

Paco saw a weight lift, and noticed how bagged-out Len's eyes were.

"You drive, Paco, I sit next to you, let you in on things."

"Cool. You real tired from plane, huh? Big stress?"

"Yeah, tired, man, need rest," said Len quietly, just to him. "Les' move."

He turned to Holly. "Ah'm ride up front, Paco drive. Talk about land, rebar, I-beams, concrete, lumber, an' things."

"Gol-*darn*," said Jimmy. "We're really gonna *do* this. *Wow!* Good thing, too, we been partyin' way too much."

Len grinned and nodded, and Paco smiled, full of visionary joy.

On the road with the sunroof open, Len began to feel warm and solid. *In the pocket*, he thought, no strangers here. Trust everyone. He felt his energies leveling as he gazed at the bright hills through green aviator glasses, and a cautious confidence came over him as he remembered the unbelievable piece of paper in the envelope pinned into his pocket. Revived and settled down, he smiled when Paco discreetly displayed a fat, perfectly-rolled bone.

Our time, he thought. Like Spengler saw for rising cultures, but in miniature, just right for Mrs. Thomas's little boy. A bone and a bonding. My people, my outfit. On our way.

"I don't smoke today yet," announced Paco gravely, reminding Len of his Step Program self. "Wait for you. Pete so surprise to see his money he throw in some personal hydroponic Canadian."

Len took the bone from his hand, lit up with ritual respect, and inhaled lightly. It seemed to him he'd hardly smoked at all since the day of the cop. *Dynamite*, he thought, *gonna put me on my ass.*

338

"Not bad, not bad at *all*."

Gently exhaling, he passed it back to Paco.

"Big news, boys. No-limit backing, papers signed. No more party 'til snow flies, twelve hour days. We gonna be scoutin' property down here, find nice land up in the hills, good pasture, set up operation. Twelve horses to start, training track, air-strip, whole deal. Everybody make enough to live right and send money home."

"Other horses," said Jimmy.

"Yeah, where other horses come from?" asked Paco.

"Foreign stock, race mostly in Europe, all good blood."

Len watched it click in his head as he was holding a lungful of smoke, then a cough brought on by a laugh, followed by a long slow smile.

"*Sheikh!*" said Paco. "He love 'Biche right away. I guess right?"

"You got it, Pook. He like that Missile jism too. He got that Commander blood in one of his studs an' had good luck with it. Turns out Commander is DeQuincy's daddy. So – we find a place to stay between here and Guadalajara, nice place for 'Biche, settle in. Pretty soon we're gonna be gettin' up early to run construction crews. Maybe hire McGoo for the hard part."

"Don' even mention name," muttered Paco.

"Y'know," said Jimmy, "I called to pick up my messages at the Office and I heard he disappeared for a while. Then he showed up at the border with some story about bandits kidnapping him. Thought maybe I call Alice."

A sardonic cackling sound bubbled up from Len's chest at the thought of his old boss trapped between an angry, pregnant Jasmine at home and Alice at the office. One hit and he was feeling silly-happy.

"McGoo deserve whatever he get," said Paco with serious pleasure. "Payback. Anyhow, I been straw-boss all kinda crews – framing, excavate, concrete, lotta experience.

"Tomorrow rest day for me," said Len, his eyes half closed. "You three scout up places to stay next few months."

Then he was asleep.

32

St. Thomas Racing covered about a hundred acres of lush, rolling green on a Sierra Madres Occidental plateau, much of it covered with trees and rich, abundant pasture. A stream separated ranch and woodland, and a wide gravel road led to the San Marcos highway. Fifty yards from the big red L-shaped barn sat a dirt track inside a grass course. Well away from this complex was the large main house, tan stucco shaded by peaceful trees. Electronic security, the Hidalgo connection, and several high-profile visits by the Sheikh and a large armed entourage discouraged local bandits.

Gamboling in the late morning sun were half a dozen two-year olds, including one from a Mexican mare, but Maximus (Max on good behavior, Imus when troublesome) already dominated. He was a solid, compact animal with large mild eyes, less beautiful than formidable. Today the eyes had a bright, lively look, as if prepared for what Holly was calling The State Visit. Announced at the last minute, it had preempted her plans for Len's birthday, which displeased her, though not visibly. Len's lack of displeasure annoyed her more, but she understood that after life with McGoohey, he'd accept Adji's appearance, which was a first, and well-intended.

It was a small group – the Sheikh, Alberto, the inevitable blonde. Walking alone across the air-strip to meet them in clean working jeans and alligator shirt, Len felt instantly underdressed. The Sheikh's immaculate dark slacks and pale green short-sleeved shirt made him a natural photo-op, but Len also sensed the cooperative warmth under the fashion plate, and he didn't miss Lakham's pleased smile later as he took in the finished result of his investment. After chatting about the general fine style of the place, he announced a little surprise.

"That aircraft we came in – it will replace the old one. Bigger and faster, and not so loud. Call it a birthday surprise."

Knows my birthday, thought Len, driving from the strip.

Gotta find out his.

"Thank you, Adji. The timing is perfect."

"You'll be needing it for U.S. travel," said his partner as they pulled up to where the horses were grazing. "I put in bigger engines and had the interior done over. You'll like it. But where is our golden boy?"

"Over there," replied Len, pointing to a distant dogleg of the pasture where Max had led his gang when the Rover appeared. "He knows we've been waiting for something. When 'Biche comes, they'll follow."

"He looks very nice in this sun," said Lakham with interest. And so does this – rancho I think it's called. This was done quickly and quite inexpensively, and the layout is very pleasing. Before, I could not really see it. Very nice from the air, too. It sits here like a little island surrounded by giant broccoli. Very nice to the eye. Holly was the designer?"

"Holly and a man from Guadalajara," said Len. "Someone in the family was an architect, and I think she worked with him summers."

Until hit puberty and the old lech starting chasing her around the office.

"No wonder she left the Lees," said Lakham. "Do you think she might care to look at another project I'm developing? I have no patience for members of the architecture profession. Their vanity. They cannot admit that they have horses for clients."

Len came close to laughing while Lakham smiled.

"I'll speak with her, she might like something like that. She's not licensed, of course"

The horses approached now, curious, but stopping well away from the rail fence, looking restless. Max was in front, tossing his head, 'Biche a little behind, all of them almost prancing in the crisp mountain air. Eight young thoroughbreds, Arabiche the Queen Mother.

"*The zigzag blaze*," said the Sheikh in a quiet, near-reverential tone. "Like the sire, but smaller. It is coming out   more now."

Then Alberto walked up, and Holly. Lakham nodded, smiled, and bowed slightly; she smiled back as if delighted. Wearing Len's ring, she was secure and happy under the new rules it that went with it.

"The Sheikh's brought us a new plane, Holly. Big   and quiet."

"That's *wonderful!*" she said, with an even more wonderful smile. "What an incredible birthday surprise." Her voice had the fulsome tone reserved for people being obliged without limit.

"Well, the plane should match everything else, replied the Sheikh, sweeping his eyes over the spread. "The old one was certainly not up to this. I was telling Len that I have another project, one that is not going well. I wondered if you might have a look at it and perhaps make some suggestions. Architects are so arrogant, and so lacking interest in the reality. The horses. It is always some kind of 'statement.'"

Searching for words, he was upstaged by Max, moving toward them again, a boy-prince surrounded by his court. From around a corner of the barn straggled Jimmy Broughton in fresh Wal-Mart clothes, checking out the interaction. Sheikh happy – no doubt about that. Everyone lookin' good, all coming together the Len Thomas way, smooth and quiet, like Saratoga. Following Jimmy was Private Pablo, on permanent leave, learning English and horses.

"And his color," observed the Sheikh in the same reverential tone. "Darker, but bright. Missile Man as a new two-year-old, still had the look of a fresh coin, but over the winter he turned golden."

He hesitated to form his thoughts, taking his time, a man whose audience never strayed.

"People use this term loosely, as if it refers to money. Well, I am looking for that other gold, Len – the legendary gold of the rainbow's end. I loved that story as a small child, and my nurse explained the difference when I was still very impressionable. The feeling I get from this horse tells me it could be possible. It was very possible with DeQuincy until he broke down. One moment Pegasus, the next moment – like Ruffian. By the will of Allah he was saved, and his line will continue."

Sees it just like Paco, thought Len, nodding in genuine sympathy as the Sheikh shook his head sadly at the memory.

"I read the accounts after you called." He paused respect-

342

fully, and Lakham moved on.

"Max is a very different type of animal, very solid for a two-year-old. The mother, of course."

"She's as sound as any thoroughbred I ever worked with," replied Len matter-of-factly. "And our Max," he continued, "I think he will be crafty, like Affirmed."

"Yes," said the Sheikh. "I see the mother in there, that intelligence and balance. Her next should be fine as well. I was thinking she could be the first to take DeQuincy's mind from his troubles, now that he moves about more easily," said the Sheikh, eyes still fixed on the golden colt, aware of enjoying himself greatly. And with Americans, in Mexico of all places!

Then Len realized that Lakham was waiting for a response from his co-owner about a DeQuincy–Arabiche pairing.

"A promising match," he replied, hearing his stilted voice like something out of a bad novel. "We should talk with Paco."

Pat's dream, he thought suddenly. *He had it right. Just too rude to pull it off.*

The Sheikh looked up into the sky.

"This sun – they have a good sun here."

"Yes, and the air is very clean. Sometimes I work outside with the men. I need plenty of sun, it's genetic, I believe."

"All of us from that region. Cancer for Europeans, health for us, eh?"

A moment later Lakham could not quite believe he had uttered that *us*. Still, it felt right. Whatever else, this partner was no infidel. The thought triggered another one, an awkward one.

"I'm curious about the name of your operation," he said, not quite comfortably.

Len was prepared.

"It's the name of the island my mother was born. She's no longer alive; it is a way of remembering and honoring. My father was abroad with the military most of my childhood, so we were close."

It left the Sheikh just slightly embarrassed, happy to leave the subject behind as Paco strolled up, turned out for the occasion in L.L. Bean gear selected by Holly. He approached the group in his usual manner, from behind via the left flank. Max gave him away with an inquiring look as soon as he came around the corner of the barn.

"Your horse-whisperer arrives?"

"Yes, as you see, they report to him."

"Ask him over. A man needs to know he has done well."

"Paco," he called quietly, "when you finish the treats, come on over."

Holly observed this male behavior in silence, with a deferential expression. Eyes on the prize, she reminded herself, keeping the little smile perfectly in place. Then something with a no-nonsense edge rose unexpectedly from deeper down.

I've been ignoring you lately, Allah, or whatever you are, taking pleasure in these gifts exactly the way my mother warned me about, as if I deserved it all for being a smart little girl, so –

The *so* stopped her, putting her in a state of sudden confusion at the edge of the group, nothing to say, glad nothing was expected. It was like that moment on the hotel patio two years before when she suddenly understood that she would lose everything if she didn't put the temptation of those Lee trusts behind her.

Get thee behind me, Satan. One of her mother's favorites, to which she added, you conniving bastard. From there it came easily, naïve and satisfying. *For all of us here, please let this generous and easy-going Sheikh continue to smile on this little world we've built him and help us make it a continuing delight for his gratification. Which it must be, first of all, as well as the means of our survival, success, and salvation. And dream come true, not subject to satire or silly games.*

And especially encourage him to see that I am his devoted employee and the capable if slightly boring wife of his trusted business partner, more than happy to assist with this equine Taj Mahal he has in mind. In return I will modestly drop my eyes whenever appropriate, and keep my ideas to myself when he's going on about you, Allah, because his intentions are beyond reproach... "

It surprised her how easily she could go on like this.

"I would like to see him work, of course," said the Sheikh, slipping into French and terminating Holly's self-hypnosis.

Len nodded and turned to Paco.

"While he is here, the Sheikh would like to see Maximus

work."

"Sure, right," said Paco, who had been waiting for this. "He already work this morning – maybe six tomorrow be okay? Would be normal schedule."

The Sheikh nodded and Len asked how much he expected, thinking of Paco's capacity to say or do anything at all if he believed it to be in Max's interest, regardless of decorum, rank, or common sense.

"Whatever he can do without harm," said Lakham a bit carefully. "A little breeze, and then perhaps a couple of fast furlongs so I can see his full stride?"

Perhaps? wondered Len. Then he noticed Jimmy listening, silent, homely and professional. *Hey, Jimmy – real glad you didn't take any rides this week.*

"Three furlongs fast, couple watches?" asked Paco bluntly, knowing exactly what was wanted. "Would be enough?"

The Sheikh nodded, his mind read perfectly, feeling unaccustomed sarcasm, the situation stripped of amenities. Len said nothing.

"The horses look very fine," said Lakham after a moment, looking at Paco thoughtfully. "Keep talking to them."

"Gracias," said Paco, respectfully, "and they thank you for this wonderful home. Max is happy here, like happy boy-child playing. He runs from love, you will see it. With his mother was different – "

Before he could finish everyone was laughing and Len was alone with his thoughts. Max was a tough, healthy horse, maturing early, but never yet pushed really hard. This test should have been at least a month or two away. As the laughter died down, he wasn't smiling.

Caught off-guard, should've seen this coming – out here in the boonies too long. Too used to agreeing with Adji. Do that too often, it stops being a partnership.

In the misty gray before sunrise, Paco went alone to Max's stall and explained what was going and why it would be his friend Jimmy on his back, and how lucky it was, that Jimmy was a special friend, very close to his mother. Then he explained how important it was for him to be the most horse he could be today, with no little games. As he was finishing this monolog, Len appeared with a cup of coffee in hand and stood silent in the doorway, unsure how best to handle him until he'd had a look. As if by natural gravitation, Jimmy appeared in riding gear, a little early, trailed by Pablo, the boy *Federale,* in Wal-Mart gear. Len and Jimmy approached Paco together.

"Thees *workout* . . . " said Paco, with a sour look.

"I know," said Len. "Not my choice. Sheikh – "

"Want three furlongs. Horse is never been push really hard by professional, is used to you. Balance changes."

"You mentioned Len pushed him pretty good couple days ago," said Jimmy.

"Ordinary day, he runs ordinary. Max not stupid horse, knows today is different. How he went up in corner to wait yesterday – never does that before. How much you weigh, Len?"

"Around one-thirty-eight."

"More."

"Gettin' kinda plump, Len," said Jimmy, to relieve the tension.

"How 'bout you?" asked Paco unswerving and unsmiling. One thirteen?"

"Little over one fifteen. Ain't et since Sheikh come."

"Good. Twenty pounds, plus different feel, more bite. What you think, Jimmy?" said Paco, ignoring Len.

"Look like he's, y'know, thinkin' about it. Kinda like 'Biche. Playin' aeound a little."

"That because he smarter than all of you."

"He ain't *awkward,*" said Jimmy, ignoring his tone. "Solid on the turns and all."

"Why Sheikh has to come now, no warning?" hissed Paco, suddenly turning on Len, who exhaled slowly through pursed lips.

"His money, his rancho, his option, come when he likes. You like your job? I like mine," replied Len, searching for eye contact. "Better than McGoo every morning."

"Pat no play games with horse if we don't want. But I cannot tell Sheikh – I am not trainer."

He had not moved or changed expression during the conversation, body set for confrontation. Len's burning narrowed eyes stayed on his, but Paco would not look at him, and the tension didn't level off.

"I don't like it either, Paco," he said quietly. "But the man wants to see what we got. Don't like what he sees, well – "

"Is racing few months, right? First race is very important. Small injury or bad state of mind can set back in development. Not necessary, timing is bad," said Paco with intensity, but almost pleading.

Len turned to Jimmy and spoke in a mild voice.

"You know we don't want that. Let him go, but don't really, y'know, *push* him. Sheikh have to live with what Max gives him. Could have consequences."

He walked away without betraying himself, leaving Jimmy to fix it. Alone at the rail, the sting of Paco's words continued. Speaking up was part of a trainer's job. And thinking fast. Alone in the quiet dawn, he recalled his carefree life before Saratoga. A dream in many ways. Easy days. *Tasty* days. Time to read, smoke, think, take a nap, enjoy ladies like Charlotte.

The memories vanished when Lakham arrived with Alberto.

"Morning, Adji, Alberto," said Len in such a mellow voice that he surprised himself. "Did you sleep well?"

"Very well, thank you," said Lakham. "It is calm up here, very peaceful. But you have a concerned look."

"Yes, I am, a little. I told Jimmy not to push him super-hard."

"You are the trainer," agreed the Sheikh, a little too respectfully. It was clear that he wasn't used to being questioned when his wishes were apparent.

"His father came along slowly," said Len deliberately, then found himself suddenly clear on the real issue. "And the horse is more important than his fractions this morning."

It came out a little harder than intended. Had he crossed a line? So be it. There was a pause.

"Yes, and there is only one of him," agreed the Sheikh. "I was looking at his half-sister. She is a little mean, I think, and certainly not very attractive. Is she worth keeping?"

"Pandora. I don't know yet, Paco chose the mother. She's quick and high-strung, a sprinter. I have hopes. The mother won local races as a juvenile, so they sent her to Mexico City. She won there, too, but went lame. She's okay now, but not to race. I picked her up for nothing, in case Pandora works out."

Then Jimmy arrived, all business in fresh white gear.

"We 'bout ready?"

His directness amused the Sheikh, who looked at Len, who simply nodded. St. Thomas was full of democratic oddities, but it was enjoyable up here without the usual half dozen security types.

They were quiet whenuntil Max danced out onto the track with Jimmy up, looking all business. Lakham felt the sacred sensation in his abdomen which came only from very special horses and women, *Inshallah*, and he was reminded that he must pray again afterward, thinking for a moment of that fine big top floor with the beautiful colored-glass windows set aside for his devotions. How wrong he had been about Holly! Then he focused on his handsome new colt. Breezing an easy lap, Max showed his father's flowing style and flawless action, along with a youthful inclination to roam the track. Green, thought Lakham, but no roughness. Then the feeling in his abdomen again on the next lap, as Jimmy moved a little higher on the horse just before the pole. Max was with him instantly, feeling command, needing to please.

With that, it was plain to the Sheikh that the class was there, the eagerness, and he felt twice blessed, as if some exceptionally beautiful woman had gone to a second climax at a completely unexpected level. Hitting the watch automatically, he observed. To his eye, the horse's acceleration seemed to continue through the turn. Perfect turn, close to the rail, no bearing out, or hesitation, just like the mother on that final turn at Saratoga. Paco was locked in position, an utterly serious look on a face built for smiling. Max thundered into the straight, flying, eyes wild, nostrils flared. And then it was over, and yhey were all a little breathless.

"I have him at 34.5," said the Sheikh, breaking the silence in a smooth, shocked voice.

"The same," replied Len, showing nothing. It was as fast as a two-year-old could be expected to run before the season. Competition fractions without the excitement of a race.

348

"That was a lot for such a young horse," said the Sheikh, impressed and cautious, aware of the tension.

Paco nodded and looked at him in a way Lakham understood perfectly, causing him to reflect on the fragility and awkwardness of unraced two-year-olds. Enough tampering, he told himself, glancing at his relieved partner as Jimmy cantered the rest of the lap before pulling up in front of them. Paco produced a shank and Jimmy dismounted, eyes bright with excitement about what he had just felt. Max was blowing just a little, but still ready to prance. Appearing from nowhere to hot-walk him was Private Pablo.

"Thirty-four five, both watches," said Len when Jimmy walked over, his eyes still on his horse and seeing nothing wrong. Jimmy nodded. Two days before, Len had thought Max felt a little like 'Biche, and now this. Exactly as Paco had indicated with those little sharp-edged remarks.

"Way to go, Maestro," murmured Holly.

Taking off his hat, Jimmy Broughton looked up at the brightening sky, it's morning haze burning away. Generations of tough dirt-farmers had bred the taciturn streak into him, and he was unwilling to do more than smile faintly, but his eyes were charged with the energy still rippling through him.

Killer horse! he was thinking. *Fucking killer horse! Shitagawdamn! Got me my break at last! Killer horse!*

When the Sheikh smiled at him and nodded, he felt even better. He felt just about as good as he could feel outside of a whorehouse. But a few minutes later he quietly approached Paco.

"It was him, Paco. He was in the mood. I only tapped him but twice to let him know, but he knew already. Felt me move up and responded before the crop come down, and I couldn't hardly *hold* him, man, I mean not with the top dog here, and he don't miss much – "

"Si," said Paco. "Anyway horse is good, everything okay, and now we know what we got. Was his best, you think?"

"No, he was runnin' for fun, man. Show him another horse, he's gonna find another gear."

Fifteen feet away was another conversation.

"The same as DeQuincy at this stage," said the Sheikh, generations of Royal blood and Public School discipline unable to keep the emotion out of his voice. "Allah is kind to me. He allows DeQuincy to survive injury and gives me this golden dream horse. And he brings me this group from the unfortunate Mr. McGoohey's Farms. What does he do now, that man?"

"The McGoohey Farms are no more. He had business reversals and gave them up, but then his wife gave him a son and I hear that all is well. He is another man, they say. Now it is the McGoohey nursery, with another on the way."

The Sheikh's chuckle released Len's tension and he smiled.

"Jimmy's got his feel just right, but I don't think Paco is very pleased with us," said Len in a different voice.

"Yes, he lets me know with his eyes. He loves Max as he loves the mother. Put his mind at rest. I rarely interfere, it is part of our success."

"DeQuincy – "

"Yes, exactly, that is it, Llewellyn. I wanted to know what we had here. But this now, this morning – this moment is perfect, the sun begins to smile at last. We must have pictures. Alberto is not bad, so long as the subject is not fearful. I had him learn some photography to avoid needing strangers about."

He turned and found himself facing his partner's wife.

"It's him," she said. "It's Missile Man all over. I didn't really see it until today. The power, and the way he moves. Everything but his mother's eyes."

He nodded and smiled. "I see it too. After dinner perhaps you could look at some photographs and drawings for our new French facility. It will be large, and there is not much land, but when I look at the drawings I know we can do better."

"Of course," said Holly, with the feeling of a great weight lifted. "With coffee, in that big room off the dining room. It has a good table for the drawings." Lakham smiled and turned back to Len.

"Someday you must tell me just how you brought this about, Len. I do not question the ways of Allah, but I am interested in them that I may learn."

"That story is so – what would you call something that begins as an Irish farce and becomes a Latin tragedy with a happy ending?"

"Whatever," said the Sheikh, cheerfully ill-read but knowing American slang and attitudes. "I sense this all occurs very differently without the hand of Paco."

His posture changed and he spoke seriously to both of them. "This is a very fine day, one to be remembered, Llewellyn. These photographs will have meaning."

Llewellyn. Len was getting to like the sound of it. *Trainer, Llewellyn Thomas, St. Thomas Racing.* Trainer and half-owner. God, but his mother would have loved it. And Jimmy Winkfield would have to be pleased to see the door finally open a little wider. Then Lakham drew him aside in a way that sent a message to the others. When they were alone he spoke quietly.

"I have given much thought to the problem that brought us together, as I am sure you have. For where we are going, the papers must be perfectly correct."

He paused.

"I lost a young brood-mare recently, Secret Letter. She can be named the mother, and we can say the foal was sent here to test my theories of altitude training. Your theories, which I will appropriate. And by luck, in my stud is a Commander son, a half-brother to Missile Man who was injured early, but a very successful sire in Europe. This story is believable, based on facts and resources we control. With Commander blood through the sire, the genetics would be at least somewhat plausible. The common genes should cause enough ambiguity that the doctors will find it convenient to moot the point."

Makes our invasion of Lee Farms look like a children's crusade, thought Len, wondering briefly if he was doing business with the Devil or just another black man doing what he had to do.

"I doubt it will come to much, Adji. The father will avoid another scandal, whatever his daughter thinks," he said. "It's perfect. The Mexicans will approve anything we put in front of them. A few Mexican races, and then maybe to France?"

"Yes – a couple of European wins and then his naturalization, or is it repatriation?"

"Another immigrant making his contribution," said Len. "If we pick his races carefully, he will enter them with the benefits of altitude training, and return soon enough to refresh them. My thinking is that too much racing would be a mistake. He is meant for the big ones, and Missile Man was not so solid in some ways."

The Sheikh nodded; his partner understood the Lakham way without discussion. "I think we have a plan then, and can release the news of Lakham's operation here at his first race."

"The Mexicans will go mad. If he's stabled here, they will adopt him and the journalists will be interviewing Paco. If Pandora is any good, she can race here. Good politics."

The Sheikh smiled and called over Alberto.

"Some pictures now. Paco and Arabiche first, and then with Max between them, and Jimmy next to Paco. The usual shots, and then a few of us all together as a group. Take several of each. And in these photographs, no way for someone to guess where we are. No mountains." He turned to Len. "It can't last, but I like it here as it is now, the privacy."

There is no question at all about that nose, he was thinking, watching his trainer thoughtfully from the corner of his eye. *The family can smile. A black trainer to go with my blond mistresses. But when we win some of those sacred classics, when we defeat those arrogant oil-Christians on their own tracks, they will see…*

He looked at the wonderful golden horse walking up to him on light Missile Man feet with his Arabiche eyes and charm.

Yes, charm, that was the word. A golden heartbreaker. The Lees would know at first glance. Unfortunate. Most unfortunate, it pulled at the heart. They had been hospitable, quite nice people, and after the near-loss of DeQuincy, he could sympathize even more fully about the death of Missile Man.

Such bad luck. Perhaps they had voted for that madman in the White House, for which Allah was punishing them.

7930633R0

Made in the USA
Charleston, SC
23 April 2011